Flight of Aquavit

A Russell Quant Mystery

Also by the author

Amuse Bouche

Flight of Aquavit

A Russell Quant Mystery

Anthony Bidulka

Edited by Catherine Lake
Copy edited by Emily Schultz
Interior designed by Marijke Friesen

Library and Archives Canada Cataloguing in Publication

Bidulka, Anthony, 1962-
    Flight of aquavit / Anthony Bidulka.

(A Russell Quant mystery)
ISBN 1-894663-75-6

I. Title. II. Series: Bidulka, Anthony, 1962- . Russell Quant mystery.

PS8553.I319F55 2004   C813'.6   C2004-903953-9

The publisher gratefully acknowledges the support of the Canada Council, the Ontario Arts Council and the Department of Canadian Heritage through the Book Publishing Industry Development Program.

Printed and bound in Canada

Insomniac Press
192 Spadina Avenue, Suite 403
Toronto, Ontario, Canada, M5T 2C2
www.insomniacpress.com

The Canada Council | Le Conseil des Arts
FOR THE ARTS | DU CANADA
SINCE 1957 | DEPUIS 1957

ONTARIO ARTS COUNCIL
CONSEIL DES ARTS DE L'ONTARIO

For Herb

Ku`u lei aloha mae `ole

`Ala mapu i ke anuhea

Aloha wau iâ `oe

Chapter 1

IT WAS A LITTLE AFTER 11 p.m. on a frigid Tuesday night. I kept the Mazda's engine running while I waited, having little desire to lose my nose and ears to frostbite. And for the umpteenth time that evening, I wondered if this rendezvous was a good idea. What was I doing here, meeting a man I didn't know on a cold, dark, stormy night? Okay, it wasn't stormy but it was really cold. He had my cellphone number and the colour and make of my vehicle. I knew nothing about him. But since I was already here, I decided I might as well see it through.

I didn't have long to wait. A dark green Dodge Intrepid, a few years old, pulled in front of McQuarrie's Tea & Coffee Merchants two parking spots ahead of mine. I watched as the sole occupant of the car released his seat belt, fumbled with gloves and pulled his hood over his head. The door of the car stuttered open just as a gust of bracing December wind, laden with razor-sharp ice crystals, bore down upon it. The man threw his shoulder into the door and successfully swung it out far enough to allow him to exit. Without hesitation he approached the driver's side of my car and leaned down to look in at me. I rolled down the window.

"You're Russell?" he asked with an accent I couldn't quite place—Aussie maybe.

7

I checked him out. He had dark eyes under heavy brows, a thick jaw covered with a later-than-five-o'clock shadow and big teeth that were very white. Maybe thirty. Something about the texture of his skin, his wintertime getup and cold-tinted cheeks made him look like a ski instructor—and given that this was flat Saskatchewan, no doubt an out-of-work ski instructor. "Yeah," I said with a smile to return his. "I'm Russell. You're Hugh?"

He only nodded. "Whaddaya say we go somewhere more private to do this?"

"Uh, sure," I agreed, lamb-like.

"You follow me, right?"

"Okay. Where are we headed?"

"Got your cell with ya?"

"Sure."

"I'll jes give you a ring if it looks you're not keeping up. Mother, it's gettin' brisk out here." He trudged back to his car, calling over the wind, "Follow me, right?"

This couldn't be a good idea. What was I doing?

The traffic on Broadway Avenue was almost non-existent as the Intrepid headed south with me and my Mazda on its tail. We passed by the darkened windows of retail shops, salons, art galleries, butchers, bakers and candlestick makers and saw only a smattering of late-nightnics entering and exiting the area's pubs and restaurants. The Broadway Theatre was just letting out a couple dozen fans of some funky foreign independent film. We quickly reached 8th Street and Hugh made a right turn, speeding down several blocks obviously not taking time to enjoy the Christmas decorations hoisted high above the street by some brave city worker. He hung a left onto Lorne Avenue and we continued our journey south. Before long I caught sight of the gaudy Las Vegas-lite sign of the Emerald Casino. Its parking lot was bursting to capacity, as it is almost every night of the year, and across the street a statue of a rearing stallion marked the entrance to Early's Farm & Garden Centre.

Suddenly the situation changed tenor.

We were leaving town.

It was one thing to follow someone I didn't know to somewhere I didn't know within city limits, but leaving the safety of the city was an altogether different matter. I had to make a decision. And time was running out. We passed the woodsy fairytale setting of the German Canadian Club Concordia and the spartan lot of the Schroh Sports Arena. And that was it. Urban street became a two-lane rural highway and our speeds quickly upped to ninety kilometres an hour. The lights of the city fell behind us like the dying embers in a fireplace. What to do?

I thought back to my first contact with the man I was now following. It was an end-of-workday phone call from a person in distress. He told me his name was Hugh and that he desperately needed my services as a private detective. He told me he was wary of meeting in public or talking too long on the phone. So we arranged to meet on Broadway Avenue. This might sound a bit strange to some, but after all, I am a detective and few of my client meetings take place between 9 and 5 in a comfy boardroom with an urn of designer coffee. But in the country after dark? Hmm.

In the end, propulsion made up my mind for me. With no ready exits or approaches, there wasn't an easy way to get off the road and besides, I had nothing else planned for my Tuesday night, so why not keep going? I maintained a several-car-length distance behind Hugh on the straight and narrow road. We were on Highway 219, that's all I knew. I wondered what the heck was out here. Where was he taking me?

As we drove in a southerly direction, a pitiful parade of two, my headlights cut a slender swath through the night. Drifts of snow passed lazily over the pavement before me like feathery ghosts. The sky was black. No streetlights or traffic lights, farmyards were few and far between and the moon had gone into hiding. There are times, driving at night, when abandoning the noise and glaring brightness of the city for the countryside brings me comfort; darkness and silence envelop me like a protective blanket. At other times, the same setting seems ominous and threatening, as if something is out there, lurking behind the curtain of night, something…not good. And tonight it was the latter knocking at the door of my brain. Funny how things can turn around so quickly. A slightly elevated pulse and body temperature, along with a general creepy feeling, slowly overtook my tough PI guy bravado.

I began to notice the distance between our vehicles growing. Hugh was speeding up. Eventually, my only guides were the two red lights of his rear end. And every so often as the Intrepid sunk into a dip in the highway I would lose sight of him completely. Was he trying to lose me? Just as I accelerated in an effort to catch up, I saw the brake lights of the Intrepid flash once, then twice, his right turn signal blinked its intention and then…he was gone.

I sped up to 120 clicks.

I followed his right turn onto an intersecting gravel road identified by a sign that simply read Landfill. I made the turn and soon found myself idling past the entrance of the South Corman Park Landfill site. The Intrepid was nowhere to be seen. I came to a stop and took a quick glance around. A chained and padlocked gate blocked access to the property and I could see no other obvious way for Hugh to have gotten in unless he'd had the key, which I doubted. So I put the car back in gear and kept on rolling. I topped a hill and about a kilometre later came to a full stop. My headlights had fallen upon the unmistakable yellow and black checkered pattern of a dead-end sign. Next to it was another sign telling me that I was at the "T" intersection of Twp 354 and Rge Rd 3055. Okey dokey. Right or left? Which way did he go?

It was as dark outside as I'd ever seen it and even with my headlights on high beam, there were no obvious telltale signs of recent travel. The snow on the road had been worn into the gravel so there were no tracks to follow. Over the sound of my engine, I could hear the lowing of the wind that every so often built itself into a powerful blast and rocked the body of my little car. For a moment I sat there, wondering yet again what madness had brought me here. It was never a good idea to be caught in the countryside, late on an ice-cold, winter night, perhaps a little lost. Had I taken the wrong turn off the highway? Or was my future client somewhere nearby, waiting for me, wondering where I was? But which way? Right or left? I had no obvious clue. But I had an idea. I couldn't see anything, but maybe I could hear something.

I rolled down the window, but the wind and car engine were still too loud. I turned the ignition key to silence the car but the wind was blowing right into my ear. I'd have to get out. I buttoned the top buttons of my coat, readjusted my scarf, pulled on a pair of lined, leather gloves, opened the door and pulled myself out of the Mazda. (I seldom wear a toque, preferring a hooded coat or earmuffs—the damage to

my hair just isn't worth it.) I rounded the car to the north side for protection and bowed my head against the wind, listening for anything
that would give me a clue as to where Hugh had gone.

It was then that I heard it.

It was all the more surprising because, despite my actions, I hadn't
really expected to hear anything except perhaps the distant howling
of a hungry coyote.

But it wasn't a night creature that I heard. It was the sound of an
engine.

There was someone else out there.

The engine rumbled and grumbled as some engines do, sounding
not unlike an animal…biding its time until it could…attack…

From the cadence I could tell the vehicle was idling. Whoever was
in the car was just sitting there, lights extinguished. Waiting.
Watching.

But why? Was it Hugh? Was it someone else? How far away? It
sounded…close. Or was this just a trick played on my ears by the
wind?

My eyes strained to cut through the night, as black as a flock of
crows, but to no avail. I could see nothing. I could feel my heart begin
to race faster. And even though it was bitterly cold, a thin line of perspiration trickled from my forehead towards my neck, almost freezing on
its way.

This wasn't good. Something wasn't right here. And just as that
thought entered my head a set of headlights illuminated, appearing
suddenly, like two bright orbs, two-hundred metres down the road to
the right of me. I shielded my eyes in a useless attempt to get a better
look, but I couldn't tell if they belonged to the green Intrepid or some
other vehicle. And then, two-hundred metres to my left, another set of
headlights flashed on.

Shit.

There were two of them.

An ambush.

Beating my own hide by several seconds, I skidded around my car
and jumped into the driver's seat, battling the wind to pull the door
closed. I glared at the two lighted sentinels, each the same distance
away but in opposite directions.

Cripes! They began to move.

They were coming after me!

I turned the key in the ignition and despite every movie I've ever seen, the rotary engine of my sweetheart of a car turned over on the first try.

They were coming, from either end of the T. I had to somehow get turned around and get the heck out of there. I tried a U-turn but only made it half way. The road was too narrow. I stopped, backed up, frustrated at losing the time, and pointed myself back in the direction I'd come from. In my haste and growing anxiety, I was having a difficult time getting the stick shift into first gear. My eyes flew to the rearview mirror. They were coming. They were coming! Both vehicles had arrived at the intersection and were turning in my direction. They were coming!

I think I swore and grimaced and somehow managed to get into first, second, third and fourth within the next few nanoseconds. My car fishtailed wildly as I accelerated and caught tufts of roadside snow and gravel under my churning wheels. If only I could get to the highway, I would feel safer.

The reflection of the chase car's lights in my rear-view mirror became blinding as they caught up with me. Holy Moses Boat Builder! They were right on my tail. We were all climbing to speeds in excess of one hundred kilometres per hour on a gravel road and the highway was coming up fast. How would I make the turn? Suppose there was oncoming traffic? Should I signal? Should I signal left but then go right? Stupid, stupid, stupid!

Not so stupid.

I had one advantage. I was in front. I could pay attention to where I was going rather than whom I was chasing. I only had time to make, consider and carry out one plan. So it had to be a good one. I slowed down to just below ninety, took a good look at where I was heading, then extinguished my headlights, making it seem—I hoped—as if I'd disappeared. In the next few seconds I was either going to (a) end up in a ditch, (b) be rear-ended by one of the other cars, or (c) make a left turn onto the highway heading back towards Saskatoon before the bad guys behind me realized what was happening.

I was shooting for (c).

It sort of worked. I made the turn, just barely missing a collision with the snow banks of the opposing ditch and, after a bit of an amusement park ride, was firmly on the road facing north. I turned my lights back on and dared a look in the rear-view mirror. As hoped, car number one had been totally bamboozled and sailed right through the intersection. Car number two, however, had been far enough behind both of us to have figured out what I was doing. He too made the turn. I had gained some distance but he was still on my tail. My only hope was to reach city limits before he caught up with me. I didn't know what he'd do with me if he did—shoot out my tires or try to force me off the road?—but I was not about to find out and become an action-flick cliché. I floored it and aimed straight ahead like a rocket bound for the moon.

About halfway to town I noticed the lights behind me getting smaller and smaller and finally I lost sight of them. Had he turned around to check up on his buddy? Did he want to avoid the revealing lights of the city? Didn't matter, at least he'd given up on me.

It was not until I was back in Saskatoon and slowed to city speed that I noticed my hands. I watched them on the steering wheel, as if they weren't my own, twitching crazily like bags full of jumping beans. My head felt odd, as if I was in the cabin of an airplane that had just lost pressure. Was it going to implode? I pulled into the brightly-lit lot of a Petro-Canada gas station. I craned my head over my left shoulder. I had to confirm they weren't coming up behind me. Who were those guys? What would they have done if they'd caught me? Was it a coincidence this had happened while I was following Hugh? Probably not. So then the question was, who the hell was Hugh and why had he set me up?

My skin shifted as the cellphone on the seat next to me began to jangle. I eyed it warily, the normally innocuous ring now ominous. I reached for it as if it were a stovetop that might be hot, finally grabbing hold of it and bringing it to my ear.

"Hello," I croaked.

The voice that answered was Hugh's, but a different Hugh from the smiling ski instructor I'd met on Broadway Avenue. In a menacing, flat tone he said, "Drop the case, Mr. Quant. Or next time…we'll catch you."

My name is Russell Quant. I'm thirty-two, a former police constable for the city of Saskatoon, Saskatchewan and I have had my shingle out as a private detective for over two years. I get to set my own hours, answer to no one and indulge my active extrovert or solitary introvert as my mood dictates. Now that being said, the life of a private detective can certainly be a capricious one. So to balance everything out, I crave and maintain a certain level of calm, steadiness and predictability in my day-to-day routine.

Enter Kay Quant, nee Wistonchuk.

Mom.

Mom is a sixty-two-year-old who speaks with a heavy Ukrainian accent replete with rolling r's and wailing ois. Even so, I've never considered myself half-Ukrainian. Not because I didn't want to be, but because my mother rarely mentioned the fact and my father, a very proper Irishman, ignored his own heavy brogue and my mother's penchant for garish colour combinations and told us we were Canadians, plain and simple. My mother is just shy of five feet tall and, although leaning towards stocky, she has generally kept the same dress size since giving birth to her last child, which was me. She sports a tightly permed head of dark hair with the occasional sproing of white, horn-rimmed spectacles and a face that can alternately scowl away a pirate ship or warm the heart of its captain.

For the first time since knowing her, which is pretty much since my birth, my mother agreed to stay overnight in my home. And not just for one night but for every night of the two weeks leading up to Christmas. When I first called and asked her if she'd like to spend Christmas together, as I do every year out of repetitive obligation, I was truly shocked by her reply. My good friend and neighbour, Sereena, was with me at the time and believed I was about to go into cardiac arrest. You see, normally, since my father's death several years ago, my mother spends Christmas with either my sister or my brother. Never with me. It just made sense. Or, if truth be told, I had never thought about it hard enough to question whether or not it made sense. I just figured she was more comfortable with the other choices: my sister, because mothers and daughters supposedly have that extra special bond, or my brother because he has two children to whom she enjoys playing grandmother. Or is it four? I can never keep track. The holidays together would be spent eating, playing cards, eating some more and then, all involved being sated, Mom would toddle off home to the farm until next year. Everybody was happy, right?

I suppose I did sometimes wonder (when I had absolutely nothing else to do) if she avoided my house because I am gay. She's known this fact for years, she doesn't like talking about it or hearing about it, but she knows. Does it make her uncomfortable? Is that why she had stayed away?

Yet this year something different was afoot. She'd said yes. After some blathering and blubbering to cover my surprise, I'd hung up, drunk the half carafe of wine Sereena'd thoughtfully set before me and called my siblings. My sister, Joanne, couldn't have Mother for Christmas because she was planning to spend the holidays in Hawaii. My brother, Bill, who lives the next province over in Winnipeg, Manitoba, said that he had made the offer to Mother but she'd refused with no apparent reason. I'd reached a dead end. I realized I'd have to swallow my feelings of…what? I didn't even know what I felt about my mother coming to visit. I loved her well enough. So what was the problem? Was I worried she'd be bored? Afraid we'd have nothing to talk about? Anxious that my Christmas would pale in comparison to my sister's or brother's version? None of those seemed quite right, but they'd do nicely until I had time to sit down and think about it. So I hired a house cleaning service, took my dog Barbra to the groomer, stocked the fridge with things I barely recognized, like butter and whole milk, and welcomed my mother into my home.

As I shuffled into the kitchen on that chilly December morning, I was still more than a little dazed from the bizarre incident on the outskirts of the city the night before. The venomous sounding words that spewed from my cellphone had echoed in my brain ever since: "Drop the case, Mr. Quant. Or next time…we'll catch you."

First of all there was the matter of the implied threat. Next time they'll catch me and what? Introduce themselves? Trade recipes with me? Kill me? And then, just for that nice added touch of confusion, was the first part of the message telling me to drop the case. The problem was, I had no case.

I'd wrapped up my most recent investigation—a fairly benign matter involving a misplaced and highly cherished curling broom (don't ask)—about a week ago and since had been toying with the idea of taking some days off. I was looking forward to using the free time to properly get into the Christmas spirit: shopping, decorating, partying, sleeping.

So what was this idiot talking about? Drop the case? What case? I'd taken some preliminary information from Hugh when he'd first called. All bogus of course, including his phone number. So now what? Even if I wanted to I couldn't do what the bad guys wanted me to. So much for the caprice part of a private detective's life. Now I needed a dose of serenity.

Nuh-uh.

As soon as my bare foot hit the tile floor of the kitchen, I knew my daily existence had drastically changed and would remain changed for the next two weeks. My usual routine is to let out the dog, prepare her food and mine, set the coffee and retrieve the *StarPhoenix* from the front walk. I then let the dog in and finally settle down surrounded by paper, food, dog and coffee in my pleasant kitchen nook to quietly welcome the new day. The first sign that things were different was Barbra. With my mother having already taken care of her doggie needs, my gentle five-year-old pepper-and-salt schnauzer was sitting in one corner of the kitchen, far enough away from Mom's busy feet to keep from being stepped on, with an odd look on her face. I think she was grinning, waiting in anticipation for my reaction to the scene in our usually peaceful home.

Instead of tranquility there was mini-pandemonium as Mom tried to acclimate herself to a new kitchen, her indigenous habitat. Most of the surfaces were covered with pots and pans and non-perishables. There were paper Safeway bags and plastic Superstore bags brimming with groceries and other items she'd brought from home—obviously things she suspected I wouldn't have and she couldn't possibly do without. She'd already brewed a pot of weak coffee and poured me a cup laced with heavy cream and a heaping teaspoon of sugar. She'd also somehow found the newspaper and was now using the Lifestyle section, my favourite for light early morning reading, to soak up the fat from a heap of freshly fried bacon. And, by some mystery, she had perfectly timed my arrival in the kitchen, as she had most days of my corpulent childhood, with the cracking of three eggs into a hot pan, spitting with butter.

Even though it was not quite 8 a.m., my mother was wearing a freshly pressed, robin's egg blue housedress under a flowery apron (not mine), what she calls house shoes (hard leather dress shoes, always black with a chunky heel) and thick nylons. Her hair was immovably perfect and her eyeglasses were magnificently shiny. I, on the other hand, had barely managed to fasten the belt around the waist of my bathrobe.

"You seet and I feex more bacon if dat's not enough," she said, her back to me, intuiting my presence in the room.

I looked at the two pigs worth of bacon sitting on my newspaper. My mother comes from a generation of prairie farmwomen accustomed to cooking meals for men who spent their days plowing fields, herding cattle and picking rocks. The closest I come to any of those agrarian activities is selecting the perfect head of lettuce—ok, romaine—at the organic produce store. I fell into a chair, picked up an unfamiliar coffee cup from an embroidered place-setting and sipped at its contents. It tasted something like a hot, mocha milkshake. Barbra and I exchanged glances. Her lips were definitely upturned on each side of her face. I began to wonder. Schnauzers aren't given to smirking unless they have very good reason. "Mom, you didn't give Barbra people food, did you?"

"Vhat kind peoples food? Vhat you mean?" She was busy flipping my eggs and I took from her tone that I was lucky she had answered me at all.

"People food, you know, anything other than the dog food in the bag in the cupboard I showed you. If she eats people food she gets sick and throws up. I wouldn't want you spending your first day cleaning that up." I tried to sound light and airy about it, but I'm not sure I succeeded, especially since hot milkshakes just don't do it for me first thing in the morning—particularly after my harrowing experience the night before.

"I haf tree egg here, dat enough? You start dese, I feex more."

No matter how many people she is cooking for, one or twenty-one, I cannot remember even one occasion seeing my mother actually sitting at a table to eat. She cooks. While others eat—she's cooks. Long after the meal is done—she's cooks. When the guests have left and are home in bed—she's still cooking. I don't get it. What happens to all this food? "Mom, I don't eat a big breakfast."

"Not beeg," she informed me as she slipped three easy-overs onto a plate along with a nice splash of boiling butter. All the better to dunk my toast in. "Tree small egg." The platter landed on the table. This was her way of giving me a morning hug.

"I'm trying to watch what I eat."

"Vhat's dat?" she said, already back at the stove. Hadn't heard a word I'd said.

"I have high cholesterol." A lie.

"Ya, okey den. Vhat I feex you? Dere's ham, mebbe nice hot porridge?" She reached for the porridge bag inexplicably within her reach. Where did that come from? Whose kitchen was this? And since when was ham a low-cholesterol food? Porridge I'm not sure about.

I stood up from the table feeling like a stranger in my own home. An under-dressed stranger. "You know what? I have to go. I have a meeting at work." Another lie. Great. My mother was in my home less than twenty-four hours and I'd already lied to her twice. Oh well. Lies are like peanuts—okay, macadamia nuts—after two it's hard to stop. "I have a client coming in. A big case." I knew she wouldn't ask me any questions about that. I don't think she really knows what I do for a living. She loved it when I was a cop. It was something she could understand. And I think it gave her certain bragging rights with friends and neighbours. My decision to leave the police force had confused her. She never understood why I did it. And never asked.

I backed out of the room as if I expected her to make a run at me with a plate of deep fried prune dumplings and hash browns. Instead, she said nothing, just added more butter to the frying pan and hummed a Ukrainian ditty. I gave Barbra one more look—that damn dog still making like a Cheshire cat—and hightailed it for my bedroom.

My office is on Spadina Crescent, just out of downtown, in an old character house that used to be called the Professional Womyn's Centre. A few years ago a young lawyer, Errall Strane, purchased the property, did some remodelling and in deference to a piece of history, renamed it the PWC Building. After renovations, PWC was left with four office spaces. Errall runs her one-lawyer practice out of the largest suite on the main floor, the balance of which is rented to Beverly Chaney, a psychiatrist. Two smaller offices on the second floor belong to Alberta Lougheed, a psychic, and me. Mine is the smallest, but the only one with a balcony and a view that more than makes up for its size. From the small deck I can look across Spadina Crescent into beautiful Riverside Park and beyond it, the South Saskatchewan River.

I parked in one of the four spots behind the building, next to Beverly's sensible sedan and Errall's bright blue Miata, and plugged in the car. Instead of taking the metal staircase that hugs the rear of the building up to the second floor, I braved the temperature of minus twenty degrees Celsius, circled the building and entered through the front door.

The reception area is a large space filled with expensive art chosen by Errall, plants donated by Beverly, and a colour scheme coordinated by Alberta's aural projections. My contribution is a pencil-holder. A massive circular desk presides over the room and divides the space in two: a waiting area for Errall's clients to the right and one to the left for all the rest of our clients. The area behind the desk is home to the ever-cheerful Lilly, our group receptionist.

Today Errall's side of the foyer was full. Half a dozen serious people in serious suits were waiting to do some serious business. Our side was as quiet as a turkey on Thanksgiving. Errall appeared at her office door, resplendent in coal-black Chanel, her chestnut hair in a severe bun. I gave her a girly wave. She averted her eyes.

I exchanged some idle chitchat with Lilly and then headed up to my office. Over the summer I'd finally given the space a bit of a facelift—a comforting terra cotta and gumleaf green colour scheme for the walls and flooring, and a new couch to replace the stuffing-less version that had been left me by a former tenant. It was out with the old in with the new, except for my beloved desk with the bar fridge holding up one end of it.

19

I had just hit the brew button on my coffee maker when I heard a soft knock on my door. I turned to find Beverly standing at the threshold with her usual friendly smile.

"Do you have a moment, hon?" she asked, her voice as close to being warm syrup without being sticky.

"You bet," I said. "Just put some coffee on."

When she closed the door behind her I knew this wasn't a social call.

"Let's sit," she said, already heading for the client chair in front of my desk.

Okay, this wasn't going to be couch-type talk either. I took my spot behind the desk and smiled at our resident psychiatrist. Beverly is a pretty brunette in her mid-forties with twenty extra pounds that look just right on her. She was wearing a plain grey skirt that showed off her curvy hips nicely and a nondescript cream-coloured blouse under an unbuttoned grey sweater that looked soft enough to be made of kittens.

"I may have a client for you."

I nodded my understanding. This was unusual indeed. Beverly and I had never before referred clients to one another. Not because we don't respect each other's abilities in our respective professions—the situation had simply not come up.

"I've been seeing Daniel Guest for about a year," she began. "Of course I won't go into any of that, but something new has come up…something very new. I received a phone call from Daniel three days ago, very early on Sunday morning. He was in an extremely agitated state and I convinced him to come see me right away." She hesitated for a brief second then continued, "These issues we're dealing with, Russell, relate to…well, criminal activity." She added quickly, "By someone else, not him."

I was about to interrupt but Beverly wordlessly indicated her desire to finish her thoughts.

"As you can imagine, Daniel and I have spent many hours over the past few days discussing this. He needs more help…different help…than I can give him. Fortunately he's now reached the same conclusion. Given the special nature of his circumstances, I suggested you. I hope you have the time to see him?"

20

Did I? What about my planned time off? What about spending time with my mother? And Christmas was just around the corner. But there was a bong sounding in my head. Was this the case Hughie and his little friend Dewey thought I was on and wanted me to drop? Well then of course I'd have the time. Nothing I like better than to pee in some pisser's cornflakes. And besides, Beverly had certainly piqued my interest. What kind of crime was this guy involved in? And what were the special circumstances?

"I guess I've got some time," I said. "And thank you for thinking of me, Beverly, but if this has something to do with a crime that's been committed, shouldn't your client first talk to the police?"

"Believe me, I've suggested it, but he wants to keep this quiet."

"Those 'special circumstances' you mentioned?"

She nodded. "Russell, I'm worried about him. What happened to him has...well, it's shaken his world. He was reticent about getting any kind of outside help at first—other than me, that is—but when I told him about you and your practice, he came around."

"You mean about how cute I am?"

She raised an eyebrow over one rim of her granny glasses but continued on without comment. "He's in my office right now if you're willing to see him."

This surprised me. "Right now? Downstairs in your office?" Nice sum up of the facts, Quant.

"Did you have an accident last night?" This interloping voice was from Alberta Lougheed, her head, a-jangle with earrings, was pushing through a crack she'd made in the doorway, her face expressing genuine concern.

"Wha...?" Was she talking about my run-in with Hugh? I have never come to a conclusion whether or not I believe in Alberta's psychic powers. I have no doubt *she* believes she has a special gift. She's no con artist. I'm just not certain she isn't just plain ol' crazy. She looks like a younger version of Beverly except for tons more make up, hairspray and peculiar fashion choices. Today she faintly resembled Elizabeth Taylor in the role of Cleopatra. "Ah, no," I finally mumbled in answer. I decided a white lie would be easier this morning.

"Oh, okay," she said, not completely convinced, and floated off to her office, likely to feed her asp.

I looked at Beverly and shook my head like a dog with fleas.

She was holding out a white envelope. "Take a look at this. Daniel gave me this to show you. He received it during an awards ceremony on Saturday night—while he was onstage accepting his award. I think it will give you an idea about his problem and why you're just the guy to help him out."

I reached across the desk and took it from her. I withdrew a single piece of paper and unfolded it. It looked a little worse for wear, as if someone had crumpled it and then tried to straighten it out.

I read the typed words and understood what she meant by "special circumstances."

Send $50,000 by December 15 to P.O. Box 8420, Saskatoon, Saskatchewan, S7T 1B5. If you don't—I will tell your wife and the whole city everything I know.

It was signed, *Loverboy.*

Chapter 2

HE WASN'T WHAT I EXPECTED. I thought he'd look like a nervous nellie. I'm not really sure what I mean by that, but it had something to do with him being both a closet case *and* an accountant. Instead, Daniel Guest, a trifle shorter than me at just under six feet, looked sturdy and athletic, in a lean baseball-player kind of way. He had wavy blond-brown hair parted on the side, crinkly green eyes behind a pair of glasses with near-invisible gold frames and a button nose that looked a little squashed to one side. Altogether a nice-looking man. He wore a stylish sports coat with carefully matched trousers and a smart tie-shoes-belt combination. He stood as I entered the office (sans Beverly) and held out a hand as I approached. He was the kind of guy who got manicures and used moisturizer. (I'm that kind of guy too—just not regularly.) We shook and he sat back down while I awkwardly made my way behind the unfamiliar desk to Beverly's chair.

Unlike Errall's ultra-chic space across the way, Beverly's office is the ultimate in homey comfort in the dried-flower, overstuffed couch, potpourri, homemade crafts, framed-prints-of-wildflowers-and-fawns kind of way. As I plopped myself into her amazingly comfortable chair I wondered for the millionth time how she made the room smell so good. I also wondered—impressed by Daniel Guest's natty

23

appearance—whether I should rethink my usual work wardrobe of wrinkle-free cotton pants and shirt.

Nah.

I slowly unfolded the blackmail note, the sound of which seemed to fill the room. Daniel's eyes fell upon the letter as if catching sight of a hated albatross that had been hanging around his neck. I heard him swallow.

"You received this at the SBA—Saskatoon Business Association, right?—awards ceremony this past Saturday night?"

He nodded wordlessly, still eyeing the white sheet of paper.

"It appears to be a blackmail note. Beverly told me you're reticent about involving the police. Which is why you're here, with me." Another nod. Had the albatross got his tongue? "I know you may be uncomfortable being here, talking to me, talking about this, but I can promise you that whatever we discuss today will remain confidential— unless you and I decide otherwise."

He appeared to be listening carefully.

"How can I help you, Mr. Guest?" I simply asked.

"Call me Daniel," he answered. His voice was smooth and deep. He may have been unhappy in the circumstance he found himself in, but his voice did not betray any readily obvious emotion. He was wary though, as he should be. "Beverly told me a lot about you, probably more than she normally would for a simple referral, but she knew I needed a certain comfort level to pursue this.

"Just so you know, Beverly did suggest I go to the police— numerous times. I can't do that. Eventually she gave in and suggested I meet with you. It was important to me to learn you're gay. I know at first that might sound trite or even foolhardy, I should want someone who is good at their job, regardless of their sexuality…but, it's not about that so much as I want someone good at their job who I also feel comfortable discussing my circumstance with. I'm hoping you might be that person. I know as an openly gay man you may have prejudices against me for being closeted or…being with a man while I am married, and if you do, I guess we need to discuss that up front."

He stopped there, a little too suddenly for me to immediately reply. His candor was refreshing. This isn't always the experience I have with the people who come through my door looking for help.

This man was putting forth a business case and, although I did not doubt his veracity, I guessed the ultra-professional attitude he was portraying was a bit of a mask for what he was really feeling.

"I don't foresee that being a problem," I finally got out. And that was the truth. I knew nothing about Daniel Guest other than what Beverly had told me. Every one of us, gay, straight, Aboriginal, white, Hispanic, lawyer, doctor, disabled, or not, has stuff to go through and we each take a slightly different route. At the end of the day I have high hopes that every one of us eventually make the right decisions for ourselves without hurting too many other people along the way. It isn't always easy to decide what's right, but it's pretty clear when you're hurting someone. Usually. I know. I've done it.

He nodded. "I am thirty-six years old. My wife, Cheryl, and I have been married for eighteen years—since we met our first year of university. We get along well. I'm a partner with the firm of Dufour, Guest, Rowan & Rowan, DGR&R for short. I make a handsome salary. I travel. I have friends. No children. I have a pretty good life, Mr. Quant."

"Russell."

"Russell." He licked his lips, a nervous habit I thought, and ticked his head towards the note still in my hands. "I have a problem, Russell, and I need help solving it."

"Tell me what happened."

"On Saturday night I received the SBA Business Builder Businessperson of the Year Award. As I was standing behind the podium—in front of three hundred people including my parents, my partners and staff and my wife—I received that note."

For the first time his voice quivered as he recalled the event. I put the note down on the desk and folded my hands over it.

"It was in an envelope along with the standard cheque the winner receives and endorses to a charity. The tradition is that the winner holds up the cheque for everyone to see and ooh and ahh over while he or she extols the virtue of the charity of choice. I wouldn't have even noticed the note right then but the applause went on and on and I happened to glance down at what was in my hands. At first I thought it was a letter of congratulations from the SBA, you know, some sort of form letter all the winners receive. But it wasn't. When I read the words, I thought it had to be some sort of crazy joke, or that maybe I'd had too much champagne." He stopped there, almost over-come with the horrible memory. He was trying mightily to avoid showing me his true feelings—and beginning to fail.

"It was the ultimate in cruel antithesis," he continued, keeping his voice under admirable control. "There I was being applauded for my personal, professional and community accomplishments yet in my hand I held something that could ruin me, my family and my career." He looked me in the eye and said, "I made a stupid mistake, Mr. Quant…Russell…and I got caught. Now, it appears, I have to pay."

Although I wasn't sure I agreed with Daniel's summation of his situation, I found that his story was sending involuntary shivers up my own spine. At one point or another in our lives, we've all done something we don't want anyone else to find out about. And we worry about being caught. Sure, the seriousness varies from breaking someone's favourite vase to high-level crime, but the fear of discovery can be just as powerful. "Your intention is to pay the fifty thousand dollars then?"

"Loverboy has made a convincing case for himself in very few words. He wants to be compensated for something he knows and I want to hide. Pretty classic case of blackmail, I suppose." I couldn't argue with him there. "I guess I've always unconsciously expected this day would come—it's time to pay the piper."

Then why did he need me?

"I don't want anyone, least of all my wife, finding out about Loverboy. And I *can* stop being with men. So if I pay, this will be over." He stopped there and gave me another piercing look. "But it won't be. Will it?"

I couldn't answer that with any certainty, but the look on my face showed him what I really thought: no way.

"At first I was in a mad rush to find a solution to my problem, to conclude that all I had to do was pay the price and I'd be released from this bloody nightmare. But as Beverly and I talked it through I realized how naive I was being. I know now there's a good chance it won't be over. To realize this person, Loverboy, has me in a vice that he can tighten whenever he wants is…unacceptable.

"Fifty thousand dollars won't bankrupt me, but it is a lot of money and I don't know if I can hide it from my wife or business partners. I can and will pay, Russell, but what happens when he decides he wants another fifty thousand? Or one hundred thousand dollars? Or a trip to the moon!" More licking of lips then, "Each time I think about writing that cheque I become angrier and angrier. At first I thought I'd pay it as a penance, out of guilt, but now I see it as capitulating to the pure greed of another human being and I don't know if I can live with that."

"I'm confused, Daniel. Are you planning to pay the money or not?"

"There are less than six days before the money has to be paid. Not a lot of time, I realize. I will pay, Russell, but only if I get what I pay for. I want you to find Loverboy and make sure he goes away forever—without anyone finding out about him or the money."

Daniel Guest, as part of his profession, was an expert at clearly and concisely identifying goals and objectives. I appreciate that. I could see why he was a successful man.

"And, I don't think finding our blackmailer will be difficult," he added. "You see, I know who Loverboy is."

"You can identify Loverboy?" I asked Daniel Guest, trying to hide the surprise in my voice.

"Not exactly." Aha! I knew it was too good to be true. "But I can tell you about him."

I must have had an odd look on my face (skepticism mixed with a healthy dose of confusion) because Daniel smiled and let out a little guffaw. He looked nice when he smiled. "Russell, there is only one candidate for the role of Loverboy," he said. "There is only one man I've slept with who could be doing this."

"But you can't identify him?"

He shrugged and looked a bit sheepish.

I thought it best to leave that alone for the moment. "Then how do you propose I find him?"

"That's what I need a detective for. In my profession I can locate a specific number in reams of financial data if I have enough clues. I'm hoping you can do the same with Loverboy."

I ripped off the top page of the pad where I'd been taking notes and poised myself over a fresh sheet. "So, what can you tell me about him? How did you meet?"

Daniel wet his lips, straightened his already straight tie and adjusted his glasses before saying, "I don't see how that is relevant."

I looked up and, meeting his eyes said nothing—very meaningfully.

He crossed his right leg over his left, then left over right. "Are you hoping for a titillating story about what a man like me must do when he wants to...in order to...meet my needs?" Suddenly he was a threatened dog, slowly backing himself into a corner, frightened, but prepared to fight. I could almost imagine the hairs on his neck bristling.

I laid down my pen and sat back in my seat. I could have been angry at his petty accusation, but all I felt was sympathy for this man. He was used to being the chairman of every meeting, the man with the answers, the person who others looked to for help—not the one who desperately needed it. Being a fish out of water is never fun to be and less fun to watch. "I'm not your enemy, Daniel," I tried to assure him.

We managed through thirty seconds of silence.

Daniel sat up straighter in his chair, a sign he was ready to talk. He placed both feet flatly on the floor with his hands clasped loosely near his waist. He began. "I met Loverboy in October. On the internet."

Ah, I thought to myself, the twenty-first century's singles bar.

"Over the summer I'd discovered a website called gays.r.us. It has a link to a Saskatchewan gay chat room. Of course I'm extremely careful in the chat rooms. I focus on men who are willing to tell me enough about themselves so I can make an informed decision as to the likelihood of our knowing one another. I look for men whose life situations are so far removed from my own that the possibility of our paths ever having crossed is slim to none. Like those who've recently moved to Saskatoon, or blue-collar types or men ten to fifteen years older or younger than me." I nodded my understanding only because I thought he needed a nod. "But even when I find a likely candidate, I chicken out when push comes to shove and it's time to arrange a meeting place." Candidate? Was he interviewing articling students? "But that night...I didn't."

"Loverboy?" I asked.

He nodded.

"Tell me exactly how it happened."

He let out a discomfited sigh and stared out a window with frilly window treatment at the frigid blue sky. "Oh...dear...I...Russell, is this going to help?"

I gave him a look that I hoped was sympathetic. I couldn't deny some curiosity. And I couldn't deny my uncertainty about what I really needed to know. I shrugged. "To be honest, I don't know, Daniel. All I know is that the more you tell me, the more chance there is I'll glean something useful to help me find Loverboy."

He seemed to accept that and haltingly began his tale. "I was home alone, on the computer doing research. Cheryl was away for the weekend, at her family's farm. Normally we go to family events together, but I was swamped with work and couldn't get away for a whole weekend so I stayed behind. It had been a bitch of a week at the office, a hundred hours and more to come." As Daniel talked, he tried eye contact as much as he could, but generally paid more attention to his cufflinks, glasses and the pleat in his slacks. "It was late, I'd had a couple Scotches and I was feeling...brave...I guess." He stopped there. Took a few deep breaths. Continued. "I had been in the chat room for about an hour when Jo came on..."

"Joe? He told you his name?" I didn't have experience in chat rooms but I doubted anyone gave out their real names.

"Jo. J.O. It was the nickname he used in the room."

J.O.? An acronym? I hid a private grin.

"Jo showed up in the chat room. I sent him a private message and we began to chat. Everything about him seemed right—he was so easy going and humorous. He was twenty-two and a drama student. The chance of me knowing him was near impossible.

"Things moved quickly. But we had a problem. Neither of us had a place to meet. I had assumed he'd have an apartment where we could get together. But he still lived at home with his parents. He asked about my place. At first I said no. I couldn't even begin to imagine it. It was looking as if it was over. Part of me, as usual, was relieved...but part of me that night was...desperate I guess. I don't know if it was the lateness of the hour, or the alcohol or what, but I began to rationalize and imagine what it would be like to invite him over. Before I could stop myself I had typed my address and told him to come over. He said okay and logged off. That was it. It was done. This man—a man I'd never met, was coming over to my house. It was...I was in shock at first."

Even though I was taking notes, I was watching Daniel closely as he told the tale. He was flushed at the memory of the assignation and

I could tell he was still affected by the experience. Was it the excitement of doing something bad—or something oh so good? "That was a big step," I said.

His face showed what an understatement I'd made. "I was petrified. I immediately began scheming how to get out of it. I thought about simply not answering the door or answering it but playing dumb. Yet at the same time I was checking out how my hair looked in the mirror and brushing my teeth."

"And he showed up?"

"Yes. And I let him in. And from the minute he started talking everything he said was like an amazing revelation to me." Daniel finally ceased fiddling with his yuppie accoutrement and faced me with unmoving hands and an almost blissful smile. "This young man, he seemed so at ease with being gay, so happy and carefree. His attitude was, 'Yeah, I'm gay, isn't it great? I wouldn't have it any other way! Let's have some fun.'"

I urged him along. "You had sex?"

"Yes. We did. In the living room." Daniel's eyes narrowed as he recalled the evening, as if suddenly understanding something he hadn't before. "You know, Russell, to him it wasn't something dirty, something you do quickly in the dark without talking or smiling, it was something you do with…rapture…like…real sex."

Daniel shook his head and his eyes were shining, as if in utter amazement of a dreamlike event. I could only imagine—and be jealous of—the fun he'd had that night. "You liked him," I pointed out the more than obvious.

"Yes," he agreed. "I did like Jo. Very much."

"Yet you think he's the one who's doing this to you, you think he's the blackmailer?"

Daniel seemed to shake himself clear of the images of young Jo and resumed the serious business at hand. "Yes."

"Why exactly?"

"Because he was in my house."

"Did he do something that night to make you suspect him now? Did he say something? Steal something? Try to contact you again?"

"No," he admitted. "None of those things. We met only the one time. But just the fact that he knows where I live, knows my name, knows about...the sex, makes him the likely candidate. The only candidate. And in addition to the obvious fact that we'd had sex together, it would have been so easy that night for Jo to figure out I was married and financially well off."

He had a point. "I suppose that's true."

"It's him, Russell, I know it."

"What else can you tell me about him? What did he look like?"

"Well, he was twenty-two. He had long, blond hair and he wore it messy-like and parted in the middle. Blue eyes. Lean but well toned if you know what I mean? Really white teeth. He smiled a lot, like it came easy to him and there was a bit of a gap between his two front teeth. Cute. He was articulate for a young guy. I guess the acting classes did that, I don't know. He seemed natural, real sure of himself, confident. He laughed a lot." He stopped there, his cheeks a peachy-pink, then added, "Do you need to know...y'know, more physical details about him?"

I may have blushed too but I doubt it. "No, I don't think I'll be needing those characteristics to identify him. But if I do, I'll get back to you."

He smiled shyly. Really, he did.

"Anything else?" I asked. "Anything I might be able to use to track him down?"

"It took him less than twenty minutes on his bike to get to my place, so he must live within that radius of my house."

I didn't think that would be too helpful. It would be a better clue in a metropolis the size of Toronto or Montreal or Los Angeles, but, if you hit the traffic right, you can get a quarter of the way across town by bicycle in that amount of time in a city the size of Saskatoon. "You said he was a drama student?"

"More than that, actually. He said he'd gotten a bit part in some local play and that I should 'check it out.'"

Now this was interesting. "Did you? What theatre?"

Daniel scoffed at the question. "Of course not." Then just as quickly realized the loss of a potentially valuable clue. "I guess I should have asked him more questions about it but I really didn't..."

He really didn't care is what I guessed he was about to say, but he let the sentence dissipate.

"This was October?" I asked, mentally figuring out how I could extract as much as possible from this bit of information. "Early or late in the month?"

"Early."

"Daniel, you're convinced Jo the drama student is our top suspect?"

Daniel cleared his throat to firm up a voice that had grown rumbly and perhaps a bit weary. "Yes, Russell. There is no doubt in my mind that Jo is Loverboy. Jo is the man who is out to ruin my life."

"The Travelodge Hotel and Banquet Facility. This is Marianne speaking, how may I direct your call?" said the cheery female voice.

"I'd like to speak to your banquet manager," I told Marianne. I was now back in my office with a contract signed by Daniel Guest promising to pay me ninety-five dollars an hour plus out-of-pocket expenses and applicable taxes as well as a retainer cheque for $1500. I like clients who show up with cheque books and aren't afraid to use them.

"That would be Natalie. Hold on and I'll connect you."

As I waited through an interminable chorus of clicks and buzzes there were enough clicks and buzzes in my own head to run an entire phone company. I had a million questions following my meeting with Daniel. We had certainly made some headway, but I sensed he still doubted the PI approach to solving his problem and in the end I decided it was best to let him scamper off to the safety of his accountant world while I did a bit of initial snooping around.

Finally I heard Natalie's phone ringing. "Banquets. Marge speaking." A less cheerful voice.

"Yes, I'm looking for Natalie."

"She won't be in 'til after one."

I looked at my watch, did some fast calculations of traffic and travel time and said, "Okay, could you book me in to see her at that time?"

Marge hesitated, as though I'd called KFC and tried to order pizza. "You want an appointment, like?"

"Sure. I'll only need a few minutes of her time."

"Well, like I says, she'll be back around one."

So did that mean I had an appointment or would it be a matter of luck to catch her at her desk? I didn't think Marge gave a hoot one way or the other. I said my thanks and hung up. I put my computer to sleep, grabbed my coat, a favourite brown suede with a faux fur lining, and headed downstairs. I found one of the homemade muffins Beverly regularly stocks in the kitchen. That would have to do for lunch today. As I waved to Lilly and told her I'd likely be out the rest of the day, I noticed Errall's waiting room was still crammed with clients. Busy girl.

Outside I unplugged my Mazda RX7, threw the cord into the trunk and, nearly frozen solid by the time I sat inside, was ever thankful for the car-warmer I'd installed last year. I let the car run for a minute. One of the benefits of having a small vehicle in a cold climate is that it doesn't take much time for the heater to do its job. I directed the car towards 22nd Street hoping to get out of downtown before the lunchtime crowd got moving. Noon hour traffic is especially fierce close to Christmas. For some reason, even though stores are open seemingly all hours of every day, everyone gets the same bright idea that they'll find that perfect gift if they can just slip out for a few minutes over their lunch break. As if there really was any chance it would only take a few minutes—or such a thing as the perfect gift.

Persephone Theatre is one of the best of several options for live theatre in Saskatoon. Even though it is illogically located in the middle of a residential no man's land near the west end of town, it's been around for over thirty years so they're obviously doing something right. And I hoped I was too.

I pulled up to the converted one-time church, grateful for the empty parking lot adjacent to the front doors. In Saskatchewan, wise wintertime parking decisions always involve keeping vehicle-to-shelter distance at a minimum. But as luck would have it, the front doors were locked. I pulled up my collar, stuffed my un-mittened hands in my jacket pockets and ran around the side of the building to where I hoped I'd find an office entrance. And indeed, up a barely shovelled walk and through a door with a cracked glass, I found what looked to be a small reception area. Behind a scarred desk that I imagined once belonged to a curmudgeonly old school teacher (I think the theatre atmosphere was inspiring my sense of the dramatic) sat a very pale girl with very black hair eating a very insubstantial looking sandwich. Butter and lettuce maybe, on paper-thin white bread.

"Hello, my name is Rick Astley and I'm the Artistic Director for Theatre Quant in Mission." I was betting she wasn't old enough to be up on her late 1980s teen idol trivia or informed enough about British Columbia community theatres to catch on to my clever ruse. And actually she looked pretty unimpressed with life in general, regardless of the decade. I continued on, hoping my enthusiasm, if not my really bad English accent, would be contagious. "I've been visiting Saskatoon and of course have made a point of seeing each of the current season's Persephone productions. Well, one of your actors has caught my eye. And now that I'm preparing for a remake of the classic *Who's Afraid of Valerie Bertinelli*, I just have to have him for one of the lead roles." I stopped there to give her an opportunity to express her amazement.

She blinked.

"So I was hoping you might help me get in touch with him. I know you will want to. Acting is such a risky career these days. Always has been actually. I used to do some acting myself, you know—Shakespeare—the exquisite bard—now that is real acting. You've no doubt heard of me?"

Nibble, nibble.

"Of course I'm better known for my roles in more contemporary classics like, 'She Wants to Dance With Me' and 'Take Me to Your Heart,' which I'm sure you're familiar with, being a part of the theatre world as you are."

Blink, blink.

"But great roles were hard to come by and I finally found myself 'Giving Up on Love,' my love of acting that is and turning to directing. And of course my reputation in that arena is...well, let me just say, 'I'll Never Let You Down.' So, do you think you can help me, Miss...?"

"Rebecca." She had finally put down the sandwich and managed a look of idle curiosity. "You're who again?"

Brave young thing. "Rick Astley. You see I have a description of the actor I am looking for, but no name or contact information."

"You saw him when?"

She must not have been able to chew and listen at the same time. Probably for the better, she might have actually recognized one of Astley's bigger hits and revealed me as a fraud.

"This past fall. You have what, three shows in the fall season?"

"Uh-huh. But, I only just started working here this month."

I was not shocked by this news.

"There's really no one else here who could help." She screwed up her face. I'm sure she was wondering if that meant she'd actually have to do something herself. "Our last show just closed and most of the management people are gone on Christmas break. They'll be back after the holidays though," she added sluggishly.

"Oh dear, well, I'll have to cast the show long before then. I'd hate for this actor to lose this opportunity to make some good money doing wonderful theatre."

She nodded sympathetically. "Yeah, yeah, that's for sure. But I don't know how we could help you without a name or anything."

Perfect, just the opening I was looking for. "Do you have a copy of the programs for the shows you've done this past season?"

"Well, yeah, sure."

"Could I take a boo?"

"Huh?"

"Take a look, dear, could I please take a look at those programs."

"What show did you say it was?" Her voice was whiny as if she was beginning to strongly suspect this might involve some effort on her behalf.

"Unfortunately I don't recall, could I see all three?"

She lethargically pulled open a drawer that must have weighed several tonnes given the effort she expended to do so and pulled out just the documents I was looking for. I quickly scanned the first one and was gratified to see that indeed the photographs of each of the actors for each production, as well as those of the staff of the theatre, were semi-glossily reproduced in miniature. I went over all the pictures in the three programs and identified five men who could conceivably fit the description of Jo given to me by Daniel Guest. So far so good. Next hurdle.

I looked up at Rebecca and judged her recovered enough from the drawer opening adventure to move ahead with a new task. "Now, I ask all actors I work with to leave me copies of their resumes, just in case I wish to work with them again. I'm sure Persephone's artistic director must do the same." I had no idea whether this was true, but I was guessing Rebecca didn't either. I laid down the three programs opened to the pages with the pictures of the actors in question. "Perhaps you might have a look-see in your files?" I knew how I would go about finding Jo, I just hoped Rebecca was up to the task. I also hoped she didn't realize I'd suddenly lost my accent. Drat, I hate when I do that!

"Well I suppooooossssse Sheila could get into the office where the files are kept." More whining.

"What a great idea!" I announced buoyantly. "Tell you what," I said glancing at my watch. "I have another appointment. Why don't I attend to it then return afterward, say in an hour or so? That should give you and dear Sheila plenty of time to find a few resumes and make copies, wouldn't you say?" I grabbed a scrap of paper and pen from her desktop and scrawled down my cellphone number. Although I didn't really expect her to call, I was on a roll and had just thought up one more Rick Astley hit I hadn't used yet. I handed the paper to her and with juvenile satisfaction said, "And if you get done early, just 'Dial My Number.'"

Chapter 3

I RETURNED TO MY CAR, started it for warmth and sat in the Persephone Theatre parking lot eating my muffin and hoping Rebecca was leaping into action. Something told me I shouldn't rush getting back. When I was done chowing down, I took 22nd Street to the Circle Drive freeway and arrived at the Travelodge Hotel in time to make my pseudo appointment with Natalie, the banquet manager. It was a short meeting.

As Marge predicted, Natalie was indeed back at her desk by 1:00, but she had little useful information about the event in question unless I was interested in the configuration of the tables or the number of bottles of red wine imbibed by the guests. She suggested I contact someone from the SBA. Although a little miffed at having made the trip for nothing, I had to admit Natalie's idea was a good one.

Back in my car I retrieved the phone book I keep behind the driver's seat and looked up the address for the SBA offices. I could have called but since I had nothing else to do for a while I decided to take my chances and show up in person. Besides, I find in my line of work that doing business face-to-face is always preferable. People have a harder time lying to me or ignoring me if I'm right in front of them. Not that some don't try.

I found my way to the Ontario Avenue building and, luckily, was immediately escorted into the office of SBA president, Lois Vermont. She was a no-nonsense kind of woman with dark hair cut short—no doubt to avoid the finicky attention required by more feminine styles—and a plain-cut, suit-and-silk-blouse set that would mix and match with all the other plain-cut suits and silk blouses I was sure were in her closet. The only outward hint of personal flare she allowed herself was a brightly coloured, oversized scarf tied about her neck. Very spiffy.

After I was seated in her orderly office, coffee in hand, she sat looking at me with her hands prayer fashion on the top of her too-organized desk, her unlipsticked mouth in a bit of a pinched position, waiting for me to speak. I debated introducing myself as Gino Vanelli but sensed that with Ms. Vermont I wasn't about to get away with anything too far removed from the absolute truth.

"What a lovely scarf." Okay, I did veer a little away from absolute truth.

Although I swore I saw the corners of her eyes crinkle with what may have been mirth, the only sparkle in an otherwise flat and bland face, she remained impassive. "How can I help you today, Mr. Quant?"

"I'm a private investigator." Her eyebrows moved a millimetre higher on her broad forehead. The private investigator thing usually gets some sort of response. There aren't many of us running around Saskatoon and everyone, at one time or another, has wanted to be part of an Agatha Christie or Nancy Drew mystery. "I'm investigating a blackmail scheme."

"Involving the SBA?"

"Not directly, but the plot involves a past SBA award recipient and originated at an SBA award ceremony."

"Interesting. How can I help?"

I liked Lois Vermont. No pretense. No gobbledygook about how the SBA couldn't possibly be involved in anything as sordid as black-mail. "I would like to ask you some questions about your award ceremony procedures."

"Are you referring to the ceremony this past Saturday? Or, if you tell me which year the blackmail relates to, I can pull out the appro-priate files. I keep detailed records of each year's event."

I winced. "Actually that won't be possible."

She nodded, not in the least offended. "You're concerned that by telling me the year of the event in question I might deduce the identity of your client—even though there are several award winners every year in varying categories."

"That's correct. I know this may make things more difficult, but…"

"This is not a problem, Mr. Quant. I understand and I will do the best I can to help you. What is it you need to know?" She quirked her head to one side, at the ready.

"The blackmail was perpetrated by way of a note sent to the victim within the envelope presented to him when he won an SBA award."

"I already know your client is a male and won the SBA Business Builders Businessperson of the Year Award within the last six years." She said this without any sign of smugness, simply as a matter of fact.

"Oh? How do you know that?" Should I suggest a guest spot on Alberta's late night TV psychic show?

"You said the envelope was presented to 'him,' so your client is male. Only the winners of the Businessperson of the Year Award are presented with an envelope. The other winners receive only an engraved plaque. The tradition of physically presenting the cheque on the evening of the ceremony—rather than at a later date—began only six years ago," she told me. "I hope you don't mind, I just don't wish to pretend to not know something that I do."

I smiled. "Thank you."

She managed a thin-lipped smile in return.

"Obviously I am interested in who could have known the identity of the winner and also had access to place the blackmail note into the envelope that was presented to that winner. It's an issue of physical access as well as access to specific knowledge."

A curt nod from Lois. "I understand. First let's discuss physical access." Lois Vermont was not the president of a business association for nothing. She got right to it. "I have been with the SBA for over ten years and I can tell you with a high level of certainty that in the last six years, since we began presenting the envelope along with the plaque to the Businessperson of the Year, the process has remained unchanged. We do things exactly the same way, year after year. It works, so why change it. I prepare the envelope in question. The cheque is actually a dummy cheque. It looks real, but it isn't. It's only for show. We do that for security reasons, because we know there are opportunities when the cheque is not under constant surveillance, that it could be stolen. We are a small organization and we are not in the financial position to maintain a fleet of security guards during the awards ceremony or any other time."

"Of course, that makes sense."

"I'm glad you think so." I wasn't certain if she meant it or was patronizing me. I decided I didn't need to know the answer. "As I mentioned, I prepare the dummy cheque. I always do it the morning of the ceremony."

"Are you sure?"

"Absolutely. I am a firm believer in lists and a system of check-off procedures. Preparing the dummy cheque is on my morning of the ceremony procedure list. There would be no reason for me to vary from this list."

I had no doubt this was true.

"So as early as the morning of the ceremony someone might have access to the cheque in its envelope?" I asked.

"No, I don't believe so. After I prepare the cheque and place it in its envelope...which, by the way, remains unsealed. We don't want winners having to fumble around with a sealed envelope."

"Very sensible."

"Yes. After the cheque is prepared and I put it in the envelope, I place that envelope in my office safe along with several other pieces of important documentation that I've prepared for that evening. So, unless your blackmailer is also a safe cracker, they would not have access to the envelope at that time. In the past six years my safe has not been broken into, or at least not in a manner I could detect. No one else has the combination for that safe."

"I think your conclusion is a sound one. When's the first time the envelope is available for someone to tamper with without someone else noticing?"

"At the end of my business day I retrieve the documents, including the envelope, from the safe in my office and I take them home with me as I do not return to the office before going to the hotel where the event is held. So, indeed, if you care to suspect members of my family,

I suppose it is possible that my husband, daughter or babysitter could have slipped a blackmail note into the envelope while I was in the shower or dressing or otherwise engaged."

"Not likely," I said.

"Not likely," she agreed straight-faced. "Thereafter the envelope remains in my possession until I arrive at the hotel, enter the ballroom, head backstage and place it on a table set up just off-stage to hold the various prizes and awards that will be distributed that evening. The envelope remains there, unguarded, until it is handed to the winner. That being said, beginning with the time I arrive, there is a great deal of activity backstage and near the awards table until the commencement of the evening's formal activities."

"Meaning there are a lot of people around?"

"Yes. Everyone from the banquet manager, stage manager, lighting and sound technicians, waiters and kitchen staff, SBA staff and other hotel personnel. The list, I'm afraid, would be a long one."

"What sort of time period are we talking about between when you deliver the envelope and when it hits the hand of the winner?"

She thought briefly before answering, ensuring the accuracy of her calculations. "Anywhere between two-and-a-half to three hours, depending of course on the lengths of speeches, dinner service, and other goings-on with indefinite start and finish times beyond my control."

My guess was that the list of things beyond Lois Vermont's control was a short one. I looked at her and gently shook my head. Her news was not good and we both knew it. Almost anyone could have had the opportunity to slip that note into the envelope Daniel Guest had received that night. But who knew it would be him who received it? That was my only hope left.

"You also brought up the question of who would know who the winner of the Businessperson of the Year award would be," Lois said right on cue. "I'm afraid my answer won't please you much better."

"Everyone and his dog?" I guessed. "Including your husband, daughter and babysitter?"

She nodded. "It is an unfortunate matter of showmanship, one that our board of directors debates heatedly every year. The winner of every other category is indeed kept secret until the actual announcement at the ceremony. But due to the importance of the Businessperson of the Year Award, we do what is necessary to ensure that the winner, with prepared speech in hand and troops of supporters in the audience, is in attendance to accept the honour."

"I take it you don't agree with this tradition?"

The corners of her lips turned up just a wee bit before she answered, "That is not my decision to make."

"So the bottom line is that anyone could have known who the winner was and anyone could have gotten to that envelope without being detected. There are no obvious suspects here," I said grimly.

"Well," she said, "just one."

She had my attention. "Oh? And who is that?"

"Me," she said. "I am the one obvious common denominator with unequalled access to the knowledge of the winner's identity and the envelope."

"Are you making a confession, Ms. Vermont?"

This time a smile did flit across her face. "No, for the record, I am not."

I narrowed my eyes. "But that in itself does not preclude me from adding your name to the suspect list." I wasn't serious about this, but I was interested in her reaction, just for the heck of it.

"I would expect no less," she responded, Vulcan-like.

"I want to thank you for your time, Ms. Vermont," I said as I rose from my chair.

"You're very welcome," she said, also rising. "I'm sorry my information couldn't have been more directive."

"Well, you never know. Sometimes the cloudiest bit of information when combined with other cloudy bits of information makes everything perfectly clear."

"I understand." And I believe she did.

I was almost out the door when I heard her call my name. I turned back and gave her a questioning look.

"Your client is Daniel Guest," she said in a hushed whisper.

I swallowed hard but hoped I gave no other outward signs of confirmation or surprise at the accuracy of her guess. "Why do you say that?"

"Don't worry, Mr. Quant, nothing we've discussed today will leave this room. It's just that I must admit I've found the idea of your profession and current dilemma quite intriguing and challenging this afternoon. I've been attempting my own internal sleuthing since you arrived with the goal of guessing who your client is. I hope you don't mind. I know it's silly." Silly was not a word I'd use to describe Lois Vermont. "I'm probably way off base, but given that I know your client is a man and he won the award in the past six years, there are only four possible people it could be. The other two recipients were women."

I was curious now too. "So why Daniel Guest out of those four?"

"When the awards are handed out, my duties include being present on or near the stage throughout the ceremony. Although it was several days ago, I remember clearly the look on Mr. Guest's face after he received his award and opened the envelope. He was smiling, but there was something else I saw, something in his eyes. It was...horror."

By the time I returned to Persephone Theatre after my meeting with Lois Vermont, Rebecca had collected a stack of five black and white eight-by-ten's (the actor's version of a resume) of blond or sort of blond twenty-something actors who'd appeared on the Persephone stage in the past three productions. Rebecca wisely would not allow me to remove the photos from the premises but she did let me photocopy them. I copied front and back—on the back of each photograph was the actor's pertinent information including name, phone number and vital statistics (likely exaggerated) of height, weight and hair colour.

Back in my car I used my cellphone to call Daniel's office number. I reached his voice mail which told me he would be in meetings or away from the office for the rest of the day.

Instead of going back to the office where I expected all I'd do is chase my tail while trying to find a comfortable spot on the sofa, I called my mother and told her to put her coat on because I'd be by to pick her up in fifteen minutes. And thirty minutes later my mother was sitting in a movie theatre seat for the first time in almost forty years. As we went through the process of selecting one of the four matinee options, paying for the tickets and buying popcorn, Nibs and drinks, her monosyllabic conversation had me worried. It wasn't until we were settled in the dim, nearly empty theatre, on the downy comfort of our coats waiting for the show to begin that I took notice of the look on her face. It was that of a schoolgirl on her first fieldtrip away from home. Her eyes were wide and shiny as they gobbled up every detail of the theatre and the few people around us. She was initially suspicious of the yellowed popcorn but was deep into the bucket's contents long before the film began to roll.

"I vas tventy-tree years old, Sonsyou—" (her affectionate Ukrainian term for "my son") "—last time I do dis. Vit Dad." I knew that by Dad she meant my dad, her husband. "Dad deedn't like. Too long for heem to seet." Her head rotated about a hundred-and-eighty degrees as she continued to behold her awesome surroundings. "Oi, vhat a ting. And before supper too!"

I smiled more that afternoon than I had in a long time. And it had nothing to do with the movie.

My house is on a large lot at the dead end of a quiet, little-travelled street. A grove of towering aspen and thick spruce neatly hide it from view of the casual passerby. Inside, the house is a unique mix of open, airy rooms and tiny, cozy spaces, each that appeal to me depending upon my mood. A six-foot-high fence encircles the backyard and at the rear of the lot, accessible by way of a back alley, is a two-car garage with a handy second storey I use for storage. My home is my castle, a place where I re-energize and take refuge from the world. And tonight my refuge smelled like pork roast, kielbasa and potatoes in cream.

After our heavy post-theatre fare, I helped my mother clean up the kitchen then introduced her to the delights of satellite TV. She was immediately drawn to the mystery channel that was showing reruns of all her favourites, like *Murder She Wrote*, *Matlock* and *Barnaby Jones*. So while she retired to her room to watch murder and mayhem to her heart's content, I took Barbra for a quick after-dinner walk, hoping to ward off the several pounds I could feel attaching themselves to my tummy like barnacles of fat.

It was one of those perfect winter evenings: not too cold, no wind, confetti-like snowflakes fluttering to the ground like ice fairies in slow motion. Graceful, bare limbed trees glittered with diamond-white jewels of frost. Decorated homes were Lite-Brite versions of their normal selves. The smoke of birch wood fires and Handel's *Messiah* floated on the air as if permanent components of nature. Magical. Tranquil. I pulled in a sharp breath of cool, clean air and wished I could maintain the euphoric feeling for longer. Christmastime in Saskatoon. A pretty terrific place to be.

We were on our way back and about half a block away when Barbra began to act up, unusual for her.

"What is it, girl? Did Little Timmy fall down the well!" It was our standard Lassie joke whenever it seemed Barbra was trying to tell me something important—if only she could talk.

Ignoring me, Barbra strained at her collar and let out a couple woofs. Another dog was running towards us. Initially alarmed until I saw that it was Brutus, her brother, I released Barbra from her leash and watched as the two dogs greeted one another with their customary nose touch followed by some rather staid frolicking in the snow.

"Errall?" I called out to the dark figure getting out of a car parked in front of my yard.

"Good timing," she called back.

As I came closer I ducked down to see if Kelly was in the vehicle. She wasn't.

"Is this a bad time?" she asked. "I should have called."

I was surprised to see Errall, especially without Kelly. Errall and I aren't the kind of friends who just drop by for unexpected visits. "Ah, sure it's okay. Come on in."

"I suppose I can't smoke in there?" she asked, knowing the answer. Errall and I both gave up smoking over five years ago but she had started again nine months ago when her partner, Kelly, learned she had breast cancer and eventually had a breast removed.

"It's time to quit again, Errall."

"I know," she said tensely, "but it'll be like last time, I'll get bitchy and gain a ton of weight."

Errall is almost always bitchy and rarely deviates more than half a kilogram off her ideal weight, but I didn't think this was a good time to point that out.

"Russell, I need your help."

This was a first. Errall and Kelly have been together for eight years. Kelly is my friend—Errall is someone who sleeps with my friend. At least that's how our relationship began and remained for quite some time. Errall and I tend to see the world in different ways, but I've also grudgingly come to admit that she, my lawyer and my landlord, is one of the smartest and most insightful people I know.

"It's too cold out here, c'mon inside. You can do without a cigarette for a while."

"Who the hell is that?" Errall asked as we made our way down the front yard pathway, dogs at our heels.

I followed her gaze. My mother's Brillo Pad head was clearly silhouetted behind the frosted glass of my front door. She was sneaking a peek, not too subtly, to see who was in the yard.

I chuckled. "Come meet my mom." But by the time we reached the house and made our way inside, Mother was no where to be found. I shrugged, and said, "I guess the commercial break was over."

After depositing our coats and boots in the foyer, I directed Errall to the living room. It's the largest space in the house, meant for grand parties of which I've had one or two. The centrepiece is a gigantic, stone-covered, octagonal fireplace. Surrounding it is a collection of couches for fireside chats with close friends, a grand piano for rousing singsongs with show-tune-loving homosexuals and women over a certain age, a fully stocked bar for that lounge-lizard atmosphere and an empty space near the windows that sometimes ends up being a dance floor and would soon become home to a Christmas tree.

"Wine?" I offered as she headed for the fireplace and I for the bar.

"You have any Scotch?"

I had some Oban I'd purchased for a special someone who'd never come over to drink it. "Coming right up."

While I poured our drinks Errall expertly laid in a small fire. Her hair was in a tidy ponytail and she wore an oversized sweatshirt and jeans. Our tasks done we retired to the couch.

We weren't small talkers so as I took a first sip of a purple and peppery Via Aurelia Cabernet I'd poured myself I asked, "What is it? Is it Kelly?"

"Sort of. I...we need a favour."

"Sure, anything, you know that."

Errall glanced over at Barbra and Brutus who had splayed themselves out with the meekness of *Penthouse* models in front of the fireplace, soaking up heat. "Actually, Barbra needs to agree to this favour too."

I said nothing. Barbra did the same.

"We were wondering if you two would mind keeping Brutus for a while."

I smiled. "Finally!" I enthused. "Where are you going? It's about time. Somewhere hot I hope." More accustomed to Barbra staying at Kelly and Errall's house whenever I have to be away for work or fun, I was more than happy to return the favour. "You and Kelly really need this after what you've been through these past months." The whole experience of the diagnosis and process to remove the cancer from Kelly's body had been stressful on both women and their relationship. The disease had curdled Kelly's usual sunny disposition. She'd become a carbonated drink gone flat. Even months after the surgery, Kelly seemed to be having difficulty getting over the dismal sense of mortality that had overcome her. Of anyone I knew, Kelly needed to get away, have some fun and learn to get on with life.

"Actually we're not going anywhere."

"Oh." So much for that idea. "Well, you know, sometimes just sitting at home and doing nothing is good too. It'll give you time to spend together, we could…"

"Russell, just stop it!" She tried to keep her voice down but she couldn't hide the raw emotion in it. And I couldn't quite identify its source. She sounded angry…but that wasn't it, not really. "Will you just take Brutus?"

"Of course," I quickly agreed. "He's always welcome. I just thought it meant you were going on a vacation."

"I know, I know." She sounded remorseful at her outburst but didn't address it. Instead she took a healthy swallow of her alcohol and stared into the fire. "I need a cigarette," she said. I thought I saw some extra fluid near her eyes but Errall is not a weeper so I figured I had to be imagining it. "Kelly just thinks it would be best if she didn't have Brutus to look after right now. She's still not feeling back to normal. She gets tired so easily. It's just one more thing she has to do."

One more thing she has to do? Kelly loves Brutus. He's family. What was Errall talking about? And even if Kelly was tired, what about her, would it hurt Errall to take the dog for a walk every once in a while?

"I've been trying to do it," she said, obviously reading my thoughts. "Trying to take care of him. And usually it's okay, but I've been so busy the last few months with some big cases…"

"Errall, it's just a dog, it's not as if you need to make gourmet meals for him…"

She cut me off with icy precision. "You don't understand, Russell. I don't always have the time and Kelly can't…or won't do it anymore."

"What are you saying?" I just wasn't getting it.

"She won't take care of him, Russell. Do you remember a couple of weeks ago when I had to go to Edmonton for a few days for work? I came home and found dog shit by the door. Dog shit! He never does that, Russell, never! Brutus would rather chew off one of his own legs than do that. I don't even know if she fed him while I was gone. The poor dog looked petrified when I walked in the door. He wasn't himself for days. I can't put him through that again." She was careful with the expression on her face, always wary about giving away too much of herself, but her eyes couldn't hide her frustration. "Did you know Kelly almost never goes to the gallery anymore? And she hasn't done any of her own work since before the operation. There are days she doesn't get out of bed or take a shower. Did you know that?"

I hadn't. I sat there, my confusion becoming worry becoming guilt.

Kelly and I had been almost inseparable throughout her illness and the beginning stages of recovery until…well, until I'd let my own life consume me. I hadn't been paying close enough attention. I just thought…assumed…that she was better now, that things were getting back to normal. My heart dropped to the soles of my feet as I realized I had no basis for that conclusion. I hadn't set foot in Off Broadway, Kelly's shop, for months and although we'd had some perfunctory phone calls, I hadn't laid eyes on my friend in almost as long.

I looked into Errall's flaming eyes. No, she wasn't angry, she was scared. And I was too. "What can I do?"

Errall took another punishing gulp of the Oban. "I just…well, take Brutus. Just for now. I don't know for how long, but it's just one less thing to worry about. I know he'll be well looked after. And he loves being here. It'll give Kelly and I some time to deal with this. Once I find out what 'this' really is."

"Of course. Anything. And I'll call Kelly tomorrow."

Errall nodded limply. "Okay, but don't...don't tell her that I told you everything. Don't push her. Not yet, anyway."

"But I could..."

She cut me off again. "Russell, just don't push her. Leave it up to me right now."

My head bobbed up and down. I glanced over at the two dogs. I saw Brutus' chest rise and fall dramatically as he let out a heavy sigh, as if sensing a momentous change was coming to his life.

A couple of hours later as I was extinguishing the house lights in preparation for going to bed the phone rang. A quick glance at a wall clock told me it was near midnight. I rushed for it, not wanting the sound to disturb my mother.

"Hello," I said into the receiver.

"Russell." I recognized the voice. It was Beverly.

She had bad news.

Chapter 4

DUFOUR, GUEST, ROWAN & ROWAN was a local firm with a total staff of sixty, fifty of which were considered professional staff, the rest administrative or support. In recent years, merger turmoil in the world of international accounting firms had fuelled the growth of smaller, homegrown organizations. Charge-out rates levied by the biggies that made sense in Toronto and Vancouver were downright ridiculous in the Saskatchewan market. So, although sometimes considered too small for larger, resource-intensive assignments, local firms like DGR&R were cleaning up by winning bids on small- to medium-sized jobs.

Located in the north end of the city, considered by some a less desirable business area than downtown, the DGR&R partners had purchased and remodelled a three-storey building they renamed the DGR&R complex. I didn't think it was much of a complex when I pulled up near the street entrance at 7 a.m. Thursday. I suppose it was pretty to look at, all turquoise-tinted glass and maroon-coloured support beams, but aesthetics eluded me that early in the morning. Besides, it was still dark and after my discussions with Errall and Beverly the previous night, so was my disposition.

I'd barely taken my first sips from a piping hot, non-fat, café latte from Starbucks when a gleaming black Beemer glided by me like a silent phantom and pulled into the empty lot behind the building. Bringing my coffee and a folder with me, I locked up the Mazda and hustled to catch up with Daniel Guest. I met him just as he was retrieving a shiny black briefcase out of the shiny black car's trunk. He was a matching fool. We exchanged curt hellos. There was a bit of "Mama—a.k.a. Beverly—is making us play together but we don't wanna" in the air, but I was okay with that. Chilled to the bone, I followed him to the back door of the building. I watched as he typed in a security code into a number pad next to the doorknob and I entered the building behind him.

We were obviously the only ones there and Daniel switched on lights as we made our way down a narrow hallway and up a few flights of stairs. I guessed this was the back exit, inaccessible to clients. On the top floor I was led down another hallway and into an atrium. Its centre looked down three storeys into what I guessed was the ground floor reception area. I had no time to find out because within seconds Daniel had directed me into an office and closed the door behind us with the stealth of a shady tax accountant fleeing Revenue Canada.

"He's stalking me!" were the first words out of his mouth after he'd switched on a set of overhead lights and fell with his back against the door.

I had gathered as much from my conversation with Beverly the evening before. Apparently Daniel had called her, yet again in a state of distress and yet again she tried to convince him to go to the police. When that failed her, they talked things through and eventually reached the same solution as yesterday: me.

I studied my client, gauging just how freaked out he was by the turn of events. He looked like a man who hadn't slept, his face an unhealthy pallor. The whites of his eyes were shot with blood, beneath which dark circles had made an uneasy home. Under his unbuttoned overcoat his suit and tie were crisp and clean, a vivid contrast to the rumpled man who wore them. I wondered if his wife had seen him before he left the house and if so, how he'd explained his appearance.

"Daniel," I said as gently as I could. "Can we sit down? I think you need to sit down."

"It was after I left work last night. I was on my way home when I noticed the same car showing up in my rear-view mirror. I circled the block to make sure. He was definitely following me! Thank goodness I noticed before I got home. Suppose he followed me home? I didn't know what to do or where to go!" This all fell out of his mouth in an uncontrollable, unstoppable stream. He was working himself into a froth. Obviously his time with Beverly hadn't released all the steam building up in this pressure cooker. I let him go on.

"Why is he doing this, Russell? He must know I got the blackmail note. It's only the eleventh today. He didn't demand the money until the fifteenth. Why is he hounding me? Does he want to show me he's serious? Well I got it, man, you're serious! Leave me alone! For chris-sakes man, what do I do?"

"Tell me what else happened, Daniel," I said, keeping my voice low and steady. "He followed you, then what?"

"I drove in circles. I went everywhere but home." Daniel ran a still-gloved hand through already mussed-up hair. "I eventually parked in front of the police station downtown. And I just sat there. For half an hour I waited. When I started out again he was gone. So I went home. Keeee-rist! WhadamIgonnado?"

"Daniel, first you need to sit down."

His eyes grew to saucer-size and his face contorted. He yelled at me, spittle flying from his lips, "I don't want to sit down! I want...I want...I want this to be over with! I want this nightmare to be over with!"

I frankly wasn't surprised at this outburst. Daniel had been too controlled the day before. He was treating the whole thing—at least with me—as if it were a meddlesome business problem that needed a tidy solution. His anger was honest. Now, I thought to myself, we can work together.

"Daniel, if indeed this was Loverboy..."

Again he railed at me, "What the hell do you mean 'if'?"

"It's unpleasant, yes, Daniel, but nothing new has happened here, nothing more threatening."

"Are you crazy?" he shouted at me, a crazed look on his face, his glasses slightly askew. "He could have followed me home! Once he knows where I live he could walk right up to my front door and tell my wife everything! He could tell my neighbours, staff, clients! Do you have any idea what this could do to my business?"

I raised my voice just a bit, only to ensure I had his attention. "Daniel! First of all, if Jo is Loverboy, he already knows where you live!"

He gazed at me with a gradual dawning of understanding, then said, "Yeah, yeah, yeah, that's right."

"And second of all, Loverboy would never dare tell your wife—or anyone else—anything at this point in the game. To do so would cost him fifty grand!"

There was a bit of settling-down silence. Even with lights on, the room appeared cast in a depressing dimness. Outside the windows, despite the morning hour, it was still the dark of night. It was too early for any neighbours to have commenced their business day and we seemed very isolated in our lone tower on this winter morning in the north end of Saskatoon.

"So why then? Why is he following me?" Daniel finally asked, having sufficiently calmed himself.

"I don't know," I admitted. "Maybe he's just keeping an eye on you, or seeking some thrill by watching you squirm now that the cat is out of the bag. I don't know, Daniel, but I think this is good news."

He shot me an incredulous look. "What are you talking about?"

"Until yesterday all we had was a piece of paper. Now we've got a real live person. He's shown himself. And if he shows himself again…well, we just might be there to catch him."

"How? How are we going to do that?"

"Leave that up to me for now. Tell me, was the car a green Intrepid?" I bit my lip waiting for the answer I was sure would be yes.

"No." My heart sank. "It was blue I think. I'm not sure of the make. Why do you ask?"

Bugger. Oh well, Hugh had a buddy with him the other night; perhaps the buddy was driving a blue car. I gave Daniel a quick run-down of my South Corman Park Landfill escapade. He doubted it had anything to do with his case. I wasn't so sure.

With the immediacy of Daniel's situation dealt with, we each took off our coats and Daniel offered me a seat while he went down to put on some much needed coffee. He'd been coveting my Starbucks but I wasn't in the sharing mood.

Daniel's office was a corner suite with a metal-and-glass desk parked in front of two large windows that looked out into the parking lot, a barren area beyond it and some indistinguishable warehouse type buildings in the distance. Given the dark outside there wasn't much to see, but I guessed the same could be said in full daylight. The rest of the room was more glass and stainless steel furniture that looked nice but not necessarily comfortable, and pale walls sporting several massive Darrell Bell originals: stunning watercolours of lazy rivers carelessly winding their way beneath turquoise skies and through wooded hills of ochre, vermilion and pumpkin umber. I couldn't help wonder if these impressive canvases were placed here to make up for the rather drab view. Although each piece was worthy of closer perusal I didn't have time to lollygag. I only had a few minutes for skullduggery.

I headed for Daniel's desk. I picked up a photograph in a surprisingly heavy silver frame. It was of four people, two men and two women. One of the men was Daniel; the other was a distinguished-looking character probably ten or fifteen years older than my client, with greying hair thinning at the top and a slightly buck-toothed smile. Next to him was a woman with short blond hair who, although not as old as the man, was definitely older than the other woman whom I took to be Daniel's wife. She had dark, curly hair and a roundish, pleasant face dusted with freckles.

"Russell?"

That was quick. I turned around to see Daniel looking a little more like his usual put-together self. I indicated the picture in my hand and said, "Just admiring the photograph." He eyed the photo as he closed the office door and took a seat behind his desk. "This must be your wife," I said about the brunette, "with all the freckles."

"Actually no," he said. "The woman next to Mick is Cheryl."

I took another look, trying to hide my surprise. Pictures are sometimes deceiving but Cheryl Guest looked several years older than her husband. Either that or she'd spent too much time in the sun. She was attractive, but...well, there was no other way to say it: she had a mess of wrinkles on her face. "And Mick, the other gentleman, is a partner here?" I asked, still trying to gloss over my obvious snooping.

"Please," Daniel said, playing the gracious host, "take a seat. The coffee's going to take a few minutes."

I replaced the picture on the desktop and plopped down in the stiff metal chair he indicated.

"The Soloways are our next-door neighbours," he told me. "Mick and his wife, Anita, are close friends of ours."

I nodded politely.

He sighed. "I'm sorry about…about earlier and for insisting on meeting you here so early and, well…"

I waved it off. "Don't mention it." I pulled a sheaf of photocopied photographs out of the leather folder I'd brought with me and placed them on the desk in front of him.

"What are these?"

"Copies of photographs of young, blond actors who've appeared in the last three Persephone Theatre plays."

He looked up at me and smiled. "You're good."

Yup. "Now it's your turn. Is one of them Jo?"

He glanced at the closed office door as if someone with X-ray vision might be behind it, then, satisfied no one was spying on us, began a careful study of each picture. He stopped on the fourth one.

"It's him," he said in a hush, gazing at the likeness.

I leaned closer and looked at the gap-toothed actor, a pleasant-looking young man. "Are you sure that's him?"

"That's him," he said without hesitation.

I reached over and flipped the picture so we could read the information on the backside.

"Now we know," Daniel uttered cryptically. "Now we know who Loverboy is. James Kraft." He looked at me and grimly said, "Go get him."

After we'd spent too much time staring at the picture of Jo/Loverboy/James Kraft and his related biographical information, such as it was, I shoved all the photographs and bios back into my leather folder and prepared for a difficult conversation. Something had bothered me since my first meeting with Daniel Guest. But now that I'd shown him some results and hopefully garnered a bit of trust, it was time to tackle it. I didn't know how to broach the subject delicately—so I hopped in with both boots and hoped for the best.

"Daniel, I know that because of what happened between the two of you you're certain James Kraft is the blackmailer, but...well...are you telling me you've only ever slept with one man?" It didn't sound odd when I first heard the question in my head, but as it rolled off my tongue I realized it might sound as if I was making fun of him. After all, he was a married man. It was as if I was chiding him for fooling around on his wife only once. "And that's okay if that's true," I quickly added, "but if not, I need to know. Because if you're only considering men you slept with immediately prior to receiving the note, well, I don't think that's reasonable."

Daniel's nostrils were flaring and the palette of colour in his cheeks was intensifying in hue. The poor man was certainly experiencing a full gamut of emotions this morning. For an uncomfortable moment we sat in silence. I decided to sit it out and see what happened.

The silence finally broke. "Why are you doing this? We know who the blackmailer is—James Kraft—I've hired you to stop him. Why aren't you just willing to do that?"

Ahhhhh crap! The answer was in his eyes. They were shifting back and forth as if trying to escape their own sockets. He'd lied to me—or at least he'd omitted the whole truth. "I've just told you why," I said, keeping my tone admirably even.

More silence, then, "There is someone else," he revealed in clipped tones as if he'd been forced to admit a dirty little secret on which he'd be poorly judged. "Someone other than Jo...James Kraft."

I swore in my head but kept my mouth shut. An uncomfortable thought crossed my mind. James Kraft obviously wasn't Hugh, but this new man he had just admitted to could be.

"I know what you're thinking," he said.

I was betting he was only partially right. I wasn't in the business of judging him or even caring how many people he slept with. But I was in the business of thinking he was a big, fat liar. Or, at the very least, a big fat...omitter of truth.

"Could this other man be Loverboy?" I asked, remaining sedate.

"I really don't think so." His face was closed. He knew I was a bit mad at him for lying and he was a bit mad at himself for being caught at it.

"Maybe you should tell me about him. Just in case."

"I shouldn't have to talk about this. I can't talk about this. I have clients to attend to."

His words were dismissive, but his face and tone of voice told me the truth. Suddenly I found myself softening towards this liar...er...client. It wasn't me he wanted to get rid of; it was his whole life for the past twenty years.

Realizing I wasn't giving up, he let out a loud sigh and gave in. "James wasn't the first," he admitted. "This past summer, late August, I met a guy in the chatroom. I'd only been doing the chatroom thing for a couple weeks. I didn't really know what I was doing. But it seemed harmless enough. It was just typing words on a computer. I never dreamed I'd ever go any further with it." Another sigh, then, "I met a guy whose nickname was...SunLover. And before I knew it I'd agreed to meet him the next afternoon at Bare Ass Beach."

When most people think of Saskatchewan, they don't necessarily think of beaches with brown sugar sand. But a little known fact is that there is such a stretch of beach, well hidden along the banks of the South Saskatchewan River. Although Bare Ass Beach is not its real name, the oft tittered-at moniker is liberally used to refer to a minis-cule portion of a beach formally known as Cranberry Flats. The shores of the Flats, ever-changing due to the ebbs and flows of the river regulated by the nearby Gardiner Dam, are located several kilometres south of Saskatoon. They're surrounded by rolling hills of arid land and scrubby vegetation one would sooner expect to find in Cape Cod rather than on the Saskatchewan prairie. Over the years, serious beach-hounds have forged a web of paths through the slopes down to the beach. It's not easy to get to, but if you're physically fit enough to make the trek, your reward can be mighty.

Bare Ass Beach, rumour to some, myth to others, is a real place to those who, still not exhausted after reaching the main beach, are willing to make the voyage, sometimes requiring portaging, to the farthest tip (although I found a shortcut some years ago) where it is said nubile young nudes, mostly male, worship the sun.

It was quiet. I looked at Daniel. He looked at me.

"You want more?" A plaintive query.

I wished for something profound to say. Having Daniel speak about his experiences out loud was like urging him to admit to his willing acquiescence in the activity of being a gay man. I came up empty. Where was Beverly when you needed her? Instead I said, "Try your best, Daniel. It might help."

"I don't know why I agreed to it. I hadn't thought through the risks," Daniel said, a mystified look covering his face. "All I know is that I was growing more and more...frustrated...each day, searching for something I couldn't identify."

All I could do was nod my head. Indeed he was right. In less than five months Daniel Guest had gone from playing a straight, loving husband to meeting strange men for sex to being blackmailed by one. This was no piddly little craving we were talking about. Whether he realized it or not, this was Daniel's true self suddenly awakened and trying to claw its way, biting and scratching, out of a deep, dark closet.

"I planned it like some sort of top secret mission," Daniel said. "The next morning before I left for work I stowed away a pair of swim trunks, sandals and a towel in the trunk of my car, all the while telling myself I probably wouldn't go through with it anyway. It was a Wednesday I think and by lunchtime it was hotter than Hades outside; work was sluggish, as were most of the staff and clients. And...I did it. Just took off and headed for the beach.

"I changed in a gas station bathroom on the way out of town. It took me a while to make it from the parking lot through the hills down to the beach and when I got there I saw only a few other people. But it was...exhilarating for some reason...I felt like a six-year-old boy with a knapsack on my back out on the adventure I'd been warned against. I walked and walked until I realized I hadn't seen anyone for several minutes and it looked like I was about to run out of beach. And I did run out of beach. End of the line. I was prepared to turn around and head back but I noticed some trails leading up into the woods. So I followed one. I almost fell over him."

"SunLover?"

"Yeah. He was sunning in a clearing near the woods, pretty much hidden by tall reeds and grasses. He was handsome, not cute or attractive, but all out handsome. Like a movie star. He was older than me I think, fortysome, maybe more. He had blond hair, thick, and sideburns, and...oh, I don't know...he reminded me of...I don't know, maybe an older Brad Pitt. Slim, muscled, nice shape, well-tanned and…well, that's all I know about him. We didn't even talk. Not one word. I never got his name and he never got mine," he added as if sealing his argument on why SunLover couldn't be the black-mailer.

"When it was over I got spooked. I was in shock at what I had done. I almost knocked him over getting out of there. I ran. I actually ran. I felt like a real jerk afterwards, for a lot of reasons." He stopped there, looking sad, exhausted.

"Can you tell me anything more about him? Did you happen to see the car he drove? Anything he had with him on his beach blanket? Anything?"

He shook his head. "I'm sorry."

"Are there any more?" I asked.

He shook his head again and lowered it, glancing at an appointment book on his desk, his eyes anywhere but on mine. I wanted to yell out, "Don't be ashamed! Please, don't be ashamed!" But I didn't. I had a lot to learn about life as lived by Daniel Guest.

As I considered SunLover, I was thinking two things. This guy would be far more difficult to track down than Jo and, unless I was mistaken about what I saw, he didn't quite fit Hugh's description. I pursed my lips in a way that would have made Sherlock Holmes proud and asked, "What about suspects other than a sexual partner?"

Daniel's brows lowered over his eyes as if the thought had never occurred to him. "Like who?"

"Well, you received the note at an awards ceremony. Wouldn't the blackmailer have to be someone who knew you were receiving the award and have access to the envelope in order to slip in the black-mail note and do it without a witness?"

He scowled at the thought. "Yes…I suppose that is true."

"Who knew you were getting the award? Who was at the ceremony that night? Was James Kraft there?"

Daniel nodded his head as if in patient appreciation of my thought process, then said, "The SBA informed me a month before the ceremony that I would be the recipient of the award. I don't know how many people in their own organization would have had access to that information, probably everyone." That jived with what I'd heard from Lois

Vermont. "I informed my business partners. And I told my wife and she told a few people. By the time I walked up to that podium to accept the award, a lot of people knew I'd be there. As far as I know, Loverboy was one of them. Maybe he works for the SBA or the salon where my wife gets her hair styled or the hotel where the event was held or who knows where. He figured out who I was, saw an opportunity and went for it. And it worked."

Although I nodded, I was not totally convinced. "What about other people who know you're...know you have sex with men. Friends? Colleagues? Family?"

He shook his head. "I see what you're getting at, but there's no way..." he stopped and stared at me. "Okay, you're doing your job. You're being thorough. I appreciate that."

"So?"

"No one in my family knows about me. There is only one person, a friend—a colleague—who knows. He's one of the partners, Herb Dufour."

"How does he know?"

Daniel hesitated for a second as if trying to remember, then answered, "I told him...well, I guess he asked. I don't know why he asked. It was about a year ago, after a staff party. Everyone had gone home and it was just he and I in a hotel bar. We'd both drunken more than we should have. He asked because his tongue was loose. I admitted it because mine was too." He shot me a look, as if revealing a truism. "And because it felt so good to finally say the words to someone. The next day when I remembered that I had told him, mixed with the horror of what I'd done was incredible relief at having done it."

"How did he react?"

"He acted as if I was just confirming something he already knew. Which I guess is why he asked in the first place. It takes a lot of courage to admit it, but it takes some courage to ask about it too."

"Yes, I suppose that's true. Is Herb Dufour gay?"

Daniel looked surprised at the question, his bottom lip dropping. "Oh no. No, I'm pretty sure he's not. He's always with a pretty girl. Not married but he dates a lot."

My eyebrows reached for my hairline, a look that was obviously lost on my new client. "How old is he?"

"About my age or a little older. Thirty-eight I think."

All I did was nod. If Herb Dufour was even mildly attractive, dressed well and could occasionally be spotted browsing in Pier 1's housewares department for no apparent reason, I had news for Daniel. But now was not the time.

"Does he know what's happened?"

A short hesitation, then the answer, "Yes. I told him a few days ago when I was considering Beverly's suggestion to hire you."

I placed the pen I was using to take notes resolutely down on my pad and said, "Daniel, I know you've been through this with Beverly—more than once—but I have to try one more time. What about the police? Shouldn't we get them involved? This is a serious crime."

"No," he answered quickly.

"Are you sure? The post office box number alone would likely lead them straight to Loverboy's doorstep."

"No. Yes. No. Not yet. Not now. Obviously I want this to go away. If that can happen without involving the police, that's how I want to do it. If I press charges it'll just bring attention to the matter, which I obviously want to avoid. But, when you find him, perhaps a well-placed threat of involving the police might help convince him to leave me alone?"

"Maybe." We'd have to figure that one out when the time came.

"I want you to deal with this, Russell. No police. Not now."

"Okay," I hesitantly agreed, "but in that case, although I'll focus on finding James Kraft, I also want to meet some of the other people in your life—people at work, family."

He ruffled at this, sucking in his cheeks momentarily. "That's impossible."

"Daniel, if I'm to conduct a full investigation, I can't be left with blinders on. I know you're convinced the blackmailer is James, but, as we already discussed, there are other potential suspects out there. I can't identify them if I never meet them."

"Who? My wife? My business partners? My secretary? Please, Mr. Quant, don't be ridiculous."

Mr. Quant again. What happened to Russell? I knew he was uncomfortable but I had to push him on this. I don't like restrictions, especially when I think they might hide the truth. "Daniel, I know you wouldn't accept a client if he only allowed you to look at some of his records but not all of them. Isn't that right? Let's cover all our bases. Let's be thorough. I'm a detective, Daniel. A good one. I can find out things without people knowing I'm finding them out. But I can't do it from the outside. I can be quite inconspicuous."

He finally allowed himself a grudging nod. He knew I was right. "Tomorrow night, we're having our annual Christmas party, staff, their spouses, some clients, how about that? You could pose as a potential new client of the firm's."

Undercover! Cool. "That's perfect."

I detected a slight shaking of Daniel's head, doubting the wisdom of what he'd just allowed me. It was time to leave. As I headed for the door, Daniel shifted his attention back to the asylum of the papers on his desk.

Chapter 5

AFTER MY NEAR-DAWN MEETING with Daniel Guest I found myself in my office earlier than normal. I set a fresh pot of coffee to brew and retreated to a favourite spot in front of the doors that open onto my balcony…well, that is they used to open onto my balcony. Sometime in November, they had frozen shut for the winter. But even from indoors, I still have a great view. Traffic on Spadina was light, but the few cars there were seemed to chug along easily despite thick plumes of exhaust visible in the icy air that made it look as though they were working as hard as plough horses. Last night's skiff had left behind a pristine layer of snow about the thickness of Kleenex.

I stood at my post for several moments, mulling over everything I'd learned from my meeting with Daniel, so recent, the scent of the Burberry cologne he favoured still lingered in my nose. And then I thought about my friend, Kelly, and what she must be going through, physically recovered from her illness but perhaps not mentally. I wanted to call her but it was too early for that. The coffee ready, I prepared a cup and took my place behind the desk to work on my case.

I booted up my trusty desktop and opened up a new spreadsheet. I created several columns and dutifully began to fill in the headings with the names—as best I knew them—of each suspect I'd so far identified. James Kraft. SunLover. Hugh. Blue Car Driver. I thought about it for half a second and added "SBA" to the top of the fifth column. The sixth column I entitled "Others," a favourite of mine for all those miscellaneous thoughts that pop into my head from time to time during an investigation. I spent the next hour or so filling in the columns with information I already knew about each of the subjects as well as ideas for potential investigative strategies. At the same time I jotted down notes on a fresh piece of paper:

Daniel's office—surveillance?

Cheryl Guest—wife

Mick & Anita Soloway—neighbours

Darren Kirsch.

The fourth jot was the first one I followed up.

Darren Kirsch is the only cop on the SPS, Saskatoon Police Service, who returns my phone calls. The rest of them just ignore me. Most cops, and I know this because I used to be one, think private investigators are unprofessional money-grabbers that will suck information out of you and give nothing back in return. And sometimes this is true. But to make a go of being a private detective, you need a friend in the police department. And Darren, a detective in the Criminal Investigations Division, is mine—even though we're not exactly on each other's list of best friends.

As I dialled his number I schemed, as I always do before we talk, on how I could get information out of Darren without revealing my real purpose. Sometimes I do this out of necessity, other times just for sport. Today was a bit of both. I wanted to confirm that what I was dealing with wasn't bigger than it seemed. I wanted to find out if the police had any investigations, ongoing or otherwise, that were similar to mine. Maybe there was a rash of well-to-do men, closeted or otherwise, being blackmailed. It wasn't a pleasant thought, but if this was the case I needed to know.

"Kirsch," he answered gruffly on the third ring.

"Darren, it's Russell." I use first names because I like him to feel like I care.

"Quant." A flat statement.

"No crimes today or is the cold keeping you indoors?"

"The weather has no..." He stopped, realizing I was pulling his chain. He was no dummy but every so often I caught him in the act.

I chuckled because it felt good. "Glad to hear it."

"Are you reporting a crime? Because if not I've got better things to do than chit-chat with you."

"I was just wondering if you guys had gotten anywhere on those blackmail cases?"

He was silent. He knew when I was playing the game and was wise enough to listen in case I actually had something to say he should know about.

"I'm handling your overflow," I told him, keeping my voice even.

"You've got a blackmail case?"

"I might," I allowed, but acting as if I might just as likely have a case of the flu.

"Details?"

"Yeah right," I answered. "How about you? Anything like that in your case files?"

"Gay guy?" he said. My ears perked up.

"Uh-huh." My being noncommittal but attentive.

"Rich?"

Shit, Daniel Guest wasn't the first.

"Blackmailer caught him on video wearing no-name jeans?"

I hung up.

I didn't want to give myself time to smart over being bested by Kirsch so I immediately dialled into the internet and scratched the itch of a distant memory by doing some archival-type research. And indeed, it didn't take long to find what I was looking for. I'm not a particularly politically savvy individual; at the best of times I can perhaps recite the name of the mayor of Saskatoon and premier of Saskatchewan, but that's about it. My research told me what I thought I'd remembered from some long ago CFQC newscast or *StarPhoenix* article. Herb Dufour currently was and had been for several years a city councillor in Ward 10. And further, he was being touted as a fore-runner in the next mayoralty race expected sometime in the next six to twelve months.

Huh.

I went back to my suspect spreadsheet and began to write in the "Others" column, thought better of it and instead labelled column number seven: Herb Dufour.

Having called to check up on my mother, my dog, Barbra, and my new dog, Brutus, Mom sounded a little lonely or bored, I didn't know which. The dogs were fine. So I again told her to be waiting for me with her coat on. This time I took her to Badass Jack's on 2nd Avenue for lunch. Another first for Mom. She'd never eaten a wrap before. Unfortunately, both the jerk sauce she'd selected for her wrap without fully understanding what it was, and the somewhat unusual name of the establishment, left her sporting a decidedly unhappy grimace. I had work to do downtown and my mother had mentioned she needed to finish up some Christmas shopping. With both our after-lunch destinations handy, I pointed Mom in the direction of the mall and sent her toddling off down the street, well-anchored in the growing winter wind by the ridiculously huge Christmas corsage of pinecones and berries she'd attached to her coat lapel.

I made my way to the corner of 2nd Avenue and 21st Street which is, despite a bank on every corner, a few fast food joints and dollar stores and a larger than life-sized bust of Mahatma Gandhi thrown into the mix, the apex of Saskatoon's fashion and entertainment district. Within a few hours, throngs of holiday shoppers would be taking advantage of the extra hours of Christmas shopping but even now, early on a Thursday afternoon, the foot and vehicle traffic was heavier than normal. I fought my way through the bundled-up and package-laden pedestrians until I reached a large sign hoisted high above street level displaying a single, elegantly scripted, black "g" on a rich, cream-coloured background. I had arrived at gatt.

Named after it's bon vivant owner, my friend and personal Auntie Mame, Anthony Gatt, gatt is a high-end menswear store from where, for a price, even the most slovenly can emerge a gentleman of breeding and exquisite taste. Anthony is a man of indeterminate age and means (I'm thinking 'round fifty with a rich, pig farmer father; bite my tongue) with a dashing Robert Redford/*Great Gatsby* handsomeness to him. He knows every word created by man and then some and speaks them with a smooth English-accented flourish. He and his partner, Jared Lowe, are vanguards of the Saskatoon society set.

The store is two storeys tall, glass from stem to stern—all the better to display the fashion candy within. As I walked through the front door I marvelled at the exquisite Christmas tree that had been erected by Anthony's warren of elves. Like everything about my friend, it was just a little over-the-top and decidedly unique. Not only was the tree twelve feet tall and only four feet at its widest, but the needles of the super slim pine were a mix of lustrous black and rich burgundy and every branch was laden with crystal ornaments that shone like diamonds. At the top was an angel of such unsurpassable beauty you might guess she'd landed there straight from heaven. In the air were the melodic strains of holiday classics and the distinct scents of Bvlgari Cologne and never-worn fabrics. I could sense the slightly intimidating presence of Hugo Boss, Bruno Magli, Alessandro Dell'Acqua, Neil Barrett and Prada. I immediately caught sight of one of Anthony's broad-shouldered, slim-waisted sales clones whose names were always Derek. He made a pointing up motion with his index finger and I made my way through racks of GQ fodder to the grand staircase that leads to the second floor.

Anthony, in all his blond glory, was wearing a tight white, silk T-shirt, faded grey corduroy slacks and grey moccasins and even from a distance I could see the glint of a magnificent diamond ring on the third finger of his right, deeply tanned hand. He was watching Maggie, the only woman I've ever known to work in the store—pretty, middle-aged, with crazy-curly, long ash-blond hair—fitting a suit jacket on a customer. The customer, a fortysomething stockbroker type with greying sideburns was staring straight ahead at his image in a floor to ceiling mirror but listening intently to Anthony's running commentary.

"Oh, Anthony," Maggie said as she knelt down to pin the trousers, giddily playing her well-rehearsed role. "I love the Armani on him. Look how nice it falls from his big chest."

Anthony's face gave up an easy grin as the stockbroker's eyes fell, on cue, to someone else's big chest. "I'm not an expert at this, Linc, but I think you're being flirted with."

Linc's face lit up and he winked—maybe at Anthony or maybe at his own reflection in the mirror; I was too far away to tell. Anthony's work was done. He looked up and cocked an eyebrow in my direction. I withdrew my hand from where it had been caressing a selection of Miu Miu sweaters and gave a little wave.

"No, no, no, no," he began speaking as he walked towards me, the intonation growing in volume and intensity with each repeat of the word. "I can't have you in here like that…or at least I can't have you leaving like that."

I looked down. It certainly wasn't the coat. I had purchased it at gatt only a couple of months ago. Had it gone out of style already? Couldn't be my shoes. If there were two pieces of fashion I paid attention to it was my outerwear and my footwear. It made sense—they were what most everyone saw. It had to be the pants. Nice cotton khakis. What's the problem?

"So boring I could pass out," Anthony said with a convincing yawn as he held forth a pair of pants he'd grabbed seemingly out of thin air. How does he do that? "Diesel Kulter black leather straight-legs or…" Poof! Another pair! "…Theory Tristan Surf indigo stretch cotton jeans. I imagine you'll prefer the jeans even though a man with such wonderfully long legs and shapely posterior should go with leather, because so few can."

I was in and out of a change room and we were heading across the street for a "wee cocktail" before I could spell my last name. We sat at the bar and Anthony ordered a martini with Bombay Sapphire Dry Gin while I opted for a glass of the house white. Having a perky drink in the afternoon is one of those "European" traditions Anthony tirelessly encourages in "the Americas."

"So, you're working the store this week?" I commented.

"Oh, puppy, it's this Christmas thing. Busy busy busy and Maggie and the Dereks have a hard time keeping up. It's too insipid to even speak of." Then, as a whispered aside, "Though, to tell truth, I rather enjoy it really." Back to his normal voice. "And what of you? Begun your yuletide vacation yet?"

"Actually no, I've just taken on another case."

"Really? I thought you'd had enough of that drudgery for a while?" he said in his most droll of Brit accents.

"I thought so too, but this one just fell into my lap."

"Aren't you supposed to be entertaining dear Kay?"

I was a little surprised to hear my mother called by her first name. Most of my friends referred to her as Mrs. Quant or "your mom." But Anthony had been partnered with my Uncle Lawrence, so in a way, he was Mom's ex-brother-in-law. They had known each other, as much as the strained relationship between brother and sister allowed, for years. "I'm trying."

Anthony gave me one of those looks where he suspected there was more to the story than I was letting on but had decided not to pursue it. "So what about this new case, what's it all about? A smoking gun? Death by untraceable poison? An homme fatal client?"

I chuckled. "No, nothing quite that exotic…or erotic."

Anthony is my unofficial liaison to the gay world. He knows what we're wearing, what we're drinking, what celebrities we're building up and which, sadly, we're tearing down, what sun-drenched holiday spots are hot, which ones are not and, most of all, he knows who is, who isn't and which of the aforementioned are sleeping together. I, on the other hand, had to be told to stop styling my hair in the George Clooney/*ER*/Caesar fringe. "Anthony, maybe you can help me."

"Wonderful. I'm a gumshoe. Shall I change? Perhaps a cloak and spiffy hat, walking stick and a pipe?"

"Have you ever heard of a guy by the name of James Kraft? Youngish. Blond. Actor."

He contemplated the name with a handsome furrowing of his brow. As I waited I noticed two women stare at my companion as they passed by on their way to the exit. Anthony was sometimes too good-looking for his own good.

"James Kraft. Hmmm…"

He was probably too young or too broke to have ever entered Anthony's radar. It was an uncharitable thought but I was peeved the women hadn't even glanced at me.

"The name sounds familiar."

"Really?" All forgiven.

"I don't know him personally, but I'm quite certain I know some-one who's mentioned that name quite recently. Is he rather new to town—say in the past few years or so?"

"Yes, that's him." I hoped.

He winked at me and threw a twenty on the countertop. "Leave it with me. I'll see if I can get you a contact." He rose and slipped on a pair of kid leather gloves, the only winter protection he'd brought with him on the mad dash from the store. "You coming along? There are some new shoes from Camper you must have."

Here was the problem: he never let me actually buy the stuff I tried on. When this happened we crossed the line from friends to rich father/poor son and I couldn't do that more than once a day. I pointed at my unfinished wine and said, "I'll be over in a minute to pick up my old pants."

He gave me one of his deadly smiles as he headed out. "Don't bother, puppy, I think they were tossed out by accident."

Cheryl Guest was the manager of J. Thames, one of several Saskatoon women's equivalents to gatt. Although I knew I'd meet Daniel's wife at the DGR&R Christmas party on Friday night, I wanted a chance to observe her on her own turf, without—as promised—her knowing.

The Midtown Plaza, anchored by Sears at one end and The Bay on the other, is two storeys of glossy shops that differ little from those in malls the world over. At this time of year the corridors are crowded, not only with holiday shoppers and recalcitrant teenagers, but with carts and booths that magically appear only at Christmastime, bursting at the seams with calendars and snow globes, knitted scarves and gloves, fruitcake and gift baskets. Then there's raffle ticket and craft tables and, most important of all, Santa's workshop, where children can sit on the knee of St. Nick and have their picture taken. For some this is the description of hell. I, however, love it. But not if I actually have to buy something. Shopping in a shopping mall in December is indeed pure misery but, as a place to soak up Christmas spirit and people-watch, it ain't too shabby.

Procuring an unobtrusive spot against the window of a negligee store directly across from J. Thames, with an Every-Watch-for-$10 vendor for handy camouflage between me and the store, I set out to observe Cheryl Guest in action. Fortunately, J. Thames has a wide-open front with easy sightlines into the store from almost every angle.

I immediately caught sight of my quarry, recognizing her from the photo in Daniel's office. She was wearing a very smart, winter-white skirt and jacket ensemble that complemented her sun-darkened skin. Her blond hair was expertly coiffed but even from a distance I could see she wore an abundance of makeup that exaggerated her already too-wide eyes and mouth to almost clown-like proportion. I watched for a while as she approached customers with what seemed a haughty attitude, which instantly became charming solicitude if they actually expressed interest in some piece of clothing or other. When this happened, Cheryl had a practised procedure. First she would take the dress or blouse or whatever it was from the potential customer, and begin by massaging and feeling up the sample, no doubt speaking of its quality fabric and the workmanship of the stitching. Next she would drape the piece on the victim—I mean shopper—and smile in such a way that indicated she had never quite seen that particular item look so ravishing on any of the other hundred people who'd come into the store before her. And all along, Cheryl made certain the distinctive blue J. Thames label (or orange if it was one the few men's items in the store) was always clearly visible to the patron and everyone nearby. In the game of retail, Cheryl was a well-rehearsed performer.

But I hadn't seen anything yet—for as luck would have it, the floorshow was just to begin.

To give the woman some credit, the store was temporarily devoid of customers when Cheryl huffed and puffed her way towards another J. Thames salesperson who'd obviously been assigned the job of displaying merchandise on a sale table. And, to be honest, even I could tell that the employee, young, sturdy-looking and with a head full of intricately patterned dreadlocks, seemed something less than enthused with her task. She was mindlessly moving knitted caps and scarves from one pile to another and then back again, all the while letting her big brown eyes stroll lazily back and forth with each passing shopper, assessing their outfit or hair or whatever else she found mildly distracting or interesting about them.

Cheryl stood behind the girl for a good thirty seconds, arms akimbo, glaring at the sluggish movements. Finally, obviously unable to take it any longer, she opened her mouth. I didn't need to be a lip reader to know she wasn't using the power of positive reinforcement. The younger woman jumped back from the table, startled, her dreads whipping her face and neck as she staggered into a defensive position to face her superior. Cheryl's eyes were bright as sparks, her shoulders thrown back indignantly, hands making vaguely threatening motions.

As I stood transfixed to my spot, witnessing this exchange, I so empathized with the berated staffer I could feel myself melting into the ground as if the attack were aimed at me. But the young woman was tougher than that. At first she just stood there, eyes growing wide and darting nervously from side to side, looking anywhere but at Cheryl's angry face. Yup, she'd been caught red-handed being bored doing a boring task. But as Cheryl railed on, the younger employee's spine began to stiffen. I could imagine her thinking to herself, "All right, enough already, it's not as if I dropped the last known sample of DNA from an extinct species." She planted her strong-looking hands on rounded hips, thrust her pelvis forward and let out a stream of something I'm sure was as colourful as the beads in her hair. She was handing back some serious attitude. How I wished I was a boll weevil in one of the nearby racks of sweaters.

For a crazy moment, as if it were frozen in time, it seemed to me that the three of us, Cheryl, her sales assistant and me, were the only ones in that shopping mall. In total, the exchange probably lasted less than a minute, but it seemed like an hour of great theatre played out on stage just for me. That is until the astounding denouement, which more than a few passersby couldn't help but notice. With an action befitting any of the great Disney cartoon mistresses of evil, like Cruella De Vil or Maleficent, Cheryl brought her many-ringed hand crashing down on the display table and, with a swoop, swept all the lovely J. Thames things onto the floor.

My ears waited for the resultant crash and more yelling. But of course, from across the way and outside the store, there was no noise to hear and there was also no yelling because the young woman, wisely I think, simply turned heel and stomped off out of my—and Cheryl's—sight.

My, my, my, I thought to myself. I now knew of another reason Daniel didn't want to be found out by his wife—she'd whop his ass.

Chapter 6

I WAS ABOUT TO DASH OUT of the Midtown Plaza when I remembered my mother. Damn! I was supposed to have met her right there, at the front doors, ten minutes ago and I was already late for my next planned bit of detective work. Could she take a cab? Did she know about cabs? I spun around like a whirling dervish trying to catch sight of her—or rather her hard to miss corsage—amongst the shopping throngs. And there she was, sitting on a chair with hands folded piously over her purse, coat buttoned tight up to her neck. The chair was meant for the Salvation Army volunteer who'd obviously been kind enough to give up his seat while he attended to his work. Seeing me come her way, my mother stood up and thanked the Salvation Army man.

"Mom?" What else could I say?

"Goot, ve go. You must be hungry."

I looked at the bare floor next to my mother's feet and asked, "Where are your shopping bags? Didn't you find anything you wanted to buy?"

She had a strange look on her face and made a move towards the front doors. I smiled at the Sally Ann guy, threw a five-dollar bill and a toonie into his drum and scrambled after my mother.

"Dees vay, uh-huh?"

73

Through the glass of the plaza's doors we could see that, although not yet 5 p.m., daylight was dimming in preparation for sunset. We made our way out and stood in wait for the crosswalk light to change. The view down 21st Street was truly beautiful. Street posts and ash trees hung with wee twinkling lights and Christmas decorations were flickering to life. Shop windows were ablaze with their colourful wares. The grandiose Bessborough, a few blocks away, was a fairytale castle. Outdoor speakers were playing "Joy to the World."

As the singers were getting to the part about repeating the sounding joy (does that lyric make sense to anyone?) I repeated to my mother, "Didn't you find anything you wanted to buy?"

"I tought dees vas Valmart. Dere's no Valmart here."

Ohmygod what was she saying? "It—it—it's a mall. There are all kinds of stores in there."

"Ya, I know dat. No Valmart."

"That's true."

The light changed and we crossed 1st Avenue and headed towards where the car was parked.

I waited a few seconds then asked, "Did you just sit there by the Salvation Army drum the whole time?" Please say no.

"Eet vas nice, I met lot of nice people. Olga Frankiw, remember, Bill's vidow? She came by veet her son, Nestor. He vas taking her to doctor. She has such poor eyes, that Olga."

Inside I was shrivelling up and it wasn't from the cold. I was beginning to realize how little I knew my mother, what type of person she was, what her life's experiences were, what she knew how to do and what she didn't know how to do, especially since Dad had died. And I had sent her off alone to shop at the Midtown Plaza as if she was one of the gals from *Sex in the City*.

So I certainly wasn't about to send her off in a cab.

Dropping her at home however wasn't much better.

"Okay," I said as I pulled up to the front of the house. "See you later."

She looked alarmed. "Vhere you going? Eet's after five. Time for supper."

Why did I suddenly feel like an eight-year-old? A naughty eight-year-old. "Actually, Mom, I'm not going to make it home for dinner."

I called it dinner because that's what we do in the big city. Lunch is at noon, dinner is in the evening—sometimes much later than five o'clock. In the country, or at least in my mother's house, dinner is at noon and supper is at five. "Work y'know."

"You vork too hard. You haf to eat. I put borscht on da stove now, eet'll be hot by time you take coat off. Dat wrap-up ting from lunch vasn't very beeg, you must be hungry, Sonsyou."

"I'm okay, I'm not really hungry yet. And I really have to do some work now. I'll just grab something later."

"Oh."

Here it comes.

The quiet.

"So I'll see you later maybe?"

"Oh. Ya, uh-huh."

More quiet. Ebenezer Quant they'd call me.

"So I leave da pot on da stove den? You can heat up when you come home."

"Okay then."

"Okay den."

As I watched my mother dig keys out of her purse, get out of the car and head in the direction of the front door I did the mind-game mambo for a while. I shouldn't leave her. I had work to do. I should go in and have some borscht at least. But then I'd miss my surveillance opportunity. I forgot to call Kelly. I didn't get to the gym today. My poor mother sat for hours beside a Salvation Army drum. I forgot about Brutus. I'm a piss-poor son. I've got work to do. I shouldn't leave her. I'm going to get fat.

I reached for the cellphone and dialled the DGR&R office number and confirmed with the receptionist that Daniel was still there. That made up my mind. Something had to. I put pedal to the metal and via the Senator Sid Buckwold Freeway Bridge and thereafter a few short-cuts through rush-hour traffic, I made it to Daniel's office building in less than twenty minutes.

After making a pass by the DGR&R parking lot to ensure Daniel's black Beemer was still there, I did a slow perimeter search of about a block's radius looking for a blue vehicle, make unknown and, just for fun, a green Intrepid. Finding neither I parked, as inconspicuously as

I could, about three-quarters of a block away from the front door of the DGR&R building and began my wait. My hope was that whoever it was who'd followed Daniel last night would do so again tonight, and I of course, would catch him.

At 6 p.m. there was a mass exodus. Nobody was doing much over-time I guess. By 6:05 there were only two cars left, one belonging to Daniel. At 6:15 p.m. Daniel pulled out of the parking lot. I kept my eyes peeled for the expected, hoped-for, second set of headlights to materialize behind his disappearing car.

Nada.

I put the Mazda in gear and tailed my client. Daniel didn't know I was doing this. I hadn't wanted to tell him my plan. Sometimes people who know they are being followed drive…well, they drive like little old ladies and that might make whoever was tailing Daniel suspicious. As it was, Daniel was already probably a little on edge thinking the blue car stalker might be behind him again. He didn't need the added pressure of knowing I was too.

Daniel connected onto Idylwyld Drive heading south towards downtown. We arrived in a few minutes and he appeared to be searching for a parking spot in the vicinity of 4th Avenue and 23rd Street, an intersection shared by the main branches of the post office, police station, public library and City Hall. I wondered which was his destination? He finally found a spot across from the library and I slipped into another spot just around the corner across from the post office. It was a perfect place from which to keep an eye on his car and anyone paying too much attention to it while he was away. Daniel hopped out of his vehicle, locked it and, watching for traffic, jay-walked across the street and into the front entrance of the library. Humph. I hadn't taken him to be a library kind of person.

There seemed to be little interest from anyone in Daniel's car, never mind someone in a suspicious blue car. I decided to risk it and leave my post for a while to check out what was going on in the library. I mimicked Daniel's route and found my answer from a poster scotch-taped to one of the front doors. It read: Saskatoon City Schools Sing! Come join us for a festive evening of Christmas favourites. Thursday, December 11th, 6:30 to 8:30 p.m. Daniel was going to a children's Christmas concert. For two friggin' hours!

As soon as I returned to my car I knew I couldn't last that long without food. I was dreaming about Mom's borscht. The next best thing was nearby. Colourful Mary's is a restaurant-slash-bookstore owned by friends, Mary Quail and Marushka Yabadochka. Within twenty minutes I had walked there and back, with a piping hot sausage and sauerkraut sandwich and large coffee in hand and had picked up my mail to boot. I nestled into my car's comfy leather seat and as I warmed my hands on the heat vent, I noted that my haul from the post office included copies of *People* magazine and *Passport*, a glossy gay travel publication. I began to think this might not be such a bad night after all. It was dark and cold out, but I had light and heat. A city worker had bothered to decorate some nearby ash trees and the glow of the coloured lights dotted the interior of my little car with a soft, psychedelic pattern. On the radio Anne Murray was doing her mellow best with a Christmas classic. I had food, drink and entertainment. No mother, no dogs, nothing but an evening of peace and quiet.

And maybe a crazed blackmailer.

I spent a rather enjoyable twenty-five minutes dining on my sandwich and coffee (and a little piece of tort Marushka had slipped unnoticed into my takeout bag) whilst reading things about *People* I had no right to know. There had been no action near or around Daniel's car. But really, how stupid was I? Chances were astronomically high Loverboy was a gay man. Of course he'd be home on a Thursday night watching *Will & Grace*. But hey, it was only a half-hour show, so I decided to stay.

Since not much was happening I decided to use my after-dinner time wisely. First I tried calling Kelly. No answer. Next I pulled out my folder that contained the photocopied likeness and bio of James Kraft, our potential Loverboy. I retrieved James' bio and found his phone number. I wanted the opportunity to meet my suspect in person without him knowing I was coming. So I yanked my phone book onto my lap and went to the *K*'s. I found a list of Krafts but none had the same number. I was out of luck address-wise. I flipped to the reverse directory. Nothing. I'd have to cold-call after all. I dialled the number on the resume. Out of service. Damn, I'd have to do this the hard way. I began with Abner Kraft and did not strike gold until Kelvin Kraft.

"Is James home?" I asked for the thirteenth time.

"I'm sorry, he's not," responded a delicate feminine voice. I think she hesitated a bit before she said, "May I pass a message?"

Although I wasn't lightning-quick on the uptake after twelve previous calls, I was prepared for this. "Oh, well I'm a friend from drama class and I have something of his I've been promising to return for ages. Would it be okay if I stopped by tonight?"

More hesitancy. I did some fast time-budgeting and jumped right in. "Say about nine?"

"I suppose that would be all right."

"See you then." I hung up. I didn't want to give her time to change her mind. Or ask my name.

As I was jotting down the Kelvin Kraft address from the phone book onto a handy scrap of paper, my cellphone rang. Damn. Maybe she had call display? Wouldn't matter. Being the wise detective I am, I'd recently had that feature blocked on my outgoing calls. I picked it up and answered with a slight Pakistani accent—just in case.

"Russell." The caller immediately identified me. I'd have to practise that accent more often.

"How did you know?" It was Anthony.

"You barely sounded Irish at all."

"I was going for Pakistani."

"Tsk tsk tsk. Oh well, it's a good thing you're pretty, puppy. Marc Driediger. A professor at the University of Saskatchewan, College of Education."

"Who's he?"

"Oh, just someone who might be able to tell you a thing or two about James Kraft." Anthony gave me the professor's number and rang off with my thanks.

At twenty-five to nine Daniel Guest, in a restrained flow of other concert attendees, exited the library. At his side was Cheryl. Where had she come from? They must have agreed to meet here after work. I watched as they huddled and chatted with another couple as only true prairie folk can, the temperature, buried deep in the minus range, a non-issue. They soon parted and headed for their cars. Again I scanned the area for a blue vehicle. Nothing. Daniel pulled into traffic and, with no obvious shadow, I did too. Ten minutes later I was on Poplar Crescent watching Daniel's black BMW pull into his garage.

The Krafts lived on Saskatchewan Crescent, an upscale neighbourhood, in a lovely Victorian across from a row of monstrous homes with football-field-size backyards that sloped into the river. The subdued lighting on the bricked walkway from street to front door was pristine, as if a flake of snow didn't dare settle on it. Although the house itself was not buried under layers of Christmas lights as were many of its neighbours, through the double-wide front picture window I saw a very tall, very thick tree decorated in gold and white. I rang the doorbell and listened to its Christmas chime, "The First Noel" I think.

A blond woman opened the door. "Hello," she said as if she wasn't expecting anyone. Perhaps this wasn't whom I had spoken with.

"Mrs. Kraft?" I said. "I called about an hour ago?"

"Yes, that's right." Her tone said that so much had happened in her life since then that it was difficult to remember that far back. "Won't you come in?"

She stepped aside and I walked by her discount haute-couture perfection into a huge entranceway with vaulted ceilings.

"Won't you join us in the drawing room?"

I had no idea anyone in Saskatoon actually had a drawing room. For a brief moment I considered the possibility that there would be other family members in it actually drawing. Instead I found myself in what I would call a rec room—bookshelves, bar, TV, couches. She asked me to sit. I did. As she went to the bar to pour me an offered glass of water a man entered the room. Also very blond and wearing a sporty outfit of well-pressed khakis and matching shirt and sweater vest. Both Krafts looked to be in their forties, and, although I had yet to be told anything about the inhabitants of the house, I guessed these were James' parents. The man walked over to me in a manly, confident way and held out his big paw.

"I'm Kelvin Kraft," he told me. Blond, gap-toothed—had to be the father. "I'm James' father." Aha, so the missus did remember enough of my phone call to tell her husband that I was someone who knew James.

"And I'm Meredith," the woman said as she handed me my water.

They perched themselves on a couch opposite my own and looked at me. I could see that James got his looks from his father. In fact they were almost identical except that the elder Kraft had short, well-tended hair, twenty extra years on his face and twenty extra pounds on his frame.

"You went to the U of S with James?" he asked.

"Yes. Has James..."

"Drama major as well?"

The questions in his drill-sergeant voice were coming at me with the quick, deadly precision of rifle fire. I fumbled a bit while I tried to recall the story I'd told the mother on the phone. "Yes, that's right."

"Kinda old for it, aren't you?"

Ass. "That's one of the great things about the career, age doesn't much matter."

"Finding any success in the field?"

I could tell by his voice that he already suspected what my answer would be. So I decided to surprise him. "Yes. It's been great."

He didn't look like he believed me. "It's not constant work, though, is it? It's not as if you get a job and keep it until you decide to quit or get a better one? You get a job, it ends, you try to get another one, it ends, you try to get another one, it ends, on and on and on, always the beginnings and endings. Nothing constant. Hard life, I'd say."

I wasn't prepared or knowledgeable enough to be an advocate for actors, after all I'd only become one two minutes ago, but this guy seemed to be a bit of a downer, especially when he should be supporting his son's career rather than denigrating it. "I'd say it's a much different lifestyle than some others. And like everything, it has its pros and cons."

"Hmphf," was his answer.

I looked at Meredith Kraft who was sitting quietly with a vacant look on her face. "Did James happen to come home since I called earlier? I'd really like to speak with him."

"James doesn't live here anymore," the father said, looking at his wife as if he'd caught her in yet another in a series of lies.

And, come to think of it, why hadn't she told *me* this news over the phone? "Oh?" I said. "I didn't know that. I guess I haven't seen him in a while."

"Lovers' quarrel?"

Yikes! Mr. Kraft was indeed crafty. He'd caught me off guard. The look on my face must have told him so. I set down my water.

"You and my son, are you boyfriends? You're kind of old for him, aren't you?"

Enough with the age cracks, buddy. "No, actually we are not boyfriends."

"You don't have to pretend with us," he said, pretty much ignoring his wife who looked as if she wanted to crawl into an oyster shell. Finding a pearl would be a delightful bonus. "We know about the lifestyle James has chosen. As frivolous as his choice of careers."

I contemplated getting into a conversation about the whole choice thing, but I could tell Mr. Kraft had had that talk before and wasn't buying it. "Anyway, would you be able to tell me how to get in touch with James?"

"If you're looking for a date, you're going to have to go a long way." Everything that was coming out of Kelvin Kraft's mouth sounded belligerent, angry, like a man itching to pick a fight. Obviously the son was gone and he needed someone to yell at. It looked like his wife wasn't much of a combatant.

"He comes home every two, three weeks," this in a quiet voice from Meredith. "He's gone to stay with a friend in New York City. He has some auditions lined up."

"Going for the big time," Kelvin Kraft said with a sarcasm-laden grunt. "Broadway! My son's going to be a chorus boy!" He laughed, but there was little joy in it.

"He comes home when he can. Every two, three weeks," the blond woman repeated. "For a visit."

"For money and clean clothes," the father corrected.

And to pick up his mail? Pick up his blackmail money to help pay for his life in the big city? Is that how he planned to afford it? I doubted his father was willing to put out a lot of cash to support a lifestyle he so obviously abhorred. Or was I out of luck? Was the fact that James Kraft didn't even live in Saskatoon anymore remove him as a likely suspect? Or could he have perpetrated this blackmail scheme from out of town? The collection address was a local P.O. Box. Why not use his New York City address? Or was he too smart for that? Would he have realized it would have been an obvious clue to his identity? If his mother was telling the truth, James Kraft might be in town often enough to be Loverboy—but then who was the person following Daniel in the blue car? Regardless, I couldn't rule him out yet.

"Listen," Mr. Kraft said, rising from his seat. "I think it's time you left."

I got up too, as did Mrs. Kraft. "Could you give me a phone number for James in New York?" One last-ditch effort to get some help from these people.

"Hey!" It was almost a yell. This was a man on the edge. "You want to date my son, you want to get into his pants, you find him yourself! I sure as hell am not going to help you!"

That was pretty clear. By the time I made it to the front door, Kelvin Kraft had it open and was making an irritating motion with his wrist indicating he wanted me on the other side of it as quickly as possible. What a jerk. Blackmailer or not, I was feeling some sympathy for James Kraft.

The wind had picked up and, after the door hit me on the ass on the way out, I stood in the protection of the house's stoop fighting with my jacket zipper when I heard it open again. I twirled around fast, worried I was about to get my butt kicked. But instead of the creepy father, it was the mousy mother. She was holding out a piece of paper. I took it and saw she had hurriedly scratched on it a phone number with a two-one-two area code. Manhattan. I nodded my thanks.

"You said you had something that belonged to my son?" she said over the whistling of the wind, pulling at a strand of hair that was being whisked across her face. Was this why she originally neglected telling me the truth about her son's whereabouts? Or had she just wanted to meet one of his boyfriends?

"What?"

"When you called. You said you wanted to return something that belonged to my son."

Shit. I looked over her shoulder hoping she'd get the hint that her husband might find her talking to me and she should forget about this stupid "something that belonged to her son." No such luck.

"Yes, that's right," I said slowly, trying to come up with something to give her. My hands were in my coat pockets searching the contents.

A loonie? Nope, not believable. Gum? Nope. Lint seemed a little inconsequential. With a sad curl in my lip I slowly eased off the silver ring from the middle finger of my left hand. It had only cost me forty bucks, but it had a neat Grecian design and I liked it. Sometimes this career calls for personal sacrifice. "Here it is." I handed her the ring. Crap.

She studied it closely, as if it might carry a reflection of her son's face on its shiny surface. Finally she looked up, her hair now a fright wig around her face. "I'll be certain to get it back to him."

Yeah, fine. "Thank you."

She nodded and closed the door.

I looked at the paper in my hand. I hoped this phone number was worth the forty bucks. I'd have to remember to add the cost of the ring to the disbursement portion of Daniel Guest's bill.

I rushed to my car and hopped in before the bracing wind had a chance to freeze me like a cod fillet and for good measure slice me up into handy grilling portions. I started it up, cranked the temperature to high and sat back to let an idle thought percolate.

Daniel Guest lived on Poplar Crescent. I was currently on Saskatchewan Crescent.

The Krafts and the Guests were almost neighbours.

I shifted into first and in less than three minutes I was back in front of my client's house. Daniel had told me it had taken James under twenty minutes to get to his house that night by bike. James had obviously taken his time. Anyone from the Kraft household could have covered the distance to the Guest house in less than five minutes.

Anyone.

It was getting late as I headed home and the streets were as empty as a gay bar before midnight. So it didn't take long for me to spot the tail. At least I thought it was a tail. It was dark out and the driver was clever, at first staying far enough away so I couldn't quite make out any details. I first saw it when I pulled away from Daniel Guest's house. It had been parked on Poplar Crescent, about a block down from where I had stopped. I didn't think much of it until I noticed the headlights, behind me on Lorne Avenue: one definitely a little dimmer than the other. Then they were gone. I stopped at a convenience store for milk. I couldn't remember what I had in my fridge but I was certain anything my mother would have stocked up on would be whole, not the one-percent I prefer. Driving away from the store I almost immediately caught sight of the lopsided headlights about a block back, heading in my direction. I decided to test my theory. I made a left on Isabella for three blocks and then another quick left on Victoria, heading towards the bridge. Nothing, nothing, nothing, then bingo! There it was. I decided to cross the bridge. It was a narrow, two-lane bridge so if I drove slow, the driver behind me would have to slow down too and stay right behind me where, hopefully, I could get a look at his face, the make of the car and a license plate number. A stupid driver that is. My stalker obviously guessed my ploy and loitered, as much as a car can loiter, until I had pretty much crossed the bridge before driving over it himself. Didn't matter, I thought to myself. Once we were both downtown, if I drove carefully, we'd eventually both get stopped at a traffic light where I'd finally get a good look at him.

As usual, it wasn't as easy as I thought and we played cat and mouse for several minutes.

While I drove I scoured my memory for any similarities between tonight's car and the ones from the night at the landfill. Did one of the cars from the night of the chase have a dim headlight? I had to admit I didn't know. Everything had happened so fast. There was however one glaring difference between the two events. Last time I was chased. This time I was followed.

When had I actually picked up the tail, I wondered. At the Krafts? The Guests? Earlier? I couldn't be sure.

And there was one more thing I couldn't be sure of: Who was interested enough in what I was doing to have *me* followed? And just then, I got my answer. Sort of. The driver finally made a timing error. We were both coming up to a traffic light that had just turned red. He'd have to pull up behind me. Knowing he'd made a mistake, he pulled a wicked U-turn and disappeared down a back alley. But not before I clearly saw the colour of his car. It was blue.

Chapter 7

AFTER LOSING MY TAIL I decided to make two more stops before going home. At both I parked half a block away and did my best to sneak up on them. I peaked in the appropriate windows and then snuck away under the cover of darkness. Daniel Guest's garage held two vehicles. Both black. One was the Beemer I was already familiar with and the other a Land Rover. More interestingly, Kelvin Kraft's garage was empty.

By the time I pulled into my own garage it was after 11 p.m. and the temperature was dipping below minus twenty degrees Celsius. I followed a path of solar garden lights that squatted in nests of snow along my backyard walkway like little fat hibernating fireflies. The house looked dark except for a light thoughtfully left on by my mother, illuminating the back deck. I let myself in as quietly as I could and was greeted by two snuffing dogs. Barbra is used to my arriving home at all hours of the day or night. She knows what a detective's life is like. Brutus, on the other hand, was a little more unsure of me, not only because of my seemingly furtive entry, but because he was a guest in unfamiliar territory. Barbra quickly moved into staring mode, awaiting indication of what was coming next and wondering if a treat was likely to be involved. Her brother however spent a few more minutes smelling the seams of my new pants and urging a few head pats before settling down. Once that was over, I tiptoed through the kitchen into the hallway that led to the guest bedroom and listened for sounds of my mother. I couldn't hear a thing and there didn't appear to be any light under the door to her room. I realized I had no idea what time my mother went to sleep. Nine o'clock? Midnight? Somewhere in between? I looked down at the dogs who had already spent more time with my mother during her visit than I had. If only they could talk and fill me in.

I headed back to the kitchen. On my usually unburdened stove-top island were three pots of various sizes. With the stealth of an international spy I lifted off each lid and inspected the contents. Borscht. Boiled potatoes. Mushroom sauce. I picked up the pot of mushroom sauce by its handle and headed for the fridge thinking she really shouldn't have left these out overnight. I opened my fridge and was stopped short. There wasn't a square inch of free space. How had this happened in only two days? I stared at the quarts of cream, bunches of celery, rows of salad dressings, jars of pickles and beets and cabbage and other unidentifiable preserves, and even more pots filled with who knew what. I returned the mushroom sauce to the stovetop. That's when I noticed the package on the counter next to the stove. It was a plate covered in foil with a note, written in my mother's halting script, taped to the top. It simply said, "For eating for you."

I peeled back the foil and my eyes couldn't believe what they were seeing. Before me was something that resembled a bucket's worth of fried chicken stuffed inside a blanket. The blanket was actually some sort of naan-looking bread or flapjack thing and it was barely secured around no fewer that four slabs of deep-fried, battered chicken cutlets, several stems of green onion, a couple slices of ham and some sliced tomato. In order to keep it from falling apart my mother had creatively tied slices of cooked bacon, pinned down with toothpicks, around the...the thing. Each end was oozing with a reddish, lumpy sauce, now coagulated on the plate. And suddenly I knew what it was. Despite all the rest of the food around the house, my mother had created this dish—her new and improved version of a Badass Jack's wrap. I couldn't wait to taste her jerk sauce.

I heated the lump in the microwave, then handed each dog a fake bone treat that they held delicately in their teeth as they followed me to the other end of the house and into my cozy den. As I entered the room and closed the door, I flipped the switch that ignited the gas fireplace and watched brother and sister head towards it like bees to a grove of freshly blooming caragana. I slipped into the nook created by my desk and several well-stocked bookshelves and set my wrap, fork and knife and pile of napkins in front of my laptop. For a moment I watched Barbra and Brutus luxuriate in the heat of the fireplace as if they were sunbathers in St. Tropez, and took my first bite of my mother's wrap. It was, as was everything made by my mother, to die for. It tasted like no other wrap, or for that matter anything else I'd ever eaten. But it was fried-goodness-good on a polar cold night. After demolishing about half of it, I turned my attention to the computer. It was time to try my luck finding SunLover. Daniel Guest had told me he'd met his Bare Ass Beach conquest on the internet through a website called gays.r.us. Although I'd heard a lot about chat lines and I even have a friend who met her husband on one, I'd never tried them out—not out of some antiquated sense of morality, I just hadn't found the time.

As I logged onto my browser homepage, typed gays.r.us into the search box and hit enter, I felt a giddy sense of excitement, as if I was about to delve into an undiscovered world. And I was. In seconds I was presented with a screen that warned me I was requesting adult content and gave me the chance to back out if I wasn't totally committed to this course of action. I dutifully read the disclaimer and told the computer to keep going. Naughty boy. I cocked my head to the side to listen for sirens or my mother's footsteps. I heard neither. Another click or two later I was given several web page options each offering a meeting with hot young guys. Would they send them in the mail? Tempted but not easily fooled, this was not what I was looking for and I knew I'd have to start again.

I returned to the browser page and entered new search parameters: gay chat. Several key taps later I was directed to a menu asking me to chose from amongst a list of "floors" on which I could choose to chat. "Men International—English" seemed the closest to what I was looking for so I clicked on that. An officious-looking dialogue box asked me for a member name and password. I wasn't expecting this. Was this going to cost me money? A monthly fee perhaps? I wondered if Daniel Guest would mind a $15.95 charge from gays.r.us showing up on his Visa every month? And was it my imagination or were the dimensions of the dialogue box actually growing and the intensity of its words brightening as the seconds passed while I tried to make a decision? I had this image of a gays.r.us security guard sitting at a computer outside the gates of the gays.r.us complex monitoring my attempt to enter and waiting to see if I was a man or a mouse—did I belong or was I an outsider? Being one who rarely fears to tread, I hit the button indicating my willingness to become a gays.r.us member. As it turned out, the membership was free, but I had to come up with a member name and password. I looked over at my furry companions and went with Brutus and Barbra respectively. I would have gone the other way around, but I didn't want the other chatters to think I was a girl.

After muddling through a few more sets of clicks and double clicks I found myself at a screen which listed gay chat room options from Brasilia to Yugoslavia. It intrigued me to think there were young Yugoslav men sitting in front of computers, just as I was, trying to hook up. Some of the locations even had sub-set rooms designed for particular chatter needs. There were rooms for chatters with certain sexual proclivities like foot fetishists and water sport enthusiasts or those looking for communication with other chatters of a certain age (Ottawa Teens Only; San Francisco Men Over Fifty) or even geograph-ically specific locations (Toronto Riverdale; Vancouver Yaletown). I guess some people are willing to travel only so far for sex. I slowly scrolled down the list, amazed at the breadth of chat activity, and low and behold, in the Canada section, I found two rooms for Saskatchewan—one simply labelled Saskatchewan, the other Saskatchewan 30+. I clicked on Saskatchewan 30+. A room counter on the upper part of my screen told me there were no participants in this room. I chuckled to myself. After all, what self-respecting gay man would admit to being over thirty if he didn't have to? I clicked on the Saskatchewan chat room. There were thirty-six participants. Not bad. It was late on a Thursday night, but apparently the Saskatchewan cyber gay scene was hopping.

I quickly figured out that, without actually entering the room, I could see the nicknames of the current participants in the room and even read their bios (if they'd bothered with one), but I couldn't interact with them. To do that, I'd have to come up with a bio of my own and ask to be let in the room. I scrolled down the list of thirty-six nicknames. They ranged from actual names like George and Dan to more creativity-challenged pseudonyms such as Guy in Saskatoon or Out of Towner. And then there were the descriptive aliases like Gym Jock, Hairy Bear and Banger in Bangor with a few in-your-face monikers like Sit on my Face and Footlong thrown in for complete clarity. I saw Horny in Humboldt, Rammy Rancher and even a Climax Here but no SunLover. What to do?

I decided if I was in for a penny I might as well get in for a pound. I knew I'd need to create my Brutus bio before entering the chat room. If I was trying to trap SunLover, I'd have to set bait as best I could based on what Daniel Guest had told me about their encounter. Obviously SunLover had been attracted to Daniel, so was that the physical type he went for, or did he simply go for anyone willing to meet at the beach—which, given current weather conditions, would be a tall order. Reviewing the bios of some of the other chat room participants, I noticed quite a diversity in what people were willing to say about themselves depending on what message they wanted to send. Some went with complete disclosure, to the extent of revealing information that looked like it'd been gleaned from a gays.r.us job interview. Likes, dislikes, physical attributes, type of sexual or non-sexual activity the chatter was seeking and, if you were lucky, accompanied by a photograph (usually nothing more titillating than a face and chest shot). Most went with something a little less committal, giving a line or two of physical description—26, bl/gr, 5-11, 175, gd lkg—or physical desire—Lkg for r/t, b/j, d/t. This was dating in the twenty-first century—impersonal, cyber-connected and chock full of short-form words and acronyms. I wondered if there was a glossary of these terms somewhere that everyone knew about except me.

I thought about what to say in my bio and decided in the end that vague was in vogue. I typed: "Attractive guy looking for same for discrete fun." I read and reread my entry, changed it, changed it back, checked the spelling of discrete and changed it to discreet and finally decided to go for it. I hit the Enter Room button and suddenly another screen opened and I was in the world of Saskatchewan gay chat. A lot happened at once. Apparently while I was busy debating my gays.r.us identity and not formally in the Saskatchewan chat room, I was not privy to changes as they occurred. There were now forty-two chatters in the room and as I scrolled down to the bottom of the list of nick-names now displayed on the right-hand side of my screen, I saw that many of the original thirty-six had come and gone while I was lolly-gagging. And for that sloth, I'd never get to meet All Man in Alsask or Big Baloney in Balgonie who'd obviously found what they were looking for and logged off. The area of the screen meant for conversation was alive with typed messages involving maybe half a dozen of the room's occupants. They seemed to be talking about a movie they'd just seen. Did all these people know one another? Wasn't this chat room stuff supposed to be about sex or were all forms of entertain-ment open for discussion? I had actually recently seen the film in question and was considering typing in my own review when the next line of dialogue read: "Hi Brutus."

They saw me. They knew I was there.

Suddenly I was nervous. I felt as if I'd just arrived at a party where I didn't know a soul.

Then Burt55 wrote, "Welcome Brutus" quickly followed by "Hey, Brutus" from Downtown Dick. How nice. How hospitable. Very friendly. I was about to respond when a new box appeared near the upper left-hand side of my screen. The header told me it was a private message from someone called Looking For Luv. He wrote, "How r u?" A second box popped up partially covering Looking for Luv's message and most of the original Saskatchewan chat room screen. It was from Dandy Randy. He asked, "Busy?" Then a third from Can Do in Canwood, also asking if I was busy. My speakers were beeping and dinging and bonging as the world of Saskatchewan gay chat enveloped me and swallowed me whole like a snake on a gopher.

My first intention was to type in polite answers, but I couldn't find which of the many open windows my cursor was hiding in. I finally decided to handle the onslaught on a first-come first-serve basis, which only seemed logical. I found my way back to the original screen and typed in "hi." I waited for a moment, but based on the script since I'd been greeted so warmly, several more chatters had joined the room and apparently Brutus had long been forgotten. Oh well, I had several cyber suitors who were willing to talk to me. I found my way back to Looking for Luv. Beneath "How r u?" was the cryptic message: "Looking for Luv has left the room or is ignoring you." Huh? No bother, I always had Dandy Randy. I clicked on his screen. After his opener, "Busy?" was a line saying "Are u there?" followed by "Where r u?" followed by a testy-sounding "Hello????????" and a downright irritated sounding "Fine, buddy" and then the line telling me "Dandy Randy has left the room or is ignoring you." I thought about changing my bio to include something about looking for someone with patience. Surprisingly the message box from Can Do in Canwood was without any remonstrations or indications of abandonment. I warily typed in "hi." Fifteen seconds later came the answer: "Stats?" I wasn't exactly sure what Can Do in Canwood was looking for so I told him I was a professional man in my early thirties, had a dog and owned my own house. That certainly sounded desirable to me. Forty-five seconds passed. Nothing. It was as if he was waiting for more. I told him I drove a convertible.

"Can Do in Canwood has left the room or is ignoring you."

Grrrrr.

This was pissing me off.

After the flurry of attention, I was left with only one window open on my screen, the one for the main chat room, and they were still talking about that damned movie. I felt as if I'd been cyber-dumped. I didn't put out whatever they'd been looking for so I'd been pushed aside and ignored like a gay man wearing acid-wash jeans at a circuit party. Well, I wasn't about to take it sitting down. I searched the options available to me from the menu bar and discovered how to initiate my own private chat. I put in a call to Mr. Can Do in Canwood.

"Is something wrong?" I typed furiously.

"Stats?" was the trite response. Had he forgotten me already?

"What do you mean? What stats do you want?"

The reply came after thirty seconds. "I'm 35, brown hair/green eyes; 6/1, 195 lbs, 6.5 in. Looking for r/t."

Ahhhhhhh, I said to myself as dawning revelation hit my brain. He wasn't interested in knowing whether or not I could afford a mortgage or liked animals. I typed back, "What is r/t?"

"Real time…like get together in the flesh right now."

"Thanks."

"Newbie?"

"Yup."

"Good luck."

"Thanks."

"Can Do in Canwood has left the room or is ignoring you."

It was after 3 a.m. when I dragged myself and my four-legged friends from the den to the bedroom. Time in the Saskatchewan gay chat room had passed amazingly quick. SunLover never showed up but I used the time learning chat room protocol as well as figuring out much of the lingo. No one would call me a newbie again.

When I woke, later than usual, on Friday morning, I felt bleary-eyed and muddle-headed. If I didn't know better I'd have sworn I had a hangover. Through the two sets of windows and French doors just beyond the foot of my bed I could see fat snowflakes floating down from a whitewashed sky, alighting on tree branches like translucent fairies. Barbra, as was her habit, was curled up near my feet, satisfied that she'd fooled me once again and slept on my bed rather than her own, a doughy looking cushion in one corner of the room. Brutus was no where to be seen. I knew where he was though. Every time he came for a sleepover he did the same thing. Although schnauzers aren't known for great displays of slobbering affection, they do possess strong feelings of attachment and loyalty. And, true to form, twenty-kilogram Brutus, stoic and proud, was desperately missing Kelly and Errall. He began each night on the floor by the bed, but soon after lights out he'd pad his way silently out of the bedroom, down the hall, through the living room and into the foyer. There he'd lie down by the front door on the off chance that sometime during the night his owners would come by to retrieve him. I'd never had him long enough to break him of this habit and I saw no reason to try.

I nudged Barbra with my foot and she opened her eyes but otherwise remained absolutely still. I slipped out from under the warm covers and trudged to a nearby armchair to retrieve my thick winter housecoat, a big wooly thing covered with a snowflake design. Barbra hopped off the bed and I let her out the French doors, gave myself a cursory glance in the mirror and winced appropriately at the less than beautiful sight. Brutus, who had obviously heard the opening and closing of the door, came into the room expectantly. I let him out too and watched Barbra greet him with a snowflake-covered snout.

In the kitchen I set the coffee then scurried out the front door to fetch the newspaper. Back in the kitchen I poured dog food into metal dishes on the floor and let in the two pooches who were now at the back door looking in with hungry desire but too proud to bark or whine. They devoured breakfast with gentility while I poured my coffee. I was almost in my seat when it hit me.

Mother.

Where was she?

Where were the spitting bacon and too-weak coffee and the pound cake that weighed a ton?

Suddenly a feeling of dread overcame me. Something was terribly wrong. I could feel doom as certainly as I could feel wind in my hair or rain on my head. I dropped my coffee cup on the island counter, almost spilling its contents over the *StarPhoenix* and rushed to the door of my moth…of the guestroom. It was shut, just as it had been last night. I put my hand on the door handle, the metal felt cold to my touch. Instead of opening the door I raised my other hand and knocked. At first quietly and then more insistently. Nothing. Terrible thoughts stampeded into my brain like ants to an anthill. Although I certainly wasn't an expert on my mother's habits, in the couple of days she'd been in my home, I knew for certain that she was not a late sleeper. So why would she still be in her bed? Was she…ill?

I turned the handle downward and pushed open the door. The bed was to my immediate right. And it was empty. Empty and made up, as if it hadn't been slept in.

Damn! Why didn't I open the door when I'd checked on her last night? Just to be sure she was there and safe and snug in her bed. But why would I? She wasn't a child and I wasn't her parent. I had no reason to expect she wasn't there. It was late when I'd gotten in, she'd been alone all night after a horrible shopping expedition—guilt, guilt, guilt—of course she'd gone to bed, what else would she do? But now she was gone. Was she angry I hadn't stayed for dinner—or supper or whatever you wanted to call it—and had gone back home to the farm to spend Christmas by herself? But no. Her suitcase was in the corner of the room next to her collection of demure shoes. I checked the guest bathroom. Empty. Living room and laundry room. Same thing. By now the dogs had joined the search but were having as little luck as I was. As I made my way through every room and nook and cranny of the house I began to call out for her but she never answered back. Back in the kitchen I found the keys to her van in the bowl where she'd taken to leaving them. So she hadn't gone for a drive. What was left?

In desperate need of caffeine, I threw out the cold cup I'd poured earlier and replenished it with some hot stuff. I leaned against the kitchen island and stared into space trying to figure out the mystery of my mother's disappearance. Handy that I was a detective. As minutes crawled by I began to suspect foul play. Had my mother been abducted? But why? Who would want a sixtyish, bossy Ukrainian woman from Howell, Saskatchewan? Or did this have something to do with me and the case I was working on? Had I unconsciously put my own mother in danger? Did this have something to do with the tail from last night or the ambush at the landfill? It all sounded too incredible. I emptied my cup and poured more. I needed the stimulant to clear my brain. There had to be a good explanation. Maybe she'd gone for a walk? Unlikely. She didn't strike me as a walker. Had she gone to visit a neighbour? I could believe she was a chatty, visit-the-neighbour sort of person, but she'd only just arrived on Tuesday. She didn't know any of the neighbours. However I had mentioned one neighbour to her—just in passing—Sereena.

Sereena?

Despite the dire circumstances I found myself laughing. Not only is Sereena Smith not a chatty, visit-the-neighbour type of person, she and my mother could never in a million years hit it off. Sereena is a complex, fantastical creature with a mythical past that no one person seems to know the whole of. How she ended up in a little house next to mine on an unremarkable street in Saskatoon, Saskatchewan, I'm not quite sure. Forty, maybe fifty, she's an imperfect, damaged, raving beauty. She lives her life without sham or deception and that's what I like about her. And, I was pretty sure, that when she and my mother met, they would instantly despise one another.

Yet, as impossible as it sounded, it was my only option at the moment. I picked up the cordless handset of my kitchen phone and dialled my neighbour's number.

"Yes?" was her greeting.

"Sereena, it's Russell."

"You're tense." Intuitive too.

"I know this is going to sound preposterous, but my mother isn't over there, is she?"

The line was quiet and I wondered if I'd lost the connection.

"Sereena?"

"Oh," she said, "did you actually expect an answer?"

"Okay, okay, I didn't think so."

"Is something wrong?"

"When I woke up this morning, she was gone. All her stuff and her van are still here, but she isn't. I'm really worried."

"Maybe she took a walk."

"I don't think so. It's too cold outside for a leisurely walk."

And just then, through the back door came my mother, bundled up in Thinsulate.

"Uh, never mind," I said and hung up.

"I start breakfast den?" were the first words out of her mouth.

"Mom! Where were you?"

"Eggs, ya?"

Was this her trying to elude my questions? "Where were you? I was worried."

"Out valking. Deed you haf goot garden dis year? My tomatoes vere so bad, oi. I haf to buy. Never as goot."

"Mom, could you maybe leave me a note next time you go out? Just so I don't worry?"

"Ya, ya, uh-huh, sedai, Sonsyou, I make eggs, ya?"

"Well, where was she?" Errall asked with incredulity.

I shrugged my shoulders. I was in her office sitting in one of the chairs meant for clients in front of her oversized desk. Errall's work-space is much different from my own. It takes up nearly one half of the main floor and is divided into three connecting areas. There's the desk area, the client meeting area and the research area. The room is smartly planned, impressive and, I think, somewhat austere. Errall was leaning forward, her elbows resting on the desk with shoulders hunched up. She was wearing a navy business suit with a blindingly white, wide-collared, man's style shirt and a string of pearls. Her black hair was in a tidy bun at the base of her neck and her eyes were disarmingly piercing as usual. It struck me then that even though Errall had taken up smoking again, I never smelled it on or around her, just the sharp, mildly spicy fragrance she always wore. I looked past her through a window onto Spadina Crescent. The early morning snow had left behind a sheet of white crispness.

"I really don't know but I got the distinct impression she was hiding something from me. She kept trying to change the subject."

"Are you sure Russell?"

I shook my head despondently. "No, I'm not. Maybe I'm being paranoid, too suspicious, a quirk of my profession. I just don't understand why she's even here, staying with me for Christmas. I'm realizing how little my mother and I know one another."

Errall quirked her head to one side and said, "Maybe that's why she's doing it."

For a moment neither of us said a word while Errall's insight sunk in.

"You know what?" I finally said. "I can't think about this right now. Listen, this isn't why I came in here anyway. I wanted to ask you about Kelly, to see how she is. I've been trying to call her but never get an answer."

Errall's face became a mask behind which I was almost sure she was hiding something. Why was everyone doing that!

"No change. She's just…well she's in a funk and she can't get out."

"Maybe she needs some help, Errall, maybe Beverly could…"

"I know. We're trying that," she said in a short, clipped tone.

"Okay." I quickly acquiesced. Getting professional help was a private matter and I didn't want to stick my nose too far in. "Maybe she'd want to come over to visit Brutus? I know he really misses her and she must miss him. She can come over anytime."

Errall nodded but the look on her face seemed doubtful. "Y'know, Russell, she needs something…some…tonic of some sort, something to give her a kick-start. She's like a battery low on juice—it wants to turn over the engine but just can't. I just wish I knew what it is she needs."

I nodded and noticed Errall glance at her wristwatch. It struck me that she and I were living similar lives. We each had personal issues begging for our attention but were being pulled away by our careers. Or…were we letting ourselves be pulled? I jumped out of my chair and headed for the door. Errall was already on the phone.

Chapter 8

UPSTAIRS IN MY OFFICE I grabbed a Diet Pepsi from the refrigerator under my desk and settled in. After making an appointment to meet later that morning with Professor Marc Driediger, the contact Anthony had set me up with, I updated my suspect chart for the information I'd learned the night before about suspect number one, James Kraft, a.k.a. Jo. I then made some notes about the landfill chase and last night's tail by the blue car. As I was still uncertain of the significance (if any) of either event, I stuck them in the Herrings file—the file I use for information I don't know what to do with but don't want to lose track of. After I was done I still had some time to kill before leaving to meet with the professor so after again failing to reach Kelly, I decided to revisit gays.r.us for SunLover. After all, what else does a beach boy have to do in the middle of winter but try to get laid?

As I clicked my way into the now familiar Saskatchewan gay chat room the thought occurred to me that SunLover might be using a different nickname. Chat rooms certainly provided a certain amount of anonymity, more so than a bar or dating service, but I suppose even the best disguises need to be changed every once in a while. If this was the case with SunLover it wasn't good news for me. It would make it harder for me to find him—but not impossible. No one calling themselves SunLover showed up in the chat room the night before, but there certainly were chatters whose bios loosely fit the description Daniel Guest had given me. I decided it couldn't hurt to pay special attention to any fortysomething Brad Pitt types.

The Saskatchewan room was much quieter on a Friday morning than it had been Thursday night. When I entered there were only seven other chatters and four of them were from Regina, two-and-a-half hours away. I studied the bios for the remaining three but found nothing even close to what I was looking for. The dialogue box was quiet, even the seven in the room weren't talking to one another, unless they were doing so in private. I kept the room open but began sorting through my mail Lilly had brought up and placed on my desk. It was several minutes later when I heard, "Bing!"

I looked up. I had a private message from someone named Big Quill. We chatted for about a minute. He was seventeen and smooth and wanting to get raunchy over the phone. I turned him down as politely as I could and surveyed the current crop of hopefuls in the main room. Sunny caught my attention. His bio was blank so I sent him a private message.

"Busy?" I typed out the standard opening line.

"No," he came back with.

"How are you?"

"Okay thanks. Stats?"

"34, bl/gr, 6, 180, athletic, gd lkg. U?" I described someone close to Daniel Guest (in case SunLover was into that particular type) but not quite (in case he wasn't into repeats).

"39, blond & green, 6.2, tan, 40 chest, 28 waist. U in Stoon?"

"Yes," I told him, I was in Saskatoon. Everything looked about right for this guy to be SunLover except possibly the age. Daniel said he was in his forties or maybe a bit older, but that was just a guess. "Where r u?"

"Same."

"Wanna meet?" I asked brazenly. If only I could be this ballsy in my real personal life.

"Okay. Do you have a place?"

Hmm. This guy used Bare Ass Beach in the summer as his meeting place, but obviously had none in the winter. I certainly didn't want him coming to my home. Then again, I suppose my mother would be happy to have someone else to cook for. "No," I replied, "Any ideas?"

"How about we meet in the parking lot at Confederation Mall?"

Huh? This was a new one. How would that work? I guess I was still a newbie. "Sure," I typed.

"Okay. Right now?"

That wouldn't do. I had to arrange for Daniel to be with me to ID the guy. I had no idea whether he was free right now. Chances were he wasn't. "Can't. How about early this evening?" That night was the DGR&R Christmas party, but I'd have to convince Daniel to join me in the parking lot before hand.

"It'll have to be late. I have a thing. How about 11:30?"

Darn. Well, at least dinner would be over and any dancing and drinking would just be starting. "Okay," I agreed, hoping I could deliver.

"11:30 Confederation Shopping Mall parking lot."

Suddenly I felt nervous and excited, like I was accepting an invitation for dinner and a movie with someone I had a crush on. "See you then."

"You'll be there?"

And now I felt bad. His question seemed almost pleading, a little sad. He'd obviously been stood up before, left sitting in a deserted parking lot in the middle of the night, waiting for someone who would never show up. At least I would show up—just not for the reason he expected. Oh well, a person had to accept certain risks when arranging blind dates over the internet. "Yes I will," I typed back. I had to get going to my next appointment. "Bye."

"Bye," typed Sunny.

Marc Driediger's office in the College of Education building was a small space overflowing with paper in every form imaginable: books, bound reports, loose-leaf, in binders, foolscap, bright white, coloured, embossed and glossy, covered in longhand, typed on and scribbled on. The man who sat behind an overburdened desk was in his late thirties with a face and body that, despite a valiant effort to thwart genetics, were thickening with age. He had covered his jovial face with a scruffy moustache and beard and his body with sedate clothes that looked as if they were about to become too tight. Marc Driediger had a wide, friendly smile, sparkling eyes behind wire-rimmed glasses and a head of curly brown hair thinning at the crown.

"Thank you for seeing me on such short notice," I said after I was seated on a chair recently rescued from beneath a stack of student essays.

"No problem at all. I owe Anthony tons of favours."

I wondered why but decided not to ask. There are very few things I don't consider my business, so when I run into one, I pride myself in letting it go. "I understand you know a man by the name of James Kraft."

"Yes, I do," he said easily. "And I'm happy to tell you about that, but not if I thought it might somehow get James into trouble."

"Is there some reason you think it would?"

He chuckled. "Anthony said you were clever and that I should watch out."

Bastard!

I gave him a clever smile. "James may be involved in a case I'm working on. I'm interested in finding out more about his character, his background." What I was hoping to find out was if James was the type of person who'd commit blackmail. "Anything you could tell me would be helpful. Anything at all."

"Anthony probably told you James and I dated a couple years ago?"

"No," I told him. "He never mentioned it." Obviously James was into older men, first this professor and then Daniel, both more than ten years older.

"Oh. Well it wasn't for very long."

Oh goody, I thought. No gay man ever had anything good to say about this type of relationship.

"It was perfect. Six really terrific months."

Bugger.

"He was a student here at the U of S. We met at a campus GLBT club meeting." He sniggered at the thought. "They host these really lame wine and cheese nights; usually a couple warm bottles of Lonesome Charlie—appropriate don't you think—and a block of dried-out cheddar. Normally about four people show up, and two of those are the organizers. It's not really my thing, but I'd been single for a while and didn't know how to meet people. So I decided to go one night and, as luck would have it, so did James. Besides James and myself, there was this really bitter lesbian and a straight, Chinese girl who could barely speak English and thought she was at a chess club meeting. Well, let me tell ya, we got out of there pretty quick, giggling like girls and with a bottle of Lonesome Charlie under James' jacket."

Aha! He was a thief!

I was grasping.

I let Marc continue. I suspected I wasn't going to get any useful information from his story but he seemed to be deriving such pleasure from telling it. "We sat in my car and talked until the wine was gone. He was such a cool guy and I was so surprised that he seemed interested in me. I mean, I'm not exactly Lorenzo Lamas and I'm a fair bit older than James is. But he insisted he was into me and couldn't we have some fun? He was still living with his folks, so we went back to my place and did just that. We had lots of fun. And I don't just mean the sex. He was such a fun-loving, nice young guy. A real sweetheart. Six months later when the term ended, I was going abroad to start a sabbatical and he was, I don't know, working in Saskatoon at a bicycle shop or something…so we just parted ways, very amicably."

I smiled and nodded. He had such an affable, easy manner, I guessed Marc Driediger was popular with his students. "So when did you next see James?"

"Actually, I haven't seen him since." Marc held up his left hand and thrust forward a chubby ring finger with a simple gold band on it. He grinned, setting his whiskers so close to his nose they must have tickled him. "I don't think Allan would approve. But I have to admit, I wouldn't mind, just for old time's sake." Then he added, almost as an afterthought, "If you see him, pass him a hello."

I left the campus wondering if I'd just wasted my time. The theory that James Kraft was some evil-monger playing havoc with Daniel's life now seemed full of holes. But then again, Marc Driediger hadn't seen James in a while. A lot could change in two years.

I used the 25th Street Bridge to cross the river and headed towards Colourful Mary's. Daniel had agreed to meet me at Mary's for a late lunch. We had a number of things to discuss. Although most of the midday diners had departed, I chose a table half-hidden behind a grove of overgrown philodendrons in case Daniel was uncomfortable being seen in Saskatoon's only publicly admitted, gay-owned and run restaurant.

Mary and Marushka had obviously spent some time decorating the place in honour of the season. The walls were covered in giant, plaster replicas of every candy imaginable and the windows were latticed with strips of faux licorice. The ceiling was now slabs of fake brown wafers covered in fake icing and fake candy sprinkles. It was what I'd expect the inside of a gingerbread house to look like.

Daniel was right on time, walking in only seconds after I was settled. He hung up his coat and scarf on a coat rack near the door. As he walked through the restaurant, six eyes belonging to two twentysomething trendy boys and one very obvious drag queen were sticking to him like glue. Was I imagining it or was he sticking out his chest and sucking in his tummy?

He settled himself, resplendent in a dashing grey suit, on a chair opposite mine. His hair seemed a little wavier than I remembered it last and I wondered if he was wearing a different pair of glasses. These were silver rimmed. They matched his silver belt buckle and silver watch. I was sure his other glasses were gold rimmed. Hmmm.

"I haven't been here in months. I'm glad you suggested it. What are the specials?" he asked exuberantly, his cheeks still flushed red from the outside chill.

I looked up at him, surprised by his ease. Colourful Mary's was a top-notch restaurant frequented by all types. I don't know why I expected him to have never been there before. Oh wait—maybe it was because someone with even a trace of sexual ambiguity might stay away from a gay-owned diner?

Just then Mary showed up with a smile that contrasted beautifully with her dark skin. She gave me a quick shoulder rub and sharp-eyed my companion. "So hons, can I get you something to drink?"

"Could I get a chai latte?" Daniel asked.

"Absolutely, dear, how about you, Russell?" She gave me a look that said, "So who's the guy?"

"Coffee please. Any specials today?"

"Marushka will be hurt if you don't try the meatballs in ketchup sauce—I'm not supposed to call it that, but that's what she uses as the base—and I'm pretty sure there are two bowls of the blob soup left."

"Blob soup? Ketchup sauce?"

Mary crossed her eyes at us for effect. "I know there's some Ukrainian name for all of it, but it's unpronounceable for someone whose last name doesn't end in ski, ka or chuk, but experience has taught me that the more unpronounceable it is, the better it tastes."

Daniel gave her a winning smile. "Bring it on."

"Sure," I agreed. "But do I get to request how many blobs I want in my soup?"

"When it comes to food in this restaurant," Mary said as she headed away, "the only one with any decision-making power is Marushka." I doubted this. Mary is half First Nations Cree, half Irish and Marushka is Ukrainian—a feisty pairing to say the least.

"I'm glad you suggested this meeting, Russell, there's something I have to ask you…and I'm not quite sure how to do it. It's about tonight."

I was glad Daniel seemed to be over stewing about the guy in the blue car, but I didn't want him changing his mind about my attending his office Christmas party. "I'm still invited, aren't I?"

"Well sure. It's just that…I've been thinking about this…and, well I hate to ask you this."

"Just ask. We'll deal with it once it's on the table."

"I want you to bring a date," he blurted out.

"A date?"

"A woman."

Mr. Liberal who sauntered into a gay restaurant and thought nothing of posturing for the boys and boy-girls was back to showing his true colours. "I don't think I understand." I did but I wanted him to spell it out. I didn't care how uncomfortable he was with it.

"Russell, it's just that…it's my workplace and it's Christmastime and people don't go to Christmas parties alone and you're too attractive to be single at your age and I just think it would raise less attention if you showed up with a woman and then no one would think anything weird about why I know you and so I was thinking last night that you could just..." He took a breath, "Just for one night..."

I let him blabber on for thirty seconds more before finally putting an end to it. I didn't have the time right then to decide whether I was insulted, irritated or simply indifferent to his suggestion. "Okay."

"Okay?" He seemed surprised.

"Okay." I could give in on this one.

He moved his hand closer to mine, such that I thought he was about to touch it but he didn't. He looked at me closely and said, "Thank you." I nodded.

"I may have found SunLover," I told him.

"You do move fast, Russell, I have to tell you. How did you do it?"

"Gays.r.us. Except the fellow I've met is going under the nickname Sunny. There's a good chance SunLover could be using a different nickname, so I've been keeping an eye on anyone in the chat room who has any of the same attributes as the man you met at Bare Ass Beach."

"Okay. So now what?"

"Now we meet him and see if it's the same guy."

"We?"

"Uh-huh. You're the only one who can identify him, Daniel. I can't do this without you."

"I...I don't know if I can do that. I don't know if I can face him again. Especially if he turns out to be Loverboy."

I thought about this for a moment. "You may not have to. All I need you to do is identify him. I can do the rest."

"How can we do that?"

"Just leave that up to me."

"Here we go, hons," Mary said as she delivered two bowls the size of woks filled to the brim with a yellowish broth. Throughout the liquid bobbed several blobs of a doughy consistency and in various sizes and shapes. It smelled amazingly good.

We thanked Mary and I caught a glimpse of Marushka's dewy red face as it peeked through the diamond shaped glass in the door to the kitchen. I winked and she smiled, reminding me of one of those fairies...Merriweather was it?...from *Snow White* or was it *Sleeping Beauty*?

"Mmm," Daniel made noises of appreciation. "My taste buds have just climaxed."

I took my first bite. It was like the best chicken noodle soup I'd ever tasted but without the chicken and with all the noodles balled together into blobs. "Of course Sunny and SunLover may not be the same person," I said.

Daniel nodded mid-slurp. Good. I wanted him a bit distracted while I brought up Plan B.

"I'll keep watch in gays.r.us, but we'll have to do more. We obviously can't go back to the scene of the liaison in the middle of winter, hoping to spot him there, so we have to come up with some other way to find him."

"Oh?" Daniel sensed a possible change in his fate and stopped eating.

"He's a gay man. We have to go where gay men go."

Daniel's lips tightened and his eyes narrowed. "There's that dreaded 'we' word again. Like where?"

"Right here for instance—Colourful Mary's. Gay people frequent this restaurant. There's a chance he might show up here."

"Oh, okay, I can do that."

"And bars."

"Bars?"

"Gay bars."

He swallowed hard (no soup this time), his resolve quickly weakening. "Gay bars?"

"Hot dance spots. Gay men like to dance."

"Dance?" He seemed to be turning into a simpering fool in front of my very eyes.

"There are certain stores gay men frequent."

"Oh yeah?"

"And cruising spots."

"Cruising?"

"Where guys pick up guys for sex."

"I can't do that!" he spit out along with a tiny bit of blob.

I frowned. "You already have. Twice at least." This was unnecessarily mean, but maybe unconsciously I was getting him back for the "bring a date" thing.

"Russell, I am not about to start hanging out in discos and dance halls and dark alleys!"

Discos? Dance halls? What decade was he living in? Dark alleys? Well…okay, I'd give him that one.

"Besides, it's too much! How can we possibly cover all that ground and expect to find one man? The chances of our being at the same place at the same time as SunLover is infinitesimal!"

I rocked my head from side to side. "If we were living in Vancouver or Toronto or even Calgary, I'd have to agree with you, but in Saskatoon I'd say our chances are much better than infinitesimal. And besides, it's the only option we have."

"I can't do it, Russell, I can't go to those places. Suppose someone saw me going in or coming out?"

"Coming out?"

"Stop it, Russell, I'm being serious."

"So am I. You hired me to find these guys and that's what I'm trying to do. But I can't do it without your help."

"No. I hired you to find Loverboy! And you did. James Kraft is Loverboy. Why don't we focus on him? I know it's him! We don't have to go lurking about in parking lots and bars to find SunLover! Let's go after James Kraft!"

"James Kraft is in New York."

That stopped him short. "What?"

"I just found out last night. James Kraft is living in New York City."

Daniel was quiet for a moment, contemplating this new information. Finally he said, "That doesn't mean he can't be Loverboy, does it?"

I had to agree. "No, it doesn't."

"Then go get him!" he said, slapping a palm against the tabletop and trying, unsuccessfully, to restrain his voice.

Mary gave us a glance from where she was chatting up a table of adoring baby lesbians, but other than her, no one seemed to be paying us much attention. "Daniel, calm down. Think about this rationally. You're only focusing on James Kraft because he's the easy target and because you don't want to step foot into a gay bar!"

"Yeah, so what? So what's wrong with that? And sometimes, Russell, and I know this from my work, just because an answer is easy, doesn't mean it's not the right one."

"How were the blobs, boys?" Not a question you hear every day. Mary was back with two plates covered with meatballs in a creamy red sauce and a hunk of heavy looking brown bread. She exchanged the soup bowls for the meatball plates and left without further interruption. She knows when to leave her patrons alone.

"Daniel," I said, lowering my voice a few notches below the last time I'd used it, "I agree with you. And we may have to go after James Kraft in New York. But there are some steps we can take right here at home that are more obvious—and less expensive."

"I don't care about the money, I just want…"

I cut him off. "I know, Daniel, I know you just want this over with. But let's be smart about this. Cross all our t's and dot our i's. If we go after James Kraft in New York, let's make sure that's the right step to take. I know you're sure James Kraft is our man. But he doesn't even live here anymore. Chances are that SunLover does. And if so, he's a better suspect than you think. I just met with an ex-lover of James'. He has a pretty high opinion of his character; he certainly didn't make him sound like someone who would do what Loverboy is doing to you. Maybe SunLover is. We should at least take a stab at finding out."

Daniel stared at his plate. He was cooling off as quickly as the meatballs were.

"And besides, if we find SunLover tonight, you won't have to go into a gay bar."

It took a few more seconds but he finally managed an "Okay."

"Good," I said warily, knowing there was a "but" somewhere in my near future.

He looked up at me, almost pleadingly. "But if things don't work out, Russell, I…I…I just don't think I can go into a gay bar. I…I…I'm afraid."

He didn't need to admit that to me, but I thought more of him for doing so. He didn't say he didn't want to be with those kinds of people, he didn't say he had too much to lose, he was simply…afraid. Afraid of what might happen. Afraid of how he might feel. Afraid he might like it? As I considered this dilemma my eyes idly wandered about the restaurant until a bizarre thought began to form in my mind. Was my client ready for this? "What if I could find a way for you to be there," I began, a smile forming on my lips, "but without you being there?"

Daniel looked confused. His eyes followed mine and understanding slowly dawned on him.

"Saturday night?" I suggested.

At first his face flushed and then he too began to smile. "That could work."

Chapter 9

AFTER LUNCH AT COLOURFUL MARY'S with Daniel Guest, I made an appointment for later that afternoon, called Sereena's cellphone and reached her doing who knows what, who knows where, with who knows who and convinced her to be my beard that evening at Daniel Guest's office Christmas party. Then I headed to the gym for a much needed workout. Although I would never say I don't have a vain bone in my body, my priorities when going to the gym are, number one, to build muscles that on occasion I need in my line of work and, number two, to keep from becoming overweight which my body type seems predisposed to.

After my cardio-heavy workout, I arrived at Aden Bowman Collegiate on Clarence Avenue a little early for my appointment. Unwilling to listen to Boney M's "Mary's Boy Child" on the radio one more time, I played the I-Spy game with myself and did not too badly. At 3:30 I left my car, entered the school and found a stray kid to direct me to the right classroom. I knocked lightly on the already open door and poked my head into the room. A woman behind a desk looked up and smiled.

"Mr. Woodward?"

"Yes," I said, approaching with an outstretched hand. I probably didn't need a fake name, but for me, that's part of the fun of the whole detecting gig. "But call me Bernie."

She stood to greet me, taking my hand. "Bernie, I'm Anita, Anita Soloway."

Anita Soloway looked even younger than she had in the photograph I'd seen in Daniel's office. Looking at her face the first thing that struck me was the seemingly countless freckles and not all squished together either, but separate, distinct freckles. So many it made me wonder how they all fit on one face, even if it was a bit chubby. Her curly, dark hair bounced as she sat back down and indicated for me to do the same in a chair she'd obviously placed next to her desk in anticipation of my visit.

"Thank you for seeing me on such short notice," I said, opening a leather folder and poising a pen above the pad within as if prepping to write stuff down.

"Oh, I'm happy to do it," she said. "If I understood you correctly, you're a journalist doing a piece on Daniel and Cheryl Guest?"

"Yes, that's right. I'm with *Today's Entrepreneur*. It's a quarterly newsmagazine published out of Vancouver, focusing on young, Canadian entrepreneurs who make a difference in their communities. We heard about Daniel Guest winning the Saskatoon Business Association's Businessperson of the Year Award and decided to do an article on his family and him."

"That's terrific," she said, "But I'm not sure how I can help, or what I can contribute. I'm sure you've already interviewed Daniel and Cheryl?"

"Daniel referred me to you." Itty bitty lie. "You see *Today's Entrepreneur* isn't your run-of-the-mill business magazine. We like our articles to have more breadth and depth; we interview family and friends and neighbours—such as yourself—to get the more personal touch."

"I see."

"You're obviously a teacher," I said, jotting down the information, "Chemistry teacher is it?"

"Among many other subjects," she laughed as if the plight of over-worked teachers was common knowledge. "But yes, chemistry is my specialty."

"And you're a neighbour of the Guests?"

"Oh, more than that," she said. "Cheryl and I go way back, back to the farm. We grew up around Wakaw? You ever hear of it?"

I had, but I was supposed to be from Vancouver. "Now where is that?"

"Oh, about an hour and some north, northeast of Saskatoon. We're both farm girls; Cheryl more than me," she said with another easy laugh. "She was a real tomboy, helping out her dad and brothers with the harvest and the cattle. She did it all. Anyway, we went to school together in Wakaw and then to university here. We were both in our first year, still in the College of Arts and Science when we met Daniel. That got her more interested in makeup and clothes in a hurry let me tell you!"

"I see."

"I of course went on to the College of Education."

"And Cheryl? She's not a teacher too, is she?" I asked, knowing full well that she wasn't.

"Ah no, she isn't."

"What college did she go to?"

Anita Soloway looked distinctly uncomfortable, as if she'd found herself in the men's room when she was certain she'd taken all the right turns to get to the women's. "Well, she stayed in Arts for a while."

"And then...?"

"Well, Cheryl didn't finish school. She and Daniel got married and well, you know."

A quickie marriage. Wonder why. "Do they have children?" Again a question I knew the answer to but one I'd hoped would reveal a more telling response from Anita.

"They...well, y'know, they tried...ah...Cheryl was pregnant, but they lost it soon after the marriage..."

Bingo. All of a sudden I had a clearer view of my client. Daniel Guest was a nice guy who might have come out when he was nineteen or so, but in his efforts to disprove his sexuality, his girlfriend became pregnant. Being a dutiful fellow, he married her and ended up a closet case. Not an uncommon story. The girlfriend, now wife, loses the baby, they never have any other kids, but they stay married because of a lot of reasons I may or may not agree with. Now, move ahead a decade or so and one of his indiscretions—big surprise—threatens to bite him on the ass. Also not an uncommon story?

Well, enough about that. "I was wondering if you could give me a snapshot of the Guest's life as couple. Who their friends are, the people in their life. Are they a typical couple or…not?" If Anita Soloway was a gossip, here was her chance to shine.

"Ah…I don't know if I understand the question." She was looking sorrier and sorrier to have agreed to this interview.

"Well, you know, are they a happy couple? What do they do for fun, who do they hang out with?"

"Oh well, I…" she stopped there as if confused, distraught, torn. "I really couldn't say. I'm sorry, I don't know if you have the right person here. I'm not being very much help, am I?"

Daniel had told me the Soloways were their good friends and neighbours. Yet Anita seemed to have little to say. Was she simply being protective or did she know something she didn't want to talk about? "Don't worry about it," I said, rising from my chair. I had hoped to get some leads on other people surrounding the Guests who might be eligible blackmailers; I hadn't gotten that, but I was leaving understanding my client a whole lot better.

Back in my office I retrieved my phone messages. There was only one.

"Russell, it's Daniel. I've just returned to my office after our lunch and I'm almost certain the same blue car I told you about from the other night was following me." Damn and I missed it! "And when I got back here Colleen told me…Colleen is our receptionist…she told me a woman had been at the office asking questions about me." Woman? "I think it was the same person…I caught a better look at the driver this time because it was daylight and it could have been a woman. I wasn't close enough to see any details but Colleen said the gal here was…I jotted down what she said…'she was short, a bit thick-waisted, dark hair, cute'…cute something…I can't quite make…oh, 'cute face' it says, 'steely eyes and no-nonsense attitude.'" Steely eyes? "And that's about it. Do you know who this woman is?" Did he think I knew every criminal-type person in the city just because I was a detective? "And why is she following me? Call me if you get this message before tonight."

I immediately tried Daniel's office number but was told he'd already left for the day. Oh well, that discussion would have to wait. As I hung up the phone I realized something important had changed in this case. Daniel, under duress, had come directly to me. Not to me through Beverly, as had been his habit. He called me.

My client was beginning to trust me.

It was already dark by the time I headed home; by the car's dashboard clock it was after six. I didn't have much time to get home, get dressed, check on the dogs and my mother, pick up Sereena and make it to the DGR&R party in time for pre-dinner cocktails. I sped up and despite the end-of-week traffic, made it home and was in my bedroom primping in eleven minutes.

Out of my closet I pulled my wonderpants. They are black, never wrinkle, I've owned them forever yet they're always in style and, most important, I've been told that they make my ass look great. I matched them that night with a cream-coloured silk shirt flocked with a vaguely Romanesque pattern, and a black jacket. I stood in front of the mirror to assess the completed product. Not too shabby. I finger-combed my sandy hair and called it a done deal. I rushed into the kitchen, called Sereena to tell her I'd be right over to collect her, petted my mother's head, kissed the dogs and ran out to meet the night.

Dufour, Guest, Rowan & Rowan held their annual Christmas party, as they do every year, in an elaborately decorated ballroom in the Saskatoon Inn, a hotel on the northwest edge of the city near the airport. Some people consider any party outside of downtown to be lacking a certain pizzazz, but the partner's at DGR&R are vigilant about supporting the north Saskatoon business community they (and the majority of their clients) work in, with as much vigour at Christmas time as any other time of year. And, as far as airport hotels go, the Saskatoon Inn is not bad.

Sereena wore a deep purple sheath she'd probably yanked off the back of some royal princess once upon a time and had bundled her dark tresses into a spectacular maze of intricate patterns at the top of her head. Her face and figure hid no secrets. Anyone who looked at her would know they were seeing one of the world's great beauties— less than perfectly preserved—but a beauty nonetheless. We stepped into the ballroom and saw a scene that would be duplicated in hotels and restaurants and halls throughout the city that night and every night from then until late December: the office Christmas party. Women in gowns of Rudolph-nose red, mistletoe green and gaudy gold that would be worn eleven times over two-and-a-half weeks of holiday events; men in the same dark suits they wore to work but jazzed up with festive ties and colourful shirts; portable bars manned by bored university-aged bartenders pouring eight dollar bottles of wine for five dollars a glass; platters of uninspired appetizers getting cold and turning up at the edges; a DJ arranging his collection of almost-hits from the '80s and '90s; a rakish-looking Christmas tree decked out in a few lights and fewer decorations; and a collection of round tables draped in bright linens topped with a centrepiece of pinecone and fake holly. I saw several women and men give Sereena the once-over. I was pretty sure one of the wait staff was checking me out.

"Swill?" Sereena suggested after having her fill of long-distance admiration.

We walked through the crowd of strangers, 150 or so of them, and eventually made our way to the front of the bar line. I saw by his nametag that our bartender's name was Derek. I wondered if he also worked at gatt. "What type of white wine do you have?" I asked.

He held up a bottle of the singular selection with a look on his face as if even he, a poor university student with a part-time job as a banquet bartender, was accustomed to far more desirable vintages.

I smiled pleasantly and told him to pour two glasses.

"So who exactly are these people?" Sereena asked once we'd found a spot to stand without danger of having our wine jostled but not too far from the bar, where we'd no doubt return.

"Most of them are staff of DGR&R and their spouses or dates, a handful of clients…i.e. myself…and their demure, close-mouthed companions…i.e. you."

"Was that humour?" she asked without apparent recognition of it being so.

"I guess not."

Her practised eye roved the room and she commented, "Care to wager on whether we'll be eating chicken tonight?"

"Here comes my client," I whispered as Daniel Guest in a black suit, crisp white shirt and bright red tie approached.

"Did you get my message?" he asked conspiratorially as soon as he was within conspiratorial range. He had to be the only man in the room who could possibly be within perfume-smelling distance of Sereena Smith and not notice her. Gay as a party hat.

"I did," I replied. "And I'd like to introduce my 'date' Sereena Smith."

Daniel shifted his attention and studied Sereena with googly eyes. He expertly commenced laying on the charm. Sereena expertly accepted it. I let them coo back and forth for a minute then made them stop before I'd need something stronger than wine.

"I'd like to talk to your receptionist about the woman who showed up at the office," I told him.

"No," he said matter-of-factly. "That would arouse too much suspicion."

"Doesn't the fact that a woman was nosing around your office and asking questions about you already raise suspicion?"

"Well yes," he admitted, "but that's different than having a PI asking questions on my behalf. I don't want Colleen or anyone to know…" He stopped there and looked at Sereena and then back at me.

"Sereena had to be told certain things before coming out with me tonight." I told him. "In case you hadn't guessed—she isn't a real date."

He looked churlish and maybe a bit sheepish at having fawned over her like a lovesick lothario when she'd already known he was fond of sleeping with men. "Oh," he said. "That's fine."

It better be fine, I thought to myself. It wasn't my idea to bring a date to this shindig.

Sereena did her part by smiling beguilingly at my client, kind of a wink-wink nudge-nudge kind of smile that I'm sure further withered his manly ego.

Daniel moved even closer into our already tight circle and spoke in a quiet voice. "I guess what's important is who is this woman and why is she following me."

"Agreed, but I have to be able to ask more questions to find out."

"Not now, not now," he whispered harshly. "Let's talk about this later."

The reason Daniel suddenly put an end to our conversation was not too subtly joining our group by threading her hand through his crooked arm. She was physically the same height as Daniel, but several inches taller with heels on. Her short, multi-toned blond hair had been curled and teased into a busy do, her toothy smile and big brown eyes were bracketed by a bevy of wrinkles, like small fissures in her caramel-tanned skin.

"I'd like you to meet my wife, Cheryl," Daniel said. "Sweetheart, this is Russell Quant and his girlfriend, Sereena Smith."

Girlfriend? Sereena and I quickly exchanged amused looks and politely shook the proffered hand. Unlike many women who, through varied means, manage twenty-eight-year-old-looking faces well into their forties but couldn't hide their age when you looked at their hands, Cheryl Guest was the opposite. Her face looked ten years older than her chronological age, but her hands were lovely and smooth, with nails professionally French-manicured. They were hands meant for teacups or Palmolive commercials.

"So you're girlfriend and boyfriend?" Cheryl purred with the friendliness of a cougar about to leap on prey. She was speaking to Sereena but her eyes continually darted back to me, assessing me like a side of beef she wasn't sure would fit in her deep freeze. "How lovely. How long have you been together?"

"Why do you ask?" Sereena smoothly shot back, unabashedly surveying the gold lamé dress barely held up by two spaghetti straps on the other woman's figure.

Cheryl was momentarily thrown off-balance by the unexpected answer, as intended, giving Daniel the opportunity to jump in.

"Russell is considering using DGR&R," Daniel told his wife.

Likely relieved to be pulled from the maw of an unwinnable battle of wits with Sereena (and if not, she should have been), Cheryl turned her full attention on me. "What's to consider? DGR&R is the best."

We all laughed lightly, except Sereena who is oblivious to the need for laughter unless something is actually funny. And even then a laugh is seldom a guarantee.

"What business are you in, Mr. Quant?" Cheryl asked.

"I'm a private investigator." I could see out of the corner of my eye Daniel beginning to squirm. We hadn't discussed the answer to this question—I'm sure he was hoping for some kind of white lie—but I'd decided I'd lied enough for him for one evening.

She lowered her wineglass, forgoing a planned sip. "Really? I've never met a private investigator before. How interesting. Do you do most of your work here in Saskatoon?"

I nodded. "Mostly. It all depends on the case. It's a small business, but growing. So I'll need a good accountant soon."

Another man drifted into our group and looked expectantly at Daniel to provide introductions. He was well over six feet and heavy-looking without being overweight, probably an impressive athlete in his younger years. With a head covered in curly greying hair I guessed him to be in his late forties, although his unlined face looked as if I might be off by several years. He had a sharp nose and strong chin. All in all a pleasant combination of features.

"Russell Quant, Sereena Smith, I'd like you to meet Herb Dufour, one of the partners at DGR&R."

I was glad he dropped the girlfriend thing. We all shook hands and he complimented the appearance of the two women in the group without seeming slimy or insincere.

"Well, it shows how naive I am," Cheryl Guest continued, not ready to leave the subject of my profession. "I wasn't even aware there were detectives in Saskatchewan. Herb, did you know that Mr. Quant is a private detective? I've always assumed the police took care of everything."

"They usually do," I told her. "There aren't too many of us around."

"Now tell me what sort of cases you work on. Is it murder and mayhem? Anything I'd have heard of? What type of people are your clients?"

She seemed genuinely interested and I was about to share some juicy details that were almost true when Daniel interrupted.

"Darling, I'm sure those sorts of details are confidential. And besides, it's about time we found our seats." He began to look around the room as if he'd just heard a dinner gong.

"Is that correct, Mr. Quant?" Mrs. Guest squeezed in one more question.

"Yes," I assured her as I would a client. "I keep a lot of secrets."

"That must be difficult," I heard her say as she was led away, smiling at me and Herb, completely ignoring Sereena.

"Mr. Quant," I heard a new voice say behind my right ear. "How interesting to see you here."

I turned to find Lois Vermont standing there in a suit that looked remarkably like the one I'd seen her in when I last met her at the SBA offices except that this one was dark green. The scarf draped around her neck was the exact same shade of green with a small red berry design along its edge. Her hair hadn't moved an inch but I was surprised to see she'd bothered with a dash of lipstick and a perhaps even a little blush. Instead of making her prettier or more feminine which I imagined was the intent, the makeup simply made her appear fake, doll-like.

"Likewise," I answered with a prim smile identical to her own.

Lois nodded curtly at Sereena, gave me an "I knew it!" look—obviously in reference to her guess about Daniel Guest being my client—and headed off into the milling crowd.

Daniel had started a trend. Most of the people in the room were heading towards tables and selecting dining companions.

"Would the two of you like to join our table?" Herb Dufour had reappeared at my elbow with the gracious invitation.

This was a lucky break. I was here to meet some of the other important players in Daniel's world and Herb Dufour was certainly one of them. As far as I knew, he was the only other person Daniel had admitted his gay experiences to. "We'd love to, thank you," I said.

Herb held out his arm for Sereena, which she expertly made use of, and led us to two seats at one of the tables near the front of the room. As we sat down I noticed Daniel and Cheryl at the next table, Daniel appearing noticeably uncomfortable with the seating arrangements. Did he expect us to eat in the kitchen? I smiled and gave him a little wave.

Also at our table was Herb's date for the evening, an attractive woman named Marilee Yuen. And, in a conspicuous attempt at mixing management with non-management, our other dining companions were an entry-level accountant and her husband and the file room clerk and his girlfriend. Herb introduced me as a potential client of the firm. Since that wasn't how Daniel had introduced me to Herb, it was evident the two men had talked about my disguise for the evening.

Not much happened for a while other than eating chicken, drinking more wine and generally pleasant but unrevealing conversation. Sereena and Marilee had met briefly at some point in their pasts and seemed to enjoy one another's company. I was busy using the file clerk's inside knowledge to learn who all the other people in the room were. Topping the list of people I wanted to meet were Shelley and Murray Rowan, the remaining two partners of the firm who were seated nearby; Nikki, Cary, James and Jill, the four managers who worked most closely with Daniel; Colleen, the receptionist who had dealt with the mysterious woman earlier that day; and Marie, the partners' secretary. I had a lot to do before Daniel and I had to leave for our meeting with Sunny.

It was after the chicken and before dessert, which undoubtedly would be Saskatoon Berry pie, when I was about to head over to the Rowan's table to introduce myself. I felt a heavy hand on my shoulder. It was Herb Dufour, who had left his seat and was standing over me.

"Russell, how about you and I go get another bottle of wine for the table?"

Overhearing him, Marilee and Sereena indicated their support for the idea by clinking together their half-empty glasses. The remaining two men at the table were too busy ignoring the women they'd come with and ogling Marilee and Sereena to care. The other two women simply scowled. I nodded and rose to follow Herb through the maze of chattering diners. At first, when we passed the bar I imagined Herb assumed I needed a pee break and was leading me to the bathroom, but when he walked right by that too and into the ballroom's deserted foyer I knew something was up.

"I'm worried about our friend," the big man said before we'd even come to a complete stop. He was standing uncomfortably close and I backed a step away.

"I'm sorry?" I said, not ready to make assumptions.

"I'm worried about Daniel. He told me why you're here, Russell. I know you're not a potential client. I know you're working for Daniel trying to figure out this blackmail thing."

"I see," was all I said, already aware of that information.

"I have to admit, when he first told me he was considering hiring you, I wasn't sure it was the best idea. But seeing as he has and you're here…well, I just wanted to tell you I'm on Daniel's side and I want to do whatever I can to help him."

I could see why Herb Dufour was a successful senior partner in a CA firm and a city councillor, positions of implied trust. The way the words sounded coming from his mouth and the look on his face made me immediately want to believe everything he said. Wanting to believe and believing aren't the same thing though. I always have to remember that in my business. Even so, I found that my comfort level with Herb was increasing—and I liked his cologne.

"I see. Well I'm sure he appreciates your support."

"Don't you think the best way to deal with this whole thing would be for Daniel to pay this damn blackmailer and shut him up—just to be done with the whole mess?"

"Maybe, maybe not," I uttered, not wanting to say too much in such a public venue. "There's no guarantee paying the money will be the end of it. That's the problem."

"You think he'll come back for more?"

I allowed myself a bit of a head bob. "Maybe, maybe not."

"So we gotta get this bastard. Do you know who he is yet? Have you found him? Do you know where he is?"

"We have some leads," I answered noncommittally.

With that he pulled a white card out of his breast pocket. "If there is anything I can do…you'll call me?"

I nodded and took the business card and, after a brief glance at the titles and letters after his name, stuck it in my breast pocket.

He slapped me on the back again. "I'm going to go get that wine we promised the ladies."

Since I was in the neighbourhood, I decided to make a stop at the washroom. Every time I enter a public loo I'm reminded of a popular e-mail joke that was liberally distributed a few years ago. It was a series of scenarios involving a row of urinals and several men standing at varying positions in the row. Based on where the men were standing, the reader had to decide which urinal he would choose to use (if any). Your choice would supposedly indicate whether you were gay or straight or undecided. Scientific? No. Accurate? Hmmm. Fortunately for me, this evening the bathroom was empty and I was spared the dilemma. I was about done my business when a black-suited gentleman entered and, despite several other options, pulled up to the urinal next to my own. Interesting choice, I thought to myself. I heard him unzip and could smell his heavy musk.

"Hey," I heard him say.

This is not usual decorum. Normally we stare straight ahead as if trying to ignore each other and what we are doing and then walk away.

"Hey," I said back, not looking at him and hoping my tone conveyed a message that I wasn't in the mood for conversation or whatever.

"What the fuck are you doing here?"

Now I looked at him.

Kelvin Kraft.

I zipped up my pants and stepped back. He was a pompous, arrogant jerk the last time I met him and I was guessing nothing had changed. I wondered if James' father was a guest at the DGR&R affair or one of the other parties being held in the hotel that evening. I tilted my head as politely as I could and turned to wash my hands at the sink.

"You didn't answer my question," he said, following me to the sink.

I calmly dried my hands on a paper towel and answered, "I make it a habit to never answer a question that contains the word 'fuck' in it, Mr. Kraft. What are *you* doing here?"

"Well I'm certainly not skulking around washrooms picking up young boys. Is that how you met my son? Huh, is it?"

Some people aren't worth talking to. I walked out. It was either that or serving him a fist sandwich and I didn't want to risk his blood on my wonderpants.

On my return trip to the ballroom I tried to judge the import of my meetings with Herb Dufour and Kelvin Kraft. Where had Kelvin Kraft come from? If he was attending the DGR&R party, then had Daniel unknowingly hooked up with a client's son? If so, had someone—maybe Kelvin himself—found out? If so, what would a man like Kelvin Kraft do?

By the time Herb and I returned to our table our companions had split and the two men were paying an inordinate amount of attention to their own dates. Herb was drawn away by a group of rowdy underlings and I saw Sereena sitting at the next table with Daniel having what appeared to be an intimate discussion. Cheryl Guest was nowhere to be seen. What happened to dessert?

After unsuccessfully trying to spot Kelvin Kraft in the crowd, sitting through a few "thanks for your hard work this year" speeches, the white elephant gift exchange and a silly skit by the lower-downs skewering the higher-ups, it was after 11 and Daniel and I had a date with a man in a parking lot. It took some re-convincing to get him to agree to join me but eventually, bolstered by cheap wine, he made some excuse to Cheryl and slipped out of the ballroom with me and Sereena. Sereena took the RX7 and drove herself home while Daniel and I took his black BMW. We headed to the Confederation area shopping mall which, by freeway, was only minutes from the hotel. If all went according to plan, we'd have Daniel back at the Saskatoon Inn before the first party-goer acted shockingly unaccountant-like.

We pulled into the near-empty parking lot at 11:20. There were three other cars spread throughout the lot but none were occupied. We found a spot to park as far away from a light standard or another car as possible and waited, me in the front seat behind the wheel and Daniel in the back. He was sitting low enough so as not to be easily seen by an approaching vehicle, but high enough to see what was happening. The plan was that when Sunny arrived Daniel would keep watch until he could positively confirm the driver was actually SunLover. Then he was to duck down into the back seat out of sight while I dealt with things. Simple.

We had a few minutes, so I decided to ask Daniel a couple of burning questions. "I met Lois Vermont at your party tonight. Is she a client of the firm?"

Daniel hesitated a second before answering, "Ah, no. We invited her as a kind of thank you for the whole SBA award thing. Just smart business."

"What about Kelvin Kraft?"

Another hesitation. "Kraft? Kelvin Kraft? Any relation to James?"

"His father."

"His father? You saw James Kraft's father at the DGR&R Christmas party?"

"No, actually I saw him in the men's room and thought maybe…"

"Huh. Well, he must have been attending one of the other events in the hotel, don't you think?"

"Yeah," I said lightly. "I'm sure that's it. We better keep it down for now. Sunny should be here any minute now."

And a moment later a blue car drove into the lot. Blue! This could be it! Daniel said the person who'd followed him twice drove a blue car. But he also thought that person could have been a woman. I tried to decide whether one of the headlights was brighter than the other, like the blue car that had tailed me, but I couldn't be sure.

"Can you see the car?" I whispered to Daniel, hunkered down in the back seat. "Is it the same blue car that followed you?"

I heard him grumble and groan as he tried to find a good position from which to see the car without himself being seen. "I…I'm not sure. It could be. Damn. Yeah, it could be. This could be him!"

The vehicle, which I could now see was an Audi, made a beeline for our Beemer as if it had a sign on it saying, "A homosexual man who wants to have sex is in this car." He parked about two car lengths away. I couldn't see the driver clearly and assumed he couldn't see me. I felt my heart beating faster. I was trying to keep my head focused on the task but it was difficult separating fact from fantasy. What was most surprising to me was that at that moment, a moment of high pitched tension, sexual proximity and a little bit of fear, I could completely understand the attraction of this activity, an activity many people, gay and straight, believe to be illicit and dangerous. But perhaps that is exactly what makes it so attractive. The hint of danger. The rush of adrenaline. The promise of pleasure. An act so contrary to the safe, routine, unremarkable lives most of us live. It's about being every outrageous, sexually free, out-there character we've ever read about or seen in a movie, even if only for a few minutes when no one—or almost no one—is watching. It's about being bad…and then being rewarded for it with sex.

For a moment that seemed to span eons, our two vehicles sat there, in a dark, snow-swept parking lot, regarding each other like two lions in a jungle meeting for the first time. Friend or foe? We kept our motors idling, partially to keep warm, partially in case a quick get-away was required. Someone had to make the first move. But who? It couldn't be me. If I got into Sunny's car I'd be without my key witness and unable to determine if Sunny was also SunLover. Another moment passed. I knew it would take a brave man to make the first move. You'd have to hope luck was on your side and that a whole host of possible scenarios didn't play out to rain on your parade. The guy in the other car could be your brother or a co-worker, he could be a weirdo or a gay basher, he might be a police officer or, worst of all, he might be…ugly.

Although I was pretty certain the other driver couldn't see me, I tried a smile and hoped I looked friendly, inviting, non-threatening.

We waited. I could hear Daniel's breathing getting heavier. My God, I thought, suppose he did that while Sunny was in the car? How would I ever be able to conceal his presence if he was making like Darth Vader back there?

"What's he doing now?" this from Daniel.

"He's just sitting in his car," I said, trying not to move my lips. "He's not getting out!"

"Maybe you should go over there."

"But I need you to identify him," I shot back, beginning to feel uneasy.

"It's gotta be him, Russell! It's a blue car. And I told you what SunLover looks like. You'll know when you see him. We can't sit here all night!"

Another forty-five seconds.

"Oh shit!" I said as the blue Audi moved away.

Chapter 10

"OHHH GAWWWDDD!" Adrenaline was coursing through me. I had to make a move with no time to think about what it should be. "He's leaving! I gotta go! I gotta go!" I whispered frantically at Daniel. "You stay here and keep your head down."

I threw open my door and stumbled out of the car as fast as I could, hoping to catch the attention of the slowly departing Audi.

It worked. The blue car came to a halt, only yards from where he'd first been parked. I gave the car's occupant a jaunty wave as I struggled to pull my coat zipper up to my neck and adjust my scarf. I swallowed a few times and took the first halting steps towards the vehicle. I kept my face expressionless. It wasn't a planned thing; I just had no idea how I should look. Should I smile flirtatiously? Should I look serious? Worried? Anxious? Who knew? I just plodded along until I came to the driver's side of the car. I heard the reassuring whir of an electric motor lowering a window. At least he didn't consider me unappealing and speed away (I take compliments wherever I can).

"Hi," I said.

"Hi," the man replied. "How are you tonight?"

Aha. A French accent, the nice soft roll of a Canadian francophone. But this wouldn't help me I realized, as Daniel said they'd never exchanged a word.

"You want to sit in for a while?" he asked.

I did a quick assessment of what I could see. Very blond, but not out of a bottle. Darkly tanned, maybe out of a bottle. Green eyes. Nice looking. Consistent with Daniel's description.

"Sure," I agreed. I rounded the car as he raised his window. The trip was shorter than I'd hoped and I considered bolting. Instead I filled my lungs with cool, clean air and kept moving. I settled myself into the passenger seat and took a good look at my quarry while he did the same. He was wearing a tri-coloured, waist-length ski jacket on top of a dark green cotton shirt unbuttoned at the neck and a pair of worn jeans, extremely tight in the style of the eighties—but trendy or not, they did him justice.

"Wow," he said. "You're cute."

With some effort, I smiled. "Thanks. You too." I wasn't lying. He was a cute man. Well, not really cute, but attractive in that rough-and-tumble, surfer-boy-just-beyond-his-prime type of way. He had big, weathered hands, solid thighs and a strong jaw just beginning to loosen with age. His body was quarter-turned in my direction with one hand resting on the steering wheel, the other on his lap, near his crotch, which was barely contained by straining denim.

"My name is Shaun," I said. As in Cassidy, brother of David, I said to myself.

He just smiled and nodded. No dummy, this guy. He wasn't giving up his name that easily.

"You do this a lot?" I asked.

He blushed. Aww shucks!

"No, I try not to," he told me. "But, sometimes I just have to. You?"

"It's my first time." Truth.

His eyes crinkled at the corners when he smiled. His teeth were a little uneven, the right incisor overlapped its neighbour, but it was a nice enough smile. "You're joking, eh?"

"No, really," I said, returning the smile and beginning what I hoped was a subtle search of the interior of the car for any clues as to this man's identity. I knew I had the license plate number, but I didn't even want to begin to imagine how much I'd have to beg Darren to run the plate for me.

"Are you a straight then?" he asked. He moved his hand from his thigh and placed it on the headrest of my seat, turning a little more in his seat, giving me an even better view of everything.

"No, I don't think so." I was finding it easy to look around the car without being caught. Sunny was too busy studying my chest and crotch to pay attention. And I suppose he assumed I was doing the same. I took a chance and glanced into the back seat. Bingo! A newspaper. From my first quick look I saw it was the *Western Producer*, a popular rural publication.

"So where do you go, if you don't do this?" he asked, his hand sliding over to my shoulder. I could feel his fingers against the bare skin of my neck above my scarf.

"Oh, you know," I answered, realizing that the content of our conversation wasn't really important at this point in the game.

"Oh yeah," he said, his breathing getting a little heavier. He had now taken his other hand off the steering wheel and placed it right over the mound of his jeans, pressing down lightly on it. "What do you like to do?"

I could see a subscriber mailing label at one corner of the magazine. But I needed to get closer to read it. It was dark in the car and the writing was small. But how could I possibly do that without raising suspicion?

"This and that," I answered vaguely. "You?"

"We should go somewhere," he said, his voice showing signs of exertion, even though he was barely moving. His hand moved down from my neck, over the front of my jacket and into my lap.

I had an idea. The things I must do for my craft. I rotated my body towards his and moved closer until I was almost on top of him. His body responded in like fashion and before I knew it, we were lip-locked. I could feel his tongue dart into my mouth and his hands on my ass. After a frantic moment of deep kissing, I manipulated my right hand so I could unzip my jacket and buried his face into my neck, at the same time, sort of kneeling over him, I brought my groin in contact with his. Despite the cramped quarters, it was not a wholly uncomfortable position and the best thing about it was that it left my head free above his allowing me to get a closer look into the back seat and at the newspaper. I kept on thrusting my body into his, not only to keep his interest up, but also to get myself closer to the mailing label. Honestly.

Luc Bussiere, Box 39, Aberdeen, Saskatchewan, S0K 0A0. Also known as Sunny...and SunLover?

I had what I came for. But now what?

I didn't have long to debate the answer for at that moment Luc Bussiere and I recoiled in terror as the driver's side door was ripped open with such force I thought it was being pulled off its hinges. A screaming dark figure reached in after us.

Our amorous intentions evaporating faster than a snowball in hell, I sort of tumbled off Luc while he tried to fight off the dark figure's flailing hands.

Had the owners of one of the empty vehicles in the lot come back? Was it the cops? God, suppose it was Kirsch! Or...a gay bashing? Was I about to experience a gay bashing? Had someone seen me approach the car of another man, watched me get in and get jiggy and not liked it?

"You son of a bitch! Why are you doing this?" the attacker screamed, reaching for me across Luc.

Shit. It was Daniel. He had cracked.

"Why, why, why are you doing this?"

"Daniel! Stop it for Pete's sake!" I screamed at him.

Luc somehow managed to avoid Daniel's hands long enough to shift the car, which he'd kept running throughout our "date," into "D" and step on the gas pedal. The car shot ahead with a jerk, throwing Daniel away from the vehicle with enough force to push him to the ground. As the car proceeded forward, Luc reached out and pulled the door closed with his left hand while at the same time trying to steer with his right. He waited until we'd crossed the expanse of the parking lot, leaving plenty of space between Daniel and ourselves, before bringing the car to a halt. He checked the rear-view mirror. I turned to look too. Daniel wasn't coming after us. I could see he had gotten up from where he'd fallen to the ground, but he wasn't moving much, just staring after us.

"Was that your boyfriend?" Luc asked, a little out of breath, his French accent thicker.

My eyelids blinked furiously as I uselessly searched for something to say to make sense out of what had just happened. What had just happened?

"Out!" he said, looking and sounding disgusted with me.

How did I get to be the bad guy in all this? I opened the door and stepped out of the car. My feet had barely touched the ground before he sped away. I stood there feeling miserable. And cold. Both had set me to trembling. I heard the sound of tires on pavement. Daniel had pulled up in the BMW. He reached across the seat and threw open the passenger side door. I got in.

"It's not him," Daniel murmured. "That man is not SunLover."

As Daniel drove me home he explained how he'd gotten a better look at Luc after I'd gotten into the Audi and knew he wasn't our man. So, to keep me from making a big mistake, he decided to play the jealous boyfriend bit. I wasn't sure if I agreed with his tactic, but, well, it was over. And time to send Daniel back to his Christmas party.

Both dogs greeted me with head butts against my thigh, looking surprised to see me entering by the front door rather than the back where I normally come in. The house was dark and a little cool. The forecast had called for temperatures in the minus twenties with wind chill clocking in at minus thirty-five. Ahhhh, a balmy weekend. I deposited my coat and boots and tiptoed into the hallway that led to the guest bedroom. All seemed quiet. Should I check on my mother? I decided not to. There was no need to develop the habit just because of one little disappearing act that morning. Instead I headed for the kitchen, turning up the thermostat on the way. I opened the fridge. Still unrecognizable. The room smelled of warm milk and icing sugar. Christmas baking or a late night treat? Treat, I decided. I made my way to the bar in the living room, poured myself the dregs from an opened bottle of Burrowing Owl Syrah 2000, a nice red from British Columbia and retreated to my den.

The dogs came with me and immediately settled down in front of the gas fireplace, looking up at me as if to say, "We're ready, make fire." So I did. With the flick of a switch a cheery blaze sprang to life in the rustic maw. I set my wine down on my desk and went to the stereo to select something melodic and Italian and operatic. That done, volume set at low, I retrieved my wine and took a spot in front of the fire on the leather couch I'd selected because the colour reminded me of soft toffee. I considered another search for SunLover on the internet but my current position with fire, wine and dogs was so pleasant I didn't feel like moving. I laid my head back, closed my eyes and gratefully surrendered to the music as it massaged my eardrums and temples.

Some moments later, I'm not sure how many, I heard Barbra let out a low, discerning "woof." I picked up my head and opened my eyes. She and Brutus hadn't moved from their spot but they were both staring at the closed door. I listened and heard it too. A soft knock. I rose up and padded to the door. Behind it was my mother. She was wearing a high-necked sleeping gown beneath a bright blue house-coat tied tightly at the waist. Her head was wrapped in a scarf under which I could see she'd set her hair into tight pin curls held in place with bobby pins. On her feet were bright pink slippers. I asked her to come in even though she clashed with the decor more than a polyester leisure suit on a fashion runway. She seemed to sense the interruption and stood stock still in the doorway, the garish light from the hallway behind her seeping into the pleasantly dim room like a lighthouse beacon. Her hands were clasping a mug of warm milk so tightly her knuckles were white and I realized that my mother was nervous.

"Come on in," I said, stepping behind her to close the door against the harsh hallway light. That helped a lot. Her housecoat wasn't nearly as blue and I didn't even notice the slippers anymore. "I was just relaxing in front of the fire with Barbra and Brutus. It's late. You couldn't sleep?"

"Ya, uh-huh," she said.

"You want to come sit with us for a while?"

"Eet's getting colder outside," she said by way of an answer. "I hope no one ees stuck outside in dis kind of cold. You cood die. You vant milk? I make for you."

"No, no. Thanks. I have some wine." I shrugged off the inexplicable feeling of guilt at admitting to my mother that I drank alcohol and realized she wasn't going to move unless I did. So I walked back to the couch and lowered myself into the same spot I'd left behind, hoping she was following me. She was. When she took a seat at the other end of the couch, the dogs, in unison, once again lowered their heads onto their paws and practised closing their eyes. For a moment the four of us—this temporary, makeshift family of sorts—sat quiet except for the music which was slowly doing its job, relaxing my nerves and filling the uncomfortable emptiness between my mother and me. As we sat there, watching the fire, I recalled that my mother's home—once my own—did not have a fireplace. Maybe she'd never sat in front of one before now, letting the dance of flames entertain and warm her. Maybe it bored her.

"Are you hungry?" she asked, not surprisingly.

I shook my head and smiled at her. "No. Sereena and I ate at the party."

"Ya, the neighbour voman, uh-huh? Nice lady?"

I knew she meant to test the waters to see if, despite what she knew about me, she should start taking Sereena's measurements for white silk. "She's a good friend," I told her, sending a definite message.

"You vere vorking? Eets late to vork."

"Ya…Yes, I had to go to a client's Christmas party."

"Vhat kind client?"

This was something new. Asking about my work. Was this my mother trying to get to know me? I gulped my wine. "Well, you know I'm not a cop anymore, right?"

"Oh ya, dat's…when did you do dat?"

"Couple years ago. Now I'm a private detective. People hire me to find stuff out for them. You know, like the TV shows you watch. My current client hired me to find someone who is blackmailing him."

"Oi, dat's dangerous, Sonsyou. Mebbe you do someting else?"

Still more wine. "That's what I do. I like it. I like it better than being a police officer."

"But dangerous, Sonsyou."

"Sometimes, I guess, but not always. Being a policeman is dangerous too sometimes."

Another silence. A sip of wine. A sip of warm milk.

"I'm glad you decided to spend Christmas with me this year," I started. Stopped. Took a deep breath. Decided to jump in. "But I'm surprised you're not spending it with Joanne or with Bill. You seem…more comfortable with them. You and I…well, we don't really know each other too well."

"Not true!" she said quickly, rolling the r with a shocked trill, surprised to think one of her children thought such a thing.

It came spilling out. "Well, I just worry, Mom, that I don't know what you like to do and don't like to do and I worry you'll be bored here. I work a lot…this case came up by surprise…I didn't think I'd be away from home so much…so I worry about you here alone when I'm not home." Then I just couldn't shut up. "I know you're uncomfortable with my being gay, just like you were with Uncle Lawrence. In all the years since I left the farm, this is the first time you've ever stayed in my home. You've always visited with Bill and Joanne, but never with me. Don't get me wrong, Mom, I'm not upset about that." Right? "I think I understand, but it makes me wonder why you would choose to come here now. If you think you can change me or change my life or change who my friends are…well, that won't happen. I have a life I love and I'm not looking to change it." Where did this come from?

I'd said more than I'd meant to, but it just came out. The words needed saying. I obviously had more on my mind than I'd realized. My mother's presence had turned my life and my home topsy-turvy. And, if I was being totally honest with myself, it wasn't just her. It was Kelly's odd behaviour and having Brutus around and working a case I couldn't get a handle on and a million other things that suddenly seemed alien to me. I looked deep into my mother's face and hoped I hadn't hurt her feelings. What I saw surprised me. She wasn't hurt, but she quite obviously didn't understand where I was coming from any more than I understood where she was coming from.

"I don't vant to change anyting," she answered quietly. "But mebbe you're right about dat one ting."

"About what?"

"About your uncle."

I had to remind myself to breathe. I had never heard my mother talk about her strained relationship with her brother, Lawrence. I only knew the strain had existed and imagined I knew why. It was because he was gay; it was because he was gay and had a lover; it was because he was gay and had a lover and didn't hide the fact. At the end they rarely spoke to one another. And now he was dead.

"I love my brodder," she told me. "But ve deedn't know vhy he deed dose tings he deed. Ve deedn't like dose tings." "Ve" meaning she and my father, "don't like" meaning don't understand. "Ve deedn't talk, ve deedn't see each odder…for long times ve deedn't see each odder. And den…he's gone." There were tears in her eyes now as she remembered a brother who had this bigger-than-life life, so far removed from anything she knew or understood or ever wanted for herself. It eventually wedged them apart. Forever. Because, for Uncle Lawrence, forever wasn't a very long time. "I geeve anyting to see heem now. To talk vit heem. Ay, Maria, but he's gone, Sonsyou."

What could I say? I didn't know what it all meant. Was I her second chance? Did she come to realize that what happened with her brother was slowly happening with me, her son? The same wedge, the same distance, the same misunderstandings? Was it too late for us too? Or not? Here she was, my mother making the grand gesture, accepting my invitation when really she would have been more comfortable, more welcomed, more familiar in one of my sibling's homes. Accepting my invitation…my fake, insincere invitation. If the truth be told, the wedge between us wasn't all her doing—it was mine too. I allowed it and maybe I even pounded it in a little further each year, by accepting and expecting my mother's non-involvement in my life.

"I'm glad you're here," I told her again, this time meaning it much more.

The next thing I heard was my mother's scream and a flurry of Ukrainian epithets. Barbra and Brutus jumped up and began to bark. All bad signs. Barbra and Brutus rarely barked and, as far as I knew, my mother rarely used the words she just had. As I jerked to attention my wineglass, thankfully empty, flew to the ground, landing harmlessly on the rug.

"What?" I called out, "What is it?"

My mother had risen from her seat and was now standing behind the couch clutching at the neck of her housecoat. "Outside, oi bojeh, outside, I saw a face!"

She pointed at the window next to the fireplace, the same one where the dogs were directing their vocal talents. Brutus had rushed up to the pane and was leaving froth on the glass as he mixed deep woofs with ferocious sounding growls. Barbra did the same at another window on the other side of the fireplace.

Someone was in the backyard.

I knew looking out the window would be useless. I raced from the room, jumped into the shoes and coat I'd taken off when I'd come home and made my way through the kitchen and out the back door in what seemed like seconds. I was fast enough to see a figure disappearing behind a clump of skeletal mock orange bushes. There was only one place he could be heading. At the back of the yard was a gate I used to access the garbage dumpsters in the back alley. Other than through the garage it was the only way out. I ran for it ignoring the bitter cold and enveloping darkness. When I arrived, the gate was hanging open. I dashed through it and, because I lived at the end of a dead end street, I knew the peeping Tom could have only turned left, so I followed in hot pursuit.

The back alley was even darker than my yard but as I galloped along I thought I could see a black-coated figure running far ahead of me. I wished I could stop, just for a moment, to listen for footsteps or heavy breathing, but I couldn't waste the time. Instead, the sound of my own footsteps in the crunchy snow and my own laboured breathing filled my ears. I kept going. Looking ahead I saw the figure as he reached the end of the alley and almost stumbled into a pool of light compliments of a nearby street lamp. Other than a dark colour coat, it was impossible to tell anything more about the runner. He made another left and I raced forward not sure whether or not I was gaining or falling behind. When I too came to the end of the alley I could see him easily, fleeing down the street. Was he heading towards a car? Did he have friends? Was this just a kid playing a prank or someone truly dangerous? Was he armed? There was no time to think about the answers to my many questions. He ran. I ran. It was easier going on the street with the shovelled sidewalks and light posts, but I knew the pursuit would have to change somehow. We seemed to be evenly matched for speed and kept an unchanging distance between us. Would it come down to who was in better cardiovascular shape?

Nope. The figure must have been thinking the same thing and turned right at the next cross street. I did the same and saw him duck into a thickly treed yard. Damn! I reached the yard and stopped. Did he just run right through or was he waiting for me in ambush? Well, I'd come this far, I thought to myself, I might as well keep going.

Bad mistake.

I had plastered my back against the house preparing to slide along its side into the backyard when it hit me. Some kind of spray. Was I being maced? Or was it...hairspray? It smelled suspiciously like Herbal Essences.

I fell to the ground like a sack of potatoes, covered my eyes with my hands and wailed. I didn't rub, I knew that would only make it worse. I turned on my tummy and blindly reached out for some snow, bringing it to my eyes to wash away the offending substance. As I did this I could hear the footfalls of my pursuee leaving the scene, escaping through a squeaky backyard gate. This time I was in no condition to follow.

Having rolled myself into a protective ball against one corner of the house, it took me a few minutes to feel comfortable enough to attempt opening my eyes. First the right one. It stung ever so slightly. The snow had helped. Then the left. Again, the sensation wasn't pleasant but at least I could see. Using the house for balance, I stood up slowly on nearly steady legs, straightening myself out and trying to get my bearings. I trudged back to the street and looked around. My eyes were tearing but I could see well enough to determine I was about two or three blocks from home. I pulled the collar of my coat as far above my icy ears as it would reach, buried my hands in my pockets and began the chilly trek home, my mind busily composing a story to tell my mother about kids playing pranks. After what she and I had just talked about, I didn't want her feeling afraid to be in my home. But...should she?

Saturday morning arrived with a thudding headache, a sore throat and itchy eyes, all results of my Friday night escapade. As I lay in bed I could hear the sounds and smell the aromas of cooking and baking even though the kitchen was at the other end of the house. There was no sign of either dog; they knew which side their biscuit was buttered on. I remained in my room longer than I normally would, mostly because I wanted to wait until the pink irritation and slight swelling around my eyes disappeared. I didn't want to worry my mother. A cold compress did wonders. While I waited I tried reaching Darren Kirsch at his office. I didn't really know how he could help me with my peeping Tom problem. All I knew was that I definitely needed to talk about this with someone. Alas, he was not there, likely spending weekend time with his wife and brood. Next I called Kelly and Errall's number, hoping I'd finally catch Kelly at home. No answer—again. Well, to heck with that.

We used my mother's van because there was no way the Mazda would have had room for the crew I was hauling. Errall and Kelly live in a two-storey house on Pembina Avenue. It's built on a hillside with a partial view of downtown and a rolling, woodsy backyard. We pulled up just before 11 a.m: me, my mother (who knows Kelly from when she and I went to Howell High together), Brutus and Barbra. When I explained to Mom about Kelly's illness she, after a brief weep, had hopped into action. We made our way up the driveway towards the front door with my mom schlepping along grocery bags brimming with medicine—plastic Becel Margarine containers filled with stews, creamed potatoes, cabbage rolls and breaded cutlets suspended in congealing gravy. As we rang the doorbell it dawned on me that what I hadn't thought to fully explain to my mother was Errall. Had she made the leap from the existence of gay men, her brother and son, to gay women?

The door was answered by a version of Errall I rarely get to see. She looks like a different person out of her hard-edged lawyer drag. Her dark hair was pulled into two messy pigtails and a plain white T-shirt was barely tucked into a pair of threadbare, faded jeans. If asked, she'd insist she feels more comfortable in her power suits, but this more casual look softened the sharp edges of her face and intensity of her blazingly blue eyes. Her pale face looked out at us with surprise, but she stepped aside and with a thin, bony hand clasping a steaming mug of coffee, she motioned us to come in.

"Mom, this is Errall, Errall, Mom," I said brightly once we were all indoors and staring at each other in the small entranceway.

My mother looked at me with a look that said, "I vasn't expecting dis, vere you expecting dis? Who ees dis girl?" Instead she said, "Very nice, hello, Carol. Very nice."

Errall gave me a look that said, "Are you outta your fuckin' mind?" But she said, "Hello, Mrs. Quant. So nice to meet you. Won't you come in?"

Errall led us to the kitchen, where most of the activity in Errall and Kelly's home usually takes place. It's a big, bright room with big, bright windows that look out onto the backyard and lots of chairs and stools to sit on.

"Can I take your coats?" Errall asked politely.

Again another, "Who dis?" look from my mother.

We gave up our coats and, while Errall left to put them away somewhere, we stood expectantly in the kitchen, my mother using her X-ray vision to see inside cupboards and under the sink.

Errall returned and served us coffee. When it came time to hand my mother her cup, she looked down at the bags my mother still held tight.

"I bring for Kelly," Mother explained.

Errall gave us her first sincere smile of the visit. "Oh, how thoughtful, thank you. What is it?"

Mom handed her the bags, which Errall almost dropped due to the unexpected weight they carried.

"Is Kelly home?" I asked. Hoped.

Errall shot me a look.

"I've been trying to call her for days. She never answers, so I thought we'd just drop by. Mom hasn't seen Kelly in years, probably since high school, and I know Kelly would like to see Brutus."

"Of course," Errall said, setting the bags on the kitchen island. "I'll go see if she's up yet." She looked at my mother and explained, "She hasn't been feeling well lately."

My mother smiled and nodded. "Dat's okay, den. Ve come back, tomorrow mebbe?"

"Oh, no, no, no," Errall said. "Let me just go see." And with that Errall disappeared and in a second we heard her clomping up the stairs.

I looked around, feeling a bit uncomfortable. I don't like showing up uninvited to anyone's house, but this was a special situation. Kelly needed to get out of her funk. Perhaps seeing her dog and having some of my mother's cabbage rolls would help. Barbra and Brutus were standing at the back door, longingly staring out at the yard. I let them out. Mom and I sipped coffee and waited.

When Kelly appeared, Errall at her back, I was unexpectedly taken aback with emotion. I hadn't seen her in such a long time and, knowing what I knew, I suddenly felt raw inside. Looking at the two women I sensed a distance between Errall and Kelly, not just a physical one, but an emotional one that was just as easy to see.

Kelly and my mother hugged and my mother immediately pulled her over to the island and painstakingly went through the contents, one by one, of each grocery bag, explaining how each was made and why it was good for her. As they did this I watched Kelly and I watched Errall watching Kelly. Kelly seemed thin, much of her stocky, muscular build replaced by an undeniable frailness. Her normally cutesy face, with the wide eyes and mouth, was drawn and wan and her hair was longer than I ever remember seeing it, the red a faded version of its former self. Errall was observing the interaction between the two other women closely, a thin, brittle smile on her lips.

"You seet down," my mother ordered Kelly after the bag inventory was done. "You seet and I show your friend Carol how to keep dese foods and how to feex dem goot, so dey be smahchneh." She almost pushed Kelly towards me while motioning for Errall to join her at the island saying, "Dees a goot stove?"

Errall looked horrified as she realized what was happening and how helpless she was to stop it. I felt sorry for her, but not that sorry and used the opportunity to steer Kelly out of the kitchen and into a nearby sitting room where we might have some privacy.

We sat in two armchairs at right angles to each other. Kelly and I didn't practise bullshit with one another so I just came out with it. "Kells bells, you don't look so hot."

"I know," she said, twisting a finger in her hair, a habit I didn't remember her having. "I haven't been to get this mop cut for such a long time and I'm not playing soccer this winter so I'm so outta shape."

"You should get out more. You and Errall are coming to the tree trimming party at my place tomorrow night, right, but how about just you and me go out for a beer next week?"

"No beers for me," she said.

"What are you talking about, no beers? You give it up? The breweries will go bankrupt!" I tried for levity.

"I've got to clean up my act, Russell."

I didn't get it. "What do you mean? The doctor say that?"

"I have cancer, Russell. I've got to watch how I treat my body." The tone in her voice was unfamiliar to me.

"You *had* cancer, Kelly. It's gone now."

She turned to face me again. I'd be happy to not remember the look in her eyes. "We don't know that for sure."

We were quiet for a moment and then she said, "You know, some doctors suggest cutting them both off. Just in case. I didn't let them. I just couldn't. The other breast is okay right now, but once you've had cancer in one the chances of..."

"Okay, stop," I told her. "You made a decision. You made the right decision for you. And in all the years I've known you, I'd say you make pretty good ones. So we're done. This is over. Each day you're going to get better and better and soon everything will be just the way it was before." I knew I'd said the wrong thing as soon as it came out of my mouth.

"Things will never be the way they were before. I have only one breast left. I've had a disease in my body that wanted to kill me. I...I'll never be the same. Ever again. You don't understand! You're just like Errall...and everyone else...you don't understand what it's like."

I nodded mutely.

"Sometimes...and I don't say this to Errall..." she said, her voice calmer, "but sometimes, Russell, I think...I may not survive this. I think I'll look back at this as the beginning of the end. I think I might die, Russell. No matter what the doctors say and how much skin and tissue they cut out of me, I think I might die."

What can you say to that? I felt helpless. I felt inadequate. I had absolutely no frame of reference to use to even have a clue as to how she was feeling. I'd never had cancer. I'd never had a part of me cut off. I'd never lived with the fear that death was hunting me. I wanted to let her know she wasn't alone and there were a lot of us who believed in her survival. But what can you say?

"I love you" is what came out.

She mouthed the words, "I know."

"Ve go now," said a voice behind us.

We turned to see my mother standing there. I could hear Errall still in the kitchen, banging around putting away the pots and pans my

140

mother had insisted on inspecting, and uttering a few choice words barely beneath her breath.

"Yes," I said, "we should go. We burst in on you without an invitation."

We collected our coats and as we said our goodbyes my mother told Kelly, "Your goot friend knows how to varm up all de food, so you eat. Vhen you vant some…" and then she raised her voice for Errall's benefit, "…just call her and she come over and cook eet for you, ya, Carol?"

"Mom, Errall lives here. With Kelly."

She just smiled and said, "Oh, ya, uh-huh, goot den. Very nice."

Chapter 11

BACK AT HOME my mother prepared us a lunch of roast beef, head-cheese and pickled beets. After that, even though my eyes, throat and head felt fine, my stomach was feeling a bit odd and my inner loner was acting up. After the tussle with Luc Bussiere, being sprayed in the eyes by an unknown peeping Tom and my discussions with Kelly and my mother, I was feeling a bit unsettled. I needed some time alone—and home wasn't the place for that. So, even though it was Saturday, I decided to go to my office.

PWC is closed on weekends unless one of us decides to work or see a client, so I had to use my keys to unlock the front door. Except for subdued sunlight the foyer was unlit, and the front desk was deserted. Perfect. For a moment as I stood there, admiring the festive Christmas decorations no doubt thanks to Lilly, I felt something suspiciously like Christmas spirit invade my body. I even debated turning around and heading for the nearest mall to do some shopping.

Nah.

For the next few hours I hung around my office, drinking coffee, looking for SunLover on gays.r.us, taking a half-hour snooze and catching up on miscellaneous paperwork. I made some phone calls, mostly leaving messages on answering machines, reminding Daniel about our visit to Diva's, the gay nightclub, that evening and everyone else about the tree trimming party at my house on Sunday night. I could have done most of this at home if I'd wanted to, but with my mother, two dogs and all those boiling and blurping pots and pans, my house seemed a little crowded. Eventually I did leave PWC for the gym and a much-needed blob-buster workout.

On the way home I took my time on Spadina, taking in the beauteous view of the park. Next to the stately Delta Bessborough Hotel, an outdoor skating rink had been carved out amidst a circle of ash and spruce in an area that in summer was a grassy plot. Where there'd been lawn was now a sheet of ice covered with a sugary dusting of snow. The trees were painted with hoarfrost, transforming them from brown stick men into delicate-looking crystalline figures. The hotdog stand had become a skater's shack and former sunbathers were now bundled up tight in toasty fleece jackets, colourful scarves and thick mittens. Skaters seemed afloat on sparkling blades, doing their figure eights, the temperature so low that twirling wisps of cloud streamed from their mouths. Although darkness had fallen on this winter city, frosted spotlights encircling the skating ring created a dome of light about the idyll. I could faintly make out the melody of holiday tunes coming from dangling speakers high above on boughs of trees, setting the scene to music. It was a real, live Christmas snow globe.

I was feeling good. I'd had a nap, a workout and some me time, and tonight I was taking a positive step in my case. Things were good.

And then I got home.

My mother was gone. Again.

After a search similar to the one I undertook the previous morning, I found myself yet again on the phone calling my neighbour.

"Sereena," I began hesitantly, almost embarrassed to admit I'd misplaced my mother yet again. "Ah...er...my mother?"

"Are you kidding me with this?" she asked, sounding a little out of breath, as if I'd gotten her away from something...strenuous?

"No, Sereena, really, she's gone again."

"Where was she the last time?"

"She said she was on a walk, but I don't believe her. Something is going on, she's not telling me something." And then the guilt came pouring out of me. "I told her I was worried about her being alone while I was away and what do I do? I go off and leave her alone all afternoon! Cripes, I can be a dolt."

"I'm afraid I'll have to agree with you on that this time," she said almost nastily. "There's a frickin' light on in the room above the garage. What kind of poor-ass detective are you anyway?"

"What?" seemed to be all I could say.

"Look out your back window. She's been up there for a couple of hours."

Sereena, although she'd never admit it, had been watching out for my mother.

I craned my neck to do as I was told. Indeed, the windows above my garage were alight. I bid my neighbour a sheepish goodbye and hung up.

Halfway to the garage, Barbra and Brutus gamely cantering behind me, I was rudely reminded I had neglected to put on a coat by the hands of a winter wind. Reaching the door we gratefully piled into the building, away from the elements, where well-insulated walls kept out the worst of the cold. The garage consists of two generously sized bays: one is for the Mazda and the other had recently been cleared of boxes and gardening paraphernalia to make room for my mother's van. In one corner is a narrow set of steps leading up to the second floor. When I'd bought the house I was told the second floor, originally built to be a nanny suite, could bring in extra cash as a rentable apartment. It was considered a selling feature—one I knew I'd never take advantage of. Having a stranger living above my garage was not my idea of enticing. I was more in the market for privacy than revenue. After buying the property, I barely took a second look at the attic-like space other than to toss in cartons of stuff I didn't have use for but didn't want to throw away.

So what on earth was my mother doing up there? I had the sneaky suspicion cleaning supplies were involved.

One by one the dogs and I made our way up the staircase. At the top I opened the door and peered in. Barbra and Brutus were more intrusive, nosing the door wider and pushing their way into the room.

I followed. At first all I could see were cartons and old furniture and dust motes set afloat by the passage of the dogs. It smelled old and musty. We rounded a collection of boxes piled to the ceiling and found a small clearing bathed in light and warmth. The light was coming from a single bare bulb dangling from the roughed-in ceiling. The warmth was coming from electric floorboard heaters. In the middle of the clearing was my mother. She had uncovered an ancient recliner chair, positioned it directly in front of the heater, crawled under a raggedy afghan and promptly fell asleep in her makeshift nest.

The dogs wandered off to snort about in some dark corner. I approached my mother's sleeping body. I knew she was sleeping because of the gentle buzzing through her nostrils. I reached out to touch her shoulder but stopped short. I don't know when I had last been so close to her face, to really look at it. Her glasses had fallen partway down her nose and slightly off to one side. Her skin looked surprisingly soft for such a tough old bird and had barely a wrinkle except for a few at the corner of her eyes and above her upper lip. My mother wore little if any makeup, and that was only when she was going out in public or entertaining guests, but I could see that her lips and cheeks, infused with the innocence of sleep, were as naturally rosy as crabapples. Her hair, although greying, was actually a dark brown rather than black as I'd always thought. My gaze moved down to her hands, one was perched on her chest, the other on her lap. They were the hands of a working woman, short nails, slightly oversized knuckles and skin toughened from lifting heavy things like bales and rocks, digging vegetables and weeds out of gardens and too much sun.

What had brought her here? What had she expected to find?

I studied her face again, trying to find mine in hers. I couldn't. I touched her shoulder and called her. My mother's eyes opened wide and for a moment she looked startled.

"It's okay, Mom, it's just me."

She threw her body up and forward urging the recliner into a sitting up position and hopped off the chair. Her hands busied themselves straightening her clothes and hair.

"It's okay, Mom, you just fell asleep," I said, feeling a little discombobulated myself. "I was worried about you. I didn't know where you'd gone."

"I came up here, dat's all, just up here, not far," she said quickly, not used to being caught doing something out of the ordinary. "You must be hungry." She glanced at her wristwatch, a thin gold one my father had given her decades ago. "Oi! Look at da time, oh dear goodness, you must be hungry."

"No, I'm okay," I said. "I was just worried. Luckily Sereena saw the lights on up here." And then I couldn't help a little admonishment. "You didn't leave a note like we discussed yesterday."

"I vas just up here," my mother repeated.

"But why?"

The dogs picked then to reappear and both approached my mother for a greeting. She seemed grateful for the interruption.

"You vere steell gone so I not vant to start da supper until you vere back," she finally answered, fussing with the collar around Barbra's neck. "And I vonder about dis room."

I was at a loss. I had no idea what my mother was talking about or if perhaps she needed medical attention of some sort. Why on earth would she be wondering about this room?

"It's just a storage room," I told her to keep up my side of the odd conversation. "We should go in now." I was feeling weird about the whole situation. And, God help me, I *was* hungry.

My mother nodded. We turned off the heaters, extinguished the light and wordlessly paraded down the stairs, through the garage, along the backyard path and into the house. After we regrouped in the kitchen, the dogs loitered aimlessly about, thinking there might be more activity forthcoming or at least a bit of sup.

"Dat's a nice room up dere," my mother, busying herself at the stove, commented with an obviously faked nonchalance. "You just poot junk up dere?"

My face paled. I could feel the blood from my head rushing south. And my life heading in the same direction.

"No, no, no, Sonsyou, I just tinking," my mother answered every possible question I could think of putting to her about why she was in my garage storage room, short of actually asking whether she was considering moving in there. She was slicing away at some fatty hunk of meat and adding it to a frying pan. "Come, seet down, ve eat, ya? You must be so hungry!"

"But Mom, what were you thinking…"

"Ay! Texoh booyd! Eat now." She wanted me to be quiet and eat. Things seemed back to normal.

By 9 p.m. mother was settled down with a cocoa in front of the television in her bedroom watching a *Colombo* rerun and I was freshly showered, shaved and squeezed into a pair of jeans from gatt and a plain black T-shirt. I slipped on some Skechers that looked like runners but weren't and a heavily lined leather coat, said goodbye to the dogs and went next door.

I was surprised when the door was opened by Jared, Anthony's partner—the model—holding aloft a martini glass full of red liquid as if it were an Academy Award he'd just won. He was wearing a dark brown outfit that clung to his body like syrup. I embraced him and, as always, marvelled at the existence of something so beautiful. The impeccable olive skin, the unique copper tint of boyishly unkempt curls, the golden-green eyes. And, also as always, I swallowed the old familiar feeling that I'd like to be in love with him. Except for the fact that he belongs to Anthony.

I followed Jared's scent into a room decorated by Sereena to resemble the lobby bar of a W Hotel; dim lighting, low slung, white leather couches, exotic topiaries and five-foot-tall, wrought iron candlesticks that looked as if they'd been filched from an abbey. Instead of Christmas muzak the sound system was blaring club tunes from the '80s and '90s. A definite party ambiance was being created here. The brushed-steel and glass bar was lit from above and below by multi-coloured halogens and around it were two women dressed to be seen. Sereena, her chestnut tresses a cornucopia of curls about her face, was wearing a champagne-coloured pantsuit that seemed to be missing it's back, perilously high heels and a stunning collection of garnet jewellery. The other woman, whom I did not know, had straight Titian hair that covered her right eye ala Veronica Lake (and sometimes Nicole Kidman) and also wore a pantsuit, but of black silk (its back intact) and a black scarf dramatically woven about her neck. She was laden with diamonds that looked spectacularly real and her lipstick was a vivid red.

147

"I'm pouring you a Red Apple," Sereena called out to me over Aretha Franklin's "Who's Zoomin' Who?" Red Apple Martinis are equal parts gin (Bombay if you have it), apple juice and red Dubonnet. Or, as Sereena is wont to suggest and I am hesitant to repeat, if you're a woman or not a sissy, substitute the apple juice with Calvados, a distilled apple cider that burns the palate.

I looked at the strange woman and then at Sereena and Jared and back at the woman, trying to wordlessly request an introduction. They weren't taking the hint and I was becoming a little testy. Daniel would likely be arriving at any minute and I didn't want him feeling any more nervous about his first visit to a gay club than he probably already was. And I couldn't understand why Sereena would have invited Jared and his red-haired friend over for cocktails when she knew we had some sensitive work ahead of us.

"Sereena," I said after I'd accepted my drink and placed it on the bar top. "Could I speak with you in the kitchen please?"

"Don't be rude, Russell, we shouldn't leave our guests alone, especially when you've only just met Clarissa."

Finally a name. I gave Sereena a tight smile and held out my hand to Clarissa. "Pleased to meet you, Clarissa. You wouldn't mind if I stole Sereena away for a couple of minutes, would you?"

"Of course not."

The music must have been too loud. It was playing tricks on my hearing. I was certain that the voice that came from Clarissa's moist, ruby lips was that of a man.

A voice I recognized.

A voice that belonged to...

Daniel Guest.

I stared at Clarissa's face. Under close inspection and layers of cosmetics, it was all there. The nose, the eyes (without glasses), the jaw. I looked further down. The well-placed scarf was no doubt concealing an Adam's apple. Further. Wide shoulders and, the most telltale sign, big square hands. Clarissa *was* Daniel Guest.

It was an amazing transformation. Daniel was an attractive man *and* a handsome woman—from a distance. The choice of black and a pantsuit for his outfit was genius, for both hid a number of obvious unfeminine traits. The makeup and hair were perfect. In a dark enough room and at a polite distance, Daniel could be Rita Hayworth. Until he spoke. His voice was deep and undoubtedly masculine.

The reconstruction of Daniel into a woman had been the plan all along (if we were unsuccessful in the parking lot with Sunny—which we were—resoundingly). I had gotten the idea from the drag queen we'd spotted at Colourful Mary's. I knew however there was no way I could pull it off convincingly myself. I needed a woman's touch. I needed Sereena. So I was glad for the opportunity to introduce Daniel and Sereena at the DGR&R Christmas party and thereafter suggest the collaboration. Daniel had been surprisingly supportive of the plan. It met all of his needs. It got him into the local gay bar where he hopefully would spot SunLover and it kept him incognito so even his mother wouldn't recognize him. And, like many a gay man, I was guessing he'd harboured a long-held desire to do drag, even just once, for the fun of it. And by the smile on his face, he'd certainly been having fun...and a few Red Apples.

"You had no idea it was me! Did you?" he shrieked, sounding excited and maybe a little drunk.

I shook my head in wonder as I surveyed Sereena and Jared's handiwork. Now I knew why Sereena had sounded distracted when I'd called earlier. "I really didn't," I admitted. "Actually, I still don't believe it."

"We wanted to surprise you," Jared said, with a companionable elbow resting on my left shoulder. "Sereena mentioned what she was doing and I just had to help. So she called Daniel and asked if he'd mind one more person in on the sham, someone with behind-the-scenes first-hand knowledge of the makeup secrets of the world's most beautiful fashion models. He agreed and then the three of us thought it would be a blast to make him up before you arrived."

"The ultimate test of our success," Sereena added. "And succeed we did. Clarissa, you are gorgeous. You make me want to be a lesbian or a straight man. Preferably a lesbian."

Daniel/Clarissa laughed and held out his glass for more Red Apple. "I can hardly wait," he enthused. "When do we leave?"

"All good things in good time," Jared told him looking at his watch. "Most serious clubbers are barely waking up about this time. We can't possibly make our entrance for another couple of hours.

Until then, we'll have drinks, pupus and scandalous gossip!" He turned to me and said, "And Anthony and Kelly and Errall will join us at the club later. Don't worry, they don't have to know anything about Daniel. We'll just tell them Clarissa is an old friend of Sereena's in town for the evening. You're okay with that, right Clarissa?"

"Except the part about being an 'old' friend," he said, hopping not-so-daintily off his barstool. "There ain't nothin' old about me tonight!" And right in front of my eyes, my accountant client began to boogie on three-inch heels to vintage George Michael.

"You sway, Mary Kay!" Jared yelled out, joining in.

Sereena sipped her drink with deeply sucked in cheeks and a smug look on her face.

I watched the scene and particularly Daniel. Like many people in costume or behind a mask, he'd become a different person. Livelier, more carefree, more willing to smile wide and let loose with a smart aleck remark or swear word. He seemed freed. I couldn't help but wonder which character—the staid, uber-professional number-cruncher or the wild, boogey queen—was closer to being the real Daniel Guest.

Diva's is the only gay bar in Saskatoon that has stood the test of time. It is gay-owned, gay-run and, although it welcomes the non-gay crowd, it has held itself aloof from giving in to the allure of the non-gay dollar as so many other gay establishments do. Gay night-spots the world over attract straight people who by simple intelligence know that gay bars are the best place to have raunchy fun and by sheer volume spend more dollars on entertainment. Slowly the tide turns and what was once a gay bar with lotsa gays and some cool straights becomes a mixed bar with some cool straights and some cool gays and eventually a straight bar with lotsa straights and a few jittery gays. In the short run you can hardly blame the bar owners, most of whom are just struggling to stay in business and make a buck. But in the long run, it seldom pays off. Most of these bars go bankrupt once all the gays are gone and the straights realize it's not so cool anymore and head out to find a new gay bar to convert. It's a sad but true vicious circle.

As the only sober member of our ABBA-like group and officially on-the-job, I volunteered to be the designated driver. It was well after 11 p.m. before we managed to finish the last pitcher of Red Apples, cover our finery with outerwear appropriate for the frigid weather and pile into my mother's van. I parked on 3rd Avenue and led my giddy group down a back alley in the direction of rumbling music vibrating off the walls of surrounding buildings. We entered an unmarked door under a rainbow flag into a long, wide vestibule at the end of which was a chest-high window kitty-corner to a locked door. Through the window we could see a pretty woman in her late forties giggling with a tough-looking coat-check chick in her early twenties. Diva's is a private club and as none of us were members we paid a reasonable cover charge and were buzzed in through the door. The music we'd heard and thought was loud in the alleyway hit us at full high-decibel force. The music is the place. It's meant to overcome you, to drive you to physical limits beyond exertion, to be the magic carpet that takes you to the moon. Well—the music *and* the poppers.

Stepping into a gay bar after midnight on a Saturday night is much the same wherever you are. It didn't matter that this bar was in a small Canadian prairie city and that it was minus thirty-three outside and our vehicle would be covered with ice when we finally decided to go home. Inside was hot and dark, packed to the rafters with people made up their best (or worst—depending on the look they were going for), the air smelled of sweat and smoke and other substances and amongst the crowd were, as always, a bare-chested boy, a bald-headed woman wearing a too-tight muscle shirt, a six-and-a-half-foot-tall drag queen, a guy who danced on the speakers and someone pretending to be straight for the last time. It was an electric atmosphere where anything could happen but rarely did. And still, as always, the promise of it was more than enough.

Errall had already arrived and was saving a table with two extra stools. The positioning was good, near both the front door and bar and with a nearly unimpeded view of the dance floor, giving Daniel the best chance of spotting SunLover. A set of stairs led to a second level loft with more tables, a pool table, bathrooms and a drink rail that overlooked the writhing dance floor. "People keep on stealing stools!" Errall yelled over the noise of the music. "I started out with enough but you're late and I was beginning to get dirty stares!"

Jared and I stood while Sereena and Clarissa sat down.

"Sorry," I said. "I had a hard time convincing the royal family here to move their asses." Now that we were gathered with our heads close together we didn't have to shout as loud to be heard. "Where's Kelly?" I asked.

"Not feeling up to it," Errall said, giving me a look that said she was more than a little pissed off about it. She was wearing a pair of tight jeans and a simple low-necked blue sweater that looked great on her. Her hair was loose around her face. She put down her bottle of Pilsner and held out a hand towards Clarissa. "Hi, I'm Errall Strane."

Clarissa shook hands politely.

"Clarissa is a friend of Sereena's in town for the night," I said.

"Oh, where are you from?"

"Ottawa," I quickly lied.

Errall cocked an arch-shaped eyebrow at me, meant to question why I wasn't letting the lady speak. She looked back at Clarissa, leaned in towards her and said rather loudly, "I love Ottawa. What part of the city do you live in?"

Clarissa pulled back and looked desperately at me and then Jared and Sereena for help.

Sereena looked Errall in the eyes and said in a way that did not invite questioning, "Clarissa is a client of Russell's here in disguise, now lay off him and get me a gin and tonic, lime squeeze."

Clarissa opened his mouth into a perfect *o*. Marilyn would have been proud.

"Don't worry, sweetheart," Sereena told him "She still doesn't know who you are. Now what are you drinking?"

"A beer...uh...Canadian," he answered in a voice that sounded more baritone than it really was.

"Mmmm..." Sereena considered the answer. "Perhaps something not in a can or bottle would be more ladylike for tonight? Get him the same as me and one for Jared. Russell will help."

I pulled Errall out of her seat and towards the bar before she had time to argue. By the time we returned with the drinks, including a club soda for myself, Jared and Sereena were on the dance floor moving to Will Smith and Daniel was watching the crowd, enthralled.

"I'm sorry," I said as I sat on one of the stools. "They shouldn't have left you alone." It was the first moment all evening that I'd had time with my client away from the questionable influence of Jared and Sereena. I tried to catch his eyes with my own to see if I could decipher what he was really feeling about what was happening to him that night. But I couldn't see anything, least of all any signs of the old Daniel Guest.

"I told them to go ahead," he said. "I'm safe under all this stuff. I feel like a hunter under a duck bluff. Besides, I wanted to stay here and keep an eye out for James Kraft."

I gave my client a sharp look. "You mean SunLover."

"Oh yeah," he said, paying more attention to the pretty boys passing by than to our conversation. "That's right. SunLover."

I shook my head. I should not have let Daniel drink. We weren't there for fun; we had work to do. And sensing that, Errall hopped off her stool and left us to join Jared and Sereena.

"Do you see anyone who looks familiar?" I asked Daniel, wanting to focus his attention, and mine, on the matter at hand.

"Nnnnnnnoooooo," he drawled, "but I do see another guy who can't take his eyes off of you."

Like a silly schoolgirl I whirled around to see whom he was talking about. And sure enough, standing against a far wall opposite the coat check was a stocky, muscular man in jeans and tight T-shirt (of course) looking at me. I smiled and gave him a quick wave.

"Do you know him?" Daniel asked excitedly.

"We've met."

"What does that mean? You've met and shook hands or you've met and," he leaned in and whispered feverishly, "had sex?"

I sipped my club soda. It was flat. "We have not had sex. We've just seen each other around."

"But you could have sex with him if you wanted to?"

"Daniel, I don't know…maybe…I suppose so…I don't know." This pubescent drag queen was actually embarrassing me.

"You are so lucky," he said seriously. It was near impossible to read the true expression on his face underneath all the Maybelline.

"I rarely have sex. Almost never with Cheryl anymore. You are a lucky man."

"Why do you say that?"

"You have all of this," he answered, raising his hands in a gesture that was meant to encompass the entire nightclub. "Right here at your disposal; you can take it or leave it whenever you want. You can come in here without a disguise; you can be who you really are. You, Russell, are a free man." He looked around and added, "These are all free people."

Although I doubted everyone in Diva's that night would agree with his sweeping statement, I understood what he meant. What he was really saying was that he was not free, he was a captive of the lifestyle he had chosen. I began to wonder if it had been the right decision to bring him there. Had I made an insensitive blunder? Was bringing him to Diva's like hauling a dieter into a bakery or taking an ex-smoker to a bingo parlour? Sometimes you don't miss what you don't see. But once you see it, it is hard to resist. But being gay isn't the same as being an overeater or a reformed smoker. It isn't bad for your health (usually). It is a state of being, no matter where you are. Denying it is like denying the nose on your face. And maybe, Daniel was finally taking notice of the nose on his face.

"Daniel," I said, "would you like to leave now?"

He looked at me in an odd way. For a moment he reminded me of the sad clown who could only laugh because that's how the makeup was drawn on his face. "No," he answered definitively, "I want to see this. I want to…I love it here."

I nodded and glanced around. The bar was getting busy as more and more people crowded in before last call, wanting to be part of the swirling, intoxicating madness that is the climax of any weekend and usually happens somewhere around 2 a.m. Sunday morning. "Do you feel confident enough to walk around, Clarissa?"

"Sure," he said, "as long as I don't fall off these shoes!"

I took Daniel's hand to help steady him and led him through the throng. It struck me that I would have never thought to hold hands with Daniel Guest when he was dressed as a man, but, although the feel of our skin touching was odd, somehow as Clarissa it was okay. We made our way past the posers on the staircase, we stuck our noses into the almost deserted pool room, we made a tour of the upper level table area, stopped in the bathroom to relieve ourselves (Daniel used the one stall in the men's room) and then slowly headed back. We came away without any sighting of SunLover but I did manage to collect a pinch from a grinch and a wink from a twink.

By the time we got back to our table, Errall, Jared and Sereena had returned. Sereena looked as fresh as if she'd just stepped from a shower. Errall, however, didn't look so good. She looked miserable actually. Daniel sidled up to Jared and Sereena to tell them of his upstairs exploits, such as they were, and I snuck in close to Errall.

"You okay?" I asked.

"Shit no," she told me harshly with a look meant to end the conversation.

I simply nodded understandingly. But I didn't understand at all.

"He's here!" Daniel shouted a little too loudly.

"What? Who?" I asked him, glad for the loud music and incessant chattering around us that handily cloaked our conversation.

He was staring towards the entrance of the club, his beautifully made-up eyes wide. "The man I had sex with at Cranberry Flats! He's here! He just came in! He's in the line for the coat check!"

We all turned our heads in unison to stare at the unsuspecting Lothario and in sync our jaws dropped to the table at the sight of the familiar face.

Chapter 12

"THAT'S HIM! THAT'S HIM!" Daniel a.k.a. Clarissa repeated unnecessarily. "SunLover is here."

Each of us made like hoot owls looking at each other with wide-eyed expressions of disbelief. Then like a crazed team of synchronized head turners we each turned to stare at Jared. He was gazing at the man identified as SunLover—the man Daniel Guest had sex with on Bare Ass Beach just a few months ago. He was gazing at his partner, Anthony Gatt. Jared was saying nothing and his perfectly constructed face was unreadable, like one of his magazine-cover photos.

What happened next was a blur. Anthony eventually caught sight of our little group from his spot in the coat check line. And how could he not, with five sets of eyes burning holes into the back of his Prada shirt. He turned and gave us his most beguiling superstar wattage smile. Under the brightly coloured mask of Clarissa's makeup, Daniel Guest went pale. He had no way of knowing that Anthony knew us, so he reached the only logical conclusion—SunLover had somehow recognized him. Jared had yet to say anything or, for that matter, register any form of reaction. I just knew that before he did, I had to get Daniel out of there. I didn't want Anthony arriving at the table and laid siege to by recriminations and accusations with my client still around to hear it all. Sereena caught my drift without so much as a verbal hint from me and gathered up her own and Clarissa's things and led the charge for the door. Errall remained at the table with Jared, glumly contemplating her drink. Instead of joining the coat-check lineup where we'd no doubt come face to face with Anthony, we pushed our way through it and towards the exit. We stopped at the check-in window to ask the white-haired doorwoman if she'd mind retrieving our coats. She did so with an accommodating smile and we were out of there before Anthony even knew we'd gone.

On the drive home Sereena and I sat in the front of the van scrutinizing the road and saying little while Clarissa was in the back, shedding her skin, slowing becoming Daniel Guest again and blabbering on with endless questions about what had just happened. I finally explained to him that SunLover was a friend of ours and therefore removed as a suspect in his blackmailing case. He kept on asking questions, but we did little more than nod or shake our heads, which for the most part seemed to appease our metamorphosing charge. I pulled into the garage behind my house and Sereena led Daniel back to her place to complete the de-dragging process. I begged off offers of a nightcap and went home.

Sunday morning dawned bright and cloudless with a much nicer temperature than we'd experienced the past few days. I knew the warm trend probably meant snow in our future. I'd had a fitful night of tossing and turning and poking Barbra in the ribs. We both emerged from the bedroom around 9:30 a.m., I bleary-eyed and feeling a little down. As we made our way to the foyer to retrieve Brutus we could smell meat frying. I was sure if my mother hung around long enough I'd eventually be able to identify a meat by its smell in the fried state, but I wasn't there yet. I was guessing it was either sausage or back bacon. Even Barbra was surprised when we didn't find Brutus in his usual spot by the front door, but it didn't take long to figure out that he was just a dog after all and probably in the kitchen with my mother slumming for scraps. We were right.

"Morning," I mumbled as I let Barbra out to do her business. Brutus went along for the heck of it.

"Dere's nice fresh pot coffee," she said, looking her usual morning self—which actually wasn't a whole lot different than her usual self at any other time of day. "I trow out da first one." That was her subtle way of saying, "The first pot went bad because you slept *so* late."

Well, it was Sunday and even if it wasn't, I had a right to sleep in whenever I had a mind to. She'd have to get used to that if she was going to move in…

Oh Gaaaawwwwwwd! Was she really going to move in? Every so often the possibility hit me like a bag of frozen perogies.

My hands balled into fists, I rubbed my eyes awake. "Sorry, I just couldn't sleep last night. Bad dreams."

"Dey say if you dreenk too much before sleep you haf bad dream." Interpretation: "You were out drinking alcohol last night, weren't you?"

I poured a cup of coffee and sat at the island. I watched her stir something in a pot and move sausage—aha! I was right—around in a sizzling pan. I sipped the coffee. Then again. Not bad. It actually had some flavour and substance. Did she send out?

And then an unexpected sensation overtook me. For some reason my mouth was watering and I realized I wanted nothing more than to be in this warm, cozy kitchen, watching my mom cook, eating fried stuff and drinking lots of coffee. What I didn't want was involvement with the outside world. I hadn't had time to chew on what had happened the night before at Diva's but I knew the experience had left a bad taste in my mouth. The dreams I'd had were actually nightmares and although I couldn't quite remember them, I remembered how they made me feel. And it wasn't good. I needed eggs and sausage and toast with butter and jam and maybe some of my mom's homemade hash browns.

I got up to let the dogs in. I saw that their food and water dishes were already full so I went back to my spot where my mother had served up a heaping plate of artery-clogging material. Yum!

I reminded my mother that I had invited a few friends over to decorate the Christmas tree that evening. She asked about the tree. I wanted to tell her that the only people I knew with trucks were lesbians, so Errall and Kelly were picking it up, but instead, I just told her it was being delivered. My mother stood to learn a lot that Christmas season.

I busied myself all day with housecleaning and laundry, sweeping off the walk, retrieving firewood and tree decorations from the garage and selecting season-appropriate music. And, despite promises to myself to the contrary, I also spent a fair bit of time fretting over my case, over what likely happened between Anthony and Jared after I left Diva's, over the state of Kelly's health and her relationship with Errall and over what plans were brewing in my mother's head. By the time my mother and I sat down for supper/dinner, I was in a bit of a state. I comforted myself with the ultimate in Ukrainian comfort food—perogies lightly fried in butter, garlic and onion and drowned in a rich, creamy sauce of mushrooms and dill.

The first to arrive was Sereena and so far my prediction was proving accurate. It was nothing obvious. There were no fisticuffs or exchange of vitriolic barbs, but after I introduced the aproned, home-permed and shrill Kay Quant to the DKNYed, salon-coiffed and shrill Sereena Orion Smith, they each made a hasty retreat to their favourite corners, my mother to the kitchen and Sereena to the bar. Barbra and Brutus wisely chose to stay near the baked goods in the kitchen on the off chance some might land in their mouths.

I slipped behind the bar and Sereena placed her delicate self onto a padded stool. We both needed a Red Apple martini—the non-sissy version.

"There are doilies in here," she said, her voice drier than the martini.

I looked down at the counter top in horror. My granite coasters had been replaced by dainty off-white squares individually crocheted by my mother. When had she made the switch? My face contorted and I croaked, "Help me."

Sereena nodded, allowing a few dark tendrils to escape from behind her diamond mine right ear. "How long?" she asked after an appreciative sip of her cocktail.

"Until the twenty-seventh," I told her, deciding not even to bring up the possibility of a much longer (as in, forever) stay. "Unless the weather is bad. Then she'll stay until the roads are safe."

Sereena frowned. "Roads? Where does she come from anyway?"

"Howell."

"Is that...a home or something?"

"Howell, Saskatchewan. It's a town. About an hour away from here. She lives on a farm just outside of town."

"Really? Have you ever been?"

I arched an eyebrow at her as high as it would go. "I grew up there, Sereena."

"On a farm?"

I helped myself to a gulp of my drink and scowled at her. The look on her face was one of concern mixed with astonishment. "You know this story," I admonished her.

"Yes, I do," she relented. "I was simply checking if you still admitted to it."

Saved by the doorbell. I left Sereena to join Barbra and Brutus at the door where Anthony and Jared were waiting to be let in. After what happened the previous night I hadn't expected them to show up. But there they were, their faces revealing nothing.

I hugged and kissed them both, accepted the proffered bottle of wine and did away with their coats while they found Sereena at the bar, like heat-seeking missiles drawn to a flame.

"Will she remember me?" Anthony stage-whispered when I re-joined them, his thumb poking in the direction of the kitchen and my mother. Someone had prepared more drinks. The eggnog remained untouched.

I rolled my eyes. I'd forgotten; yet another possible source of friction at my happy-go-lucky Christmas soiree. "Who knows," I said. "How many times did you meet her while you and Uncle Lawrence were together?"

He clicked his tongue as he thought. "Handful, perhaps. As you know, puppy, Lawrence and Kay never got along well."

"Why was that?" Jared asked. "Was it because he was gay?"

Anthony shrugged and wiped away a piece of imagined fluff from the collar of his pricey Cavelli shirt. "I don't really know. Sometimes I wonder if it wasn't just because they lived such vastly different lives that they simply didn't know how to talk to one another. They may as well have been from two different species."

I nodded absentmindedly, paying more attention to the interaction between the two men than the words coming from their mouths.

Where was the damage that follows any accident—in this case the accidental revelation that Anthony had fooled around on Jared? I felt a need to say something. But to which one? Certainly Anthony and I had known each other the longest and were closer. But Jared was the obviously wronged party here.

Again saved by another bell. I excused myself and dashed for the phone.

"Russell? It's me, Daniel Guest. I'm sorry to bother you at home."

Oddly I was relieved to switch my brain to thinking about work rather than my friend's dilemma. "No problem, Daniel. Has something happened?"

"Not yet," he said. "But there's something I want to talk to you about. Not tonight, but I was wondering if you could meet me in my office tomorrow morning?"

I cringed. Was this going to be another dawn meeting?

"Say about nine-ish?" he suggested.

That's better. "Sure, no problem. Is everything okay, Daniel?"

"I've got to run. Nine o'clock." And he hung up.

I heard a knock and the front door opening and then over the strains of Bing's "White Christmas" came that good, old traditional yuletide greeting: "Hey, I need one of you twinks to help me with this tree!"

Apparently Errall had forgotten that my mother was visiting.

I replaced the phone receiver. Jared and I met her at the door and I doled out coats and gloves from the closet. Errall's hair was tied back with a ribbon and two powder-blue muffs were where her ears should have been. She wore a down vest over a thick, patterned turtleneck sweater and tight, black stretchy pants. Her pale face was flushed pink with cold and delicate snowflakes decorated the crown of her head and eyelashes.

"I let Barbra and Brutus out front," she informed me. "They're having a ball in the fresh snow."

"Where's Kelly?" Jared asked as he slipped on his boots. They were black things that looked warm, but about a million years old. It's another one of those things I like about Jared, away from the runway he never plays "model."

"At home," she answered, her voice tight. "She's not feeling well."

Crap. She had all but promised me she would get off her ass and come tonight. Where in the world was our old Kelly?

We followed Errall out to the street where she'd parked Kelly's Dodge Ram truck. In the back was a healthy-looking six-and-a-half-footer. "The guy at the place helped me get it on here," she said through lips puckered around a freshly lit cigarette. "He just gave it a fresh cut so we can put it right in water."

"Mayfair Hardware on 33rd?" Jared asked in between catching snowflakes on his tongue. Mayfair Hardware is a bizarre little store, circa small-town 1930. You can easily spend an afternoon in its cluttered aisles rifling through overflowing bins and dusty shelves collecting the coolest stuff you must have and will never use. And each December, stuffed into a crowded back lot, they have the best and cheapest Christmas trees in the city.

"Yup," she answered as she lowered the end-gate and hoisted herself up into the truck's bed.

Jared and I took positions on either side and pulled while Errall pushed. Feeling as butch as that guy with the blue ox—Paul something?—we delivered our trophy to the living room, depositing it directly into a heavy metal tree stand I'd placed in the perfect spot ahead of time. While Jared and I battled to position the slightly bowed tree trunk to make it appear straight, I couldn't help noticing my mother and Anthony having a tête-à-tête near the kitchen. I would have given up the chocolates I was bound to eat that evening to hear what they were saying. I could tell nothing from the look on their faces or body language, my mother with a plate of cookies in her hand, Anthony a snifter of brandy in his.

"We'll have to let it sit for about half an hour to forty-five minutes," Errall instructed. "So that all the branches settle to their normal position."

And then it happened. We stood there, staring at one another. Between what had happened at Diva's the night before, Kell's absence, my mother's strained history with Anthony and all the blasted doilies, there was not only a giant pink elephant in the room we were all pretending not to see, but a spotted giraffe and flying zebra as well.

Surprisingly it was my mother who saved the day.

"Den we haf time to eat and mebbe some Kaiser." She'd left Anthony behind and was already laying out cards and food platters on my dining room table covered by a lacey tablecloth I'd never seen before. We followed her like calves to a water trough. "You and Carol play da vinners."

She was referring to Errall and me. The other three took seats at the table looking pleadingly to me for help. My mother sat at the head of the table and began to shuffle the cards like a Las Vegas shark. If I didn't know better I'd have sworn that her spectacles were fogging up from the intensity of her concentration.

"You feex everyone dreenks," she ordered us as cards whizzed from her hand, landing in perfect piles in front of Sereena, Anthony and Jared. I know enough about Kaiser to know you do not play the game with a full deck (I'll regretfully deny myself the obvious joke here). My mother must have either brought the deck along with the doilies and tablecloth and entire contents of her farmhouse pantry, or she'd planned this ahead of time and doctored one of mine.

Errall and I took and filled drink orders and made sure the serviettes in front of each player were heaped with cold cuts, cheese and gherkins. Once done with that, we recognized the huge entertainment value of my Ukrainian mother teaching a fashion model, an ex-jet-setter and a clothing-store magnate the finer points of trump and no trump, the joy of the five of hearts and the evil of the three of spades and pulled up two stools to watch.

"Wow, I can really smell the pine needles now," I said after about half an hour, taking a deep whiff. But no one was listening to me. They were all too focused on beating my mother at her own game. And thankfully the evening passed with pleasantness. Pleasantness, a pink elephant, a spotted giraffe and a flying zebra.

When I was ushered by the receptionist into Daniel's office on Monday morning, I noticed something different in my client. He was wearing a light grey-green suit, a solid green shirt and a matching patterned tie. He rose, held out his hand and smiled as he always did. It was nothing obvious. But it was there. Was it his manner—relaxed and open? The glow in his eyes? The way he carried himself with vigour and confidence? Had his experience on Saturday night as a drag queen visiting his first gay bar changed him?

"Russell, thank you for coming. I appreciate you taking the time."

"Well, I am working for you, so I guess my time is your time. Is something wrong? Were you followed again?"

"No, no, nothing like that. I'm sorry. I should have given you more information over the phone. You see, I've made an important decision that I think you should know about," he announced.

Oh, oh. Was he about to come out of the closet? As a drag queen named Clarissa? What had I done?

"As you know, it's time for my payment to Loverboy and...I've decided not to make it. I'm not going to mail the cheque." As he said this his chin rose a tad and his voice was triumphant.

I wasn't immediately sure how I felt about his decision. "What convinced you to do this?"

"Nothing...and everything. I think it's the right thing to do. The only thing. I want this to be over, Russell, and I think this will help. I know you'd never suggest it because of the possible danger to me, but it is a good idea, isn't it? I mean, this might help flush him out, won't it? He'll have to contact me again to find out what's happened to his money and when he does that, hopefully he'll screw up or leave some clues for you to follow."

"You're right, Daniel, there are dangers to you. You risk making Loverboy angry and doing what he's threatened to do all along— make your homosexual activities public. Or worse, he could become more threatening or even violent. He might change the terms of your agreement and ask for even more money. That's the problem with a criminal you know nothing about, there's no way of knowing just what they're capable of. Maybe we should wait before making such a bold move, give my investigation a little more time. I've only been on the case less than a week. Something will turn up."

"No," he said, his shoulders squared off like a warrior's. "Besides, it's too late. The payment was due today, the fifteenth. When Loverboy checks his mailbox, it'll be empty. I don't think he'll do any-thing rash...at least not right away. He won't want to jeopardize his getting the fifty thousand eventually."

I took a deep breath. I was nervous for him. And worried. "Daniel, are you sure? This is a big step. Do you really understand the possible consequences?"

"I know you're going to find him, Russell, before anything untoward happens to me. I just know it."

His confidence in my abilities was generous. But was it misplaced? I would find the blackmailer. But would I find him before he damaged Daniel Guest's life forever?

"Let's go over the candidates again," I instructed as we took seats around Daniel's desk.

"You're convinced SunLover is out of the picture for sure?" he questioned.

I thought about Anthony and my stomach lurched involuntarily. I nodded. "Yes. SunLover is not Loverboy."

Daniel nodded, seeming to accept my decision on this point. "So that leaves James Kraft. And you know what I think about him."

I did.

"It has to be him, Russell. It just fits. Besides, with SunLover eliminated, he's the only one left."

"You're forgetting that there might be other possible candidates."

He sighed impatiently. "I know. I know. You think people I work with could be involved. But you met the lot of them at the Christmas party. See any potential Loverboys in that crowd? I doubt it."

"I'm not so sure yet."

"Are you saying you think James Kraft cannot be our Loverboy?" He was twirling a ballpoint pen between his fingers like a mini baton; his voice was challenging and he was frowning.

"No, that's not what I'm saying."

"We agreed to hold off on going to New York to find James Kraft until we thought we'd taken care of business at home and concluded it was the right move. Well, if I have a vote, and I think I do, I think it is the right move. Now."

I nodded. It was time to acquiesce. After all, he was the client and I had so far failed to come up with a more plausible local lead. Besides, he was right. James Kraft was our most likely suspect. And I felt better about making the trip, now that I'd done some preliminary work on the case and gotten a better feel for it and my client.

"I don't mean to be a hard-headed jerk about this, Russell, but he's the only candidate we've got right now and…well, I just want this over and done with as soon as possible. Could you go to New York this week?"

I thought about my mother. I was unsure about leaving her, but I nodded nonetheless. "I'll arrange it."

"Great. Let me know when and where you're staying. We should keep in touch. If James Kraft *is* Loverboy I want to know about it right away."

Daniel's phone rang and he answered it. He listened to whoever was on the other end for five seconds then put them on hold. "Listen, I have to take this, it's a conference call. Is there anything else we need to discuss?"

He was the one who'd called this meeting, so, I guessed, he could end it. I shook my head and took my leave.

I was about to head towards the staircase that would take me down into the reception area, but stopped myself. The walls of the atrium were a deep purple and the matching carpet a thick berber. The only sounds I could make out behind the closed doors lining the corridor were the clicking of computer keys and the odd muffled voice on a phone. Chartered accountants at work. Instead of turning left to the staircase I turned right and found what I was looking for in fairly short order—a door with a nameplate that read: Herb Dufour. I tapped lightly on the door and opened it about a foot, sticking my head in far enough to catch sight of the man behind a desk even bigger than the one in Daniel Guest's office. I wondered if the size of your desk was some sort of status thing with accountants or a sign of virility like a monster truck?

"Mr. Quant," Herb Dufour greeted me. He hurriedly came out from behind the impressive piece of furniture and approached me with an outstretched hand. We shook. "I didn't know you were in the building."

How would he, I couldn't help wonder. When I'd cased the building—as was my habit (just in case I'd need to break in one day)—I hadn't come across any hidden cameras or microphones. Perhaps it was simply a figure of speech. Perhaps I was being an anal detective. "I was here meeting with Daniel and thought I'd drop by to say hello." I could see by the look on his face that he wasn't really buying my reasoning. But, so what.

"Would you like a coffee or something else to drink?" He motioned me to sit in a chair that was dwarfed by his massive wooden edifice. As I took my place he returned to his own seat of power. I took notice of an impressive array of plaques and degrees and commemorative framed photographs on the walls, many relating to his years as a city councillor.

"No thank you. I won't stay long. I'm sorry for stopping by unannounced. I know how busy you must be."

He grinned a pleasing grin that made his big-boned face appear softer. "Actually, come this time of year I like to take it a little easier and cruise gently into the Christmas season. I have a Christmas party, concert, come and go, wine and cheese or dinner every night from now until the twenty-fifth. It's all I can do to make it into the office in the morning."

"Somehow I doubt that," I said. Herb Dufour was a successful man who struck me as one of those guys with boundless energy and stamina. He could probably work until 1 a.m., go out with the guys for drinks afterwards, then go home, watch some TV before bed, wake up at dawn for exercise and review of the morning news programs before heading back to the office to do the same thing all over again.

"What can I do for you, Mr. Quant?"

"I forgot to ask you something the other night at the Christmas party. I was just wondering if you happened to be at the SBA awards ceremony the night Daniel received the blackmail note."

He looked at me steadily but did not answer.

"So…were you?"

"Yes," he said slowly, drawing out the word. "Why do you ask?"

"Well, I'm interested in talking to anyone who might have been there that night. They might have seen something or noticed someone who shouldn't have been there or was acting strangely."

He appeared to be thinking this over. Finally he rubbed his wide chin with his wide hand and answered. "No, I can't say that I did."

"How about Marilee?"

He frowned. "Marilee?"

"I'm sorry," I said, "I just assumed since she was with you at the Christmas party that she might also have been...?"

He regarded me carefully before saying, "No. Marilee was not there that night. I had another escort that evening."

"Oh," I said. "Who was that?"

He looked at me as if I'd asked him what he did on a particular Thursday afternoon seven years ago. "I don't recall."

"I see."

"Have you been having any luck on the case, Mr. Quant?" he asked in an obvious attempt to get off the subject of his varied unmemorable escorts.

"Yes." I always say yes to a question like that, even if the answer is something different.

"Well, I hope you remember my offer to help you in any way possible."

"I do and I'm sure Daniel is grateful to have the level of support you've shown for him. Obviously you have no issue with his being a homosexual?" It was a loaded question and a little out of right field. My favourite kind.

He volleyed back with ease. "Daniel, as always, has my full support. He is my friend as well as business partner. I may not understand everything he's done to...find himself embroiled in this situation...but I would do *anything* to help him out of it." His words and tone of voice were unwavering—a politician's expertise.

"I hope that won't be necessary, but I guess we'll see what happens now he's decided not to pay the blackmail."

Dufour's face suddenly changed. If it wasn't for his long sleeve shirt, I'm sure I would have observed the hairs on his arms bristle. This was obviously unexpected news. "He what?" he boomed.

"He's decided not to pay the blackmail."

"Don't you consider that completely foolhardy and...and dangerous, Mr. Quant? I hope you're talking him out of it. If he doesn't pay how does he ever expect this...this horrific experience to end? My God, man, he's not thinking this through."

Was it anger or was it concern for his friend or was it something else that was making the man's cheeks and forehead grow redder by the minute. He no longer looked like any of the images portrayed in the commemorative snapshots on the walls around us.

"It's too late. Daniel has already made up his mind and withheld payment. The money was due today."

Herb snorted through his nose and looked away. After a moment he said, "I'm sorry for my outburst. I'm just worried about Daniel and this mess he's gotten himself into."

"And worried about what the effect would be on DGR&R if the blackmailer makes good on his threat?" I wasn't being paid to be Mr. Nice Guy.

We stared at one another.

Dufour relented. "That…is not…wholly unimportant, it's true, but my concern, first and foremost, is Daniel's well-being. You can choose to believe that or not, it doesn't matter to me."

And with that we shook hands like gentlemen and I left.

I spent the next couple of days checking up on DGR&R employees and spending oodles of time pulling surveillance duty outside the post office watching P.O. Box 8420. With payment due on the fifteenth, certainly Loverboy would be anxious to collect. But all I managed to accomplish was an over-familiarity with the upholstery of my car. More and more I was becoming convinced that Daniel's idea of going to New York to find James Kraft was the most worthwhile course of action we had. I managed to book a seat sale flight to New York and Sereena, who'd been to the Big Apple many times before, decided to tag along to do some Christmas shopping, visit friends and maybe show me a thing or two in one of her favourite cities in the world. I even played around with the idea of dipping into savings and bringing my mother along with us. Sereena was a sport about it, promising to research the best "colourless dress stores" for my mother's shopping pleasure. But in the end, my mother convinced me she would be much happier staying home for the couple of days I'd be gone, taking care of the dogs and catching up (?) on Christmas baking. And, smarty-pants that I am, I used the situation to get Kelly out of the house by making her promise me to physically check in on my mother (not just phone calls) at least once a day.

It was the Wednesday afternoon before my trip to New York City when I gave up on the post office for the day and returned, bug-eyed and dejected to the office. As usual at this time of year, PWC was empty even though it was not yet 5:30 p.m. I was about to head upstairs when I first heard the noise. I was wrong. PWC wasn't empty.

There was someone else in the building. And that someone was in my office.

Chapter 13

THERE IT WAS AGAIN. The sound of shuffling from upstairs. Someone was definitely in my office.

I racked my brain to think of who it could be, what they were doing here and how they'd gotten into the locked PWC building. Was the intruder the Herbal Essences peeping Tom? I was not in the mood to be hairsprayed in the eyes again. Could it be the unknown stalker in the blue car?

Step by careful step, I skulkingly topped the staircase and gazed about for something to use as a weapon. My gun, as usual, was nowhere handy, but that was probably a good thing. I don't like playing with guns—unless my playmate has one too. There was nothing, no baseball bat, no heavy brick, not even an umbrella. What I did have was a three-foot tall, plastic candy cane Lilly had hung from the stair banister. A three-foot candy cane and the element of surprise.

Brandishing the faux candy treat like an axe, I slipped soundlessly across the small second floor landing to my office door. I could see a light coming from beneath it. Pretty bold move on the bad guy's behalf to be using lights. I shifted the yuletide weapon into my left hand and grasped the doorknob with my right. In one motion meant to startle, I turned, pushed, burst into the room, brandished the red and white armament in front of me and yelled out, "Hold it right there!" (a term left over from my days as a policeman...and watching too many episodes of Angie Dickinson in *Police Woman*).

And there, jumping up from a chair in alarm, was someone I knew—and the last person I expected to see.

Cheryl Guest stared at me with wide eyes. The air was heavy with her gardenia scented perfume. I decided she looked better than she had at the DGR&R Christmas party—without her hair stretched and pulled into a shape it didn't want to be in, no excess makeup attempting to hide her collection of deep wrinkles or over-the-top designer clothes on her non-designer body. She wore a light beige pantsuit, no doubt compliments of J. Thames, which nicely camouflaged her ample hips and small chest and complemented her café-au-lait tan. Her hair was combed back from her face and except for a few stray strands around her forehead, held there by a pair of tasteful diamond pins. It was a simple hairdo; almost refreshingly honest in how it revealed her face in all its age- and sun-damaged entirety.

I laid the candy cane to rest against a bookshelf and approached her. Even though she'd surprised me as much as I'd surprised her, I couldn't help feeling sorry for her; the startled look on her face some-where between tears and terror. "I'm sorry, Mrs. Guest, I thought you were an intruder. The front door was locked, the lights were off, I...I...I just thought...well, how did you get in here?"

She placed a delicate hand over her beating chest and attempted a smile. "Oh my."

Uh-huh. Not quite the answer I was looking for.

She fell back into her chair, so I went to mine, directly across from her behind my desk. I offered her coffee or water, which she declined. I stared at her tight smile.

"I apologize, Mr. Quant. In some ways I'm a compulsive person and when I make up my mind to do something I just go out and do it whether it makes sense to or not. And, particularly this...I...well, I wanted to do it...to be here...before I changed my mind. When I got here it seemed everyone had left for the day except for...Alberta? Is that her name? Anyway, I am grateful to her for allowing me to wait in your office. I think if I'd been in the waiting room...so close to the door...I would have been long gone by now."

I glanced over at my phone message machine and saw a blinking light. No doubt Alberta telling me she'd deposited a client in my office and then up and left her alone in the building. For anyone else, a bit unusual, for Alberta, not so much. "I see." At moments like this I find it best to say as little as possible and allow the other party to babble on and fill the silence.

Mrs. Guest pulled a Kleenex from her purse (which matched her outfit nicely—the purse, not the Kleenex) and dabbed both corners of her lips. She was acting and sounding like she was nervous, but there was something else about her performance I couldn't put my finger on. Her eyes were on me like honey on toast, assessing me. "I was glad to meet you at the party the other night, Mr. Quant. As I think I mentioned then, I've never met a real private detective before. I've only seen them on TV or movies or read about them. Saskatoon seems so...safe to have a need. But I guess I'm naive about that sort of thing. Sometimes when I read the newspaper in the morning I'm amazed at the goings on in certain parts of the city and realize how far removed I am from it all. You know...like the...the west end or down 20th Street. But it's mostly bad kids and the...well, the Native population, isn't it?"

I wasn't about to answer her and give credence to her obvious prejudices, racial, geographic and otherwise.

When she noticed my silence she simply nodded as if agreeing with herself and continued on. "Anyway, meeting you had an impact on me. It has pushed me to make an important decision about something I've been thinking about for a long time."

Now this was getting interesting.

"A decision that involves you, Mr. Quant. I'd like to hire you."

"Oh?" Still sticking with the "don't say much" bit.

Although her well-tended hands moved constantly from purse to lap to hair to lapel of her suit, her cocoa eyes remained steadfast on my face, anxiously searching out some kind of information she'd come here to find. "I'm afraid I don't know how this works now, Mr. Quant. You'll have to help me. I don't know what comes next. Do I make an appointment to see you again about this...this matter? Do you require a down payment or something? It's...it's...well, it's Daniel. I believe he's having an affair and I want you to find out if it's true and who she is. I have to know the truth. It's all so obvious. He's been distant for some time. But you know how it is, you probably see it all the time, the wife is the last to know…or at least the last to accept the truth. This past weekend for example. At his own office Christmas party—it was after you'd already gone, I think—he disappeared for over an hour and barely even managed a half-baked explanation as to where he was. And then the very next night he tells me he has to work late—on a Saturday—and comes home in the middle of the night. He'd gargled with Listerine but I could tell he had alcohol on his breath. And I think there was a trace of lipstick on his face!"

I almost choked on that one. Little did she know the lipstick on her husband's face was likely his own—or rather Clarissa's.

"So as you can see, I need help, Mr. Quant. I need your help. And quickly. I want to save my marriage."

Throughout her speech my mind was racing like a rabbit from a fox. I wasn't expecting her visit and I certainly wasn't expecting what she had to say. Part of my mind was feverishly composing a response to her request to hire me and the other was assessing the implication of her suspicions on my client and my case.

"I'm afraid I can't help you, Mrs. Guest."

She looked surprised, almost baffled. "D…did I do something wrong?"

"No, of course not. However, given that I know your husband and am considering using DGR&R as my accountants, I just don't feel it would be ethical at this point for me to accept the job. I'm sorry."

Her eyes narrowed and lips tightened. "Are you covering for him? Do you know about the affair? Do you know who she is?"

I felt sorry for Cheryl Guest. She was desperate. She was angry. She was trying whatever she could to find answers. And I was in a difficult position. I hate outright lying (well…sometimes), but in this case my first loyalty was to my client. "I'm sorry, Mrs. Guest, I have no information for you. I wish I could help you, but I can't."

She seemed to accept that. She rose, keeping her back stiff and straight and I followed suit.

"Then I guess I shouldn't be here. I'm sorry about all this. I'm sorry to have taken up your time," she said as she headed for the door.

I followed her and opened the door to let her out. "Not at all." I wanted to say something like "It was nice to see you again" but by then it seemed trite.

She was almost over the threshold when she turned and faced me one more time. "Will you tell Daniel about this?" It was an interesting choice of words. She wasn't asking me not to, only if I was planning to.

"Of course not." Ouch. That hurt, because I knew I was lying again. In my job a lie here and there is part of the territory. That doesn't make it any easier to do.

"Why do you do it?"

My heart stopped. Her gaze cut into me.

"What?" I asked weakly.

"Men. Why do you cheat? I've watched Daniel turn into a mess. He's not sleeping much, he doesn't eat, he pretends he's okay, but I know he isn't. Never mind what it's doing to me. Is it worth it, Mr. Quant?"

I had no answer.

Without another word, she did an about-face and marched across the small landing and descended the stairs. From over the upper floor railing I watched her progress until I saw her leave through the front door. After she was gone I returned to my desk and pulled a Great Western Light from my desk-fridge along with a mug and small container of clamato juice. I mixed the beer and clam into the frosted mug and reclined in my chair to think about what had just happened. I was relieved Cheryl Guest hadn't requested a referral for another private investigator after she learned I couldn't help her. But that didn't mean she wouldn't find someone else to do the job herself. And if she did, well, Daniel was in trouble.

Although Daniel had told me he hadn't slept with another man since receiving the blackmail note, I had no way of knowing whether he was telling me the truth. But even if it were true, I was betting Daniel still managed some sort of activity that a detective worth his or her salt could uncover, like maybe he bought gay porn magazines or parked his car in known gay cruising spots to watch the action. And if that were the case, Daniel Guest would soon be outed. Maybe the better choice was for him to come out before some PI discovered all his secrets? At least then he'd have an opportunity to control who got the information and how.

I also had to wonder, if Daniel Guest decided to come out, at least to his wife, what that would mean to my case. Would I even have one? The more I thought about it, and sipped my beer, the answer to that was probably yes. Daniel might be convinced to tell his wife about his dalliances with men, but he certainly wouldn't be keen on having everything revealed to the public in a *StarPhoenix* exclusive.

Even telling Cheryl Guest the truth had risk, other than the obvious ones to their relationship and marriage. Right now she suspected another woman, not a man (or men). What would she do knowing her husband was bisexual? Would she want to cover it up or would she want to rant and rave and tell the world just to hurt him? Both were possibilities and no matter which was true, the experience wasn't going to be a barrel of laughs for my client.

Today was the seventeenth, two days past the due date for Loverboy's payment and he'd apparently not yet gone to Cheryl Guest with his revelations. If he had, I doubted she'd have come to my office. Or she'd have been asking about an affair with a man, not another woman. So why not? Why hadn't Loverboy made a move? I knew Daniel hadn't heard anything from the blackmailer. Had Loverboy been bluffing? Had he gone running? Or was he still hoping to find the money in the mail?

I fixed myself another beer and clam. Office hours were long over so I took my drink with me downstairs to raid the kitchen for supper...I mean dinner. I found an apple, a plastic container of brown rice that looked relatively fresh and a slice of carrot cake. I knew my PWC mates wouldn't mind. Actually they counted on me to keep leftovers in the fridge from going bad. After giving the rice a quick blast in the microwave, sprinkling it with soya sauce from a plastic, take-out pouch and selecting utensils, I gathered my meal onto a tray and took it back to my office.

I decided to keep on working while I chowed down and picked up the phone.

"Kirsch," the black-bear voice answered.

"Quant," I replied, mocking his serious tone.

"Geez, Quant, it's been a few days since I last heard from you. I was beginning to think maybe you'd run off with the gay circus or something."

Ha. Ha. Not so funny. "You wish." Great witty comeback by me.

"You bet I do. But you're lucky today, I'm in a good mood, so what can I do you for?"

"What's with the good mood? Was there a double episode of *Cops* on TV last night?"

"Hilarious, Quant. Now whaddaya want? I got tonsa paper work here and it's time for me to go home. So make it quick."

"What happened to that good mood? It disappear already?" I asked, shovelling some rice into my mouth.

"You have that effect on me," he said dryly.

"Listen, I had a bit of an altercation the other night."

"That's what happens when you use outdoor parks as singles clubs."

I ignored the slur. "It just so happens I was attacked."

"Oh?" His voice was immediately alert and concerned. Despite everything, Darren is a good cop and, although I hate to admit it, probably not a bad person either. "What happened?"

"I was at home on Friday night with my mother...no smartass comments please...and she saw a peeping Tom. I chased him down the street. When I caught up with him I got sprayed in the face with something."

"Mace?"

Damn. I hoped I wouldn't have to tell him this part. "No. It smelled more like hairspray."

"Excuse me? Did you say hairspray?"

"Uh-huh."

"So your attacker was a gay hairdresser?" His voice lost its concern.

"Darren, I'm not kidding. This happened. It really scared my mother." I added for dramatic effect, "And me too."

"Okay, okay. You had a peeping Tom. Any idea who it might have been?"

"None."

"Could you describe him?"

"I'm afraid not. It all happened so fast. And it was dark out." I freed the carrot cake from its Saran wrapping and began dessert.

"Could it have been a woman?"

"What? A woman?" Sexistly I had not even considered that. "Why would you think that?"

"The hairspray. Not many men…real men…carry hairspray around with them, especially if they're planning to do some peeping rather than primping. If it was hairspray, or even if it was mace or some other such defensive spray, the chances are good your peeper was a woman. That MO just doesn't fit a man."

Darren was making sense. I should have seen it myself. And perhaps my female peeper was the same woman who showed up at the DGR&R offices asking about Daniel. But who was she? And why peep in my windows?

"You could be right." I hated giving him the compliment. "So, do you know of any female peepers in town? Any other instances of the same thing on the dockets?"

"Gee, let me search my memory of everything there is to know about crime and criminals in Saskatoon."

"Hey, you're doing better with the sarcasm."

"Good teacher. I'll check around…maybe…and don't call me like in half an hour…I'll get to it when I get to it. Don't expect anything."

"Never do."

Sereena's carry-on was smaller than mine. I couldn't figure it. How can such a high-maintenance person require so little? We were on the three-and-a-half-hour flight from Saskatoon to Toronto. From there we'd catch a connection to New York City. I don't know how it happened, but after Sereena flashed a card or two and maybe some shapely thigh, we were bumped up into Air Canada executive class—wider seats and better treats. As soon as we settled in with our champagne and orange juice, I spent my time gazing smugly at passengers embarking after us and heading for the back of the Airbus while Sereena began to accoutre herself with the necessities of *le grand voyage*. She nestled her politically correct silk-lined fake-fur coat around herself like a luxurious nest and proceeded to pull from pockets and bags and places so hidden not even Sir Edmund Hillary could find them, a selection of moisturizers—some for the face, a different kind for the hands and yet another for the fingernails—a magazine on fine art, bottled water (which I wouldn't be surprised to find was laced with vodka), a palm pilot that contained a dizzying array of personal and business information and a hardcover book about how globalization was the system replacing cold war geopolitics as the defining force in world affairs.

Landing in LaGuardia Airport after the fifty-five minute flight from Toronto was like landing in Sim City. Having seen it all before, Sereena had kindly allowed me the window seat. Everything I knew about this place I'd gleaned from movies and books and magazines. I gazed down at the countless buildings, like the pieces of several puzzles squeezed into one, and thought it was a dream city—not quite believable. As the plane descended, quiet apprehension over the appearance that we might land atop one of those buildings, gave way to ascending excitement. This was New York City! At the mouth of the Hudson River and bordering the Atlantic Ocean, here was the USA's most populous city. Downtown! Midtown! Uptown! Harlem, Chelsea, Gramercy, Tribeca. The Financial District, Garment District, Theatre District. East Village, West Village, Greenwich Village. China Town, Little Italy and Brooklyn. Laid out before us like a map of the world on a stamp-sized piece of land, each colour-coded section as distinct from its neighbours as tall buildings are from short, heavily treed parks are from concrete jungles, bohemian is from couture, and haves are from have-nots. The shopping, the museums, the shopping, the historical sights, the shopping! How could it all be in one place? Sereena reached for my hand and held it on our way down, her fingers near my quickening pulse spot, as if hoping for an infusion of a first-timer's excitement. She answered my many questions with knowledgeable precision and seemed quietly pleased with my appreciation for the behemoth below, about to swallow us like a beast of grandeur.

We made it through the airport with surprising ease and found a cab—promising an incense-free environment—to take us to our hotel. We were dropped curbside on bustling Fifth Avenue, across the street from Central Park and The Plaza Hotel and next door to The Pierre at our equally exquisite, temporary new home, The Sherry-Netherland. Sereena had insisted on "The Sherry" and supplemented my client's per diem to make it so. I stepped out of the vehicle in a daze, barely registering the driver who was attempting to free our amazing haul of luggage from where he'd bungee-corded it into his trunk. Sereena was making jovial small talk with the doorman with whom she seemed well-acquainted.

Although the air was cool, there was no snow on the ground and barely a trace of wind. Tropical by Saskatchewan December standards. I pulled in a deep whiff of city-scented air. Nothing like it on the prairies. Despite the hoo-hah about polluted city air, I always find it oddly exhilarating; city air is air that has lived. And this, the air of New York City, especially so, having swirled around masses of people doing exciting things, floated through world-class museums and theatres and restaurants, this is air breathed in and out with vigour, this is air that has tasted the money of Wall Street, the sorrow of Ground Zero, the passion of a million honeymoons and the intoxication of a thousand opening nights. I was, immediately, under its spell.

The Sherry-Netherland is an elegant building still reflecting the glory days of old-world class. The heavily gilded and chandeliered front entrance is not so much a lobby as a well-appointed check-in area with a pair of gold-doored, staffed lifts to the right and down a short hallway from a discreet front desk. According to Anthony (in training mode), unless you plan a change of clothes between the airport and hotel, you should always know your hotel and the impression you wish to make upon checking in, and select your airplane wardrobe accordingly. So, although I was sharply dressed to make my first entrance into a swanky New York City hotel, with the best accessory of all, Sereena, and though I had the strong desire to walk in like Joan Collins in an episode of *Dynasty*, I'm sure I appeared as the worst of tourist trash, stumbling along behind her like a poorly trained poodle, gawking at the muralled ceiling, priceless paintings and intricately tiled floor. And of all the glory, the most curious to me was a door. It was on the right as we entered the exclusive sanctum of The Sherry-Netherland. The door was curious because of how completely out of place it appeared in this ornate palace. It was just a door. No adornment whatsoever, just a plain old door. So plain it seemed to hope not to be noticed.

"Members-only club," Sereena commented as she swept by. "Want to slip in for a drink? And that," she nodded towards another, better-marked doorway next to it, "is Harry's. Of course we'll have dinner there one night." I later learned "Harry's" is Harry Cipriani, a supposedly famed Italian/Venetian restaurant.

"Ahhhhhh...I guess we should check in first?" I answered although she didn't seem to be waiting for it.

"Yes, yes, let's do that," she said, already at the front desk.

The woman at the counter was officious and efficient and deferred to any comment made by Sereena like a peon would to a queen. After receiving our room keys and being told our luggage had already preceded us to our suites, we were directed to Alfred, the hunched over, octogenarian elevator man who patiently awaited the pleasure of our company. We entered the golden cage and all was right with the world until, as Alfred pushed the appropriate buttons and knobs, I had the sense of being watched. And in the instant before the doors closed I thought I spotted the prying eyes of a dark-haired woman standing by the revolving doors of the hotel. She was looking right at me as if she knew me—in a city of 7.5 million strangers.

Chapter 14

WHEN THE ELEVATOR STOPPED on Sereena's floor, Alfred announced the floor, courteously held open the door with his white-gloved hand for her departure, and as she sashayed past, he said, "Good afternoon, Ms. Ashbourne." Ms. Ashbourne? I was sure I saw Sereena's three-inch heels break stride but then the door slid shut and she was gone.

"I'm sorry," I said to the old man, "but do you know my friend?"

"I know everyone who has stayed at The Sherry-Netherland during my time here—more years than I care to count," he answered pleasantly.

"But you called her Ms. Ashbourne. That's not her name."

He looked at me strangely and almost gratefully shifted away when the elevator thumped to a halt and he announced, "Sixteenth floor."

Although I should have stayed with Alfred to pursue the matter, I got off. Sereena and I had agreed to meet back in the lobby in an hour and I wanted to make a few phone calls before then.

As the door closed he said, "I was obviously mistaken, sir. My apologies."

Using the phone number given to me by his mother, I had called James Kraft before I'd left Saskatoon and set up an appointment to meet with him. Despite the attraction of the destination, I wasn't about to travel that distance on my client's dime (and some of Sereena's) without some assurance I'd get what I was going for. I'd told him I was a Canadian talent agent visiting New York and had been impressed by some of his work (which I could recite from the handy resume on the back of his photo). He seemed excited to meet. When I got to my room I tried the number again to confirm our appointment for the next afternoon but only reached his voice mail. I left a message repeating the details of our meeting and telling him where I was staying and the room number in case he needed to contact me. I then used my SaskTel calling card and dialled my home number.

"Ya, hello?"

"Mom, it's Russell."

"Oi, ees everyting alright? Vhere are you?" she sounded worried.

"I'm fine, Mom. I'm in New York. We had a good flight. Did you get home from the airport okay?" Mom had volunteered to drive us to the airport in her van. She's not overly confident with city driving, particularly in the winter and, although she seemed to do well getting us there, I was concerned about her getting back home without our navigational aid.

"Oh ya, uh-huh. I drive slow and get here."

"Oh, good. Is Kelly coming over today?"

"Ya, ya, she call. She come for supper."

"Oh good. Okay, I just wanted to check in, make sure you're okay."

"Ya, ya. You haf safe treep, I pray for you."

Back at ya.

After a quick shower to freshen up from the journey and a change into one of my "New York State of Mind" outfits, which was basically an over-priced, stretchy top with my wonderpants and a cozy leather jacket appropriate for New York winter conditions, I headed back to the elevator. When the door opened I joined a new elevator man—considerably younger and less dried out than Alfred—and a wizened gnome of a woman hidden beneath a beehive bouffant and a sumptuous chinchilla coat. The Sherry-Netherland, in addition to being a hotel, was also home to a number of owner-occupied suites and it was from one of these I guessed this interesting creature had emerged.

"Main floor," I told Hunky. His name tag said "Seth" but I preferred Hunky.

"Yap! Yap! Yap!"

I looked down at a something that could best be described as Chewbacca sperm. It's two front paws grazed my shin and its two rear paws rarely touched the ground as it hopped up and down like a furry wind-up toy on amphetamines.

"Oh, Shelby, stop flirting with the man," a voice made of gritty sauce slithered out from somewhere in between the bouffant and the chinchilla.

This was flirting? I smiled at the pile of hair and then down at its spawn. The dog kept on yipping and looking like it was about to hop into my arms and chew my nose off.

"Oh really, Shelby, such manners for a lady!" More gravel from the woman.

Under the spell of some crazed compulsion, I leaned down and reached out for Shelby. Wondrously the movement seemed to appease the dog-like thing and she shut her trap as soon as my fingers made first contact. But as my hand ran over her quivering body I could barely conceal my surprise. She was...crunchy, as if she'd been shellacked or covered in...hairspray. Her owner, in preparation for a walk in the windy park, had hairsprayed her dog's hair! I looked up at the woman's own hair and realized the styles and colour were not dissimilar.

As I straightened up the elevator came to a stop and the woman and her Mini-Me dog stepped out. As they scuttled away from us I overheard her chastise her pet, "Shelby, you are such a slut."

I looked at Hunky who appeared unfazed.

A New York moment I'd say.

Sereena was a vision in head to toe cranberry-hued leather as we made our way across Fifth Avenue at 59th in a swirl of feathery snow that had just begun to fall from a cotton-batting sky. It wasn't particularly cold out, but she'd pretended it was to rationalize a must-stop at the Plaza's Oak Bar for an Offley Port. She expertly led the way through the maze of horse-drawn carriages, movers and shakers and hawkers and gawkers that littered the area in front of the hotel. And although no less awed than the tourists outside, I tried my best not to be waylaid by the grandness of the interior of the hotel when we marched smartly through the foyer, as if we did it every day, and down a corridor or two to the unassuming entrance of the bar.

After soaking up ambiance and pricey port at the Oak Bar we buoyantly walked arm in arm to West 54th Street between Fifth and Sixth Avenues where Sereena (and The Sherry-Netherland concierge) had managed to get us a table at Aquavit, reputably the grandest of New York's Scandinavian restaurants. It claims to raise the level of eating Swedish food to an art form. And as my entire experience with Swedish food consisted of cheese fondue (or is that Swiss?) from Safeway, this was bound to be a treat for me.

After relinquishing possession of our coats, the maître d', a charming man with an unpronounceable name and matching accent, seated us at a lovely table for two near a wall of water cascading in shimmering sheets from an enormous height. In no time our server, with the very pronounceable name of Joyce, came by to chat. She was friendly and sincerely thrilled (good training) to have a New York first-timer (me) and Aquavit first-timers (both of us) in her restaurant. She was so knowledgeable about the menu and how each dish was prepared that we eventually put our fate in her hands and requested she bring us her favourites. And drinks.

Normally I wait until liquor is served before bringing up serious topics, but I couldn't stand it anymore. Except for the tree trimming party where little of substance was discussed, what with all the zoo animals in attendance, I had spoken little or not at all to my friends who were at Diva's the previous Saturday night.

"I'm worried about Anthony and Jared," I began. "I almost feel like it was my fault. If it wasn't for my client…"

"What's that? What are we talking about?" Sereena quipped back.

"Diva's…Anthony and Jared…the whole Anthony-sleeping-with-my-client thing?" I shook my head. Not much got by Sereena. I didn't know why was she playing so dense.

"They were sleeping together?"

Duh. "Sereena…you know this. You heard it too."

"They had sex, Russell, they weren't sleeping together. It wasn't an affair, was it?"

I sat silently. Sereena's eyes moved over my shoulder to someone or someones trying to attract her attention. She pasted one of her famous mirthless smiles on her face and nodded at a table of diners she obviously knew—or who knew her—and quickly returned her full attention to me. At first she said nothing, seeming to concentrate on the topic I'd brought up as if she'd only just recognized it as worthy of thought. After a few seconds of that she said, "What happened was unfortunate. Surprising to some, awkward I suppose to others. But is this a big deal, Russell?"

Of course it is! "Don't you think so?"

Her head moved slightly from right to left, her bright eyes intently resting on mine. "It had no effect on me whatsoever. Except that it prematurely ended what was a rather pleasant evening—that was unfortunate. The rest of it—well, that's none of my business." She stopped short of saying, "Or yours" and instead said, "What do you think?"

"They're friends of mine. How can it not affect me? And as a friend I should care and worry about what's going to happen next. Isn't that what friends are for?"

"Not always."

At that point Joyce returned, balancing a tray so large I'd have thought it was impossible for one human to do so. I was grateful for her appearance. I definitely needed a drink. Like a magician pulling rabbits out of a hat, Joyce revealed her enticing delicacies with a dramatic flair.

"I know you'll want wine with dinner," she said, "but first, as an aperitif you must have a Flight of Aquavit, a house specialty." She placed in front of us two small, metal-and-wood racks, each containing three glass containers that looked like test tubes brimming with different coloured liquids. "A Flight consists of three shots of Aquavit, each uniquely flavoured. My choices for you tonight are boysenberry, orange and spicy cinnamon." She then set down two bottles of Carlsberg beer. "We recommend following each shot with a beer chaser," she announced joyfully. Next she revealed two platters that looked suspiciously like slate floor tiles and positioned them on the tabletop. "This is your starter. I had the chef throw together a special smorgasbord plate of assorted Swedish delicacies and a herring plate. We have here several types of herring, gravlax with a little red beet sorbet and espresso mustard sauce; some rare, seared tuna and scallops with taro root chips and sea urchin beurre blanc; caviar osetrabeluga with potato pancakes, egg, and crème fraîche; and a selection of sauces and pastes for dipping."

We ooooed and ahhed as appropriate and asked a lot of questions about what she'd brought and eventually let her go when it seemed other customers were being slighted.

Sereena pulled a test tube from her rack and held it aloft as if it were made of the finest crystal. "First, before we continue our conversation, let's take a moment to salute how marveleous it is to be here together in one of the greatest cities in the world. Skal!"

And that is one of the reasons I love Sereena Smith—she never forgets to recognize the moment.

I repeated the Swedish toast and we downed the Aquavit. At first the unusual flavour and heavy texture of the alcohol seemed strange in my mouth. For a brief panicked moment I wondered if I would be able to keep it down. But then, just as quickly, the warmth of it engulfed me and the half-second of resistance became insatiable desire and I swallowed it hungrily, immediately wanting more. As instructed, we followed with healthy sips of beer to calm the fire on our tongues and walls of our mouths.

"Have you considered," Sereena continued as if we'd never been interrupted, "that your worry is not what you think it is?"

"What are you talking about?" I asked, even though I could hear a discordant bell ring somewhere in my head.

She gazed appreciatively at her second test tube and quaffed it, forgoing the beer. Only Sereena can play bottoms up with a test tube full of booze distilled from fermented potato and make it look as if she were sipping Dom Perignon. "You've had a schoolboy crush on Jared Lowe ever since you laid eyes on him. And you revelled in the safety of that crush. As long as he was with Anthony, he was unavailable to you. You felt you shouldn't and wouldn't and couldn't do anything about it. Oh, my dear, what a wonderful thing unrequited love can be."

"Wonderful? What's wonderful about it?" I asked, waving a piece of herring at my friend.

"Think about it. In retrospect, unrequited love is always much sweeter than the actual thing. It is innocent. It is a fairy tale. It is dreamlike. And, I'm sorry to say, it's usually a load of hogwash. But so what? If only we could enjoy it while it's happening instead of wishing it were over. Because when it is, things can never go back to the way they once were. The illusion is shattered. The fairy tale becomes reality. And reality is definitely not dreamlike." Sereena rolled a marble or two of black caviar onto a petite triangle of toast and nodded at another patron who was moving intentionally close past our table. Then she continued. "You heard Daniel's accusation against Anthony and you immediately began to think about yourself."

"I...I don't...oh hell." Was she right? Could I subconsciously have sunk that low? I had more Aquavit and beer.

"You began to wonder if the unrequited status of your relationship could possibly change. And, rightly so, that scares you. And it gives you guilt. Anthony is your oldest and dearest friend and a trusted mentor. To think that way would be treasonous, a betrayal. Maybe your worry is simply guilt."

Gulp.

Sereena waited until she'd thoroughly chewed her miniature-sized toast and added with a touch of offhandedness, "Or maybe not."

"You think...do you think something might change between Jared and Anthony...between Jared and myself?" And in my head I thought, "Between Anthony and myself?"

She laughed then, a throaty sound that I'd known at times to draw looks from others hoping to share in the atmosphere it created. "My God, Russell, how on earth would I know that? That's what makes relationships, of any kind, so difficult. They're like a crazy puzzle where every time you finally put the pieces together you get a picture different from the one you were expecting. Anyone who tells you they know what's going to happen now between Anthony and Jared and you is witless. There are no guarantees on how things will turn out. You know that, Russell."

I didn't know that. At least not as well as Sereena probably. She seldom gave details of what she'd been through in her life, but I knew her words came from experience. A lot of it.

"And then there's the matter of my mother," I added to the conversation, just to make matters even more confusing. "I think she may be considering moving in with me...well, not with me...into the room above my garage."

Joyce and a helper appeared then to clear away our floor tiles and test tubes and replace them with a fragrant and chalky Petit Chablis and the main course. The Ocean Curry of bass ceviche, lobster, tuna duck terrine and shrimp ball and a hot smoked Arctic Char arrived decoratively perched on top of four-inch thick, glass bricks. I had to wonder if someone in the kitchen was in the middle of home renovations.

"Just to let you know," Joyce cheerily informed us, "the wine is compliments of Mr. Parkridge."

Sereena wordlessly pulled a pen and small card from her purse (as if always prepared for such a moment), jotted a quick note on the card and handed it to our server, along with a five-dollar bill for her trouble. "Please give this to Mr. Parkridge the next time you see him, dear."

When Joyce departed I gave Sereena a questioning look which she chose to ignore. I knew from history to accept that response.

"Is that good news or bad news?" Sereena asked. "Your mother moving in."

I nodded thoughtfully as I mulled this over. "You know, I guess I'm not sure. With everything else going on right now, Christmas coming up, the case I'm working on, keeping Brutus for Kelly and Errall, my mother being here, I feel like I'm falling behind on my 'thinking things through' time."

"Those are bits of life, Russell, not excuses for why you're not thinking things through."

I knew she was right but I wasn't happy about it.

"You're trying to balance career and home life, you're concerned about Anthony and Jared, you're witnessing a difficult time between Errall and Kelly, you're trying to figure out the intentions of your mother. Of course it's not easy. But it's not impossible. And certainly not the worst of possible situations. You're going to be okay, Russell. I know you are. I think we'll be needing another Flight of Aquavit."

I felt like a true New Yorker (whatever that is) heading off to meet James Kraft at The Townhouse restaurant late Friday morning. I was hoofing it, alongside regular, workaday New Yorkers a little off the beaten tourist track on East 58th, coffee and pretzel in hand and without a map in sight (I did have one hidden in my jacket pocket just in case the "easy-to-navigate grid system" failed me. The pretzel, which I'd purchased from a comically surly street vendor for a couple bucks, was yeasty and salty and warm and the perfect companion on my chilly walk.

As I descended the two steps down from street level into the restaurant, I could only hope James Kraft would be there. And why wouldn't he be? Any unemployed actor living in New York City—or anywhere for that matter—would be crazy not to show up for a meeting with a talent agent. As I shooed a few flakes of snow off my shoulders, I noticed a sign instructing would-be diners of the dress code—no hats, workout clothes, sleeveless shirts, cut-offs or torn clothing of any type. I was good to go. I had chosen The Townhouse because Anthony and Jared mentioned it as one of their favourite places, describing it as a "gay version of '21' where discerning and discreet gentlemen meet." It had to be worth a look.

My first thought as I stepped into the room was that this was where beige had gone to die. Beige floors, walls, table linens. Was I in the right place? Gay people came here? The restaurant was actually a series of rooms, end to end. The first consisted of a twelve-seat bar and long, narrow booth seating against two walls with beige chairs opposing and a few small tables in between. The adjoining rooms were similar but without the bar. I walked through the lounge past a collection of already soused middle-aged regulars of the pink-shirt-and-ascot variety. They were lined atop a row of stools that creaked noisily (both the stools and the regulars) as they swivelled to cast not-very-subtle glances in my direction. I felt like a prize Jersey at auction. A surprisingly lovely sensation. Beyond the bar I could see tables of mostly mixed couples, many a little long in the tooth, and even though it was only lunchtime on a Friday, many of them were enjoying cocktails or sharing a bottle of wine. Again I wondered if I was in the right place. But what did I expect? A scene from *Queer As Folk* or Sodom and Gomorrah with chintz and a brunch special?

Just as a pixie-faced youth came over to greet me with menus in hand, I spotted James Kraft. The publicity picture I'd gotten from

Persephone Theatre and Daniel's description told me exactly what to look for. And there he was, in his full youthful, blond, blue-eyed, gap-toothed splendour. He'd obviously taken some care in grooming for our meeting. His shoulder-length hair (which Daniel had said was messy) had been combed back off his face into a tight ponytail that sat obediently at the nape of his long neck. He was wearing a conservative striped shirt, buttoned to the neck and a pair of olive-coloured khakis. His Sunday best. He was a beautiful kid, no doubt about it. I indicated to Pixie Face that I saw my party and he motioned for me to go ahead with a flirtatious wink that was probably more out of habit than real intent.

Like a seasoned businessman James Kraft stood and held out his hand when I approached the table. "It's a pleasure to meet you, Mr. Quant," he said eloquently. "I'm James Kraft."

We shared a firm handshake, exchanged further pleasantries and sat down. As soon as we had, our waiter appeared offering drinks, menu suggestions and more flirty winks (none of which were free). We both ordered iced tea and I asked for the pea soup and mussels while James requested fried calamari and Caesar salad.

"How are you enjoying New York?" James asked. "Is it your first time here? I'd be happy to give you some suggestions of things to do or even show you around a bit if you'd like."

Boy, he really wanted whatever it was I was supposedly offering! I was going to hate disappointing him, especially after he was being so charming. I decided it was best to get it over with right up front.

"James, I'm not a talent agent. I'm a private investigator from Saskatoon. I work for Daniel Guest and I know you're blackmailing him." I had also decided to do a bit of bluffing and see what happened.

The young actor was momentarily speechless. He stared at me; his blue eyes registering something that wasn't quite surprise or even worry. It was more like...curiosity.

"Really?" he finally said. "A real private eye?"

"Yes."

"Is this some kind of joke?"

"Nope."

The waiter brought our drinks and we both smiled and said thanks as if we were having a normal, pleasant, everyday type of conversation.

"You're really from Saskatoon?"

"Uh-huh."

"What province is it in?"

"Saskatchewan."

"Spell it."

I did. Flawlessly.

"Why is there a big tent by the river in the summer?"

"Shakespeare on the Saskatchewan Festival."

"What is Wanuskewin?"

"A First Nations' Heritage Park."

"What slogan is on the Saskatchewan licence plate?"

"Land of Living Skies."

He asked two or three more rapid-fire questions until he seemed satisfied that I was indeed from his hometown. Then he sat back in his chair and stared at me again, letting his eyes rove freely over my face and upper torso. He seemed undisturbed by the silence.

"What was the other stuff you said?" he finally asked. "Something about blackmail?"

"I know you are blackmailing Daniel Guest. And I'm here to make you stop."

The corners of his mouth turned up into a wry smile, displaying a beguiling gap of tooth. "And how do you intend to do that?"

Was he admitting to being the blackmailer? To being Loverboy? Did I have him? My plan was to reveal, without doubt, that James Kraft was Loverboy. Once I'd done that I'd deal with him appropriately. But it was the "without doubt" part that I was still unsure about.

"My client is willing to make one small payment." I didn't say how much. I didn't talk about the fact that the due date for the original $50,000 demand had come and gone. "But that's it. If that is not sufficient, or if you ever demand more, we go straight to the police."

"Why not go to the police now?"

This was a suspicious question. If he was Loverboy, he wouldn't have to ask it.

"Are you Loverboy?"

He laughed now. "Loverboy? Well I guess that depends on who you ask." Now it was his turn to wink. "Maybe you'd like to find out?" His smile was part lascivious, part sweet, part mischievous. Undeniably bewitching.

"Have you been blackmailing Daniel Guest?"

He slowly shook his head, still smiling at me as if he were having two conversations at the same time, one with his smile—a private one between he and I, and another with his voice—a public one dealing with the boring other matter at hand. "I don't even know who that is," he said.

Liar!

Got you.

Chapter 15

I NOW KNEW JAMES KRAFT WAS A LIAR. Now—was he a blackmailer too?

I leaned closer and lowered my voice. "Daniel Guest says the two of you had sex a couple of months ago. In October. You met in a chat room, he invited you over, you arrived on your bicycle and you had sex together. Ring any bells?"

James's eyes squinted as he obviously recalled the interlude. "Ohhhhhhh...him. I never knew his name. Daniel, huh? He was a nice guy. We had fun."

"Are you telling me you are not blackmailing him?"

"Blackmailing him about what?"

I studied the face before me, searching for signs of deception or insincerity, not sure if I saw either.

"We had a good time," he said with ease. "That was it. It was fun. What would I blackmail him about? I'm an old-fashioned guy, Mr. Quant, I generally don't blackmail someone after I have sex with them." Now he leaned closer too so that our faces were less than a foot apart. "If you and I spent some time together, you'd find that out."

"Hey lovers," the waiter announced as he shoved plates of food between us. "Time to eat." He seemed offended that we were paying more attention to each other than to him.

We smiled gratefully and sat up straight in our seats.

"I tend to like guys a little older than you," James told me as he popped a golden ring of squid into his mouth, "but I'm thinking it's time to make an exception."

I sipped at my soup and tried to look elsewhere. Based on the two men I knew about, Daniel and Marc Driediger, James's attraction to older guys was bona fide. I was about a decade older than James was, but I couldn't decide whether he knew that and was playing with me or not. Regardless, I couldn't help a smile. "That's not what we're here to discuss."

"Okay, okay, Mr. Private Dick, suppose I am the blackmailer, what's the offer? How much money are we talking about?"

I felt my spine stiffen. Was this it? The shakedown? Was he finally tired of the game? Did he know the $50,000 was late and wanted to see how much he could negotiate for? Or was this a trick?

"What's to stop me from taking the money and running? Even if I'm not the blackmailer. How could you prove I am or not?" Good question. "And I am a starving actor after all. I could use the cash, no matter how much it is."

"Well, you see," I said, "there's a skill-testing question."

Another squid entered his mouth. His lips shone fetchingly with a fine layer of grease. "Okay, lay it on me."

"What did the blackmail note say?"

James's face became serious. He laid down his fork and looked to his right and to his left, as if taking a quick poll of whether anyone could hear our conversation. He made a deliberate show of finishing chewing his food and swallowing before reaching into a pocket and pulling out a pen. He searched for something to write on and finally settled on the white paper napkin sitting under his iced tea. He wrote on it, folded it over once and handed it to me with a somber look on his face. This was it. Despite all the playful banter back and forth James Kraft was about to reveal his true self. I had to admit, he had me puzzled. This was a young man who played sweetness to the hilt, but underneath the candy coating could very well be a criminal with sour intent. Above all, this young man was a survivor. And he needed money to survive in New York City. I didn't think Daddy was giving him any. So, blackmail might not be out of the question.

I pulled the napkin to me. I gave him one last look. His face revealed nothing. I flipped open the napkin. In neat block letters he'd printed, "Will you go out with me, Mr. Quant?"

I looked up from the napkin to the gap-toothed grinning face of my lunch companion. I shook my head and went in search of mussels amongst the steaming shells in the bowl in front of me.

A pretty New York City actor had a crush on me. But I had to maintain a professional distance. So when he offered, after our meals were done, to show me around town, I regretfully declined. He told me where he'd be "partying" later that night, just in case I changed my mind. I promised nothing, left money to cover the bill and left him at The Townhouse smiling bedazzlingly at me.

Sereena was spending the day catching up with acquaintances at restaurants, bars and shopping plazas from one end of the island to the other, so I had some time on my own. After a quick stop at the hotel to pick up an extra sweater and a warmer pair of gloves, I set out to discover the Big Apple, or at least a tiny slice of it.

The first thing I did was poke my nose into Central Park, the south end of which was directly across the street from our hotel, but decided it was too big and the weather too cold for a day in the park. I looked longingly at the Plaza but knew that as wonderful as it might be to spend a lazy afternoon inside the warm and cozy Oak Bar, I had places to see.

I re-crossed the street and headed into FAO Schwarz—the mother of all toy stores. The atmosphere enveloped me like a 1950s' holiday movie. Next to this, Toys"R"Us would look like an understocked discount outlet. The place was streaming with holiday shoppers in brightly coloured coats, hats and scarves. Traditional carols fa-la-laed us into jubilant moods. And it was there—on the lower level of FAO Schwarz, as I contemplated which country King Wenceslas was such a good king of—that I caught sight of her behind a mountainous display of board games.

At first I thought she was one of those someones who looks annoyingly familiar but you can't quite figure out whom they remind you of. But then I realized that wasn't the case at all. She looked familiar because I'd seen her before, glaring at Sereena and me, when we got on the elevator in our hotel only the day before. I dashed round the towering heap of merchandise, but she was gone. I headed upstairs and wandered into the educational toy area. There were only six shopping days left until Christmas. I was in the best toy store in the world. And I did have nieces and nephews. With lightning-quick mental prowess I connected these random thoughts. I quickly selected five or six items meant for varying ages and sexes (I'd get it right in the mix) and got in line to pay. As I stood there, I caught sight of my stalker once again, this time on the other side of a cheerfully decorated display window. She was outside on the sidewalk looking in at me. She was short, dark-haired and had on this massive coat: one of those arctic parka type things with fur rimming the hood and multi-coloured embroidery encircling the cuffs and bottom hem. Not too chic. But she didn't look like she particularly cared. With what I had decided were beady eyes—perhaps even steely—she burned a hole through the candy-cane-coated glass and right into me. But when she noticed me noticing her she quickly scurried off. I debated dropping my merchandise and taking chase, but decided it wasn't worth it. She'd be long gone before I got to the street.

After making my purchases I continued down Fifth Avenue where between 50th and 58th I paid homage to the mystical procession of some of the grandest retail establishments in the world. Beginning at Saks Fifth Avenue and ending at Bergdorf Goodman, I went forth and gaily partook of their wares. Weighed down by packages but high on adrenaline, I schlepped south, making a slight detour to 6th to see Radio City Music Hall and further down to one of the most famous public areas in North America, the Rockefeller Center. Although I was disappointed at how small (by Canadian hockey-rink-on-every-corner standards) the ice-skating rink is, the Christmas tree perched above it made up for it. And there, continually insistent on ruining my burgeoning yuletide spirit, three quarters of the way down one side of the walkway bordering the rink, and standing behind someone who looked amazingly like Tony Bennett, was *that woman*. I'd had enough. It was time to go a-wassailling on her ass! I tightened my grip on my colourful bags filled with fetchingly wrapped goodies and started after her. She did a double take and headed in the opposite direction almost knocking over Aretha Franklin, Pat Boone and his daughter Debbie (of "You Light Up My Life" fame). Well, it could have been them. This *was* New York City after all.

As I undertook this crazy pursuit, jockeying down the streets of a totally unfamiliar city, carrying seven armloads of Christmas presents that were getting heavier and less desirable by the minute, I wondered again who this woman might be and whether she was dangerous. Was it a coincidence that she began following me immediately after my lunch with James Kraft? Was he more sinister and better connected than I'd given him credit for? Was my accusing him of being Loverboy a big mistake? Had he put a hit out on me? On the other hand, if this was the same woman I'd seen in our hotel the day before I even met James Kraft, that theory didn't hold water. So then who was she? Who in New York City would have reason to set a tail on me?

Parka Woman circled back onto Fifth Avenue and kept on trucking south towards 42nd Street where she turned right before the New York Public Library, passing Bryant Park with its charming bistro tables, merry-go-round and imprisoned typewriters. I knew Grand Central Station and the Empire State Building were somewhere nearby too but I didn't see either.

A couple of blocks later she turned right again onto Broadway Avenue. She was no dummy. She was undoubtedly accustomed to the amazing sights to be seen on this world-renowned street. I, however, was literally agog.

Dorothy was no longer in Kansas.

Broadway is a paradise of sorts. Even in the light of day it shines with the brilliance of newly coined money. Like a photograph enlarged for a closer look, the proportions are larger than life-size. Any of the buildings plopped down into any other city, large or small, would look to be a dinosaur amongst pygmies. Broadway Avenue itself isn't about the theatres. Most of the theatres are actually half a block or more off Broadway on one of the side streets. Broadway Avenue is all about the signs. They are everywhere, they are big, they are bright, they are in-your-face, they are like billboards falling from heaven, advertising all the world has to offer.

And it's about the people. Crowds of people moving at high speeds in every direction like ants escaping a shot of Raid. And not just tourists and not just fashion models and not just artsy-type actors and their nebbishy agents, but rather a swirling mixture of all human subtypes from the society madam to the mohawked skateboarder. The one thing they all have in common? They move fast.

Parka Woman was looking to lose me. And she knew just how to do it. She led me to Times Square. I swear I looked up for only a moment, distracted by movie, television and singing stars, beckoning me from a menagerie of signs on high, to see their career-rejuvenating turns in *The Naked Producer from Chicago on a Hot Tin Can of Hairspray*. When I looked back down…she was gone. And all the while I was still moving forward, propelled by the momentum of the crowd. I tried to stop, get my bearings, find the only parka with fur and embroidered trimming in New York City, but to no avail. It was hopeless.

For a while I wondered what would happen if I allowed the wave of people to carry me. Where would it eventually deposit me? Or would it? Maybe we'd move along together forever. I fought off an uncharacteristic shot of panic. With a brisk and purposeful pace, I was able to regain control of my own destiny (and destination). I knew however that if I ever gave it up, even for a moment to debate which way to go, I'd be sucked back into the maelstrom and end up transported several blocks past where I wanted to be. Wherever that was.

At 57th Street I caught a break in the human train and veered off Broadway. By this point I was so weary from carrying my shopping bags, each of which had somehow turned into cast iron, I barely stopped to examine Carnegie Hall. I thought about hailing a cab but I could sense I was close to Fifth Avenue and managed to trudge along until I saw The Sherry-Netherland sign. No sweeter sight.

After my strenuous afternoon, jockeying about Manhattan chasing the elusive Parka Woman, I was happy to start our evening close to home at the hotel's restaurant, Harry Cipriani. That decision made, there was only one question left to answer. Perhaps the biggest question of all when dining in New York City. Do you eat before the theatre or after the theatre? The "in" crowd eats after—a more likely time to catch sight of a star (if you aren't one yourself)—but by the time your play has ended and you've made it to your restaurant of choice (if you can even get a reservation) it can be close to midnight. And *then* you start eating? Who are these people? They must not get home until 2 a.m. Don't they have jobs to go to in the morning? Sereena informed me that it was absolutely respectable to eat prior to a show and that's just what we did. Besides, I had already spotted Pat Boone and daughter Debbie. What more could I hope for?

Although not a landmark establishment, I quickly realized that Harry Cipriani has its own "in" crowd. And with Sereena on my arm, I was part of it. Cipriani's was created in the image and atmosphere of some place called Harry's Bar in Venice, Italy. I'd never heard of it, but if the replication was genuine then it too has delicious Italian fare and delicious Italian men who greet you at the door in a rough and brutish maître d' sort of way.

A big man named Mario who, with an inexplicable glint of recognition and complicity in his eye, addressed Sereena as "my dear and lovely, Missus Smith," boisterously welcomed us. He was a fully maned lion in heat, six-foot-three and simmering with nearly unrestrained sensuality. He looked comfortable in his black tuxedo but you could easily imagine him chopping up hunks of red meat in a butcher's shop. Sereena did her part, wearing a creamy white piece of clingy material that hung off her shoulders by way of strings of sparkling, multi-coloured gems, and was cut extremely low in front and even lower in back. Her hair was dramatically pulled away from her face, proudly showing off the signs of life that lived there, including a tiny scar at the apex of her chin. Women, men, staff and guests alike stared at her when she entered the room and for some time afterwards. My new suede jacket barely registered—though I'm quite certain more than a few eyes looked covetously at my wonderpants.

After we were seated in the centre of one of the two main dining areas—better for all to feast on the dish called Sereena—I began to notice a certain well-designed regimen, a play of sorts, acted to perfection by the Harry Cipriani people. Immediately following our arrival a group of six arrived. They were obviously well-known to the maître d', for he flirted with the women in a most obvious and lascivious way and with the men he alternated between hearty back slaps, whispering something into their ears, and slipping something (who knows what—cigars maybe?) into their breast pockets. He then made a cacophonous production of showing them to one of the many "best tables in the house" and yelling for a server (of equally hirsute and husky proportions) to shower them with attention, but only after convincing them to begin with an impossibly, excruciatingly perfect bottle of red. And that wasn't the end of it, for throughout the evening this roughhewn host would often return to the table as if he'd only just caught sight of the group and would fawn at their sides with exaggerated solicitude.

The next diners to arrive, two men and two women, although equally spiffed up for a night on the town and looking as if it'd been a while since they'd set foot in a Burger King, received a much different treatment. The host was not familiar with them and, although amazingly charming, he was reserved compared to his earlier behaviour (although both seemed quite sincere). He asked a few pointed questions to determine their intentions towards his restaurant and the evening, expertly categorized them in an instant (tacky tourists, show goers, wannabes, money spenders, no-fun-nics) and then seated them accordingly (in a quiet corner in the room next to ours).

Our meal sounded like standard fare, veal and pasta, but tasted gloriously unlike anything I had ever eaten before. I ate ravenously between furtive glances about, checking for Parka Woman. Sereena did little more than look at the repast, busy as she was being flattered and courted by most of the men in the place. Afterwards we donned our coats and caught a cab arranged by our gracious host. Minutes later we were at the St. James Theatre for the 8 p.m. performance of *The Producers*. Although Sereena didn't roll in the aisles with laughter with the rest of us, she certainly cracked a smile or two.

There are probably a million (small-town-boy exaggeration) gay bars and restaurants in New York City but it seemed my experience wasn't going to be that varied. The Townhouse nightclub is only a short walk from the restaurant of the same name where I'd met James earlier for lunch. Before we'd parted he'd told me he'd be at the club waiting for me. I had offered no promises, but now, buoyed by the excitement of being in New York City on a Friday night, fresh from excellent entertainment, food and drink, I'd decided to find what there was to find. Besides, I assured myself, this was work. I had to make certain James Kraft was not Loverboy and hadn't sent Parka Woman to follow me.

Leaving Sereena with some friends at a champagne bar called Flute, I caught a cab to The Townhouse. After being deposited on a dark street I found and scooted up a set of stairs that took me into the bar. Upon entering I hesitated for a moment to take in the scene. I was Neil Armstrong landing on the moon. One small step for gay man, one giant leap for gay mankind from Saskatoon. Inside was an unusual combination of gay nightclub and sedate Boston fern bar. The space was long and narrow and divided into several distinct areas like the restaurant, but unlike the restaurant it was crowded and noisy. Gazing down the tunnel where I stood to the farthest corners of the bar was like looking through a rotating kaleidoscope, the swirling mass of men like so many pieces of colourful glass and paper constantly moving and changing shape as they flitted about their playground. And I wanted to play.

I initially moved through the collection of partiers with ease but found the going rougher with each successive room, the noise growing louder, the writhing more pronounced, until finally I reached the last room where suddenly, as if protected by some invisible barrier, the din disappeared. And there I found James, sitting on a stool next to a small table situated under a painting of a hunting dog and hunter. He was nursing a beer and listening to a piano player who was maybe in his early twenties but singing standards in a voice that was three times his age. I gave the sedate room a once over and noticed that most couples were of the old-rich-guy-in-shirt-and-tie (and in a few unfortunate cases a smoking jacket) and very-young-guy-in-tight-jeans-and-T-shirt variety. I scored a beer from a goateed bartender and approached James. He was wearing tight jeans and a T-shirt. His hair, now released from ponytail bondage was a glorious blond tangle around his surprisingly patrician, aristocratic-looking face. He might have been a Roman emperor surveying his gladiators or a young prince assessing his subjects. When I slid onto the chair next to him he gave me a sly sidelong look and easily slipped his left hand into my right and continued to focus on the music. The simple gesture was astoundingly seductive. I reacted inside as if I'd just been presented

Jeff Stryker on a platter. No, strike that, I wouldn't know what to do with a porn star. I made a show of being at ease and pretending to listen to the piano player but really I was studying the compelling features of James' profile and quelling the butterflies in my stomach.

Finally when the set was done James turned to me with a warm smile and said, "You met my parents."

"What?" I sputtered.

"You're the guy who showed up at their place last week saying you were an old friend of mine. My mother gave you my phone number. That's how you found me."

There was no use in lying to him. Obviously one of his parents, probably his mother, had told him about my visit and he'd put two and two together since we'd met that afternoon. I nodded.

"Do you know how I knew it was you?"

I shrugged. I could feel his index finger slowly running up and down the top of my hand. It made me shiver and my mouth went dry.

"Because she told me the man who visited was very handsome." And then, without further preamble, he leaned over and gave me a light kiss on the cheek. Before he pulled back I heard a pull of air as he stole a gentle whiff of my skin. "It had to be you," he murmured. He sat back and let his eyes caress me. This man was inexplicably beguiling, far beyond his years. "I'd like to kiss you, Russell," he said.

I swallowed hard. "I think you just did," I said.

His head shook so slightly it would have been easy to miss. "Not like that. I'd like to kiss you on the lips. In private."

I was flattered. I was horny. I was weak in the knees. But I was also thirty-two years old and knew how I'd feel in the morning if I let my hormones overrule my professional goal in this situation. So I over-compensated. "My offer still holds," I said.

If only I hadn't said that right then. Or in that way.

"Offer?"

"Money, James. My client is willing to offer a great deal of money to put this business behind him."

I could see the hurt building in his eyes as certainly as snow gathers on a doorstep during a blizzard. And no amount of shovelling was going to stop it now. He didn't say anything. He first looked away, then back at me, then away. He withdrew his hand from mine, slid off his stool and left The Townhouse bar.

Nice one, Quant.

The several blocks back to the hotel were as cold and miserable as any December night in Saskatchewan, heavy on the miserable. But truth be told, it wasn't so much the temperature or biting wind as it was how much I felt like the biggest louse in the world. My Friday night in the big city had not ended up the way I'd planned. It had come close, but as if on purpose, I screwed it up. But did I have a choice? If James had been anyone other than a suspect in a case I was working on, perhaps I'd have been in a much warmer place. Instead, since James Kraft had a crush on me, I turned around and crushed him. What a guy. But what if James *was* Loverboy? He was an actor after all. How hard would it be for him to put on an act in order to distract me from my real purpose? Someone who was capable of blackmail was certainly capable of trouncing on my feelings to protect themselves. The problem was, I didn't know which was the accurate scenario. In my heart I felt James Kraft was innocent, but was my heart the best judge when it came to an attractive man? Especially an attractive man who found me attractive too. Had I failed? Had I come all this way and failed in what I'd set out to do? Was my inexperience as a private detective beginning to show?

Sure, I had found out the identity of Jo and tracked him to New York, but then, my options were limited. What would have been the best way to find out if he was the blackmailer? I'd tried to bluff the information out of him. The trouble with a bluff is that you can never be one-hundred-percent certain whether or not the bluff worked if the bluffee is actually innocent. Perhaps I should have found a way to be invited to James' apartment—to find some incriminating evidence. Whatever that would be.

I let the elevator man take me to my floor without exchanging more than a few words. I was not in a chatty mood. By the time I reached my door I was seriously considering calling James. I didn't care that it was after midnight. There was something about him…the way he ran his finger over the back of my hand. I shivered again at the thought. What was happening to me? I would call him. I just had to. It would make me feel immeasurably better. But as soon as I entered my room and closed the door behind me, I felt much worse.

The attack was quick and brutal and wholly unexpected.

I was thumped to the ground with surprising speed and force. The right side of my face scraped against carpet and I felt an agonizing burn. Before I had a chance to react, my assailant grabbed my wrist and wrenched my right arm behind my back and pushed it up with one knee while the other knee pressed into my lower back.

Pain receptors began to fire all over my body.

I wondered if I would survive.

Chapter 16

ONCE THE INITIAL SHOCK WORE OFF, I realized that whoever was on my back wasn't very heavy. Probably a woman or small man. I also realized that when I stopped struggling, he or she stopped pushing and pulling my body parts in every conceivable way that could possibly cause me pain. So I did.

"Who are you?" I asked. The right side of my head was squished against the carpet so the words came out like I was speaking through guppy lips.

"Never mind." A woman.

We remained in that awkward position, my right arm pinned between my back and her torso, for another few seconds. I knew that with not much effort I could probably just stand up—but I didn't know whether she had a weapon (other than her pseudo-brute force). I didn't think so, or else why would she have jumped me?

I had to give her credit though. If this was who I thought it was—Parka Woman—then she had a lot of balls to think her five-foot-nothing frame could keep me nailed to the floor. Even though she'd only said two words thus far, I could tell from the tone of her voice that she was flustered. I had probably surprised her as much as she had surprised me. I would bet her intent had been to get a look around my room—not to confront and attack me. She hadn't expected me back so soon, but when she heard me coming she'd had little choice. It was take or be taken. Unfortunately for her I probably had sixty pounds and over a foot on her. She didn't stand a chance in a hand-to-hand battle. I could just sit on her (not unlike what she was doing to me now). I imagined she knew it too. I almost smiled as I thought about her sitting up there slowly coming to the grim realization that she was a dachshund trying to take down a St. Bernard. That's why she didn't want to talk. She was dancing as fast as she could, trying to decide how to get out of this without damage to her physical being or pride. As for me, I saw the situation as a temporary advantage. As long as she wasn't yanking on my arm too much I wasn't in any particular discomfort other than a smarting cheek. And from this position I'd get more information out of her than if I was chasing her down a hotel stairway. So I tried again.

"Who are you?"

"Would you shut up already?" Her voice was feminine but more deep and strong than soft and high. "What are you doing here, Mr. Quant?" I could hear some hesitation as if she were wondering why I wasn't fighting back or if maybe I was too stupid to think I could.

"So you know my name," I pointed out the obvious. "Why are you following me?"

"What are you talking about?"

Oh puh-lease. "I know you've been following me. First here at the hotel, FAO Schwartz, then Rockefeller Center. And certainly you haven't forgotten our little foot race down Broadway Avenue?"

"Yeah well, maybe you're seeing things. I've never been to Rocketfellow Center."

My ears pricked up. Rocketfellow Center? Rocket-fellow? Certainly no New Yorker would call it Rocketfellow Center. Who *was* this woman? Where was she from?

"I want to know what you're doing in New York City, bub. Are you here alone? Are you meeting someone? And who's the fancy broad?"

She'd obviously seen me with Sereena. I didn't think most women liked the term "broad"—but obviously my attacker was not most women. "What are you talking about?" I thought I'd use her own line against her. See how she liked it.

"Shit!"

"What?"

"You made me tear my parka!"

"I…?" I couldn't believe what I'd just heard. "I *made* you tear it? Like I asked you to lay in wait in my hotel room and jump me from behind like a wild hyena!"

I don't know where the hyena thing came from but it did the job.

"Hyena! Who the fuck are you calling a hyena? Just because I don't have a twenty-two inch waist? You sexist pig-dog bastard!"

She tightened her grip on my arm and pushed it a little further up my back. I grunted accordingly like the pig-dog bastard I was.

"I want to know why you're here in New York City!"

"I'm doing my Christmas shopping."

"Don't be a smartass!" She said with growing frustration. How did she know? "We're on to you, bub, so just spill it."

We? Hmm. I turned my face as much to the left as I could and strained my eyes in that direction to get a look at the woman on my back. She leaned away so I couldn't see her face. I'd had enough with playing prisoner. I said frankly, "I think I'm going to get up now."

The chuckle surprised me. Her too, I think. But she knew she couldn't keep me down unless she had a couple friends helping her. She released my arm and crawled off my back. I half expected her to run, but she didn't. I rolled over onto my back and she was holding out her hand. I grabbed onto it and let her pull me up. As I'd guessed, it was Parka Woman. Up close she was prettier than I remembered, but she still had the look in her eye of a WWF wrestler and an untrusting set to her jaw. Despite a diminutive stature, this was someone who wasn't used to letting people get the best of her.

After helping me up she began fussing with the tear on her parka sleeve and her hair which had gotten dishevelled during our tussle.

I reached over to switch on the light so we weren't standing in dimness. "You know who I am," I said. "Now will you tell me who you are?"

She stopped playing with her sleeve and gave me a baleful look. "I'm Jane Cross."

"You're not from here, are you?"

"Regina."

"Saskatchewan?"

"Do you know of another one?" she asked, presenting a snarly attitude that I thought was mostly a bluff.

"Well, actually I do. Are you telling me you followed me all the way from Saskatchewan to New York City?"

"I ain't telling you nothing, bub. Not until you tell me a thing or two."

I wished she'd stop calling me bub. "Like what?"

"Like why are you here? I'm not buying this 'shop 'til you drop' bullshit. Although God knows you've done enough of that!"

Aha! "How would you know that if you weren't following me?"

She tried an Elvis lip curl. "Is there any store in this goddamned city you didn't go into? You're such a woman."

"Now who's a sexist pig-dog bastard?" And since I'd scored what I felt was a winning blow in that particular discourse, I decided a little bit of truth might not hurt as a segue into a more useful conversation. "I'm a private investigator and I'm in New York working on a case."

That seemed to shut her up for a few seconds.

"You're on a case?"

Interesting. She didn't seem surprised to learn I was a detective, but she was surprised I was here on a case. She'd obviously done her work on who I was. What she didn't know was what I was doing. "Uh-huh."

"I'm a private investigator too." She admitted slowly as if she was paying more attention to something in her head than to what she was saying. But after a second she shook it off and asked, "What case are you working on? Who's your client?"

"If you're really a private detective, you know I won't tell you who my client is, but I will tell you the case I'm working on involves blackmail. I'm here investigating a suspect."

"Blackmail?" Her face looked as if she was working on a particularly hard arithmetic problem. I imagined sprockets and coils whizzing and whirring in her head as she tried to figure out what was going on—and whether I was telling the truth.

"What about you? Who is your client? What case are you working on?"

She frowned at me, looking a little bit like a garden gargoyle. "That's none of your beeswax."

Ah. Nothing like some good old give and take and fair play and all that. "Look," I said, "I think we need to share a little more information or we're never gonna get anywhere."

She thought about this for a moment and obviously agreed—sort of. She began, "I'm not going to tell you who my client is either, but…well, for your own sake so you don't go chasing your tail for too long, why I'm here has nothing to do with no blackmail." She raised an unplucked eyebrow high on her forehead and finished off with, "You sure you're not here for some other reason?"

Huh? "Huh? Like what?"

"Okay, never mind," she said, sounding a bit prickly.

I tried disarming her with a smile. Didn't work. "Jane, I think there's been a big mistake here."

She didn't look any friendlier, but her head was slowly bobbing up and down. "I'm beginning to think that myself."

For a moment we were mute. The air was electric with uncertainty and mistrust. I was sure that if I touched her I'd get a shock. Although our instincts were telling us that if only we'd talk we'd figure out some important stuff, they also told us to keep our backs up like barnyard cats.

"Who's the dame?"

Gawd! Was she channelling Mickey Spillane or something?

"If I answer a question will you answer one?"

"No promises, bub."

"The dame is Sereena Smith, a good friend of mine." And for the first time another thought hit me. Was this not about me or my case at all? Could this be about Sereena? Suddenly I was sorry I gave away her name. "Why do you want to know?"

"Next question."

I took a stab. "Do you drive a blue car?"

She stepped back and stared at me in a way that told me I had guessed correctly.

"What kind of hairspray do you use?" I asked, not too friendly like.

She took another step away and gave me a "whaddaya talking about?" look.

"It was you who hairsprayed me in the face, wasn't it? You're the peeping Tom!"

She pursed her lips and looked at something, anything, over my shoulder. It *was* her! I tried not to get too mad. The one good thing she had going for her was that I was in the same line of work as her and could understand the possible need to hairspray someone's face better than the next guy.

"What about the landfill? Was that you too?"

She held up her hands in mock surrender. "Hey, I know nothin' about no landfill. You can't lay that on me."

I wasn't in the mood to trust anything she was telling me. "You've been tailing me for…how long now? A week? More? What are you looking for? Who hired you?"

She glared at me but didn't utter a word.

"You haven't found whatever it is you're looking for…so that's why you followed me here!" The words came spilling out of my mouth as quickly as I could think of them. "You probably thought this was your first big break in the case. You thought I'd become careless once I was away from Saskatoon. I'd never suspect you were behind me. In time you'd catch me at whatever it is you and your client expect I'm doing! Wow, this is very Jane Bond double-oh-seven of you."

"Are you making fun of me?"

I said nothing.

"Are you making fun of me, bub?"

Oh, oh, I was a bub again. And each time she repeated the phrase she got angrier and a small vein began to pulse at her temple.

"Don't blow a gasket, Jane, I'm just pointing out the obvious. Whatever your client is looking for, they're wrong. There's been a mistake. You have nothing."

"I can't fucking believe this!" Jane began pacing the room, shaking her head like a wet dog fresh from a bath.

"You know I'm right." I was just blowing smoke, I didn't really know what I was talking about but Jane's reactions seemed to be telling me I was on the right track. There had been some mistake. She had made the trip for nothing.

"And that makes you some kind of hero?" she spit out.

I knew she was mad at the situation, not me—well not much at me. I wanted to cool her down. Despite everything, I kind of liked this little spitfire. "C'mon, why don't I see what sort of drinks I can find in the mini bar and we talk this over? Besides, how unlikely is it that two private eyes from Saskatchewan find themselves pitted against each other in a New York City hotel room?"

"About as unlikely as me having a drink with you! I'll catch you later, Russell Quant." She turned on her heel and headed out the door.

"Later, Jane Cross."

She grumbled an inventively abusive turn of phrase and was gone.

After helping myself to that mini-bar drink, a shot of whiskey, I plopped down into a club chair and tried to put together the pieces of my night. James Kraft. Jane Cross. Sereena Smith. Related? Unrelated? Was I in some spinning vortex of confusion from which I'd wake tomorrow morning? Hoped so. After several fruitless minutes I noticed a red light on my phone blinking. Message. With barely the strength of a Raggedy Andy doll left in me, I pulled my body up from the chair and allowed it to topple onto the bed (without spilling a drop of my drink) from where I could reach the telephone. I pulled the handset to my ear and pushed the button.

"Russell? It's James," the recorded message began.

My heart did an involuntary leap. Why did it do that? Stop it, Russell.

"I just wanted to…I wanted to apologize for walking out of the bar like that, I know you're just doing your job and…oh, hell, Russell…"

It was quiet for a bit, but I could hear rustling. He hadn't hung up. Then, "Russell, I…can you just call me, man? As soon as you get home? I don't care what time it is. If…if you're not pissed with me or whatever, call me. Okay?"

He hung up.

It was 1 a.m.

I went to the bathroom, finishing my drink on the way. I peeled off my shirt and threw cold water on my face and chest. My cheek looked a little raw from being grated against the carpet, but no blood.

I went back to the bed and sat on the edge, pouring myself another shot from the tiny mini-bar whiskey bottle. I pulled off my shoes and socks. Ran my hand over my face and fell back onto the bed. I reached for the phone and dialled.

"Hullo?" It was a sexy voice, thick and slurry with sleep.

"James?" I whispered.

"Russell. I'm so glad you called."

There was a moment then between us. We said nothing but it was the beginning of a new set of rules.

"What are you wearing?" he asked.

We both laughed.

"I hope you don't mind that I called your room like that?" he said.

"No. Not at all." I propped the tumbler of liquor on my chest and watched it gently rise up and down. The cool drink ring on my skin felt good. "I was a real jerk at the bar," I said. "I'm sorry."

"You were doing your job, man. I understand. You got no reason yet to believe me. I know that."

Yet. He said yet. It was a little word but it brought colour to my cheeks. Was our history together being written starting today? Was it going to be something more than it was until now? Jeez, I was being schmaltzy about this.

"It's just that I like you, man," he said. "There's something about you that I really dig. I know it seems crazy because we just met, but I like the whole package man. It's for me. You're it for me."

Ohhhhhhhhmaaaaaaaaaaannnnnnn…

I was melting at the sound of his voice. This guy did not beat around the bush.

Quant, you've got a job to do!

Ah, shut up.

Voices in my head. I may need pills for this.

"James." That was all I had. My mouth was dry, my ears were pounding and I could feel each of the little hairs on my body quiver. I put the glass of whiskey on the nightstand—it was no longer stable on my chest.

"Come over," he said in a hoarse whisper.

Part of me was already hailing a cab.

"I can't, James," I said.

"Why? Don't you want to?"

"I do," I admitted. "Yeah, I do."

"Come over." He told me his address.

"I can't." I didn't sound very convincing even to myself. I memo-rized the address.

"I'll be back in Saskatoon before Christmas."

Why did he tell me that? As a warning to Daniel Guest? Or to tell me this didn't have to be just a one-night thing if we didn't want it to be. My mind was all over the place. This was all wrong and all right for a million reasons.

"Come over." Again.

"James, I just can't tonight."

"I wasn't kidding," he said then, his voice never losing its sexual fullness.

"About what?"

"What are you wearing?"

This time neither of us laughed.

Saturday I toured a minuscule portion of the Frick Collection, lunched in Chelsea, had a passerby take my photo at the corner of Christopher and Gay Streets and shopped in SoHo all without the company of Jane Cross. At least not a Jane Cross I could spot. Had she given up and gone home? Was this something for my Herrings file or a hairy tail of a big fat mouse? Sereena was—well, I don't know where Sereena was, but we'd promised to get together that evening. When I returned to my room early afternoon the message light on my phone was blinking once again.

"Russell." And once again it was James.

My cheeks reddened.

"Actually I'm kinda glad I reached your machine, this way you won't be able to say no this time," he said with his easy laugh. "But I don't think you will anyway."

I stared at the phone, wondering what was coming next.

"After…last night, I thought I owed it to you. I've got something you've been looking for."

My mind crashed. James. What are you saying?

"I've got plans earlier, but why don't you drop by my apartment later—my roommate is out of town until after the holidays—say about midnight? I'll see you then."

And that was it. What the hell was that? He had something I've been looking for. I was looking for one thing. Loverboy. But no. I had all but concluded James couldn't be Loverboy.

Or was it just that I didn't want him to be?

That evening after a pan-Asian/fusion dim sum dinner at Ruby Foo's, I was led by Sereena (with no little bit of trepidation on my part) to some dim den of a theatre so far off Broadway the locals spoke a foreign language. We saw a musical about a family of gnomes that prostituted themselves as a means of religious expression (you figure it out). I wasn't the best of company because I was still on the lookout for Jane Cross and more than a little distracted thinking about my midnight meeting with James. But Sereena was, as always, understanding and a trooper and kept up more than her fair share of the conversation.

With about ninety minutes to kill before cabbing it to James', Sereena and I returned to The Sherry and said our goodnights on the lift. As was becoming a habit, when I entered my room the telephone message light was flashing.

"Russell, it's James." This time, the third, his voice sounded much different. It wasn't sleepy, it wasn't sexy, it wasn't oozing with sensuality, all of which I'd experienced in the past twenty-four hours. Instead, this voice was melancholy and…desolate.

"Russell, I've decided to tell you the truth. I am Loverboy…"

I was stunned. My heart sank and my knees buckled. Luckily the bed caught me. I placed a steadying hand on the bedstead and stared at the phone as if it were a snake about to bite me.

"I am so sorry for what I've done…"

My chest began to heave as I heard the unbelievable. And beyond my mind, the mind that was listening to the stilted words, was the rest of me, beginning to feel the pain, the betrayal.

"What I did was wrong. And it will stop…"

Oh shit. Shit. Shit!

"Tell Daniel he has nothing more to fear from Loverboy."

And then somehow I knew. The dread built up in me like an explosion, and I began to shake before I even heard it…

The shot.

It was over.

Loverboy was dead.

I did all the right things. I called the police. I jumped in a cab and got over to James' apartment as fast as I could. The cops were already there. They let me through when I told them who I was. I had to see the body. I was the only one there who could identify him. I didn't know who his friends were or who else he knew in New York City. I really knew very little about James Kraft. I was able to tell the police how to reach his parents. At least they wouldn't have to see him…that way.

As a former police constable, I've seen death. I've seen it in many horrific forms. But it's different when it's someone you know. Even for just a little while. And now, I carry that picture of James wherever I go. Along with the sound of the shotgun blast that ended his life. It's always there, lurking, somewhere in the back of my mind.

The cops were interested in me for more than one reason. Not only had I called in the emergency, I was familiar with the victim, could give background as to the events that had led up to his death and there was a gift-wrapped box found in James Kraft's apartment with my name on it. That "something you've been looking for"? My ring. The ring I'd given to his mother. Thinking it was something he really wanted back, she must have couriered it to him.

After spending the night with members of the NYPD into the wee hours of Sunday morning, they reluctantly allowed me to return to my hotel room in time to pack and catch my flight back to Toronto with the proviso I make myself available to them any time during their investigation. They couldn't rationalize holding me for a suicide. After all, I provided them with the proof—I'd heard it happen.

By 10 p.m. Sunday, a rather sombre Sereena and I were back in Saskatoon where pan-Asian was something you bought in a kitchen supply store and midtown, uptown and downtown were all the same place. I dragged my bags from the cab and through the frost-covered jungle that was my front yard. The house was dark except for an outdoor light left on above the front door. I let myself in as quietly as I could so as not to wake my mother and was affectionately nuzzled by two half-asleep schnauzers. I sank to my knees and sucked up their warmth and affection like a brittle sponge desperate for water. When I looked up, there was my mother, in her bright blue housecoat, those crazy slippers and her head wrapped in a babushka. As soon as she saw my face she could tell something was wrong. Something I couldn't tell her about. But as I rose to my feet and she embraced me, I realized I didn't have to. She knew all she had to. Her sonsyou was in a bad place and needed some comforting.

We didn't say much after that. I eventually sent her off to bed and I transported my luggage from foyer to bedroom. Once I'd slipped into my thick, cozy housecoat, I trundled my way into the den. I couldn't sleep. The memory of my short time with James Kraft, from start to gruesome finish was like a horror flick on endless playback in my mind. If it didn't end soon, I feared I might go crazy. I needed a distraction.

I sat behind my desk and pulled the top copy of a pile of three *StarPhoenix* towards me. My mother had taken to putting the newspapers there (rather than using them as drip pans for bacon) if I didn't get a chance to read them in the morning. I glanced at the Saturday headline. Yet another slam-dunk project for the south downtown development site had fallen through. Most of the front page and many within were filled with reactions from talking heads. I couldn't concentrate on the meaningless words and eventually tossed the paper aside.

Making sure I had a pen and pad handy, I activated my voice mail. Several messages were blanks. A couple were early Christmas greetings from out of towners. The final call on the machine was from Daniel Guest. He said he was calling from his office on Friday afternoon—two days ago—asking that I call him back—but not at home—on an urgent matter. That was odd, I thought. Daniel knew I was going to be in New York looking for Loverboy. It was now after 11 p.m., beyond the polite hour for a telephone call. Besides, he'd said he did not want to be called at home. It would have to wait until tomorrow.

I glanced at my desk calendar and saw, with shock, that Thursday was Christmas. Was I ready? Where had the time gone? What happened to all the fun Christmasy stuff I'd planned to be doing? Ahhhh crap, I was in a lousy mood, about to start seeing ghosts of Christmas past, present and future.

I rose from my desk and headed for the cabinet that housed my entertainment centre. I knelt in front of it, pressed on the power buttons and began rifling through the satellite music channels until I came to one titled "Traditional Seasonal." I selected it and heard the strains of "We Wish You a Merry Christmas"—the part about "figgy pudding." I hit the off button. The silence fell on me like a heavy cloak. I hung my head and had a little cry.

The next morning I was up and out of the house before my mother cracked the first egg. I couldn't sleep. In my car I tried Daniel's office number; I wanted to tell him the news about James in person. But it was still too early and I reached the night bell answering service. With no where else to go, I headed for PWC and was in the kitchen before 8:30 a.m. refilling the coffee mug I'd emptied on the drive in. I have an adequate coffee maker in my own office, but every so often I have a hankering for the flavoured stuff Lilly makes for the clients. Plus, at this time of year, there is always a big selection of home-baked goodies to fill my face with. A habit of mine when feeling depressed. Choosing between a peanut butter cookie with a Reeses Pieces face and a slice of banana loaf crammed full of cranberries and walnuts, I had my back turned when I heard someone walk in. I swivelled around. Errall. She looked tired and pale and if I didn't know better, thinner than when I'd last seen her. She was holding an unlit cigarette in her left hand.

"Errall, hey," I said with little enthusiasm.

She just looked at me with little of her own in return. She poured coffee and gave her cup a suspicious sniff, wrinkling her nose at the Mocha Grand Marnier blend. "What the hell is this shit?" And she walked out.

I guessed we'd talk later.

I heard Beverly and Alberta chattering as they headed into the kitchen. I hoped for a friendlier reception. I needed something positive, uplifting this morning to pull me out of the dark place I was in.

"Hi, Russell," they greeted in unison.

"Have you tried Beverly's cookies?" Alberta exclaimed as if I'd die if I hadn't. "They are the best I've ever taste...Russell, what happened?"

Must have been the look on my face? Was my cheek still raw? Or was my psychic aura pure black?

Beverly sensed something too or else she just instinctively trusted Alberta's lead. She approached me and reached out to give my forearm a squeeze. "Russell, did something happen in New York?" her voice and face pure motherly concern.

I gave them a sketchy outline. They were, of course, horrified, particularly Beverly who I'm sure guessed the suicide had some relation to my working for Daniel Guest. After a minute or more of comforting, Alberta picked up half a dozen peanut butter cookies, stuck them in a crocheted pouch that hung at her hip and left. Beverly remained behind and fixed herself a cup of coffee.

"I'm glad we're alone, Russell," she said quietly after she was done. She was leaning against the counter with her arms crossed so that her coffee cup was suspended just under and to the left of her chin. Her brown hair was in a controlled wave as usual and she wore a nondescript mauve sweater and skirt set. "Is there anything I should know?" Her words came out slowly. I was surprised to hear them. This was murky territory as far as client confidentiality was concerned—even though we were both working with the same client—and Beverly was a stickler for following rules in this regard. I looked closer at her face. It looked...different. There was an unspoken message there. What was she asking me...or...what was she telling me?

I swallowed hard. We stared at one another. I slowly shook my head and asked, "Is there anything I should know?"

"You really should try one of those cookies, hon," she said and walked out of the room. And as she did, I heard a sound escape from under her breath, a whispered, "Yes."

I went back to my office without a peanut butter cookie. Somehow I didn't think I could get it down. My first matter of business was to contact Daniel. I couldn't be certain how soon the local news would pick up the story of a local man committing suicide in New York City—if at all—but I wanted him to hear about it from me. And, of course, I had to tell him that, as I'd been hired to do, I'd found his Loverboy.

"Russell, thanks for calling," Daniel sounded amiable, no hint of the urgency apparent in his phone message.

"Sorry I didn't return your message sooner…"

"I know, I know, you were in New York finding James Kraft and I want to hear all about that…" He didn't know yet. "It's just that I was upset at the time and forgot you were away."

Upset? "Did something happen? You could have called me at the hotel."

"Yes I know, but when I settled down and thought things through rationally, I realized there was nothing you could do until you got home anyway. And even so, there's nothing you can really do."

"What is it? What happened?"

"While you were gone," he said, "I was contacted by Loverboy."

Chapter 17

HIS STATEMENT SENT A SHIVER THROUGH ME. How could this be? How could Daniel Guest have been contacted by Loverboy in Saskatoon at the same time I was with him in New York City? And, more to the point, how could this happen now that Loverboy was dead?

"When? How?" I blurted out.

"A note was hand-delivered to DGR&R sometime on Friday morning. Before you ask, no one remembers who delivered it or exactly what time it arrived, but there was no postmark, so it wasn't mailed. The receptionist handled it like any other message or package and it eventually ended up in my in basket Friday afternoon."

"Was the receptionist the only person who could have seen the note delivered?"

"Well, not really, but I didn't want to make a big deal of it. I didn't want to go around questioning everyone and getting them suspicious that something weird was going on."

"Something weird *is* going on, Daniel."

"You know how I feel about involving the staff here."

"Okay, never mind that for now. What did the note say?"

"Where is my money?" Daniel began, obviously reading. "Don't be a fool. Send it now. Or else life as you know it is over." I couldn't see it, but I was betting all the words were written in caps.

I asked him to repeat it then let out a low whistle.

"Yeah," he said, "Loverboy is mad."

"I'd say so."

"At first I was worried. That's why I tried to call you. And when I didn't reach you and remembered you'd gone to New York, I just thought, to hell with it and wrote out a cheque."

I nodded. Obviously James had somehow orchestrated this last-ditch effort before he and I'd met and before he'd put a gun to his head. "I'm sorry this happened while I was away, Daniel."

"Don't be. I didn't do it, Russell. I didn't send the cheque. I stopped myself. I remembered why I didn't pay in the first place. And I remembered about the risks we talked about. Well, the day has come. We expected this. I'm scared, y'know…but exhilarated at the same time?" I could hear it in his voice. "Does that make any sense at all?"

"Actually it does, Daniel. It does." But it was too late for heroic acts.

"So I suppose this means James Kraft, because he's living in New York City, is off the hook?" he asked.

My mind was going crazy with possibilities. James Kraft admitted to being Loverboy then killed himself over it. Yet just days before he somehow arranged to have another threatening letter delivered to Daniel Guest's office? Did it really make sense?

Or…was Loverboy more than one person?

"I have something to tell you, Daniel."

"What happened? Did he remember me? What did he say?"

"Daniel, James Kraft is dead."

Silence.

"Daniel?"

"Yeah…How? When?"

I told him the story with a voice as devoid of emotion as I could muster. James was a charming, alluring, appealing young man who'd lost his life way too early. But James was also Loverboy. A blackmailer.

Or was he?

"So it's over?" Daniel said dully when I was finished.

"Maybe," I answered.

"Maybe? Why maybe? Loverboy is dead."

"It doesn't add up, Daniel." The more I thought about it, the more I wasn't buying the whole thing. "Why would James send you a message demanding the money, then two days later kill himself?" I didn't bother telling him the part about my ring. But that too continued to bother me. Would James go to the effort to wrap up the ring and invite me over for what sounded like it might be a romantic evening then commit suicide just hours later?

"It's obvious, isn't it?" Daniel said. "I don't want to make you feel responsible for his death or anything, Russell, but think about it. He must have figured out I wasn't going to pay the fifty thousand, so he sends the message, then you show up, he figures the jig is up and he does himself in."

I made a doubting sound. "I suppose that could be true. But it sounds drastic to me. We both met James. He was such a positive guy. He loved life. I just can't picture him killing himself over this. Especially since I didn't exactly present an airtight case against him. I was bluffing. And he knew it. And there's more. The message you received—it was *hand* delivered to your office. Who delivered it? We know it couldn't have been James. He was in New York with me."

"What are you saying? Are you saying someone else was in on all of this with James? An accomplice? Are you thinking...this accomplice...Russell, do you think someone killed James Kraft?" His voice was definitely tinged with panic now.

"I don't know, Daniel. I'm just saying it's a possibility." And indeed, at this terrible moment, the possibilities seemed endless. Did James act alone? With an accomplice? Did the accomplice kill James and intend to carry out the blackmail and get the money for himself? Or was James' confession and death all a ploy to throw our attention off the real blackmailer? And would the real Loverboy be coming after Daniel? Who could that be? We were fresh out of suspects.

Daniel's voice came through the phone in the key of dread. "But how will we ever find this accomplice? It could be someone I don't even know! Someone I've never met! How...how...oh, God, Russell! And I though this was over."

"Daniel, it might be. I could be wrong about this." I waited a moment and only heard breathing. I had also meant to tell Daniel about his wife's visit to my office but...well, maybe he didn't really need to know that right now.

"So what do we do now?"

"Well, if you still stand by your decision not to pay the money, I think Loverboy—if there still is a Loverboy or a replacement Loverboy—will be forced into making another move. Soon."

"And until then?"

"Until then we try to come up with some new suspects. And…be careful."

I stood at the balcony doors of my office for a long while, contemplating the slushy street and gloomy sky outside, both the same shade of grey. The forecasters were predicting a massive snowstorm and the clouds looked heavy, like overfull bags of grimy laundry, but a single flake had yet to fall.

Although I try never to encourage dangerous behaviour by my clients—that was my job—I silently approved of Daniel's decision not to pay Loverboy; assuming someone other than James Kraft, who was now out of the picture, was involved. The letter Daniel'd received was the first sign the plan had merit. By breaking the routine of acquiescence, Daniel had forced Loverboy to take action and the more activity Loverboy was forced into, the more likely it was that he would either screw up, show himself or be scared off. I was hoping he wouldn't be scared off. I didn't like the idea of a blackmailer remaining unpunished. However, with increased activity, came increased risk that Loverboy would make good on his threats and tell the world that Daniel Guest liked having sex with other men. Yet Daniel seemed willing to take that risk. Why? Was he really so intent on catching his blackmailer? Or was there something else going on here? Maybe, deep down, he wanted to be found out. Maybe he wanted his wife to know the truth. Maybe he thought it was easier to be outed by a blackmailer than rallying the courage to say the words himself. If the reaction wasn't good, he could simply deny it all, whereas if the words came out of his own mouth, well, that was harder to do.

Pulling my gaze from the mesmerizing swirls of grey, I made my way to my desk. After conversing with SaskTel directory assistance, I dialled a number.

"Jane Cross Investigations. How can I help you?" The pleasant voice belonged to a woman.

"I'd like to speak with Jane. It's Russell Quant calling."

"What do you want?" The pleasant voice morphed instantaneously into the hard-edged tones used by the tough little brunette detective I'd met in New York.

"I missed you in New York. You never said goodbye." I said affably. I was about to add something about her running off with her tail between her legs but wisely held off.

"I'm sure Ralph Lorent and Johnny Versocky kept you good company."

"Are you referring to Ralph Lauren and Gianni Versace?"

"I asked what you wanted, Quant."

"So you're out of a job and back home in Regina with nothing to do?"

"Is there a point to this call?" she asked impatiently. "Other than to irritate me?"

I really wanted to answer in the negative, just to hear her reaction, but concluded it probably wasn't a good idea to make her mad. "Listen, Jane, I'm looking for a bit of professional courtesy here, a favour. I know you can't tell me anything about your case or who hired you…right…?" Couldn't hurt to try one more time.

I could imagine her pulling the receiver away from her ear and looking at it with incredulity before finally smacking it on her desk-top a few times to ensure it was working. "That's right, bub. And what on earth would ever lead you to think I'd do you a favour?"

I didn't like the tone in her voice. "Hey, wait a second, Cross, I think you *do* owe me something! Not only have you scared my mother out of her wits, sprayed me in the face with hairspray, and physically attacked me in my hotel room, but you've disrupted the progress of my case under the false assumption that you knew what you were doing when in reality, you didn't!"

She made a sound that reminded me of an angry bull. "You wait one second, Quant! I'll have you know that I was only doing my job and you should know that better than anyone! You were, after all…" And she stopped there, on the edge of saying too much.

"I was what?"

"You know, Quant, part of my job was to find out who the hell you are. Well…now I know. You're an asshole!"

I laughed.

She laughed.

We seemed to have the same sense of humour. I could work with that.

"Will you help me?" I asked once I stopped guffawing.

"What do you need?"

"Are you still on me? I just want to make sure I'm not missing something. Things have gotten a lot more serious here. The guy I told you I was following in New York City is dead. I want to make sure that what you were after—whatever it was about me you were looking for—has nothing to do with my blackmail case."

She sighed. "If I tell you, you'll owe me."

I was about to argue with the logic of that conclusion but decided against it. "Whatever."

Stony silence.

"Yeah, alright, okay, I'll owe you."

"I've been called off. For now. And like I said before, it had nothing to do with no blackmail. Best I can do, Quant."

And that…would have to be good enough. For now.

I spent the rest of the day going over every scrap of information I'd collected and stored in my paper and computer files. I returned to my suspect chart several times and tried out every possible scenario I could come up with, sensible or not, for whodunit and howdunit. It was gruelling and mind-numbing and ultimately unrevealing.

Done with banging my discouraged head against the wood of my desk and resisting an evening of companionship with the alcoholic contents of my desk-fridge, I shrugged myself into my winter garb and headed to my car. And there, in the parking lot behind PWC, my perfect day took a turn for the sublime. Somehow looking like a dispirited version of its usual self was my innocent, little Mazda, defaced and deformed. Each tire had been slashed, a sharp instrument of some sort had travelled up and down both sides of the car's previously pristine silver body, the block heater cord had been sliced and the windshield had been egged and now, after hours in sub-zero temperatures, resembled a very sturdy meringue pie. For a moment I stood in shock, not believing what was before me. For a moment I felt like a helpless child. For a moment I was empty, hurt, pained.

And then I got mad.

But that only helped so much.

I went back into PWC and called the cops and the garage and later a cab.

Merry Christmas.

It was a little after 8 p.m. by the time I made it home, tired, grouchy, hungry and liable to spit. As I exited the cab and trudged towards my front door, I saw that my house was obviously in a much better mood than I. All the exterior lights, Christmas and normal ones, were ablaze and through the front window I could see the Christmas tree we'd decorated shining with the intensity of a thousand silver bells. It was, after all, the twenty-second of December, I told myself, so despite my bad luck and disposition, the house had its right to be happy.

I had no idea who they were, but they were in my living room, lined up on the couch like a collection of life-size dolls. The one on the left, in her early sixties and tiny as a bird, had eyeglasses the size of small dinner plates and thicker than ice cubes. Through them I could make out two unfocused pupils. On the right was the oldest woman I have ever seen (who was still upright). She kept the few strands of hair she had left pulled into a tight, white mini-bun at the top of her head. Both ears were plugged with monstrous-looking appliances that I took to be the first hearing aids ever invented. They must not have worked too well because I noticed that when the others spoke they habitually raised their little old lady voices beyond their natural ranges and directed their words in her direction. The one in the middle was as wide as she was tall with a wattled face like Plasticine. Her eyelids and lips were thick like freshly risen dough and her hair was a purplish helmet. I found myself continually having to ask her to repeat herself, claiming to have missed her words when I really hadn't. She spoke with a heavy Eastern European accent and as if she'd downed too many vodka shooters.

They were the "See No Evil," "Hear No Evil," "Speak No Evil" monkeys.

And moving about in front of them like a busy bee was my mother, serving tea and dainties to this threesome she called "the neighbour ladies," even though I'd never laid eyes on any of them before.

"You must have some of your mother's tea," screamed Hear No Evil. "It is absolutely delicious! The best tea I've had all day!" And then she laughed uproariously at her little—very little—joke.

"Oh, well, that's very kind, but I just…"

"Dyew leave herewidda dyermodda?" this from Speak No Evil.

I looked desperately at my mother for help.

"Oh no," my mother answered for me. "Dis is Russell's home. I'm just veesitor."

I looked sideways at my mother then nodded agreement at Speak No Evil.

I watched as she poured out some hot brown liquid and realized I'd never known my mother to drink tea, never mind offer it to guests. It all looked like some bizarre little-girl tea party that had gone on for *way* too long. If I didn't know better I'd say my mother was trying her hand at what she'd consider "city" entertaining. Was this what she thought these neighbour ladies expected from her? In the country having the folks from the next farm over in for a cup o' java or whiskey shot was a regular occurrence, but not here. At least, not in my neighbourhood. And where had she come up with the elaborate tea service? Each saucer was embossed in gold with a subtle monogram: SOS. SOS? Where on earth did my mother get these—off the Titanic? It certainly wasn't from my cupboards. And even from a distance I could tell the delicate pieces hadn't come from Superstore where Mother gets most of her fine china.

"You look just like your mother, dear," See No Evil said to me as she adjusted her vision-aid apparatus for a better look. "Except you're so tall for a girl."

Hear No Evil thought this was hilarious and roared with laughter. "Oh Virginia, this one's a boy, not a girl!"

"I thought Russell was a peculiar name for a girl."

"Itzak ahand soaman fercrysakes! Whycanyewnot seethees?"

"Don't talk to me like that," Virginia complained to her Pillsbury Dough friend with a mightily mean-looking frown.

"Now, now," my mother cooed, her accent smoothed into some refined dialect unrecognizable to me, "haf more tea."

The doorbell rang.

What the heck was going on around here I wondered, feeling more than a little dazed and confused. Were there more cronies yet to arrive? I decided it was none of my business and headed for my den with the dogs while my mother answered the door.

The discord was sudden, each shriek setting off another until it was a choir of shrill pandemonium. It started with my mother's resounding "Oi, bojeh!" This got Barbra and Brutus aroused. They took off out of the den for the living room, barking their response to what sounded like an alarmed call for help. Then came the yowls and screeches of the monkey ladies. I too sped for the living room, all the while thinking two things: what the hell is going on today and what the damn hell is that reeking smell!

As I ran into the living room, the four women and two dogs were running out, escaping…what? Danger? Another peeping Tom? Was it Jane Cross again? No. They were fleeing the malodorous molecules that now pervaded the room. Sitting on the coffee table, next to the exquisite tea setting, was a lovely package, wrapped in red paper. The lid of the package, topped with a large green bow, had been lifted off, no doubt by my mother. The box had been rigged so that when some-one did that, voila, a most unpleasant scent, like aging human waste, was released. Not harmful, except to the senses.

A stink bomb.

It took an hour to clear out the smell; it took a significantly shorter time to clear out my mother's guests. Amongst them they couldn't see, hear or speak, but they could all most certainly smell, and this was one odour they wanted nothing to do with.

My mother described over and over how when she'd answered the doorbell, there was no one there, only the package on the doorstep. It was not addressed to anyone and although she would normally have assumed it was for me, Kelly had promised to drop off some baking and somehow she thought this was it, just in time to serve her new friends. Wrong.

After the peeping-Tom incident and now this, I was pleasantly surprised by just what a resilient old bird my mother really is; not at all faint of heart. I explained to her that both incidents were no doubt related to my current case, that things like this sometimes happen in my line of work, and she seemed to accept that without much problem. She didn't like it, but she accepted it. I however did have a problem. I was beginning to seriously worry about her safety. I now knew that our peeping Tom had been Jane Cross and although I still didn't know why she'd been sent to spy on me, I was convinced she was harmless, a little rough around the edges, but harmless. But now this. Where did this come from? Who would have done this? Was this just kids playing around? Coincidence? Or had I royally pissed someone off?

I woke up on Tuesday morning with that uncomfortable feeling I get in the pit of my stomach when I sense I've done something wrong or missed some important thing or date but can't quite put my finger on it. Although I'd never admit it out loud I was beginning to worry that I was out of my league, that somehow this investigation—if it still was one—had gone hurdling out of my control and I wasn't going to be able to stop it. Had I made a mistake somewhere? What was it? What was I missing? What clue wasn't I listening too? Without opening my eyes I used my foot to nudge Barbra. She weighed a ton this morning and her bulk had me pinned under the blankets.

"Sheesh," I said, finally opening my eyes and trying to sit up, "what has my mother been feeding you!" I was about to shoosh her off the bed when I realized the bulk against me wasn't only Barbra. With his head resting on her hindquarters and his back tucked up against my right side was Brutus. I looked at him. He looked at me. We both knew a line had been crossed. He had never stayed the entire night in the bedroom before, never mind on the bed. I didn't know what I felt about having double the dog poundage in my bed every night, but for now I didn't want to make a big deal of it. I was touched that he'd come to feel comfortable enough in my home and with Barbra and myself to spend the night with us. It was either that or…he had given up on Errall and Kelly.

After what happened to my car and the stink bomb I felt a need to protect my mother, but I had a lot to do and didn't have time to stay home to babysit her. So, once I got myself together and found her at her usual station in the kitchen, I tried to convince her to at least spend the day at Kelly and Errall's house. But she was having none of it. She reminded me how she had won a showdown with a scraggly old coyote who once upon a time deigned to steal hens from her chicken coop. How can you argue with that? We finally agreed she would stay in the house while I was out (using her van), but with the doors locked and that she wouldn't answer the door or phone and would call Sereena if she had any worries at all. It wasn't perfect, but it was the best I was going to get.

When I was shown into Daniel's office later that morning he was not alone. Sitting near the desk was his partner, Herb Dufour. The faces worn by the two men told me they had been discussing serious issues.

"I'm sorry to interrupt," I said, "I can wait until you're done."

"It's okay, Russell," Daniel said, indicating for me to take the chair next to Herb's.

I nodded a hello to the other man as I took a seat. The eyes over his sharp nose were distressed and his brows were knitted tightly together.

"We were discussing the latest development," Daniel said.

"You mean about what happened in New York?" I asked.

"No," Daniel answered. "About these." He gestured towards a bouquet of flowers, still in the paper wrapping they'd arrived in, lying on Daniel's desk. "They came this morning. The envelope attached was addressed to me. Thank goodness our receptionist didn't open it."

He handed a small card across the desk for me to read.

To Daniel Guest,
Love,
Your Boyfriend,
Loverboy

I cringed inside. There was no more doubt.
Loverboy was still out there.

Chapter 18

LOVERBOY WAS BACK.

The words left little up to the imagination. The message and accompanying flowers from Loverboy were a warning. It was a taste of what was to come if Daniel continued to disobey and withhold payment. It was also proof positive that James Kraft was not Loverboy—or if he was, someone else had taken over the role after his death. I looked up at my client. I knew what was going to come next. He was going to give in. He was going to pay the money. We were now no closer to finding out who Loverboy was than when he first hired me. And he couldn't afford to wait any longer. He couldn't afford to play this dangerous game at the risk of a similar bouquet showing up at his home or something worse happening. And I can't say that I blamed him.

"I've made a move," Daniel announced. "I know I should have waited until I could talk to you about it, but…well, I did it anyway, because I know it's the right thing to do."

I exchanged glances with a silent Herb Dufour. His heavy jaw moved slowly from side to side. Obviously whatever Daniel had done did not sit right with his business partner. Daniel handed me another piece of paper across the desk.

I took it and read:

Dear Loverboy,
I have received the flowers. In return, I am willing to send you one
payment of $10,000.00. If I hear from you again, even once, after your
receipt of this payment, I will immediately call the police and reveal to
them and anyone else necessary the details of the events of this
blackmail scheme. I will, at risk to my own personal reputation, career
and marriage, most happily ask them to pursue you, apprehend you
and incarcerate you to the fullest extent possible under the law, which,
after all, is on my side.
If you are agreeable to this arrangement, send me a letter with the
appropriate details.
D.G.

While I reread the letter a second time, Herb Dufour came to life.
"Russell, you have to tell him how dangerous this is. The blackmailer
will not accept this. There's no reason for him to be open to negotia-
tion. He set his price." He turned to Daniel. "Daniel, you've got to pay
it. If not, he will take your ten thousand and come back for the rest of
it, if not right away, eventually. Or, even worse, he'll accept the ten
thousand and spill the beans anyway because you didn't meet his
original demands."

"Why would he do that?" Daniel shot back. "What good would it
do him?"

"Oh come on, Daniel," Herb said, "this is a blackmailer we're talking
about. He doesn't live life by any moral code of ethics we'd recognize.
He'd do it for sport, to see you ruined, humiliated, while he laughs all
the way to the bank with your money. He's not going to buy your bluff.

"Russell has been at this for less than two weeks. Give him a
chance to find this asshole. When we know who he is *then* we can
figure out how to deal with him, maybe get your money back." Herb
shifted in his seat and brought the full power of his attention to bear
on me. "You must have some idea. Who is this guy? Who the hell are
we dealing with?"

In a sudden motion Daniel stood up behind his desk. With a bang
he slammed both palms down on its surface and leaned towards us,

staring at us with an unflinching gaze. He calmly spoke the words, "I—am—not—bluffing."

A hollow silence filled the room. Daniel straightened up but did not sit down. This had to stop. We were getting nowhere. "Daniel," I said, "could I speak to you alone for a moment?"

Herb did not wait for an answer. He jumped up from his chair and headed towards the door where he stopped, turned and said, "You're making a big mistake." And with that he was gone.

Daniel fell to his seat like a boxer returning to his corner of the ring after a punishing ninth round. With his hands against his face, steeple fashion over his nose and mouth, he gazed at me and asked, "Do you think I'm making a mistake too?"

"I don't know, Daniel. I wish you had waited to talk to me first, so we could have decided together whether or not it was the best strategy at this stage of the game. But what's done is done. What we need to do now is focus on the right next move."

He let out a big sigh. "Thank you, Russell."

"For what?"

"For everything," he said. "For everything you've been doing for me. I know I haven't been the easiest client to deal with. But through all of this, the one thing I've come to rely on is you. That you are looking out for my best interests. Even when I'm not always sure myself of what those are."

"You're welcome" seemed insufficient. I nodded. I looked closely at Daniel. His perfect hair. His perfect suit. His perfect pinky ring. But underneath it all, this was a man whose whole life, whole being, was slowly being recast. He was becoming someone different from the man I first met. Someone he himself was having a hard time recognizing, a hard time living with—at least for now.

I spent the next few minutes telling him about the damage to my car and the stink bomb sent to my home. At first I thought the two unfortunate incidents were simply that. But no more. The vandalism and stink bomb were meant to send me a message. They were thinly veiled threats meant to say, "Yoo hoo, I'm still here, I want my money and you'd better stay out of it."

We needed to come up with some new possibilities. I goaded and pressured and urged Daniel to think of someone else, someone he might have missed or discounted for whatever reason, someone we could look into, a family member, an employee, a business colleague or long forgotten acquaintance, perhaps another sexual partner he'd failed to mention. But he came up with nothing. And as I left the DGR&R building the same feeling I'd woken up with came back to haunt me. I had all the pieces but they frustratingly refused to fit together.

"Even if you run really fast on a treadmill, you still don't get anywhere."

Errall had caught me slumped over my desk, staring at my computer screen. And she was right. I did feel like I was exerting myself like crazy, but getting no further for it. I was thinking about my case and the frenzy of dead ends, suspects that weren't suspects, and the growing pile of stuff in the Herrings file. I wordlessly raised my chin off my forearm and looked at her. It had been a while since Errall had made the trip upstairs and stepped foot into my office. It was after four in the afternoon and I'd forgotten to turn on an overhead light. The room had become dim as the churlish grey snow clouds congregated over the city, effectively blocking out the sun.

"I was wondering how Brutus was? Is he doing okay?" She had ended up in front of the balcony doors gazing out at the encroaching storm. She stood with her back to me, hands on slender hips.

"You didn't come over with Kelly when she was checking on my mom while I was away?"

Her head swivelled towards me, a surprised look on her face. Did she even know about this? Didn't Kelly tell her?

She turned away. "No. I didn't," was her only answer.

I let her off the hook. "He's doing great. Barbra loves the company and so does my mom." I decided not to tell her about the sleeping in the bedroom thing. It would only make her feel guiltier than she obviously already was. "You know you and Kelly can come over to see him anytime?"

"You know what?" she said, approaching the desk. "The real reason I came up here was to…Gawd, I don't know, I guess to get some adult conversation about anything other than this. I am sick to death of thinking about it. Sick of it."

That much was obvious. I changed tack. "So work is busy?" I asked, somehow glad we had still not switched on any lights.

She grimaced and sat down. "Actually no. Most of my clients have either gotten 'nice' for the holidays and don't want to sue each other, or else they've left town. I'd be working half days just like everyone else around here seems to be doing this week…except, well, home's not a great place to be right now, so…How about you? You were looking mightily perplexed when I came in. Give my brain something to do. Give me an update."

Since moving into PWC, Errall has acted as my business and personal attorney. That arrangement of legally bound confidentiality allows me to talk freely with her about my clients. It's at times like these where my relationship with Errall becomes something much different from our usual state of agreed-upon acrimony—something neither of us cares to inspect too closely. So I gladly gave her a run-down on what had transpired over the last couple of weeks. A cathartic experience.

"And you have no other suspects?" she asked when I was done.

"No solid ones. And none endorsed by my client. He's having a hard time accepting the fact that Loverboy might be someone other than SunLover or James Kraft."

"Could he be right?" she asked, her sharp blue eyes glinting like sparks in the almost-dark room.

"Well," I began, rolling the possibilities again through my mind, "James was the one Daniel had pegged as the most likely candidate to be Loverboy. But when I met him in New York, he seemed genuinely in the dark about any blackmail scheme. And living there would have made it difficult for him to perpetrate the crime. There was the threatening note *hand*-delivered to Daniel's office. And then this morning, the bouquet of flowers from Loverboy—well after James' death."

"Those could have been sent from anywhere in the world and ordered at any time, even before James died. Did you check the florist?"

"There was no way to identify which florist was used—if at all. As far as we know, Loverboy himself could have purchased and delivered the flowers."

"What about an accomplice?"

"I've thought of that too. But the more I think about it now, the less likely I think it is. It seems pretty risky to carry out a blackmail scheme and then leave town and have a buddy handle all the cash. I don't know, it doesn't feel right to me. I think Loverboy, whoever he is—or was—acted alone."

"You have circumstantial evidence, but no proof, Russell. James Kraft could still very well be your Loverboy. Everything that has happened since could have been arranged by him before his death."

"Except the stink bomb and my car getting trashed."

"He coulda hired that out...and besides, we don't even know for sure if that has anything to do with the blackmail. There was no note making a threat or claiming responsibility with either one, right?

I shook my head.

Errall opened her mouth to say something but I saw her catch the words before they left her throat. We both knew why.

"Could it be him?" Errall whispered in the darkness. "Could Anthony actually be Loverboy?"

I wanted to chastise her for even suggesting our friend could have played such a heinous role. But I couldn't. For I was wondering the same thing.

She took my silence as tacit permission to go on. "Unlike James Kraft he was physically present throughout the blackmail period," she said. "And, he has nothing to lose."

I stood up. Now it was my turn to stand at the balcony door staring out. "That's where you're wrong," I said, placing my hand on the back of my neck, rubbing the lumps of stress that had grown there. "He does have something to lose. Jared." There was quiet behind me. I didn't turn around. I couldn't bear for us to be talking about this; I couldn't bear to look at her while these words came out of my mouth. "It would however explain all his money," I admitted. "People have always wondered where it all comes from. It can't just be from the stores. They do well enough, but not that well. It's retail for Pete's sake.

"Maybe he operates a whole blackmail ring, with several men on the hook. A few thousand here, a few thousand there. Pretty lucrative game if you think about it," I said, warming to my theory. "Jared is away so much of the time on modelling assignments, it'd be easy enough for him to pull it off without his lover knowing. God, Errall, it could be Anthony, it really could." I'd obviously been considering this scenario, somewhere deep within my psyche. And now, I'd revealed it out loud. I was pathetic. Anthony was my dear, dear friend, the love of my dead uncle's life, my hero, and here I was, suspecting him of blackmail. How could I? I felt ashamed. The shroud of darkness overcoming the room seemed ever so appropriate for our ugly words of betrayal.

"Russell." Her voice came from right behind my ear. She had come up behind me. "You're only doing your job. And you'll be happy to know that when it comes to Anthony being the blackmailer, you have no proof of that either. Either of these men might be Loverboy. And you have to consider both of them as serious possibilities. It's your job."

I twisted around so I could look her in the eyes. "How can I do that? How can I investigate my own friend?"

"Don't think of it as proving him guilty. Think of it as proving him innocent."

Our eyes hugged for what seemed like a long time. Finally she backed away and disappeared. I turned back towards the window. Still no snow.

I waited until six o'clock. I called my mother to excuse myself from the evening meal—which, actually she seemed to be okay with—and then headed for DGR&R. On the way I slipped by the drive-through McDonald's window for a low-fat salad thingy, low-fat muffin and a Diet Coke (my mother's cooking and NYC dining extravaganzas were turning me into…well, into me at fourteen).

I chowed down on my meal parked about a half-block down from Daniel's office building. I had a good spot. I could see the parking lot and most of the office windows on two sides. I was willing to wager that this being two days before Christmas, there wouldn't be too many slowpokes out of the office. And I was right. By just after six-thirty the last vehicle pulled out of the lot and the only light visible was a night light through the first floor reception-area window.

I took the last slurps of my drink and manoeuvred my car behind the building, up close to the back door where most street traffic wouldn't catch sight of me. I hopped out and raced to the door and, fingers crossed, typed in the security code I saw Daniel use the morning we'd met at this same spot. Opening the door I was greeted by the welcoming arms of silence. So far so good. And then, like a thief in the night (as opposed to an intruder at dusk, like me) I stole up the rear stairs, down a hall into the atrium and into Daniel's unlocked office.

It wasn't just a need to do something, anything, that had led me there. It was a number of things. Loverboy was still out there; I could feel him. With Daniel's decision to bait him with a $10,000 payoff letter, the chances of our blackmailer responding quickly and negatively were high. Our main suspect was dead. The others were...doubtful. My client was not cooperating in helping to identify alternatives. But, most of all, there was one thing that was driving me to do this, to break into my own client's office—an action which I'm sure is frowned upon in the *Being a Private Eye for Dummies* handbook. That one thing was Beverly. In her own incorruptible, honourable, scrupulous way, she had been trying to tell me something the day before—without really telling me. There was something about Daniel I did not know. And needed to.

The search of his office was slow, particularly since I, to be careful, was performing it by flashlight and really had no idea what I was looking for. Being an accountant, Daniel had an abundance of paper in his life—but to be fair, it was meticulously organized paper—tabbed, labelled, colour-coded, filed and bindered. And, it was in paper where I eventually found something. I was searching a file cabinet drawer, unlocked, in a file labelled Royal Bank Statements. What alerted me that this was somehow different from the several other banking-related files I'd riffled through was that the account was in his name only, whereas the others were office-related accounts or joint accounts with his wife. Nothing libellous about that, but worth a look.

At first the bank statements seemed innocuous enough, revealing not much other than a series of modest deposits, withdrawals and Interac charges. That is until a pattern emerged, a pattern that began twelve months earlier and stopped sometime in July. In that six-month period there were regular Interac charges for the Riviera Motor Inn. Sometimes five or six times a month. The amount was always the same. About the cost of a hotel room.

Cheryl Guest was right. Her husband *was* having an affair—long before his assignation with Anthony Gatt or James Kraft.

The problem was this: How to get my client to tell me who he was meeting in the Riviera Motor Inn Motel without letting him know I'd broken into his office and gone through his personal records? As I drove home from DGR&R I resisted a temptation to simply call him at home and confront him with it. We didn't have time to fool around and I didn't have time for a client who was keeping things from me. I chastised myself for not being more wary of this possibility. It wasn't the first time Daniel Guest had withheld information he thought I didn't need. In the end though, I had promised not to call him at home so as not to arouse his wife's suspicions even further, and it was still in the best interests of the case to keep that promise. And with all that was going on, I wanted to go home to check on Mom.

By 8 p.m. I was comfortably laid out on a loveseat in my living room, alternating my lazy gaze from the crackling fire my mother had set in the hearth and the clacking crochet needles she was manipulating into creating another in a lifelong series of, as far as I could tell, identical doilies.

Never looking up from her toil, my mother said, "I tink about leaving da farm."

Just when you think it's safe to go home.

I was astounded. When my father died, everyone—the kids, friends, neighbours, relatives—expected Mom to move away from the farm—perhaps into a small house in Howell, or even a condo in Saskatoon, or maybe to move in with Joanne or Bill with his house full of ready-to-be-spoiled children. Instead, she stayed where she was and, with the exception of renting out the farm land, continued on as if nothing had changed. She grows a garden that could feed Prince Edward Island, keeps chickens, a few pigs, a milk cow, a dog and some cats and still tirelessly maintains a house and yard meant for a family of five even though it had dwindled down to one. She never complains, never asks for help and accepts visits from her children with surprise rather than expectation. Her health is good and it seems, in her early sixties, she'll be able to go on in that same fashion for many years.

Still, my siblings and I worry about her being alone in a somewhat remote location. But we also realize that everyone makes choices in life. Some not as obvious or safe as others, but still valid. That was what Mom had done. She'd sooner risk being scared or sick or lonely than be holed up in some apartment in a city far away from the familiar surroundings she loves so much. So to hear her suggest a change was a shock.

I sat up on the loveseat and stared at her and her busily crocheting hands. "What are you talking about?" I asked. "You've never talked about leaving the farm before. Did something happen? Are you feeling okay?"

"No, no, no, all goot," she answered as if she were discussing nothing more serious than a recipe. "But I tink about tings. Tings change. I'm old lady already."

"That's not true. You're only in you're early sixties. You just need to slow down. You don't need to put in such a big garden. Buy your veggies. Get rid of that damn cow. Milk is cheap."

"But de cream, Sonsyou, noting like goot, fresh, farm cream."

"Welllllll...you shouldn't be using so much cream in everything anyway. It's not good for you." Where was this going? "Don't you like it on the farm anymore?"

"I do, ya, uh-huh," she said. "But I could leeve for tventy more years."

I nodded. She could be right; my grandmother had lived into her nineties. "Exactly, so why give up now?" I challenged her. "You have a lot of good years left on the farm. You don't have to give it up."

She finally laid down her handiwork on her aproned lap and took off her glasses to clean them with the partially completed doily. Aha, so that was what they were for! "But mebbe dat's not vhat I vant to do vit tventy more years."

This was as surprising to me if she'd told me I had wings. But, come to think of it, she did used to call me her angel.

"When Dad died, Eva Demchuk tell me...you remember Eva? She bury two husbands, poor Eva. She tell me, don't change anyting for one year. After den you decide. So dat's vhy I deedn't leave de farm.

For years. And I vas happy. But I vonder vhedder time for change has come."

"You're going to sell the farm?" I asked, still shell-shocked.

"No, no, no," she said. "Are you hungry, Sonsyou?"

I frowned.

"I sell notting. The farm is for you kids," she said.

"Mom," I said, "you know none of us are interested in becoming a farmer. You don't have to save it for us."

"Your dziadzio came to dis country to claim land for de family name. Not for sale, de farm." Barbra came up alongside Mom's chair, seeking one of the head pats she tends to solicit sporadically throughout any given evening. Mom complied then resumed crocheting. "To sell...vell...I leave dat up to you kids—if dat's vhat you vant."

My mother: fiendishly clever buck-passer and guilt-monger.

I wasn't about to get into an argument about how the world had changed since Grandpa had come to Canada. Instead I stayed with current-day reality. "You have no other income, Mom, you need the land for yourself. If you're serious about moving away from the farm, the money from selling the land would help you buy a new house or condo somewhere and nicely supplement your pension income."

"No house."

What? What's this? Then where would she go? She couldn't realistically be thinking of a retirement home at her age. Bill's? Joanne's? There was a third choice. A choice I had soundly ignored. Why? Because I thought she'd be more comfortable with Bill or Joanne? Or maybe...I thought *I'd* be more comfortable too. But why? It didn't have to be that way. Was I being a homophobe about this? Had I automatically downgraded my ability and appeal as a provider and companion for my mother just because I'm gay? There *was* a damn fine third choice. THE ROOM ABOVE THE GARAGE. She wasn't saying the words, but I was hearing them loud and clear in my head. I had ever since the day I'd found her up there. And then, even louder words were telling me what I had to do, should do...wanted to do?

"Well, you'll just move here then. The room over the garage, we can fix it up, it'll be perfect."

"Ya, uh-huh," she murmured, heavily concentrating on her work. "You hungry, Sonsyou?"

I smiled and lay back down on the loveseat, letting my gaze burrow comfortably into the fire. "No, thanks, Mom." I felt so very good inside.

At 9 p.m. Mom retired to her room to watch reruns of *Matlock* and *Murder She Wrote*. I decided to try for the Christmas feeling to go with this new-found familial instinct I was developing. I dug up Barbra's Christmas collar—a ruffled thing of red and green silk which she dutifully wears every year with a minimum of apparent indignation. I found a red bandana at the bottom of my underwear drawer (don't ask) for Brutus. For myself I snuggled into my favourite holiday sweater, a worn and cozy thing with a trail of tiny reindeers scampering around the threadbare collar, cuffs and hem. That done I stacked celebrity-sung Christmas tunes on the CD player and retreated to the kitchen to pour myself a glass of eggnog heavily laced with Gosling's Black Seal dark rum. I had just restoked the fire and settled in with my thoughts when the front doorbell rang.

"Hey," said a fellow beneath a utilitarian winter coat, knitted toque and thick, brilliant burgundy scarf. "Sorry to bother you." He was a little out of breath.

"That's okay," I said. "Come in." It wasn't too cold out but the darkness made it seem so and the heavy clouds were finally beginning to deposit their cargo in the form of butterfly-sized snowflakes.

"Oh no, no thanks," he said. "I live down the street."

I looked closer. With all the winter paraphernalia covering him all I could really make out was a fringe of dark hair sticking out from beneath the toque, small dark eyes and an indistinct nose. I supposed he looked somewhat familiar so I gave him an "oh, of course!" sounding "Oh, hello!" First it was the three monkey neighbour ladies and now this guy. Where had I been the last few years? Who were these people? I'm not a "can I borrow some sugar" kind of neighbour, but I'd always thought I could at least recognize most of the people who live on my street.

"I hate to bother you—I've tried a few other houses on the block but no one seems to be home tonight. Out Christmas shopping I guess," he said.

"I guess," I agreed agreeably.

"The problem is that I only have the truck for an hour before I have to take it back." This said he used his head to indicate an area in the general direction of the street. Of course, with all the trees surrounding my front yard, I couldn't see a thing. I took his word for it and continued to listen. "You see I had a desk made special for my daughter for Christmas and I borrowed a truck to pick it up. The guy at the studio helped me load it into the truck but I forgot I'd have no one to help me get it out of the truck and into the house. It's a surprise for her. It's got space for her computer and printer and all her other stuff. Cherry wood."

Oh, oh. Woodworking. Guy stuff. "Very nice," I said.

"So, I kinda need a hand?"

"You want me to help you get the desk out of the truck?" I clarified.

"Yeah, if you could. Out of the truck and into the house. Before my daughter and her mother get home. I hate to disturb you…"

"No, no, that's okay." It wasn't exactly a sleigh ride in the park, but helping thy neighbour seemed like a sufficiently Christmasy thing to do to fit in with my theme for the evening. "Won't you come in while I get my coat?"

"No, no, I'll just wait by the truck. It's the big one down the street. You can't miss it."

When he turned to leave I shut the door to keep Barbra and Brutus inside while I threw on the nearest coat in the foyer closet, a pair of boots, a kicky, striped Gap scarf and some gloves. Instructing the disappointed dogs to stay indoors and listen to Celine Dion, I left the house and followed my neighbour out to the street. Indeed, about halfway down the block was a massive three-ton truck, its box covered by a flat, metal roof, probably to keep snow off the desk. The tailgate doors were open, revealing a gaping, black hole. Somewhere in that hole was the cherry wood desk.

"Big truck!" I said when I'd caught up. "Just how big is this desk?" I joked.

"Hand-crafted," he said by way of questionable explanation. "Maybe you could get in and start untying the bungee cords we used to hold it in place? I have to get my gloves out of the cab." He stood and waited for my response.

"Sure," I said, peering into the back of the truck where I could see a faint square outline.

"Russell!"

We both turned around. The voice had come from behind us. A familiar voice. One I wasn't expecting.

"Jared!" I called back.

Jared had pulled up in a black Jeep Cherokee in front of my house and was now striding towards us. He was wearing a bright yellow ski jacket, jeans and a pair of Nikes. Even in the dusky light given off by the street lamps his face and hair shone with vitality and life.

"Hi," he greeted when he reached us.

I checked his face for signs of anything amiss. I hadn't had a chance—on purpose or not, I don't know—to talk with either Jared or Anthony about what had happened at Diva's. Was that why he was here? Had something happened between the two of them? He didn't look stressed or sad or worried or anything but he did look like some-one who was ready to have a good, long talk. "Hi," I said back.

"What are you up to? Sorry to just drop by, I would have called but..." And he smiled impishly.

"I'm helping my neighbour get a desk out of his truck," I said rather proudly, gesturing towards said neighbour.

"I'll help you," he readily offered along with a wide smile at both of us.

"Oh no," the man said. "No, that's okay. Why don't you two have your visit? We can do this some other time."

"No problem, sir," Jared said politely.

"I thought you said you only had the truck for an hour," I said. "With Jared here it'll take us two seconds."

"No really...I can get someone else..." he began, but we'd already hopped into the bed of the truck.

The desk was surprisingly small. I could have pretty much done the job myself but I was glad to have an activity to delay the inevitable discussion with Jared. I needed time to think about what to say to him. After we unhooked the bungee cords holding the desk to the floor, I hoisted one end, he the other and we began our moving-man shuffle. That's when we heard the sudden loud clang and everything went dark.

"Russell?"

"Jared?"

"I just wanted to check I hadn't passed out and didn't know it. What's going on?"

Although we were only inches apart the blackness was so complete I couldn't make out his face.

"The tailgate doors must have been thrown shut by accident," I said. "Come on, let's put the desk down and help him. Those doors looked heavy."

"It's so dark in here I can't tell which way is the front of the truck and which is the back," Jared said as we lowered the desk to the floor of the box and bumbled our way around, often bumping into one another.

When we reached the tailgate I pushed on it. But it didn't budge. It was the type with two doors that swing open to the sides. There was a storm coming and I surmised the rising wind must have ripped the doors from their moorings and slammed them shut.

"Push on it," I instructed as I continued to do the same.

"I am," Jared answered from somewhere next to me in the dark. "But it's not moving an inch. What's your neighbour's name? Let's call out to him. Maybe he got into the cab to warm up and doesn't even know what's happened."

"I don't know."

"You don't know what? His name?" he asked, incredulous.

"No," I admitted sheepishly, bearing the full weight of my ignorance.

"Hey sir!" Jared yelled out.

Nothing.

We both began calling out, hoping our voices were loud enough to carry through steel.

Nothing.

We began to bang.

And then the body of the truck lurched.

"What the hell was that?" Jared asked, suddenly alarmed.

In the utter darkness of the box, unable to see even my own hand in front of my face, it was as if a ghost had appeared in front of me and pushed me backwards. I fell with a resounding thump onto my ass. A similar sound to my right told me the same fate had befallen Jared. He let out a mew of pain.

"You okay?" I asked, concerned.

"I landed right on my tailbone. Man that hurts. But yeah, I'm okay."

"That desk isn't made of cherry wood," I commented flatly, a creepy suspicion having invaded my brain.

"Huh?"

We sat there not saying anything for a few seconds. We listened to the telltale sounds. Although we couldn't believe it, we both knew what was happening.

The truck was moving.

We were being kidnapped.

Chapter 19

I THOUGHT OF ELISABETH KUBLER-ROSS and her well-known, oft-quoted research on the stages people go through when dealing with death: denial, anger, bargaining, depression and finally acceptance. Although no one had died, as our trip in the blackened bowels of the three-ton truck continued, I hit all five—several times. After getting back to our feet we banged away on the locked tailgate doors and sides of the truck box, yelling at the top of our lungs, certain this was some sort of mistake or stupid joke. But after twenty minutes, grim awareness set in—there was nothing funny going on. For a while we dumbly stood where we were, not saying much to one another, listening to the sounds and swaying with the motion of the truck. At the beginning there were a lot of stops and starts. City driving. But then the truck's speed rose and there were no more stops. Highway driving. We were being taken out of the city! This was a discouraging realization. Having looked for and failed to find a way to escape our steel prison we were rendered inactive. And we were cold.

The longer we stood in the back of that truck, the colder it seemed to get. We searched for anything that might help keep us warm, but there was nothing. All we had was each other. And a desk. We found a spot no more comfortable than any other in the barren space and slumped down next to each other for warmth, our knees close to our chests. Jared was worse off than I. I had a coat, gloves, scarf and a good pair of boots. All he had was a jacket that was more stylish than warm and a pair of Nikes. Not good winter wear if you're planning to be kidnapped and held captive in the box of a truck so cold it might as well have been a refrigerator. But who knew? I offered to share my clothing bounty but he refused, claiming he was okay as long as his hands were in his pockets, and that he had really thick socks on under his running shoes.

It was a unique sensation being back there, in the dark, not knowing where we were going. To lose sense of sight and control of your own immediate destiny is not a pleasant thing. They say when you lose one sense the other four are improved. Hoping that was true, I began to focus on what else my body was telling me. The only thing I could smell was Jared. For all the years I've known him, he's always worn the same cologne. I've never known what it's called or, to my knowledge, smelled it on anyone else. I like that because I always know when he's near. It's a subtle, spicy, manly smell. Pleasant. The only nice thing about what was happening to us. As far as taste, well, the only thing I was tasting, and in abundance, was fear. That left touch and hearing. I decided that for my purposes feeling the movement of the truck throughout my body was like using my sense of touch. And together with the sound of the vehicle it could tell me a lot. I could gauge how fast we were going, in what direction, and on what type of surface we were driving: pavement or gravel, snow covered or clear.

Judging the starts and stops from the first part of the trip I'd guessed that we'd left the city heading east. We'd then driven only a short distance, maybe a few kilometres, before stopping again and making a left turn. Then we drove for about twenty minutes before we slowed down to make a right hand turn. The best I could figure it, that put us smack in the middle of...nowhere.

We were in the middle nowhere and I couldn't even be certain this whole thing was even related to the blackmail case at all. But why else would someone want to kidnap me? Or...could this be about Jared? Had he really just come along at the wrong time? Just as darkness filled the back of the truck, it now coloured my thoughts. Horrible thoughts. Maybe this *was* about Jared. Jared *and* me. Maybe Anthony was Loverboy and I was too close to finding him out. So he was getting rid of me—and Jared, the cuckolded lover—at the same time.

Shit, no! What a load of hooey! I was letting my imagination run amok. I was allowing fear and anxiety to eat away at reason and logic. First I accused my friend of being a blackmailer and now a murderer? Preposterous! I knew him. I knew his character. I knew he wasn't capable of any of this. It had to be something else, someone else, I told myself. Maybe it had nothing to do with the Daniel Guest case at all. Maybe it had something to do with Jane Cross—a woman who'd ambushed me, sprayed me in the face with Herbal Essences hairspray and attacked me in my hotel room. I really knew nothing about her. Who was she working for? What did they want from me? Maybe I'd made a mistake in judgement. Or what about the man driving the truck? How did he tie in? Who was he? Was he the second driver during the landfill chase? Obviously he'd lied about being a neighbour. If not, then I was living in a pretty rough area and would have to seriously consider a move as soon as…if…we got out of this mess. And at the least, under no circumstances would he be getting an invitation to my Christmas party!

It had been close to an hour since we'd turned off the highway. We seemed to be on a series of country roads that twisted and turned and rose up and then down. After about fifteen minutes more of this the truck finally came to a halt.

"Thank God," Jared exclaimed.

"I wouldn't do that just yet," I said, all my senses (except sight) on high alert.

For a moment we sat in dead silence except for the sound of whooshing gusts of wind slamming the truck broadside, buffeting the huge vehicle from side to side.

"Now what?" Jared whispered as if worried our captor could hear us.

"I don't know," I hated to say.

Then came the sound of metal against metal. It lasted maybe two seconds, then stopped.

"What was that?"

I began to rise to my feet but immediately fell back down. The cold had settled into my bones and rendered me arthritic and ancient. "I think it may have been the lock on the tailgate doors." I tried again to stand, more carefully this time, gingerly straightening myself up. I held out a hand towards Jared. "Come on, let's check it out."

Jared, in runway model shape, had an easier time getting up, but I knew he was colder than I. Not only were his clothes less protective against the elements, but he had less than one percent body fat and that couldn't be good in these conditions. Finally, eating my mother's cooking was paying off! After bumping into the desk, we inched our way towards the tailgate. When we reached it, I held out my gloved hands and applied pressure against one of the doors. As it swung out, it was grabbed by the wind and flung wildly away from me. A shattering bang followed as the door slammed against the side of the truck. And then another as the other door was also thrown open. We both jumped back from the precipice created by the opening, startled by the sound, startled by being let free, startled by the raging elements before us. Outside was Mother Nature gone wild. Billions of pinpricks of snow danced crazily before our eyes. The wind was a violent force, and sounded like a howling pack of starving wolves looking for prey. The storm had arrived.

"Is he letting us go?" Jared asked. "What's happening? Are we supposed to get out?"

A fear colder than ice shot through me.

That was exactly what he wanted us to do.

"Get back!" I yelled at him, grabbing the sleeve of his jacket. But it was too late. I heard the sound. The sound of our doom. The hoist. Imperceptibly at first we felt the floor beneath us quiver. "Shit!" I screamed. "Get back, Jared, get to the back of the box!"

"What is it?" he yelled. I could hear fear in his voice.

I kept a vicelike grip on Jared's jacket as I pulled him towards the rear of the truck bed. But it was no use. I could feel the upward motion, slow but steady. "He's using the hydraulics! He's emptying the box!"

"Emptying the box? Why is h…" He stopped there, the sickening answer all too obvious. We were being dumped like a load of garbage.

It didn't take long. As the end of the box nearest the cab rose higher and higher it became increasingly difficult for us to stay upright. We desperately searched for anything we might hold on to that would keep us from sliding out of the truck's box and into the blizzard nightmare. But there was nothing. Only the desk. And it was the first to go. We watched it slide, at first jerkily, then with increasing speed, towards the end of the box, then disappear over the edge. It landed with a thump on the frozen, snow-covered ground, waiting for us to join it. My eyes darted about the floor, ceiling and walls of the box, hoping against hope to locate something, anything, that we could attach ourselves to. If not, we'd end up outside and…well, I didn't want to think about that option. But eventually, like the icy fingertips of a cold and lifeless hand, the wind found us. It reached into the tilting truck bed, grasping at us, pulling at us like an evil accomplice, howling its laughter at the hopelessness of our plight.

And finally, with no other choice, we gave in.

Unable to resist gravity we fell to our backs. We looked at each other, saying nothing. We reached out and held hands as we slid down the length of the box and finally over its edge. We landed first on the desk and then toppled painfully over it onto a crusty bank of snow. I was definitely back to stage two: anger. Despite a jabbing pain in my right side where I'd hit that damn desk, I jumped to my feet, intent on running to the door of the cab, tearing it open and pulling Neighbour Guy From Hell out into the snow with us. Although I didn't know his real name, I had a few others I wanted to try on for size.

But I was too late. As soon as we'd landed on the ground, the truck began its escape, the box still elevated on its hydraulic lift. I tried to catch the lumbering beast but, disoriented and trying to run against the wicked wind on slippery, fresh snow, the truck proved too fast for me. I watched in horror as the truck disappeared from sight behind a curtain of snow. After a brief moment of self-pity, I looked back to where I'd left Jared and the desk, two grey lumps in an otherwise black and white landscape. Neither was moving. Despite exhaustion and paralyzing cold, I ran back, worried that Jared might be hurt. When I reached him I fell to my knees next to where he was splayed against the desk.

"Jared! Are you okay? Are you hurt?"

He looked up at me and I saw that a patch of his copper hair was matted against his forehead with red. A stab of fear jolted me. Blood. His golden eyes looked brown and his olive skin was drab.

"I'm okay," he croaked. "But I think I may have hit my head kind of hard on a corner of the desk when we fell out of the truck." For a moment I thought I saw his eyes roll up into his head, but then he recovered, seemingly alert. "How about you?"

"I'm okay," I assured him as I gently tried to clear away some of the hair around his wound to see how bad it was. "Just hold still if you can."

The cut wasn't big but it had bled a lot, though it seemed to have stopped. Still I was worried he might faint from the loss of blood, and being this cold would not help. Any type of trauma can easily contribute to faster onset of hypothermia. Living in Saskatchewan I am well acquainted with the dangers of being caught outdoors in the winter without appropriate protective clothing. Normally I'm careful to avoid that happening, but neither of us had expected this and we were poorly prepared to deal with it. I knew we had to get out of our miserable situation as soon as possible or we were in for a nasty case of frostbite or worse. With an injury and poor clothing, Jared was even more at risk than I was.

For the first time since we'd been dumped, I closely studied our surroundings. But other than dark, snow and the desk, there was nothing to see. I assessed our situation with the little information I had. It was night, we were on a deserted gravel road, over an hour away from Saskatoon during a raging winter storm. The temperature was dropping fast and I couldn't decide which way was north and which was south. We were definitely lost. We were definitely in trouble.

"What can we do?" Jared asked, still in his prone position. I could tell from his voice that he was pushing the limits of his energy to speak. "What about the desk? Can we use that for shelter?"

I looked at the crappy piece of furniture. I should have known it was too much of a piece of garbage to be a Christmas gift for some-one's daughter. Cherry wood my ass. It was nothing better than a Salvation Army reject. "It's too small to get under and one of the sides broke off in the fall," I told Jared. I should have known I was being set up! There was something about him…I was mad at myself, but I'd have time to admonish myself later—if there was a later. "You didn't happen to bring a cell phone with you, did you?"

"I left it in the Jeep," he said. "Sorry. Can you see any lights? There must be a farm or town somewhere nearby."

I had already scanned the horizon, which, under these conditions was a lot closer than usual. I'd seen nothing but more swirling snow and the oblivion of a full-blown Saskatchewan blizzard. I shook my head.

"So what do we do?" Jared said. "Don't they say if you're stuck in a snowstorm you should stay where you are and wait for someone to come for you?"

Unfortunately that advice was only good if you were stuck within the relatively safe confines of a vehicle or other protective covering. We didn't have that luxury and I didn't know of any other rules meant for this particular predicament. Should we just wait here and hope for a passing car? Or should we pick a direction and start walking? Should one of us go for help and the other stay? Should we separate or stay together? How was one to decide? At least we had options. None of them good, but at least we had some.

"I think we have to try to find help, Jared," I said to him, assessing the wound on his forehead again. "We should keep moving. If we stay here we'll freeze to the spot. It's gotta be minus twenty out here and worse with the wind chill. Without better clothing we're not going to last long. We have to find shelter of some sort."

He nodded agreement and winced in pain as he made a move to get up.

"Let me help you," I said, slipping my arm around his back. When we were standing I pulled off my gloves and handed them to him. He shook his head but I pushed them towards him. "We have to take turns with these, Jared. Do you have a hood on that coat?" He shook his head. "Let's switch," I yelled over the bellowing wind.

"No!" he yelled back. "I'm not going to let you freeze to keep me warm.

"Jared!" I said, grabbing him by each shoulder and bringing his face close to mine. "You're hurt! You're bleeding! I can already see that you're shivering and getting glassy-eyed. You could be going into shock or getting hypothermia! Most of the body's heat escapes from the head. You need a coat with a hood. Mine has a hood. And you need to take my boots too."

"No way!" he argued.

"Listen, we don't have time for this! I'll keep the scarf! And I promise I'll take the coat and boots back when I'm feeling cold." I was already feeling cold and I hadn't even taken them off yet, but I knew I was right. I had to keep him warm or he'd never make it. Rather than wait for his rebuttal, I unzipped my coat, slipped it off my shoulders and handed it to him.

He hesitated and then thinking better of it made the switch. I showed him how I could pull the turtleneck of my reindeer sweater high over my chin so that most of my head (up to my eyes—which I was planning on using) was covered. Then I fashioned my scarf into a protective turban/headband thing ala Norma Desmond in *Sunset Boulevard*. I leaned against the desk and began taking off my boots. Fortunately our feet are about the same size. After exchanging footwear I pointed in the direction the truck had disappeared and said, "Well, time to head home?"

"Thank you, Russell."

I avoided his eyes. I shrugged and laced my arm through his and we headed north…or was it west?

The going was tough. The wind pushed and pulled at us, flailing us about like two puppets in a whirlwind. Sometimes it came at us so hard and cold we could barely breathe through our burning nostrils. We'd stop and bow our heads against the onslaught until we managed to pull in enough oxygen to continue. The falling snow was not the soft, fluttery kind, but rather like a hail of hard little pellets that pinged off our bodies as we struggled through it. And even though we pushed ourselves onward, it seemed we weren't progressing an inch. The scenery never changed. Everything around us looked just as it did when we began—white and miserable.

Although we were travelling on a road, we had yet to see a car— or any other moving thing for that matter. I concluded it was probably either an old country road rarely used at the best of times, or, more likely, the savage weather, not made for man or beast, was keeping everyone safely tucked away in their homes. Which was exactly where I was supposed to be, curled up with my dogs in front of a blazing fireplace, listening to Christmas tunes and enjoying a yuletide evening with plenty of eggnog and rum. What had happened to that? How quickly everything had changed.

As we trudged forward I tried not to think about how cold I was. "How are you doing?" I called out. I had taken to asking the same question of Jared every minute or so. Although he was still on his feet he was wrestling to keep pace. I needed to keep him moving.

No answer.

"Jared? How are you?" I said it louder, thinking the screeching wind had stolen my words.

He stopped and I did too. He turned towards me, his eyes, sad and serious, glared out at me from beneath the sheath of his hood.

"We have to keep going, Jared. We shouldn't stop. Keep going!" I demanded.

"I just realized…"

Even though I could see his lips moving, the rest of his words were lost to the noise of our surroundings and the scarf protecting my ears. I leaned into him, the bounty of his coat's hood creating a cocoon around our faces. "What did you say?" the words slipping out of my mouth so thick with cold I could almost see them.

And then, when I finally heard the words, I pulled back as if their meaning had physically repelled me. I stared at him, horrified. "Slowly, but surely," he uttered, "you and I are being murdered."

With the heavy blanket of the snowstorm threatening to cover and suffocate us, Jared and I looked at each other and I knew he was right. This wasn't a misunderstanding. This wasn't a joke. This wasn't even an idle threat. This was the real thing. This *was* murder. We weren't meant to find our way to safety. We weren't meant to survive this. We were meant to die.

I made some useless moves to tighten the ties of the hood around Jared's head, my freezing fingers bungling the effort, and announced, "We're not giving up!"

He nodded supportively but with little real confidence and pulled me close. As we embraced I looked over his shoulder and that's when I first saw it in the far distance. A silhouette. Jared must have felt my body stiffen and released me to look in the same direction. With our hands protecting our eyes from stinging snow we tried to make out the shape. Was it a house? A barn? Maybe a large piece of machinery? It didn't matter. It looked big. Big enough to afford us at least some shelter from the wind that was thieving the warmth from our bodies and turning us into human snowmen. But there was one problem. To get from where we were to where it was would mean travelling cross-country. We'd have to leave the road. In most places higher than the fields that bordered it, the road had remained surprisingly free of significant snow build up and had allowed us comparatively easy passage. It also gave us a sense of security (however false) and hope that perhaps a vehicle might come by to rescue us. Leaving the road would be a major decision. And what if we were wrong? What if the shape we were seeing was some kind of winterscape mirage? Would we be able to find our way back to the road? Or would we be lost to the unnavigable snowdrifts of an abandoned and desolate field?

"We've got to go for it, Russell," Jared said, his words slightly slurred. "No one is coming to get us. We have to try to save ourselves." I'd noticed earlier that the skin around his eyes and mouth was turning grey and bloodless. He needed to get out of the cold…fast.

"Here!" he said leaning over to pull off a boot.

"No!" I bellowed through the howling wind. "I don't need it. I'm fine. I can make it."

"Tell you what," Jared bellowed back, amazingly revealing a smile on his blanched face. Was the cold making him delirious? "You take one, I'll take one."

It seemed stupid, but why not I thought to myself. I had been wearing the Nikes for several minutes and was beginning to lose feeling in my toes. Extremities. They're the first to go. Besides, there was no more time for this stand off. We exchanged a boot for a shoe and then took the first steps into the field. We were like two non-swimmers diving into water of unknown depth and turbulence. I said a silent prayer, hoping we weren't making a last, fatal error.

Seconds passed like hours and minutes were an eternity. The snow in the field was deep, at times hard enough to walk on but then unexpectedly soft, giving way and dropping us into a frothy mess up to our waists. We'd fight a rising feeling of panic, knowing what it must feel like to slowly be dragged beneath the killing mire of quicksand and pull ourselves out only to find that our goal, the elusive dark outline, seemed to have moved further away. We trekked and traipsed and oftentimes pulled and pushed one another beyond reasonable endurance, but we kept on going. The conditions seemed only to worsen. We trudged ahead, like two machines that had stopped performing the function they were meant for but still had a few ounces of battery juice left to keep them moving forward. Jared became quieter and slower. And then, just as my hopes were collapsing, I saw the barn.

Reaching shelter was better than arriving in Mexico in the middle of a Saskatchewan winter, better than showing up at your own surprise birthday party, better than reaching the summit of any mountain in the world. Reaching that barn meant we might live. That barn was our world.

From the little I could see through the wild snowstorm around us, the structure, with siding and shingles of weathered grey wood, looked one step from complete dilapidation. But it was still standing, and that alone was no small feat in the current weather conditions. It was a standard 1950s' barn design with large sliding doors on either end, a row of tiny, square windows running the length of each side, and a high domed roof beneath which was probably a hayloft. At each corner of the aged structure was a clump of trees, branches grotesquely gnarled, probably all that kept it from falling down. When we reached the end of the barn closest to us we threw ourselves against it almost as if to hug it, but more likely to keep ourselves from falling down. Our energy level was extremely low but reaching our oasis in the snow buoyed our spirits.

The feeling didn't last.

We saw it at the same time and both gasped in incredulous disbelief. A thick chain fastened with a medieval looking padlock joined the two wooden handles of the sliding doors. For some insane reason, the owner of the building had decided to protect his disintegrating investment like a castle fortress. I told Jared to stay put while I checked the doors at the other end of the barn. The going was rough and slow as the snow had accumulated to four or five feet in some places around the building. At the other end I found the same thing. I was devastated. Why did this have to be so hard? We were trying to save our lives for crying out loud! Didn't we deserve some help? Some divine intervention? Rather than one obstacle after another!

I hated the thought of having to go back and disappoint Jared, but that is what I did. By the time I returned he had slumped to the ground with his back against the barn. His hood had fallen askew to one side of his head and he hadn't even bothered to put it back in position where it might do some good. He was losing energy and warmth faster than a colander loses water. I adjusted the hood as best I could and knew I had to do something fast. I considered the windows, but even if I could get up high enough to break one I was pretty sure they would be too small for either of us to crawl through. In a fit of desperation I clomped over to one of the nearby trees and hacked at a branch with my fists until I loosened a good sized branch. Weapon in hand I unleashed the power of my frustration on the padlock. What a time to be without my lock pick set. As I tried to slaughter the heavy metal lock, Jared seemed oblivious. I thought about shaking him awake, but the grim reality was that if I didn't find a way into the barn it wouldn't matter anyway.

I slashed away until the branch was but a splinter. Ultimately the battering of the lock did not work. In a war of metal against wood, metal always wins. There had to be another way, I thought to myself.

Aha.

Instead of attacking metal that was constructed to withstand the pressure of a hundred men hitting it with a stick, why not attack the ailing wood it was attached to: the door handles themselves. After procuring another branch, I shoved the narrowest end under one handle and used the leverage of my weight to begin a jerking motion meant to convince the handle to pry away from the door. Almost immediately I could feel it working. The handle was loosening! I kept at it and in under a minute the stressed chunk of wood fell to the ground releasing the chain. I whooped with joyous enthusiasm. Still no reaction from Jared. No matter, I thought, we were close to home!

Feeling like Superman and Wonder Woman rolled into one, I grabbed the edge of the door and gave it a mighty tug.

Nothing. It didn't budge.

I pulled and pushed and tugged at it some more. The door stayed resolutely in its place. I am not a man easily given to tears, but I was close to it at that moment. I began to pace back and forth, every two seconds giving the wretched doors a hateful kick and tried to figure out why they wouldn't open. Were they locked from the inside? Was there another chain and padlock I hadn't seen? Was the devil himself holding them closed? It was only after I disposed of all those possibilities that I noticed how simple the answer was. Right in front of my eyes. Over the course of the storm the blowing snow had drifted up against the building and was blocking the path of the sliding door. It was stuck. The door was stuck! This I could fix! I fell to my knees like a penitent sinner on his first day back in church and began digging gopher-like until the hillock of snow that was blocking the door was reduced to a small trough that, hopefully, would make way for the door panel to slide open. I jumped up and tried again. And joy of joys, it moved. Stubbornly at first, but I knew I had it. I had won!

Eventually I made a space large enough to wedge my arm between the two doors and then my shoulder and then my entire body. Jared had fallen into a near solid stupor, his eyes fluttering as if he was battling to stay conscious. I knelt next to him, threw his left arm over my shoulder and coaxed him up. I helped him towards the opening I'd made and pushed him in like a square peg through a not-quite square hole. It took some doing but he was finally inside, and then, so was I. Ignoring our new surroundings, I focused first on closing the door to shut out the storm that threatened to follow us in. I expected a struggle, but the door slid closed as if it had been recently oiled, lubed and maintained and had never caused anyone a spit of trouble in all its days. I hated that door.

The first thing I noticed was the silence. I hadn't been aware until that moment what an unrelenting auditory invasion the winter storm had been. Who says falling snow is silent? My nose filled with a pungent smell unique to old barns—a tangy mixture of straw, aged manure, rotting wood and rusting metal. Immediately to my right I noticed a ratty-looking horse blanket hanging from a nail on a beam support pole. I yanked it down and flung it around Jared's shoulders, lowering him to a sitting position on an overturned, empty five-gallon pail. Although he seemed barely awake, he shrugged into the warmth of the blanket, pulling it around himself as if he was naked. I took that as a good sign.

"You okay like this for a while?" I asked him. "I want to take a look around, see what else I can find to keep us warm."

"Yeah, I'm fine," he mumbled into the folds of the blanket. He seemed aware but not fully conscious.

I gave him a pat on the back and left to investigate. Although it was long past sunset, the barn was dimly lit by an otherworldly glow coming through the windows. Likely from moonlight or its reflection off the copious amounts of bright, white snow being deposited around the building like a mantle. Without insulation the inside of the old barn was not significantly warmer than outside, but the lack of wind and falling snow made it feel like a veritable sauna. I saw that one of the barn's stalls was stocked with square straw bales and another with loose hay. My first priority was to get some warmth back into our bones and this looked like just the place to do it. I used a pitchfork to shove the hay into the stall where the bound bales were and spent the next several minutes rearranging the bales like building blocks, to fashion a straw fort complete with walls, roof and a floor lined with the hay. The physical activity was beginning to thaw me out.

Retrieving Jared from his five-gallon perch, he shuffled next to me muttering undecipherable comments on the short trip to our new campsite. I helped him crouch down and manoeuvre into the makeshift fort. He lowered himself onto the soft hay bed with a grateful sigh. Once both of us were within the small and cozy space, I fluffed up some of the hay to cover the entrance, leaving us completely surrounded by the stuff. The smell was strong, yeasty, but not wholly unpleasant. I lay down next to him pulling the horse blanket over us both and snuggled up against him. Gently as possible I placed a kiss on the soft spot right next to the corner of his lips. They twitched and maybe even turned up just a bit. Maybe not. It didn't matter. We had been targeted for murder, but we were still alive and, if not kicking, at least twitching. I lay my head back on the hay pillow, thrust my hands deep into my pants to the warmest spot I could find on my body and fell into a strangely satisfied slumber.

It never occurred to me that we might never wake up, having frozen to death in our sleep.

Chapter 20

WAKING UP ON A BED OF STRAW with my friend's partner in a barn in the middle of nowhere justifiably made that particular Christmas Eve day the most peculiar I'd ever had. Many of my friends, especially the gay ones, profess to prefer the period leading up to Christmas rather than the actual two days, being Christmas Eve and Day. I think this is because they often end up having to spend those two days being dutiful sons and daughters, brothers and sisters, nieces and nephews, aunts and uncles at a whirlwind of family events, often without the most important member of their own family—their partner—with them. Since I rarely spend holidays with relatives, I am spared all that nonsense. So consequently I quite enjoy December 24th and 25th. I usually spend the twenty-fourth ODing on carols and eggnog, lounging beside a pine-scented fire while calling out-of-town loved ones on the phone and making last-minute preparations for my annual come'n'-go on the twenty-fifth. This year however, it was becoming quite apparent my plans would have to change just a wee bit.

I looked over at Jared whose eyelids were half-open, revealing the golden green beneath. Our faces were so close that the tips of our noses were almost touching. I could see in his eyes that he was well. I sighed relief.

"What was that for?" he asked. His voice had a sexy morning sound to it. "The sigh?"

"I was just glad to see you looking better. You do feel all right, don't you? I'm worried about you."

"How could I be anything but with you looking after me?"

I noticed he hadn't moved his face away from mine. It was still chilly in the straw house I had built, but definitely warm enough to survive without necessitating such closeness. I too did not move. I focused on the cut on his forehead. "Head feel okay?"

"I'm fine, Russell. I can't believe this…this place. It's terrific. And warm. I can feel my toes again."

I was coming to realize that our arms were around each other, my right and his left under each other's heads, my left on his chest and his right on my hip.

"Thank you, Russell," he said with gentleness and kindness in his eyes—eyes that stared deep into me. "For everything you did."

I nodded a curt response, my throat having grown dry. Despite our still desperate circumstances all I could think about was that I was suddenly feeling inappropriately aroused. Hard to disguise. Damn male anatomy!

Our noses touched.

Our lips came close and touched. I could feel his hand move a little further down my side, from hip to thigh. We kissed lightly.

"You're welcome," I croaked. Oh shit, oh shit, oh shit, were the only intelligible thoughts that came to mind.

Quiet.

I grinned and pulled myself into a sitting position.

"Time to get up?" he asked innocently.

"I'm just gonna go check things out." I couldn't lay there with him any longer. For many reasons—most of which were unclear to me but shouldn't have been. I only knew it was time to get out. I carefully shifted to a crouching position, mindful not to disturb the roof of our lodging and rearranged the horse blanket around Jared who watched me with wide, untelling eyes. "Stay warm," were my wise parting words.

Like a series of identical pale grey postage stamps, the windows were frosted over but letting in even more light than they had the previous night when we'd arrived. Everything else appeared unchanged. The stalls, the cream separator, the rolls of wire; all still there. I don't know what I expected. Maybe an espresso machine, toasted bagels, a pile of fuzzy blankets and a snow blower? But there was *something* different. I just couldn't put my finger on it. I made my way to the malefic door I'd battled the night before. I leaned my head against it listening for sounds of the storm. That was it. That was what was different. No wind. No howling, no rattling rafters, no roof preparing for flight. Was the storm over? I pulled on the door and met with resistance. Oh shit! Not again! I could guess what the problem was. I'd dug away the snow to let us in, but it had continued snowing and obviously piled up again making the door immovable once more. But this time we were inside and I wouldn't be able to get to the snow to shovel it away.

Freaked at the thought of being locked in, I grasped the door again and pulled with all my might. It yielded so easily I stumbled into a heap on the floor. Recovering quickly I pulled it shut again to keep the cold out, leaving a space only big enough to stick my face through. There was good news and bad news. The good news was that indeed the storm had abated. The bad news was that it had apparently obliterated the rest of the world leaving only this barn in the middle of a blaring white void. Either that or everything was covered in snow.

"What do you see?" I heard the voice from behind me.

I pulled my head back into the barn and turned around to see Jared, swathed in the horse blanket. "You should be in bed," I told him.

He chuckled lightly. "I think I need to walk around a bit, get rid of the kinks. So what's out there?"

Again I felt a sense of gratitude to see my friend up and about, clear-eyed and rosy-cheeked and well. "Take a look for yourself."

I stepped aside and let Jared take his turn with his head out the door.

"What do you think?" he asked when he finished perusing our surroundings and pulled closed the door. "Any ideas on what to do now?"

"Well, I think I'm going to go out and take a look around, get a sense of where we are."

"I'll go with you."

"No, you should stay as warm as possible. Even if you're feeling better, you're still wounded and its much colder out there than it is in here and the two don't mix well."

"Okay, but you're going to take some of your winter clothing back."

We exchanged some clothing with me ending up with most of my stuff again including the hooded coat, gloves and boots. My colourful scarf was once again around my neck where it belonged, rather than wound around my head like some kind of gay bandage. I headed outdoors. It had begun to snow again but lightly and, unlike last night, there was no wind to blow it around like a blender full of flakes. The first thing I noticed with alarm was that any sign of our arrival the night before, footprints or trampled trail, had been wiped clean by the storm. If anyone was looking for us, they'd have no clue we were here. As I began to tread my way around the barn, past the bare-branched bushes, I began considering tentative plans for attracting the attention of would-be rescuers. Perhaps a big SOS carved out in the snow with urine? And then, like one of those unrelated thoughts that sometimes come unbidden and inexplicably to the forefront of my brain, I thought of Sereena. And my mother's mysterious tea service embossed with the letters S-O-S. The answer came to me. The expensive tea set belonged to...Sereena...Sereena Orion Smith—SOS. I had never before connected Sereena's full initials with the well-known international request for help. For a bizarre moment something inside me told me it was no coincidence at all. But I let it go. I had more pressing matters to attend to at the moment.

As I rounded the corner of the greying structure I looked for the tallest thing around. Anything would do, a tree, an abandoned piece of farm machinery, anything I could use to get myself high enough to get a lay of the land and maybe spot a nearby village or farmyard where we could find help. Then I saw something immeasurably better. A house.

An hour later we were moved in. The old farmhouse, obviously obstructed from our view last night by the storm, was as deserted and aged as the barn. It had no electricity, little in the way of insulation and didn't even have any straw, but it had a wonderful wood fireplace complete with well-stocked woodpile and several boxes of wooden matches. It didn't take long for the one-room shack to heat up. When we were sufficiently warm I presented Jared with another surprise. I'd found in the cupboards a veritable gourmet meal of canned goods. There was tuna and mushrooms and Vienna sausages and corn and a can of peaches for dessert. And no meal is complete without half a 1.75 litre bottle of Canadian Club rye whiskey, cut with snow melted over the fire. We were so famished that for several minutes we sat on the overstuffed couch pulled near the fireplace and ate with barely a word between us.

"I have never tasted a better sausage in my life!" Jared enthused as he chowed down on the last of the rubbery pink encasements. "It's my new favorite food."

"That's good. There's plenty more in the cupboard. We may have to live on them for a while." I checked my watch. "I can't believe we're getting tipsy on C.C. at eleven in the morning."

"All we need is a two-four of Pilsner and this would be the perfect white-trash Christmas Eve."

"Should we sing a carol or something to make it official?" I asked as I licked tuna juice from my fork.

Jared winced. "Let's save that for the made-for-TV movie version of this escapade."

I laughed and passed him the corn.

We fell silent for a few more minutes, eating our grub and enjoying the fire licking at the logs. A lot was on my mind. Not only the obvious— our precarious situation—but something possibly even more precarious, assuming we lived. For the moment I could think of nothing more to do to get us out of our situation, so as I was busy sating my need for food and warmth, I allowed myself a few minutes of idle wonder. Wonder about that kiss. Was it simply a thank-you kiss? A desperate "we're gonna die so let's kiss" kiss? Or was it something more? All of this got me thinking about what had happened at Diva's two Saturdays ago. Jared had found out, in a most humiliating and public way, that his partner of five years had had sex with someone else. I had no idea what had transpired between Jared and Anthony since that shocking revelation. Had they been fighting? Had they broken up over it? It was time to find out.

"Jared," I began hesitatingly, "I wanted to say I'm sorry for what happened at Diva's."

Jared eyed me carefully over the can of corn but took the time to eat another spoonful before saying anything. "Why are you sorry?"

"I guess I feel responsible. If it wasn't for me and the case I'm working on…it wouldn't have happened…I mean…the thing at Bare Ass Beach would have hap…but, well, you wouldn't have been at Diva's and Daniel wouldn't have seen Anthony and…well, you know." I can be extremely eloquent when the situation calls for it.

He ate a peach sliver.

"I'm sorry you had to find out the way you did. I'm your friend and I should have been there for you. And I should have been there to kick Anthony's butt."

Jared repositioned himself on the sofa so as to be directly facing me. "Russell, I knew about it."

Knock me over with a feather boa. "You did?" Suddenly the flames of the fire seemed to be licking at my cheeks.

"Yes. And why would you want to kick Anthony's butt?"

I stumbled over words for a bit. "Well, for what he did to you. For fooling around on you. But I guess…but…You knew?"

"Yes." His voice was calm and revealed nothing, but his eyes had turned an unusual shade of green.

"And…you're okay with it?"

"I have to be, Russell. It happened this summer…when Anthony and I weren't a couple."

I had raised my glass of watered-down rye to my lips but lowered it again afraid I might gag. The fire was all over my body now and I could feel perspiration form at my temples. "What are you talking about? You and Anthony have been together for years!"

"Not this summer we weren't," he said, his voice soft.

And I didn't know about this!

Shit. I didn't know about this.

How did I not know about this?

"What happened? Did you find out he was cheating and leave him?" I cannot believe the garbage that sometimes comes out of my mouth.

The look Jared gave me then was odd. It was sad. It was critical. It was discomfited. "I did leave him. Not because he was cheating. But because I was."

I'm sure my eyes grew as big as they do in cartoons. My throat tightened and all I could do was stare at him.

"It has always been a challenge, Anthony and I, with our careers, especially mine, keeping us apart for such long periods of time. I come back to Saskatoon and he sometimes flies out to my location shoots, but it isn't perfect. And I began to think it was too hard. I foolishly thought love should be easier. So when I met a man, another model, who seemed to be…easier…I decided to end it with Anthony."

I finally found my voice and some whiffs of good sense and said, "I was just so used to you being away, sometimes for months at a time, I never noticed you were…really gone. And Anthony didn't say anything. It's hard to remember but I don't recall anything obviously amiss this summer."

"That could be," he allowed with a sad bob of his head. "We talked about what to say to people after we, or rather I, made the decision. But we never got that far. We were still very much in love but it took Anthony's persistence to show me that love still counted for something. I was such a knucklehead. But he kept on calling, just to talk, just to see how I was, no judging, no histrionics, no accusations or pleading to get back together. Sometimes we'd be on the phone every night for hours at a time. He really believed in us. And I discovered that something worth having is worth working at, no matter how hard. So you see, when Anthony and your client had their thing on the beach, he had every right to be with another man, because I was too."

I took a punishingly huge gulp of my bitter drink and contemplated my shame. Had I been prepared to believe the worst about Anthony in order to fuel a childish fantasy of a possible future with the lovely Jared Lowe? I had believed it possible Anthony was a philanderer and a blackmailer and maybe even a kidnapper. I sunk under the weight of how incredibly selfish and down right stupid I had been.

"In the fall," Jared continued, "we got back together, stronger than ever and we're very happy, Russell—as really, we always have been."

I nodded mutely. What a fairy tale this turned out to be. My knight, sitting next to me beneath a tattered horse blanket, had revealed the chinks in his not so shiny armour. My maligned friend Anthony turned out to be the injured party and ultimately heroic character. As for me? Well, I turned out to be the fool. And the kiss? Who knows for sure what it was, perhaps an intimate act of thanksgiving for our survival.

"I'm glad it's turned out that way," I said, realizing without a bit of doubt that I was being completely truthful.

"Me too," he said, reaching out to take my hand in his and giving me a meaningful look.

"Someone will come for us, Jared," I told him, wanting…needing to change the subject.

"Do you really believe that? Who? Who will come for us? No one has even the foggiest idea where we are."

That was when the banging started.

Despite our history of congenial dislike, I was never so glad to see someone as I was that Christmas Eve morning to see Darren Kirsch, coming through the door of that shack with two RCMP officers at his heels.

"Are we disturbing something?" were his first words as he directed a bemused stare at our surprisingly cozy situation: cuddled up on a couch in front of a roaring fire, full of corn and tuna and a little slap-happy from downing rye shooters.

"How did you find us?" we both asked at once, shocked by the men's appearance and jumping up from the couch like two teenagers caught in a half-nude embrace.

"We've got a snowplow and two cruisers waiting outside," he told us matter-of-factly. "I'll fill you in on the way back to town." He stopped there and gave us a careful once-over. "You guys okay?" he said, barely disguising something not dissimilar to genuine concern in his voice.

We nodded and hurriedly gathered our meagre belongings while one of the RCMP officers put out the fire and Darren and the other officer performed a quick search of the farmhouse. I don't know why they were searching it, but I didn't really care. I just wanted to get the hell outta there.

An hour or so later when we arrived at the Saskatoon police station downtown, we were greeted by my mother, Anthony, Kelly and Errall. Apparently, the Saskatoon cops first became aware something was amiss via—in a roundabout way—James Kraft. NYPD officials had contacted Darren to tell him to keep an eye on me because James' death was now being ruled "suspicious," and I, given my involvement with the case, was topping their list of people they wanted to investigate. Darren called the house to give me a heads-up and reached Errall, who had come over with Kelly after Mom, in a state, had called Kelly fretting about my whereabouts. And then, not long after, Anthony had called about Jared. But it wasn't until early the next morning when an anonymous caller gave the police our approximate location that they had sufficient cause and information to make a move.

We spent some time being interviewed by Darren and his team of investigators, giving a detailed description of how the kidnap occurred and how we survived. They were working on trying to identify the anonymous caller, a woman, but had yet to have any luck. Eventually they released us into the welcoming custody of our loved ones.

As I moved into the embrace of my mother, Kelly and Errall, I was struck by the thought that only a short while ago, if I'd have gone missing, no one would have been the wiser. At least not right away. And by then it might have been too late. Instead, I was amazed to find that what I had been struggling with the last couple of weeks—an increasingly crowded life, particularly the presence of my mother—had actually demonstrated in a dramatic way exactly how it made my life better—by saving it.

My mother knew of my tradition of hosting a Christmas Day come'n'go and, even while I was missing, insisted on keeping the stove busy in preparation for my undoubted safe return and a party to celebrate it. (In actuality, I think it was my mother's way of coping—some of us eat when we're stressed, my mother cooks.) So that evening, after a quiet dinner together, she returned to the kitchen to putz and I retired to my den with Barbra and Brutus to think through my case in front of the fire. We stayed like that for a long time and finally, the seemingly depthless cold that had invaded me, body and soul, over the past twenty-four hours began to seep away.

Christmas morning, instead of being a groggy, draggy mess as I expected after the previous day's ordeal, I awoke with a clear mind. I lay in bed for another twenty minutes listening to the comforting sound of canine snores and calmly considered all that had happened over the past two weeks.

By the time I made it to the kitchen, my mother was in full holiday gear: red dress and shoes, green earrings, necklace and apron. Our guests wouldn't be arriving for several hours but she informed me that with all there was to do to prepare for the day she'd have no time later on to get herself all "gussied up."

While my mother fed the dogs, I searched kitchen cupboards and drawers and finally came up with an apron of my own. It was sleek, black, made of raw silk, tailored to slim one's hips and emphasize one's chest, and wholly inappropriate for anything other than show. But I didn't care. I was gonna bake and cook with my mother on Christmas morning. In that bliss we remained for about an hour, laughing and chatting about nothing while we toiled like Santa's elves. And then she said it. It was an innocent enough comment but it was just the lubrication I needed to fit the pieces of the puzzle slipping and sliding around in my brain into place…well, almost into place.

"What did you say?" I asked her to repeat it.

"I said I hafn't made dese kind cookies seence I vas girl in school. Dere so simple to make, but so goot, ya? You like, uh-huh?"

"Oh yeah," I said as my mind focused on three seemingly disparate things: a bomb, a scarf and high school chemistry class.

"Mom, are you under control here? Would it be okay if I went out for a little while?"

"On Chreestmas?" She sounded like she was not in favour of the idea, but I think deep down she was happy to get me out from under foot.

I made one call and then headed out to solve my case.

Chapter 21

I KNEW THERE WAS A RISK that a knock on the door on Christmas morning might elicit nothing more than dead silence, but as it turned out, luck was on my side. The man who answered the door was fiftyish with wavy, thinning hair turning grey at the temples and in flecks throughout. "Merry Christmas," he greeted with a toothy smile when he saw I wasn't his mother-in-law (that was just my guess).

"Mr. Soloway?" I asked, almost certain this was the man from the photograph I'd seen in Daniel Guest's office a couple of weeks ago.

"Yes, that's right. How can I help you?"

"I'm sorry to be bothering you on Christmas morning, but I'm an acquaintance of your wife's and I was wondering if I could have a brief moment of her time."

He was wearing one of those over-the-top Christmas sweaters married men wear only once a year at the urging of their spouse. He'd probably worn it on Christmas day for the past five years and would do so for the next five. It bore a psychedelic arrangement of bright colours made even brighter against the skin of a man who normally wore grey or navy business suits. "Well, we're just about to head out for the day," he said, sounding a bit protective, uncertain about my intentions. "What is this about?"

"I interviewed your wife for a magazine article," I answered, trying to sound serious but not ominous. "And I really need to confirm some quotes before we go to press this afternoon."

I'm sure this seemed odd to him given the day it was, but he was too polite to say so. (I often rely on the politeness of strangers.) "I see, well, won't you come in?"

I stepped into a modest foyer with stairs at the far end leading up to a second floor. Next to the staircase was a hallway with a doorless entryway on each side through which I could see a formal sitting room to the left, dining room to the right.

"Anita!" Mick Soloway called out in the direction of the hallway. "There's someone here to see you."

I watched the expression on Anita Soloway's pleasant, freckled face change in slow motion from wonder to wariness as she came down the hallway and recognized my face.

"Oh," she said as she sidled up next to her much taller husband, like a baby bird looking for protection under its mother's wing. "Hello," she cheeped. "Mr. Woodward?"

"Anita," I said quickly, "how nice to see you again and to meet your husband. I was just telling him that I had something to discuss with you in private. You know," I said with a wink, "that little matter we were talking about?" It wasn't smooth, but at least I was giving her the option to discuss her recent activity in private if she so chose.

She was a little slow on the uptake. Still surprised to see the reporter from *Today's Entrepreneur* in her front foyer I guess. "Are you talking about the article you're writing about..." she began to ask, her eyelids blinking madly as she began to make certain connections in her head.

"...about how to make stink bombs," I finished for her, shooting an innocent grin at her husband who was again beginning to look a little concerned about what I wanted with his wife.

"Oh that!" she finally said with a follow up lopsided smile in her husband's direction. I'm sure that smile couldn't have come easy at that particular moment in her life. "Yes...yes, that little matter, yes, that...thing."

She needed help. "Perhaps we could discuss it in private?"

"Welllllll...we were just about to go out and it is Christmas morning..."

I gave her a look that told her she was pushing the limits too far with my not-infinite patience.

"But of course, why don't you come in here," she said with a flourish of her arm indicating the sitting room. "Mick," she said to her husband who was now looking entirely confused, "would you mind giving us a few minutes? It shouldn't take too long."

He shook his head good-naturedly and said, "Of course. I'll just go up to my office."

"That's fine, that's good, yes, we won't be long," Anita Soloway said, her face now so pale even her freckles were disappearing.

We wordlessly watched her husband mount the stairs to the second storey and out of sight and then entered the sitting room. We sat on matching armchairs next to an unlit fireplace, facing each other.

"Now what's this about?" she asked, going for the bewildered innocent approach. I'd have probably done the same. She crossed her legs showing off stylish going-out-for-Christmas-lunch shoes.

"I know about everything," I said, trying to look almost bored, "I just want to know why."

Her hands played nervously with one another on her lap. "What do you mean? What are you talking about?" Her delivery was as bad as you'd expect from first day in acting class.

I didn't have time for games. I had Christmas plans too. "You delivered a stink bomb to my home, Mrs. Soloway. And not only did it smell bad, but also it frightened my mother and her friends. I want to know why and I want to know how you're involved in the black-mail of Daniel Guest."

She stared at me in a way I imagine Little Red Ridinghood first looked at the Big, Bad Wolf.

I could understand how she'd be confused. As far as she knew, I was a reporter doing a story on the Guests, not the person whose house she had delivered her stink bomb to. "Mrs. Soloway, my real name is Russell Quant. I'm a private investigator." I pushed harder. "I know you're involved in the blackmail and possibly the kidnapping and intended murder of my friend and me."

By this time the woman had turned near scarlet in colour. "No, that's not true! None of it!" she cried, but kept her voice low for fear of her husband overhearing us.

I shook my head unbelievingly. "It was the stink bomb, Mrs. Soloway, that put me onto you. A silly move. How many people— adult people—know how to make a stink bomb? But they might remember, I suppose, if they're a chemistry teacher...which, suspiciously enough, is what you are."

"I...I...I...what are you talking about? Of course I'm a chemistry teacher, but what does that have to do with you or...or the rest of this nonsense?"

"You delivered your stink bomb to my house?" I said again.

Her face blanched as she sputtered out, "I did not deliver the bomb...I just...I just made it for her..." She stopped there, knowing she'd gone too far and said too much...and that ultimately it was too late. "But that's all! I don't know anything about blackmail or kidnapping or murder! For God's sake, you've got to believe me!"

"If you didn't deliver the bomb, then who did?"

"I don't know!"

"Mrs. Soloway, who did you make the bomb for?"

She was silent, looking down at her lap for the next few seconds.

"Mrs. Soloway? This isn't going away. I'm not going away. Some serious things have happened. I know you're involved, I'm just not sure to what extent. Who was it? Who?"

Her voice was so quiet at first I didn't hear her answer. I asked her to repeat it.

"Cheryl."

It was the answer I had expected. A bomb, a scarf and high school chemistry class. Anita Soloway, Cheryl Guest and the driver of a three-ton truck. All tied together by a brilliant burgundy scarf with a bright orange J. Thames tag. I'd seen it around the neck of the man driving the kidnap vehicle. A gift from Cheryl Guest to her collaborator?

"Cheryl left the bomb at my house?" I questioned Anita further.

"I guess, I really don't know. All I know is that she asked me to make one for her."

"Why? You must have asked. She's your best friend. I'm sure she didn't just order up a stink bomb without you wondering why."

She hesitated. I was asking her to betray her friend. Well, too bad.

"Why?" I urged once more.

"I told her...I was the one who told her about Daniel."

"Told her what?"

"She had no idea Daniel was gay. None of us did. They seemed like a pretty normal, happy couple. But it was me who found out."

"How?" I asked.

"One weekend Cheryl was away, Daniel stayed behind to work. Cheryl asked me if while she was out of town I wouldn't mind taking him over a hot casserole or something. She knew he'd be too busy to cook and if he even bothered to eat he'd end up ordering in crappy fast food. I love to cook and I didn't mind doing her a favour so I did. I made a meatball casserole and walked it over there. I passed right by their living room window." She stopped there to catch her breath before continuing. I could see her chest begin to heave as she contemplated getting to the next part of her story. "It was dark out and there was a lamp on inside and the drapes weren't quite closed. I saw the movement as I was passing by and I could just sense there was something weird about it so I took a closer look." She stopped again and looked down at her hands, a rose bloom appearing on each cheek.

"You saw Daniel Guest having sex," I guessed, hoping to help her over the tough part.

"With another man!" she hissed. "At first I thought it was another woman because...well because that would make more sense and because the other person had long blond hair, but I looked closer to see if I could recognize who she was and...well, it was *not* a woman."

The part of me with a warped sense of humour wanted to laugh, but I knew that wasn't a good idea, so instead I swallowed it and asked, "And then what did you do?"

"I ran home and took my casserole with me. There was no way he was going to get my food! I didn't know what to do then. I didn't know if I should call Cheryl, or contact the police, or tell my husband or what. So I did nothing. Until about a week later. Cheryl had come back and we were having coffee like we do a few times every week and I just couldn't hold it back. She's my best friend after all. And she had a right to know. For a lot of reasons."

"How did she react?"

"You can just imagine. It's a good thing I told her first thing in the morning while Daniel was at work, because if he'd been home, I think she would have ripped his...she would have hurt him somehow." She gave me a look that invited my imagination to conjure up one of many possible blood-and-guts scenarios. "It took her all day to calm down. She just yelled and screamed and threatened to do all sorts of things to him and to herself. Eventually she calmed down and we began to really talk. Apparently the sex between she and Daniel had never been that great and by then almost non-existent. It hadn't been a marriage in a long while. She admitted she'd been thinking about divorce. She'd been trying to make it work, trying to make it appear to the world she and Daniel were the perfect couple...so much so that Daniel probably believed her too. But this was it, the end of the line for her."

Blackmail time, I thought to myself. "So you hatched the plan?" I coaxed her on.

"Well, yeah, I guess. She wanted a divorce. But she wanted proof of what I'd seen first."

"Proof?" I was getting confused.

"Yes. She hired a private investigator."

Ta-da! Jane Cross. But why was Jane chasing me? I hadn't been the one having sex with Daniel. And what about the blackmail and kidnap? "Then what happened?" was all I said. I didn't want to put words in Anita's mouth.

"I don't know really. I didn't hear much from Cheryl for the next little while. She was understandably withdrawn. I thought it best not to push her about it. But she must have found out something from whomever she hired because she came to me a couple days ago and asked me to..." She had the sense to look a little penitent here. "She asked me to make a stink bomb for her so she could teach somebody a lesson. I assumed it was for whoever was fooling around with Daniel. I thought...well, I thought it was harmless and the least I could do to help my friend through this miserable thing. A little wifely retribution is necessary every once in a while y'know. Kind of like *The First Wives Club*."

I always thought there was something deeply disturbing about that movie.

That being said, I found myself believing Anita Soloway. She knew nothing about the blackmail or the trip from hell into the frozen countryside. She was simply an unwitting accomplice in Cheryl Guest's voyage of fury and revenge.

I looked out the window and saw Darren Kirsch along with two SPS police cruisers pull up curbside.

Darren and I were standing on the doorstep when Cheryl Guest opened her front door. The other constables remained in their vehicles for now. I wondered if Anita Soloway and perhaps her husband too were sneaking peeks from next door.

At first Cheryl said nothing, taking her time to assess the situation, glancing behind us at the police cars near her driveway and taking a half step forward to look both ways down her street. Was she worried about which of her neighbours were witnessing what was sure to be a spectacle?

"Mrs. Guest, I'm Constable Darren Kirsch of the Saskatoon Police Service."

I shot Darren an aggravated look. I thought we'd agreed on the phone that I would lead the confrontation with Cheryl Guest because…well, because I'd figured out what was going on (sort of) and he hadn't. Jeepers.

"And this is…"

But she didn't let him finish. "Yes, I'm familiar with Mr. Quant. My husband's…private detective." The way she said the last two words made the profession seem almost scurrilous.

Without inviting us in she turned and took a faltering step away. Stopped. A hand on a hallway table, the other in a fist on her hip. I saw her back slowly rise and fall as she took a deep breath, and then, much to our surprise, she threw back her head and let out a deep, sorrowful roar, like a wounded lion. For a brief—very brief—second afterwards, with the aggrieved sound still hanging in the air, I felt sorry for Cheryl Guest. Despite all she'd done, here was a woman wronged, a victim of perfidy, outraged and filled with unfathomable sadness at the lamentable outcome of her useless vengeance.

We stood there for a moment, Darren and I, staring at her back as it shuddered. Eventually she moved forward and we followed her into the house. Despite its owners, a gay man and a woman in the fashion industry, the home (or at least what we could see of it) lacked pizzazz. They were trying for an English Butler/The Bombay Company—authentic fake antique—look but had somehow missed the mark. They had the pieces, but they just weren't put together right. Not, I mused to myself, unlike their marriage.

Ending up in a sitting room, we each took an offered seat while Cheryl excused herself to get a glass of water. When she returned, she was not only rehydrated but looking remarkably composed following such a harrowing fall-apart. She sat down on a settee opposite us and gave me a curious look. I wondered if she was simply surprised to see me alive after having me dropped off to freeze to death. My earlier sympathy for her was quickly waning. She then turned to Darren with an expectant gaze. "Well," she began, "what is it?"

Ah, the woman had balls.

"We know what you've done," I began before Darren could hop in. "We just want you to fill in the details."

"Oh?"

"Where is your husband, Mrs. Guest?" Darren asked.

Drat, good question. I should have asked that.

"He's at a meeting with a colleague."

"On Christmas morning?"

She cocked her eyebrows at him and shot me a look.

"We know you found out about Daniel's affair with a man and hired a private investigator, Jane Cross, to find out who that man was," I started again.

"And what a useless waste of money that was," Cheryl said bitterly. "That woman couldn't find her way out of a brown paper bag."

Oooo, I'd really have to share that tidbit with my new bud, Jane.

"I wanted to have proof in hand before divorcing the bastard, but I got nothing from her. I was worried if we started proceedings without it, Daniel and all his high-priced professional friends would find a way to hide all the money and I'd get nothing. And I wanted to show everyone what a horrible man he is and how he'd fooled me, how our marriage was a sham. But that wasn't working…at least not quick enough. So I decided to take further steps."

"Blackmail," I said.

"Not just that," she responded, a tightness developing around her mouth and eyes. "Humiliation."

"You knew about his award so you devised a way to get the black-mail note into the envelope he received at the SBA awards ceremony."

"Not that difficult, believe me." She spent a second rearranging her hair and checking the tabs on her pierced earrings. "I wanted to see him squirm, in front of everyone. And let me tell you, Mr. Quant, it was worth it. And yes, it was about the money too. I wanted to get at least the fifty grand out of him up front, tax free—my accountant husband taught me the importance of that—just in case."

"But then you came along." She gave me a snarling look. "I met you at the Christmas party and I was certain you were Daniel's lover. Young. Handsome. Fake date."

Hmphf. How had she seen through Sereena and me?

She kept on going. "You didn't have the long blond hair Anita told me about, but gay guys get new hairstyles all the time, don't you?"

I wanted to shoot her a raspberry, but propriety won out.

"So I sicced Jane on you. Surprisingly she'd already been on your tail since spotting you outside Daniel's office. I began to realize you were something more than a roll in the hay."

I winced and said through gritted teeth, glancing sideways at Darren as I did so, "I was never a roll in the hay."

Cheryl ignored this and went on. "When Jane found out you were working for Daniel I began to worry you would counsel him not to pay the fifty thousand."

"So you came to my office under the guise of wanting to hire me. Why? To riffle through my files to find out what I knew?"

"And, by good fortune, I also found out you were going to New York City."

Crap! I had my electronic ticket and hotel confirmation information sitting on my desk.

"I didn't know if you were going to New York for a romantic weekend that Daniel'd tell me some cock-and-bull story about at the last minute before he got on a plane to join you, or if you were going to meet some high-powered divorce attorneys or blackmail specialists or whatever. All I knew is that I had to know what you were up to. So I sent Jane after you."

"When did you find out about James Kraft?" I asked. I sensed Darren tensing at the mention of the potential murder victim's name.

"Who?"

The look on Cheryl's face told the story. She had no idea who James Kraft was. How could that be? She was Loverboy yet James had also admitted to being Loverboy. The NYPD had now labelled his death suspicious. Up until then I thought there had to be some connection, but what if there wasn't? Did James call himself Loverboy simply because I'd put the idea in his mind? Was it one last irreverent jest from an unbalanced actor before he killed himself?

"Who is he?" Cheryl spat out. "Is he Daniel's lover? I have a right to know."

"No, Mrs. Guest," Darren said with quiet authority, "you do not."

While she huffed at that, I asked, "So Jane Cross comes home empty handed and then what?"

"Well, by then everything was falling apart. Jane could find nothing on you in New York…which cost me plenty let me tell you…and the date for the money from Daniel had come and gone. I couldn't believe it! The asshole didn't pay up! After all he'd done to me! I didn't have the cash, I didn't have the proof I needed to ensure a good divorce settlement and I didn't really want to make good on my blackmail threat." She leaned towards me then, her eyes ablaze with hatred. "And it was all your fucking fault! You told him not to pay! You were still fucking my husband for all I knew! You were making a fool of me! Of me!"

"So you left a stink bomb on his porch?" Darren asked, not bothering to mask how ridiculous he considered the move. "Vandalized his car?"

She gave me a sour look. "I wanted to hurt you whatever ways I could think of. But of course none of it was enough."

"So you hired someone to kidnap Mr. Quant and Mr. Lowe?" Darren said.

She turned to Darren and told him, "I didn't hire anyone. That was my brother. But don't get all worked up about that. He didn't know what he was doing…other than helping his wronged sister get a little harmless revenge."

"You call dumping us in the middle of nowhere to freeze to death harmless?" I asked incredulously.

"That was me," she said, looking me straight in the eye. "All my brother did was bring me the truck from the farm and get you boys...your friend was obviously a mistake...loaded up in the back. I told him you were having sex with Daniel...which of course did not go over well with him...and that I was just trying to teach you a lesson. After he got you on the truck, he left. I was already in the cab."

I shook my head in disbelief. Cheryl Guest had, by playing the wronged wife, gotten her best friend and brother to unwittingly help her commit her grand criminal schemes.

"You left us to freeze to death, Cheryl," I said plainly.

Suddenly her eyes were everywhere but on us and her fingers were knotting around one another with nervous energy. When she finally spoke her voice was so quiet we both had to lean forward to make out the words. "I didn't sleep all night. Everything I'd done seemed surreal. I began to wonder if it'd really happened at all. But of course it had. And I knew it was wrong. But I didn't confront myself with it until the morning, after Daniel left the house. When he did, I just fell apart. And I finally admitted to myself that I'd attempted...murder."

She looked at us then, not crying, but her eyes shone with unshed tears. "So I drove to a payphone and told the police where I'd left you. I didn't want you dead. You have to believe that." She looked at Darren but his face remained an expressionless stone. "And I don't want...to...go...tooooooooo jaaaaaaaaiiiiiiiilllllllll..." And the tears began. Without a tissue or handkerchief she simply let them pour from the corner of her eyes, over her cheeks and past her trembling lips.

"Do you know a man by the name of Hugh?" I asked, desperately trying to tie together several loose ends before Darren took over.

She shook her head, unable to speak.

"Drives a green Intrepid?"

Nothing.

Darren stood up then and went to the front door to motion in the other constables. I sat across from Cheryl Guest—the long elusive Loverboy—and said nothing.

I spent the next hour in my office unsuccessfully trying to find Daniel by phone. While I did that I went through my files on the Guest black-mail case, checking things off, getting it clear in mind who had been naughty and who had been nice. In the end I was satisfied I'd earned my money and done what I'd been hired to do, which was to find and stop Loverboy. All well and good except the stubborn suspicion in my mind that the fat lady had yet to sing. Sometimes as a detective you have to reconcile with the fact that there are truths you may never discover, answers that can't be found. I hate that. And there was stuff in my Herrings file that just wouldn't allow itself to be ignored.

There was James Kraft. Did he commit suicide? Or was he murdered? Why did he refer to himself as Loverboy in his last phone call to me? If he did kill himself, why do it—for all purposes—in front of me?

The landfill chase. Who was Hugh in the green Intrepid? Was this related to the Guest case at all? Common sense would say no—the chase occurred before I was even hired by Daniel—yet Hugh had warned me off a case I didn't have at the time. Why? And who was in the other car?

And what about Daniel Guest? Who was he meeting at the Riviera Motor Inn for six months?

Even as the idea entered my mind I knew it was wrong.

Beverly. She knew something. Daniel had revealed something to her in their private sessions that somehow influenced my case. And she knew it; she'd hinted at it when I returned from New York. But what? What was it and how could I find out? Did she mean for me to ask her more questions? But asking her to reveal a patient's confidences in order to help me would be contrary to our professional relationship and personal one. I couldn't put her in such a position. Then what? How could I find out what she knew?

And so, my treacherous scheme: break into Beverly's office, on Christmas day when I was sure not to be caught, and riffle through her files on her sessions with Daniel Guest.

I made it as far as her office door, my lock picks in hand, before I stopped myself with a most hearty chastisement. To do this would be wholly unacceptable. My housemates trusted me, we trusted an other and to do this would be a breach of that trust. I turned away from her door with the intention to slink upstairs and think up some other means to my end, when a memory shot across my brain like a subliminal advertisement, barely there but still leaving an impression.

The newspaper! When was it? When had I seen it? I rushed into the kitchen and to the closet where we stored used newsprint for recycling. It was the Saturday I was in New York...the twentieth...I'd come home and read the article...about the south downtown vote...I found the paper I was looking for and yanked it down from the shelf where it was stored with about two months worth of old *StarPhoenix*, causing several other issues to spill onto the floor. I spread the paper on the kitchen table and quickly found the front-page article I remembered. As with most big stories in Saskatoon, much of the news coverage consisted of comments and opinions of local politicians and professional wags. I hurriedly flipped pages to where the story continued on page B6.

And there it was. The mini-headline read, "City Councillors Weigh In." My finger raced down the column's verbosity to the end where I read, "Councillor Dufour was unavailable for comment. He was in New York City on business."

Like coins into slots, I could hear the phop, phop, phop of missing pieces falling into place. And then I remembered a startling bit of information. Cheryl Guest had told us Daniel was meeting with a colleague. Daniel Guest was with Herb Dufour. Daniel Guest was in danger.

Chapter 22

I SWISH-TAILED OUT OF THE PWC parking lot onto icy Spadina and sped towards the north end of town and the DGR&R office building. The going was quick as most people with any sense were home on Christmas day with their loved ones, rather than out on the streets collecting guests for the local police holding tank. But I was on a mission. There was a good chance my client was in mortal danger. For some reason he'd agreed to meet Herb Dufour that morning. I could only guess that their meeting place was DGR&R, likely abandoned on December 25th.

Daniel was correct in assuming Herb was not Loverboy, but he was sorely unaware—as I had been—of another subplot burbling beneath the surface of his wife's blackmail scheme. By simply being caught having extramarital sex with another man, Daniel had unintentionally set off numerous chains of events that resulted in blackmail, kidnap and murder. Daniel had much to fear from Herb Dufour.

At least that was my theory.

I knew Daniel had been meeting with someone at a local motel for six months prior to his rendezvous with Anthony. I sensed James Kraft had not committed suicide but had been murdered for some unknown reason. And I knew someone didn't want me to take Daniel's case and nearly ran me off the road in order to convince me.

From the *StarPhoenix* I learned Herb was in New York City at exactly the same time I was; at exactly the same time James was killed. Coincidence? Bullshit. But how did he know I'd be there? How did he know that James Kraft was the most likely suspect to be Loverboy?

The same way he knew I'd be offered the case of finding Loverboy before I even did.

Daniel Guest had told him.

Daniel and Herb were business partners, friends and, I was betting, ex-lovers who'd had a six-month affair which had played itself out at the Riviera Motor Inn. An affair that someone, likely Herb, called off when it became too serious or too close to becoming revealed. This was probably about the same time Herb was just becoming highly touted for the top job in Saskatoon—mayor.

But then what? Blackmail? No, it was Daniel's wife who'd been blackmailing him. And Herb would have no logical reason to blackmail Daniel. He wasn't in obvious need of the money. And a threat of revelation could only hurt his own chances of anonymity in the whole matter. It didn't make sense.

But it was about to.

I parked on an empty street half a block away from DGR&R and made my way to the back door of the building on foot. I was gratified to see I was right. In the parking lot was Daniel's black BMW and another equally ostentatious car that I assumed belonged to Herb Dufour. I used the now-familiar security code and gained entrance into the building and made my way up to the partners' offices. As I inched open the third-floor door I could hear a low murmur of voices. Although there were no overhead lights on, the hallway was grey with dull daylight. I crept down the passageway and peeked around the corner into the atrium. And there, standing at the entrance of Daniel's office were two men. Embracing.

Daniel and Herb.

I couldn't make out the words between them. Their voices were low and muffled by kisses and caresses. I was wrong. I came here thinking I might be saving Daniel's life. I was almost certain Herb killed James and now intended to kill Daniel too. But a murder was definitely not what I was witnessing. I pulled back into the hallway, utterly confused. I heard a thudding noise and quickly stole another glance around the corner. Herb had pushed Daniel against the jamb of the door and while covering his face with sloppy kisses was slowly pulling his shirttails out of his pants. Daniel's hands were also busy a little lower down. On the floor between them was a 750 ml bottle of Scotch, a third empty. This was a party, a tryst, a reunion.

I slunk back down the stairs. Something didn't add up and I was bad at math. But unless I was planning to become a voyeur (which under different circumstances would be okay) I had no course left me but to leave. Although I doubted they'd hear me over their growing moans, I managed to reach the back door and let myself out with little noise.

I should go home, I said to myself. It's Christmas day, I was expecting a house full of guests in a few measly hours, Loverboy was behind bars, what else did I want? And just as I rounded the corner of the building to head for my car I saw it coming.

Danger.

The green Intrepid.

I pulled back and felt my chest begin to heave. I had only seconds to react. I dove behind Daniel's black BMW just as Hugh pulled up near the back door of the building. What the hell was he doing here? Who had sent him? Whatever the answers, this could not be a good thing for the two men upstairs.

I heard the door of the car open and close as Hugh stepped out of the vehicle. I laid flat against the frozen ground, my right cheek smarting from the chunks of gravel and ice against it, and watched his black-booted feet move to the rear of his car. With as much stealth as I could muster, I pulled myself up and dared a peek over the hood of the BMW. I was just in time to see Hugh pull a rifle from his trunk.

I reacted, smartly or not, brawn over brain.

I had surprise on my side when I leapt, cougar-like, from behind Daniel's car onto Hugh's back. I may have even growled a little bit. Hugh went down like sack of potatoes, but unlike a bag of spuds, he was ready for bear. He hunkered up with amazing speed, throwing me back far enough to give him a chance to turn around and face his aggressor. Unfortunately my original attack had not knocked the rifle out of his hands and, now that the shock of the unanticipated assault was dissipating, he was coming to realize he had a weapon of destruction in his hands and could use it against me. I couldn't let that happen. I rushed him again. Rifles are okay weapons I suppose, but not as agile and responsive as smaller handguns. Before he was able to manoeuvre the gun into a pointing-at-me position, I was on him, the gun between us flat against both our bellies. I used it as leverage and took hold of it at each end, allowing me to lean back and bring the full weight of my knee up and into his crotch. His eyes, only inches from mine, went wide and for a second he just stared at me in disbelief. Unfair fighting? Below the belt? You bet, asshole! I'll pull your hair too if I have to.

Hugh fell away from me and down to his knees, dropping the rifle, grasping for gonads before they totally receded up into him. I used the tender moment to grab onto his shoulders and, utilizing my knee one more time, made contact with the left side of his chin. He let out a yowl of pain so loud I wondered if Daniel and Hugh would hear it three floors above us. I scooped up his gun and watched as he rolled onto his back. I ran to the trunk of his car hoping to find something to tie him up with. If not I'd have to keep with the knee bashing until he passed out and I wasn't a fan of that level of brutality.

I found what I needed all too easily. Not only was there an abundance of rope in the Intrepid's trunk, but also a large roll of burlap and a mid-size plastic tarp. I had the sinking feeling Hugh was planning on spending Christmas day transporting bodies.

I made quick work of the rope, expertly hog-tying Hugh where he lay moaning. I retrieved the rifle from where I'd left it leaning against the car and and headed inside. I had to warn Daniel and Herb, in case more Hughs were on the way. As I reached the door I shot a last look over my shoulder at the captive, lying there, shivering in the cold. Pitiful? Not quite. But I couldn't just leave him there like that. I ran back and threw some burlap and the tarp over him. That done, I entered the DGR&R building.

By the time I made it upstairs again I'd expected the two men to be *en flagrante delicto* on the carpet in Daniel's office. But when I peeked into the atrium from the hallway, instead of having moved inside the office, they'd moved nearer the centre of the atrium where...

And instantly I knew.

Daniel Guest was about to fall three floors to his death. Hugh was here to help dispose of the body. And, if Daniel's body was ever recovered from wherever they planned to stash it, he'd be in a dishevelled state with alcohol in his system. Was it an accident or suicide? A seemingly stray but well-timed comment from his grieving best friend and business partner would hint at some mental anguish over the sorry state of his marriage. No one would think too much more about it.

I pulled back my head and thrust forward the barrel of the rifle. In a he-man kind of voice and with the best Australian accent I could muster, I called out, "I'm here."

At first there was silence except for some furtive rustling of clothing. Then I heard Daniel whispering, "Who the hell is that?"

A hesitation.

Then, "You asshole! I told you to stay hidden until I called you." Herb.

Gotya, jerk off.

I stepped forward, revealing myself to the two men. They were standing near the atrium railing, too close to it for my comfort, staring in my direction, bewildered at my appearance, but for very different reasons. "Sorry," I said. "I've never been very good at following orders."

Daniel spoke first. "Russell. Have you gone crazy? What are you doing here?"

I had to give him that. I probably looked a little bit nuts, standing there brandishing a rifle, my hair dishevelled and with fresh bruises and cuts from my scuffle with Hugh.

He tried a nervous laugh as he said, "I know you think Loverboy could be someone I work with, but really, man, breaking in here like this, on Christmas day…come on!"

I looked at Herb whose eyes were whirling in his head as he tried to figure a smooth way out of this one. "Care to explain, Herb?"

"Russell," from Daniel again. "Herb is not Loverboy. Okay, he and I had an affair earlier this year; I'm sorry I didn't tell you about that. But you didn't need to know. It had nothing to do with why I hired you. As a city councillor, in order to survive politically in this town, Herb can't afford to have something like that get out. You couldn't know. No one can know. You've got to understand that. He is not Loverboy."

"I know he's not. Loverboy was arrested this morning."

"Thank God," Herb uttered, giving Daniel an empathetic nod. Yeah right.

"Wh...what? Who? Who was he?" Daniel asked.

"Yes, tell us," Herb said.

It was just what Herb wanted, a discussion about Loverboy to divert attention away from himself.

"Why don't you first explain to us about Hugh," I said, ticking my head towards Hugh's rifle in case he'd forgotten.

"Who's Hugh?" Daniel asked.

"I have no idea," Herb said. His hands were down by his thighs clenched into fists. Preparing to fight? Ah, I got a firearm here!

"He's not coming," I said to Herb. "He's tied up downstairs waiting for the cops." Actually I hadn't called the police yet, but he didn't need to know that.

Daniel turned on his partner and said, "What's going on, Herb? Who were you expecting?"

Herb obviously wasn't quick on his feet when it came to thinking his way out of an unexpected confrontation. Not a good feature in a future mayor. So I helped him out a bit. "Herb was the first person you told about being blackmailed, wasn't he, Daniel?"

"Yes," he said. "The only person aside from you and Beverly."

"But you told him before you even hired me. Was he for or against the idea?"

Daniel didn't have to think long. "He hated the idea. I couldn't quite understand why, but he tried to convince me not to do it. He wanted me to just pay and be done with it."

"I'm thinking...and by the way, Herb, just hop in and stop me if I'm wrong about any of this," I said with a sideways glance at Dufour. "I'm thinking he was worried that a PI snooping around in your private matters would uncover your affair. An affair that ended when Herb decided to take a run at the mayor's chair."

Daniel looked at me and then at Herb, back at me, then Herb. "I promised you I'd keep your name out of it. And I did that. I didn't tell Russell about us."

But I bet he did tell Beverly. That's what she thought I needed to know.

"I know how much your political career means to you, Herb," Daniel said. "I'd never do anything to jeopardize that, you know that."

"I know, Danny, I know," Herb said in a low voice, as if he didn't want me to hear. "But I couldn't take the risk. You couldn't promise that, you couldn't control everything this joker did."

Hey!

"So he came after me," I said. "He couldn't convince you not to hire me, but maybe he could convince me not to be hired. So he rounded up a local thug, Hugh, and together they tried some scare tactics on me. Remember the chase on the landfill road I told you about?"

Daniel simply nodded. The two men were now avoiding each other's gazes, standing before me emanating guilt, fear, anger, resentment, fury, so heavy it filled the air like bad cologne.

"But I took the case any way. Which I'm sure pissed him off. So all he could do was act the supportive business partner and keep as much in the loop about what was going on in the investigation as he could. He'd failed to dissuade you or I, the only way to make it all go away, was to stop the blackmailer himself."

"But we all wanted that!" Daniel said.

"Not exactly," Herb shot back. "You started crowing about not paying him or negotiating a better deal! And your detective I'm sure would have gotten the police involved somehow. I needed the blackmailer gone! For good! Your way he would just keep on coming back to haunt us. And if the cops got called in there'd be no saying what they'd dig up about you...about us. How could you expect me to run this city, have any respect, if they discovered my involvement? There's no way."

Daniel's face began to crumble as the horrid truth began to dawn on him. "I...I told you about James Kraft. I told you he was, without any doubt, the blackmailer. I told you about Russell going to New York to find him. I...you..."

"It would have been perfect, Danny," Herb said, almost pleadingly. His fist making had stopped and he was holding out a tentative hand to his ex-lover, a hand that was being soundly rebuffed. "If it had turned out right, if James Kraft was Loverboy—like you swore he was—you would have thanked me for getting rid of him. It's only because it got all fucked up—because you were wrong about the kid—that you're pissed off!"

"Don't blame me for any of this!" Daniel railed at the other man. "I sent Russell to find out for sure if James was Loverboy and find some way to convince him to stop. I didn't send him—or anyone else—to kill him!" Daniel grabbed onto his forehead as if struck with a migraine. "Oh shit, the poor kid! Oh shit!" Tears were forming in Daniel's eyes. "Herb, you son of a bitch! You bastard! You killed him!"

Herb did not deny the charge.

I kept on, "Then, you got back home, thinking you'd put an end to both the blackmail and my investigation, only to find out Loverboy was still alive and well and actively pursuing Daniel."

Herb sniffed loudly, glared at me and again began with the fist-making.

"You couldn't convince Daniel not to hire me, you couldn't stop me from taking the case, you'd killed the wrong Loverboy, there was only one thing left to do to stop the whole thing," I said. "Kill Daniel."

Daniel whipped his head to the side to get a full bead on Herb. He tried, but no words formed on his lips, just a strangling kind of sound. Herb was looking only at me, his nostrils flaring like a derby horse after an exhausting race. I was sure sweat was beginning to lather around his neck.

"So you asked Daniel here today to do it. What did you say? That you missed him and wanted to get back together? Your plan was to get him drunk and push him over the atrium railing. Your friend Hugh was around with a gun, just in case the fall didn't quite do him in? And then you'd leave him to clean up your mess while you headed out to attend a family Christmas?"

"Shut up," Herb growled at me.

"You were going to kill me?" Daniel was finally able to speak. His face was crestfallen.

Herb refused to look at him. "I want to speak with my lawyer."

I'd say that was a yes.

Given that it was Christmas day, Darren took pity on me and let me out of the interrogation room much sooner than he'd probably have liked to. Besides, within the past forty-eight hours I'd been kidnapped and almost killed, caught a blackmailer, solved a murder and prevented another; I deserved a little special treatment. And, I promised to come back early the next day.

I made it home in time to help my mother with the final touches for our—whoa, where did *that* come from?—for *my* Christmas party and change into something festive—wonderpants, red sweater with white piping and a jaunty Santa hat. The storm Jared and I had been dumped in was long gone leaving in its wake a sparkling veneer of fresh snow. Freezing temperatures had also migrated north leaving sunny Saskatoon to enjoy balmy temperatures in the minus teens.

It was when I'd gone into my mother's room to retrieve some table linens she'd brought with her from the farm and needed for the party that I saw them. There in full view, two pieces of luggage—hers—were open on the bed, half filled with her things. I stood there for a minute, my mind whirring with possible explanations for what I was seeing.

"No find?" my mother asked me when I returned to the kitchen empty-handed. "You look in drawer? Dey dere."

"Mom...your bags?"

"Ya?" She was kneading a puffy mound of raw dough.

"Mom...I thought you were moving in...I thought..."

"No," she said simply, heaving over the pliable white lump with little effort. "I go home day after tomorrow."

"Mom, I want you to feel welcome here...I think..." Oh my God, was I going to say it? "I think you should move in." And I meant it.

"No, no, no, not time yet."

"What? But you said you liked the garage apartment and you said..."

"I say notting. You say."

"But the other night, when we were talking..."

She powdered the dough with more flour and continued her task. "Ya, ve talk. Only talk, Sonsyou."

I shook my head in frustration. What was going on? Hadn't my mother said she was moving in? Maybe not in so many words, but..."Mom, you are very welcome to move into the room over the garage...or into the house if you want. No need to think anything over."

"I only look at garage to see vhat it like. To see if dere's room for me vhen time comes. Den you say I move in. But I vait, I tink. Not time yet."

"No?"

"I'm only sixty-two, Sonsyou. I need de farm. I need my garden and flowers and lady friends. Not noise and smoke in air and city craziness. But vhen eet's time...I know. And den...mebbe den...I come here mebbe."

I nodded. I think I understood. I could see not wanting to live in Bill's house with four kids, all of whom one day soon would be teenagers. And I've long suspected Mother and Bill's wife, Adrian, only tolerate one another. As far as Joanne is concerned, she's still looking for herself and enjoying a swinging single life. She switches jobs, apartments and cities more often than most. And, she obviously isn't anxious to leave Saskatchewan. Moving away from the farm would be a big enough step for her when the time came. So that left...me? Had I somehow become the child with the most attractive and stable lifestyle? How could that have happened? True, I didn't have a hoard of human noise-makers running around the house, I did have a comfortable home and a garden and a nice quiet dog (or two) that I returned to every night (almost) and I did live only an hour away from the beloved farm.

Oh my gosh. It was true.

I smiled—big.

"Sonsyou." My mother had stopped with her doughy ministrations and was looking right at me. "Dyiakyou for vanting me."

"You're welcome."

"I love you, Sonsyou."

I always knew my mother loved me and I her, but we rarely said the words. And to hear it at that moment, in my home, both of us knowing that some day we'd end up together, just as we began together, was pretty powerful. Powerful and wonderful.

Which meant the conversation was over. My mother went back to her cinnamon-bun-making and I went to check my hair.

The first to arrive was Sereena who entered with a flourish of crinoline and taffeta in tones of rich burgundy, mistletoe green and Devonshire cream. Her head was covered with scores of precise ringlets and sparkling, jewelled hairpins. She was Mrs. Claus' younger and more stylish sister.

"Here, I brought you a little something," she said as she deposited her silk wrap in my waiting hands along with a crumpled brown paper bag.

I peeked inside and pulled out a bottle of golden liquid. Lysholm Linie Aquavit from Norway. I gave my friend a fond and appreciative grin.

"I thought it was an appropriate reminder of our time together in New York."

"Shall we?" I said, eyeing the bottle like Groucho Marx—minus the eyebrows.

She tilted her head enticingly and purred, "There's no time like the present."

But at that moment the doorbell rang again. I placed the bottle on the foyer table and opened the door. It was Kelly and Errall. I hugged Kelly and felt an unfamiliar stiffening. But before I could think too much about it, the parade began. Mary and Marushka came next, followed by Anthony and Jared. Barbra and Brutus were the first to welcome everyone with feverishly wagging tails. As the day moved from early to late afternoon, the noise and activity level in my little house grew in intensity as more people come'd'n'go'd. Drinks were imbibed and food was scarfed down, calories be damned. Amongst the holiday revellers were Alberta and her Indo-Canadian snake-charmer date, the three monkey ladies, and Lilly and Beverly and their husbands and kids and about a dozen others.

When the mass had grown big enough that I knew I wouldn't be missed if I slipped out, I grabbed Kelly and asked her to join me for a walk. She wasn't happy about it. She knew what was coming but complied anyway.

Once we were bundled up appropriate for the weather and on the street heading nowhere in particular, I began. "Kelly, I need to know what's going on with you. I'm worried about you and I want to help. But I can't do that unless I really understand what's happening. I know you're still dealing with your cancer, but there's something more."

Surprisingly she readily agreed. "You're right."

Okay. Hmm. Now what? "So what is it?"

"That's part of the problem, Russell. I don't really know. You're right though. I am still freaked about being sick. I'm afraid that will never go away. And if it does…if it does I don't know who I'm going to be."

I watched puffs of air escaping Kelly's mouth, the only things making sense to me right then. "What do you mean?"

"I'm a different person than I was before the cancer, Russell. And I might never be the same again. I can't explain it. It's like I can see the woman I am right now, I can see what she's like, what she's doing. I can see she's not me. I don't even like her very much, but it's like I'm powerless to leave her behind, to go back to who I was. Can you…can you understand that at all? Probably not, it sounds crazy even to me, but it's exactly how I feel right now."

This was the most I'd ever heard Kelly talk about herself at one time. That alone was different from the Kelly I'd always known. And what she was saying was disturbing, maybe even a little frightening to me. But I could see it myself. This woman was different. I wrapped an arm around her and again felt the stiffening. I so wanted everything to be perfect or at the very least, the way it used to be. It was Christmastime for Pete's sake. My case was solved. My mother and I had come to a new level of understanding with one another, an understanding that someday would change my life—but not right now. It had taken an evening of nearly freezing to our deaths, but I had also come to some important realizations about my feelings for Jared and respect for his relationship with Anthony. I now had two dogs and that was okay; I was up to the responsibility. So why wasn't Kelly jumping in line, completing the picture of my life in good order?

We walked on and talked some more, but there were no easy answers to this one—and, like in my line of work, I had to accept that sometimes there are none.

As we retraced our steps and approached the house, we both saw a car idling nearby. A black BMW. Before I'd departed the police station I'd left a note for Daniel asking him to join our party when they'd finished with him. He'd lost both his wife and…friend?… lover?…that day. Who did he have left to spend Christmas with?

"Someone you know?" Kelly asked as we came closer.

"Client," I told her.

"I'll go in then," she said and started to head towards the gate that leads to my house.

I pulled her to a stop and into a bear hug. No stiffness this time. It was a start. I hoped.

I waited until I saw Kelly step into the yard before I walked up to the driver's side of Daniel's car. Daniel got out and we fumbled through an awkward handshake-come-hug. "Merry Christmas, Daniel!" I couldn't help wonder how the recent events in his life would effect him. Would he too be forever changed? But for him would it be for the better?

"Merry Christmas, Russell. I got your message to stop by. Thank you."

"No problem. Why don't you come in? Get ya some food and drink."

"I'm afraid I can't stay."

"Is everything all right?" Stupid question. Of course everything wasn't all right. "How did things go at the police station?"

"It was...it was okay. There's a lot to talk about. Going back tomorrow. Right now I just feel utterly exhausted. I don't want to face anyone right now, I know you understand. I need to be alone. But I wanted to come by and thank you for all you did."

"I know it's not how you hoped things would turn out, Daniel, but at least it's over. And I'm sure the police will do their best to keep the details quiet."

He shrugged as if that was the least of his worries. And he was probably right. "I need to go." He turned away then stopped himself. "Russell—I want you to know—you've given me a very special gift this Christmas."

"Oh?" I said, unsure of what he meant.

"You've opened my eyes to a new way of life. You've shown me that who I might be inside is...well, maybe he's not such a bad guy." Might be? Maybe? I was disappointed. Hadn't the last couple of weeks taught him anything at all? "I want to be happier, Russell. I don't know what's going to happen...with me...with Cheryl and me...but, well...I don't know." He laughed nervously. "But thanks."

I could see by the look in his eyes that his familiar, closeted lifestyle was luring him, tempting him with its shallow promise of safety and ease.

298

"Daniel, I want you to remember there are people around you who can help you and support you through this. Including me."

On the spur of the moment I decided we needed a gesture, a seal, a token of some sort to commemorate this moment, celebrate it. "Hold on a sec," I said, turning around and dashing into the house. I returned in a moment brandishing the bottle of Aquavit I'd left on the foyer table along with two glasses. I poured out two shots and placed the bottle to rest on the hood of the car. How festive! How jolly!

"A little Christmas cheer to toast the season," I said holding my glass aloft. "Here's to you, Daniel, a truly free man!" I wondered if he'd remember our conversation in Diva's. I may have been overstating the case, but if nothing else, I wanted to give him something to shoot for, perhaps a New Year's resolution in the making.

"What is this stuff?" he asked, giving the liquid a suspicious sniff.

"Aquavit," I told him. "The water of life." The translation was appropriate I thought. I remembered when I first tasted the liqueur in New York with Sereena. At first I resisted it, but then its warmth and flavour overtook me. An acquired taste, perhaps, but it would forever be a favourite of mine. As for Daniel, maybe this moment would signify his transition into a life he was always meant to live, a person he was always meant to be. Or was I hoping for too much? If he took anything from this experience, I hoped it was the courage to try.

I downed my drink in one gulp, as did Daniel.

He wordlessly opened the driver's side door of his car and got into the still-running vehicle. He didn't roll down his window, but mouthed the words, "Thank you" one more time and drove off.

And as the car moved away I realized Daniel had indeed taken something with him.

A Flight of Aquavit.

Atop the vehicle was the bottle of Aquavit. I watched as it jerked from the sudden motion of the car's departure, precariously close to falling...and then...it did.

Acknowledgements

The many who gifted me with some of the best days in a writer's life—thanks for showing up, laughing at the right spots, paying attention, braving the Sask lineup, flowers, cards, hugs, e-mails, messages on that day *and* long after, the rose brigade, I will never forget it

The wondrous booksellers, store managers, event coordinators, festival organizers in all the cities, who provided a warm, welcoming place to land—especially Beryl, David, Tom, Jackie, Beth, Louann, Henrietta, Gaylene, Susan, Gord, Jennifer, Janine, Mark, Charlene, Paul and Holly

All the reviewers and interviewers and columnists and news reporters for their time and attention

Carolee and Carol for your invaluable promotional efforts—you put a poster where?

The most amazing network of supporters across Canada and beyond, created through the power of e-mail and friends—special thanks to Darrell, George, Judy, Rob

Ginette my goddess of French, Carol for Timmy's in the well and countless more, Cal—you Cheekay Monkay, Dori for T-shirts+BFF, George & Jim for the first flowers and tallest slices of cake, David—ever grateful for the window display, Ptown fun, perpetuating the BV myth, & Dick, Gord & Mary for being there, Shelley & Murray for showing up where I least expected, Shelley & Linda for champagne at the Arc, RQ Fan Club—Dylan, Jenn, Dan, Judy (I still wear my button), Pat & Mike—my New Yorkers, Marv & Ginette—what a cake, Dana—bon voyage dear man, Fran—for behind the scenes efforts-above & beyond, luv ya, Mom—for being brave, flexible, smart, loving, for learning from & embracing life, Family & Friends—xo always

Heather—keep writing, Gordon—good health, Claude—thanks for the call

Insomniac Press—Mike, Adrienne, Marijke, Emily—my eternal gratitude, you rock

Catherine Lake, editor and friend, whose skill made this book better and whose kindness makes it shine

For you, thanks for picking up this book and being a reader

And Herb.